Praise for
Dark Things I Adore

"A smart, nuanced exploration of victims and villains, inspiration and theft, and the intersection of these things in every artist. Pay attention to Katie Lattari. She's the real deal."
—Sarah Langan, author of *Good Neighbors*

"I felt like I was being physically pulled into a dark forest while reading this psychological cat-and-mouse game, always aware that more danger lay ahead. With a constant sense of foreboding and lush imagery, *Dark Things I Adore* is a haunting, mesmerizing tour de force, everything about it a brutal sort of beauty."
—Zoje Stage, *USA Today* and international bestselling author of *Baby Teeth* and *Getaway*

"Gorgeous and absorbing, *Dark Things I Adore* is a stunningly executed tale of art, trauma, and revenge. At once propulsive in plot and lyrical in style, it's the kind of novel you'll want to savor every sentence of—dark and deeply satisfying."
—Katie Lowe, author of *The Furies* and *Possession*

"Pulsing with seductive menace, *Dark Things I Adore* is a beautiful package, set to explode."
—Eliza Jane Brazier, author of *Good Rich People*

"This vengeful tale that pits artistic genius against mental health and happiness will captivate fans of dark suspense."
—*Library Journal*, STARRED Review

Dark Things I Adore

Dark Things I Adore

Katie Lattari

sourcebooks
landmark

Published by Sourcebooks Landmark, an imprint of Sourcebooks
P.O. Box 4410, Naperville, Illinois 60567-4410
(630) 961-3900
sourcebooks.com

The Library of Congress has cataloged the hardcover edition as follows:

Names: Lattari, Katie, author.
Title: Dark things I adore / Katie Lattari.
Description: Naperville, Illinois : Sourcebooks, [2021]
Identifiers: LCCN 2020056407 (print) | LCCN 2020056408 (ebook) | (hardcover) | (epub)
Classification: LCC PS3612.A924 D37 2021 (print) | LCC PS3612.A924
    (ebook) | DDC 813/.6--dc23
LC record available at https://lccn.loc.gov/2020056407
LC ebook record available at https://lccn.loc.gov/2020056408

Printed and bound in Canada.
MBP 10 9 8 7 6

For Kevin, who always believed and did the believing for me when I couldn't muster it

Author's Note

This book addresses themes of abuse, mental illness, and suicide. If you or someone you know is struggling with mental health issues, engaging in reckless or suicidal behavior, or a victim of abuse or assault, please seek support. If you're not sure where to start, here are a few resources:

National Domestic Violence Hotline
www.thehotline.org
1-800-799-7233

Love Is Respect
www.loveisrespect.org
1-866-331-9474

National Suicide Prevention Lifeline
www.suicidepreventionlifeline.org
1-800-273-8255

National Resource Center on Domestic Violence
www.nrcdv.org
1-800-537-2238

National Center on Domestic Violence, Trauma & Mental Health
www.nationalcenterdvtraumamh.org
1-312-726-7020

Prologue

Excellent Friends

Audra

A smudged, barking pattern—male.

My vision is pulled back into focus by a voice, louder than the others, in the room behind the closed door. I blink the water stain on the ceiling into something with sharp, definite borders. It looks like a tree or a hand, tendrils grasping outward. I'm lying on the old couch outside one of the institute's larger lecture halls, fingers laced beneath my head. The couch is ratty but comfortable, and because it's *art school*, it has panache, covered and saved by years and years' worth of weird little fabric patches and guerrilla embroidery jobs—furniture Frankensteined. The lecture hall across the way is a sixty-seater set aside for visiting speakers, conferences, and large workshops. Right now, faculty from across departments and disciplines are gathered in there, having their second and final all-faculty meeting of the academic year. I'm out here because Max Durant is in there. My handsome professor. My dedicated mentor.

Professor Durant told me before class this morning that I should wait for him after the meeting. He told me he wanted to see me. That *we should talk*. Maybe even grab dinner. I let him know he could look for me when he got out.

A muffled scrape and shuffle rise behind the door; bags are being gathered, friendly chatter is breaking out. I look at my phone—it's almost six in the evening. They were supposed to be done by half past five. I push myself to sitting and look up and down the vacant hallway. It's the Friday before spring break, so everyone has split. I rub my face and mindlessly check my email while I wait. Junk, spam, coupons, one message from a fellow student with the subject line: *thesis prospectus??* I put my phone away in my jacket pocket, and as I do, my fingers brush the corner of an envelope I've had stowed in there all day: a letter addressed to a man I know back home, from an old friend. I withdraw my hand quickly and rest it on the outside of my jacket, feeling the outline of the envelope like a mite burrowed under flesh.

"But if the Warhol is going out on loan, it means prime space is empty in one of the most prestigious rooms in our own gallery." Hearing his voice stirs me from my torpor. That's him. Max.

My hand presses over the shape of the envelope harder. I'll post this tonight.

Max's voice is loud and animated—even through the door. I smile. He's always wound up about some goddamned thing. I try to listen more closely, but the crush of movement crescendos when faculty members push through the double doors, first in drips, then in groups of threes and fours, holding laptops and notepads under their arms, some talking about their break plans, some shaking their heads dubiously at each other as they unpack whatever it is they've just talked about in there. Dr. Grant gives me a wave and smile, which I return. She's only a few steps past me, a couple colleagues at her elbows, when I hear her speak in a hushed tone.

"We all had the chance to make our pitches back when we first found out the Warhol would be going out on loan—I'm not sure what makes Durant think he's some special case. I mean, the *Polk Room* for god's sake." She laughs. At him. "God knows we all did enough begging. Let it rest."

Professors Wilson and Zapata exit right behind them, chatting clandestinely to each other and peering over their shoulders at the apparent commotion inside the seminar room. Soon everyone has exited and streamed by me. Except Max. And whoever he's haranguing. They're just inside the door, at an angle I can't see. But I can hear them.

"Well, I have no idea who said that to you. Who in their right mind would promise that?" The voice is the confident staccato of Dana Switzer. Jesus. He's haranguing the head of the whole damn school. She was a professor in Max's department, Painting, for many years and then was chair for a while. Five or six years ago she became the president of this place, the Boston Institute for the Visual Arts, but that was before I ever got here. I've never formally met her. A wave here, a hello there. She teaches very infrequently these days. "The Warhol will be out on loan, but that doesn't mean its spot will remain empty," she continues.

"That's what I'm saying. My work should go there. *Architecture of Radiance* should go there." I can hear the fight in him. The thinly veiled frustration. I've come to know his energies and emotions well over the many months we've been working together. "I've earned it. In all the years I've been here, I've never made it into the Polk Room at all, forget about the Warhol spot. I know there is precedent for faculty art being shown in the Polk Room. You can't tell me there isn't precedent."

"There is precedent, yes, but faculty art hasn't been hung in the Polk Room in more than ten years. It just isn't done anymore. You know that, Max. I've been here a long time, but so have you. You know how it works." She sounds tired. Like this is an argument they've had many times before. "Trust me," she sighs, "nearly every one of your colleagues has asked for that coveted spot. None of them will get it. It's not personal. We have the Warhol, those few Picasso sketches in there, and the new Amy Sherald—"

"I am the institute's most renowned faculty member and artist," Max steamrolls her, his voice echoing down the corridor. I press my fingers to my lips, amused by his pluck. "It's *my* faculty picture you push to the front of our website during admissions season every year. It's *my* paintings and awards and write-ups and reviews you feature in alumni newsletters. Not Okende or Grant or Fitzherbert." I smirk. He *has* got some name recognition, and they use that to maximum benefit around here, it's true. But he's not the only one. And, to be honest, most of his notoriety is two decades behind him—and everyone knows it. Even Max. *Especially* Max. He was short-listed for the Guggenheim's Hugo Boss Award in 1995 and hasn't let anyone forget about it since. Most of what he's done since then have been…lesser versions of those evocative works. As one of my crueler classmates put it, Max is an artist somehow derivative of himself.

"Max—" Switzer hisses, their voices echoing into the vacant corridor. "Stop this. You're overstepping. We have a full roster of dazzlingly talented and well-regarded faculty here at our school. This is not the Max Durant Institute for the Visual Arts. This is the Boston Institute—"

"May as well be the former, and you know it." I have to cover my mouth to keep from laughing my astonishment out loud. My eyes dart around the empty, gaping maw of the pinned-back double doors. They must be *just* off to the side. I can imagine Max, hands on hips, defiant, glowering down at the petite, choppy-haired Switzer, who no doubt is giving him as weary a look as he is giving her a ferocious one. "I helped make this place what it is. I've been here fifteen years. Fifteen years."

"Yeah, I know how long you've been here, my friend. I got you the job, if you'd care to remember." She sighs. I can imagine her rubbing the bridge of her nose, trying to ward off a growing headache. I hear her starting to move toward the exit. I spring up lightly and jog down the hall a little, leaning into a dark alcove so I can watch them unseen. What a fun bit of theater my Max is constructing. She breaks into the hall first, followed hotly by Max.

"What a fucked-up thing to say," Max says. "You didn't *get* me anything."

"You know what I mean. I've been here for twenty-four years, Max. I was instrumental in getting you a position here—" Max starts to growl in protest. "*Which* I was happy to do because you are a credit to this institution," she says firmly but quickly, trying to head off his anger. "But this institution is also a credit to you. None of us should ever forget that."

Max runs his hand through his black hair. It's flecked with gray and long enough to have a handsome, foppish part. He tries another tack. "Think of the renaissance this place has undergone during my tenure."

"Without a doubt. But you did not do it alone." It's like she's talking to a petulant child.

"But I'm *why* you manage to get your grubby little hands on

7

Picassos and Warhols and Sheralds in the first place. The Polk Room has the exclusivity it has because of people like me who have worked to make this place a destination. Even you must see that!"

"My grubby little hands," Switzer growls, her voice dropping to something more secretive, angrier. "Max," she says with barely contained rage, "we have known each other for many years. Many, many years. You are, somehow, one of my best friends. And that is the *only* reason I am not going to formally reprimand you. But remember yourself, man. I am the president of this school. I am your boss. So you'd better chill the fuck out." Switzer has her laptop pressed to her side under one arm and is pointing directly in Max's face with her other hand.

Max's jaw grinds. "If I don't get the Warhol spot in the Polk Room in *our own* Boston Institute Gallery over the summer, there will be hell to pay. And you will pay it. You." He points right at her.

"Is that a threat, Max?" Switzer stands a little taller against his increasingly out-of-control tone.

A wolfish smile curls onto his lips. "No, *Dana*. No, of course not." His voice softens, almost seductive. An about-face. "I—" He takes a breath, shakes his head out. It relaxes his countenance, makes him handsome and almost gentle again. "I'm sorry I lost my cool." He breathes in through his nose, puts his fists on his hips. "You're right—we are good friends. Excellent friends. We go way back. Which is why I know you will do the right thing here—"

"Max..." she groans, rubbing her eyes.

"I just feel that after all this time," he pushes on, "and after all I have meant to the school, my body of work should speak for itself. That if there were ever a time for this institution to make a gesture on my behalf, after all I have done to bring acclaim to this place, that time would be now. That gesture would be this." The two painters and professors look at each other. Switzer softens minutely at Max's deep-blue eyes. I know the power of those eyes, of what they can do. I barely remember to breathe. Max and I have discussed this very thing many times at this point—his work going in the Polk Room. I know what it would mean to him. A silence has fallen between them, and Switzer seems to be relenting. "It would cost you nothing," he goes on gently. "Nothing but a little humility. Which I know for you is asking a lot." His tone shifts sharply, venomous.

Oh, Max. So close.

"You know what, Max, *Professor Durant*, why don't you go take a flying leap." Switzer turns away from him and storms around the corner. She's completely disappeared within seconds. I look at Professor Durant, astonished at what I have just so publicly witnessed. To talk to the president of the institute that way—even if they do consider themselves friends.

He looks pleased with himself. I study him in this secret moment, in this hidden frame in the film reel, and I see that he is relishing the small pain he has caused her. He made her fight him, soften, and then take a sucker punch. But then the bright glimmer of pleasure on his face drops away as quickly as it came. Something stormy moves in within seconds. The pleasure of the snipe is gone. He's left only with his failure. With that empty wall in the Polk Room. He grabs the edge of a nearby table and violently lifts and slams its legs once, twice, three times into the floor. I jump at the noise as it echoes around the hall. He lets go, sucks in air sharply between his teeth, and pulls his hand up—it must be bleeding. He sucks on the skin between his thumb and forefinger.

His eyes finally fall on me.

Max Durant sees me. He removes his hand from his mouth,

and like a mask, slides the charming smile I have come to know so well back on his face. His brow loses its storm, his vague snarl clears. Seeing me brings him back to himself.

Oh, yes, Max sees me.

And I see him, too.

One

Souvenir

Max

Audra's voice floats to me like the scent of roses across a dark, abandoned garden; first sensed, then followed. "We're stopping just up here." It takes me a moment to come to the words, to apprehend their meaning. I've been very far away, fallen into the deep crevasses of my own thoughts and memories and preoccupations, clouded things, and now she is throwing a bright, silken rope down, beckoning me to climb back up to her out of the murk.

I blink a few times out at the blur of scenery going by my window—it is so terribly vibrant. We are moving so very fast. The farther into Maine we've gotten, the tenser my muscles have become. I feel their gentle protests as I come back to myself in the passenger seat of her little Volvo wagon; she's driving us onward and onward, farther north, further wild.

"Ground control to Major Tom—are you there, Major Tom?" Her voice is supple: deep as a river bend, scratchy as an alto sax, able to convey everything or nothing at all depending on her mood.

"Yes, reporting for duty. And stopping for a moment sounds good," I say, adjusting myself in my seat.

"You can even stay in the car," she says quickly, as if not wanting to inconvenience me. "I really just have to use the bathroom."

"No problem. Might get out to stretch." I rub my hands on the thighs of my jeans and yawn, looking back out the window.

Towering balsams, firs, and pines in varying depths of green all shimmy like '20s flappers in the stiff breeze, birches wrapped like mummies in what looks to be peeling papyrus lean this way and that, grand oaks, maples, and chestnuts muscle in on one another, flared in their autumn robes; a motley conflagration under the dazzling mid-October sun. We are in the middle of a beautiful nowhere, digging into sprawling hinterlands, into territories of wild earth.

The rolling, winding roads away from Bangor took us through towns with names like Charleston, Dover-Foxcroft, Monson, and Shirley, all with their own quaint, beautifully cinematic set dressing. It was like each was curated from grange hall flea markets and movie sets rife with small-town Americana. Stoic stone war memorials. American flags. Whitewashed, chipping town hall buildings from other centuries. Church bell towers in the actual process of tolling, gonging, calling. To me, the sound was ominous in a remote sort of way, unnameable.

I glance over at Audra again, consider her, and wonder if my other students have found out about this little trip. They'll be upset to hear I've undertaken this effort to work with and see Audra. They know I would never do the same for them. The admirers and the sycophants hate Audra. They deride her, mock her, belittle her and her work behind her back. But they're mediocre, deluded self-consolers. She is better than them in almost every way. And they know it.

But I understand her. Because I *am* her. Or was. Twenty-plus years ago, just starting out, full of ideas and energy and hunger and pure, unbridled talent. Dedicated to the work. I can cultivate her. I can make her greater than she ever could have been on her own. None of the others afford me that; not a one.

When Audra first proposed this one-on-one visit, I'd been pleasantly surprised, even a little triumphant. But things couldn't help but flicker back into memory like sunlight breaking through clouds. Images. Emotions. Colors: cadmium yellow, alizarin crimson, prism violet, cerulean blue. Just snippets, catches of history. I'd *lived* in Maine for two years, as a matter of fact—but as a much younger man. Barely more than a boy. It was decades ago; many bottles of wine and lovers and lines of cocaine and gallery showings and awards and lectures and semesters ago. So much has happened. So much has grown in the space between me and that capricious boy so far down the tunnel of time that he feels almost entirely obscured from me, insignificant to the man and artist I've become. I didn't tell Audra any of that because my experience here all those years ago holds realities she might consider a little ugly. I didn't want to ruin our fun. I didn't want to ruin the potential such a trip might hold for us. I still don't. So I'm treating this adventure like a clean slate, made just for me and her.

"It's another mile or two until we stop," Audra tells me as her eyes track a big pickup roaring by. We pass the mouth of a private dirt driveway. POSTED: No TRESPASSING No HUNTING, a sign at its edge says. The dirt drive cuts a winding path up a steep embankment, through trees and gone, a scar in the hillside. Halfway up the densely forested slope, I see whorls of gray smoke lifting into the crystalline sapphire sky. I gaze over at Audra again, thinking of the desolation, the beauty, the shocking potential of pure *color*.

"I can see you here," I tell her, nodding. "I see you in this place."

"You do?"

"Yes. I thought you were mad to not go abroad to complete your thesis. Absolutely mad. Every young artist—every *good* artist—needs difference. It pushes you forward, opens up the imagination to go out there and see the world!" She smiles faintly, sagely as she listens to me, to the bite-size version of this speech of mine she's heard many times before.

"I know what my paintings need. They don't need Istanbul. They need"—she takes a deep breath and then gestures around us, breathing out a sigh of pleasure—"this. And all of the money from those departmental awards will keep me comfortable right here."

"Seeing it now, like this, my guess is you're right. It suits you. It suits your work."

"And wait until you see what I've been up to since my last update. Any doubts will be cleared away." There is a devilish little twinkle in her eye. Reminds me of myself right before unveiling a masterwork to a hungry audience. The anticipation. The excitement.

"You sound confident."

"I am confident," she replies, sure as granite, light as a summer breeze. *As ever*, I think, not without some prickliness. But the sudden, joyful flash of her teeth and the uptick of her lips into a smile, the way her hair flares in the sun plunges me into wild, raw infatuation, that just-born kind of infatuation you feel at the beginning of every one of your own very best love stories. The sensation is of a rose reblooming, an egg re-cracking, a sweet, delicious pressure released. It has been this way with me since I met her. This inability to look away from her and what she creates. Even her sheer, bald confidence—I admit I'm the same way. Unwavering about my art. But where I am hotheaded, Audra is all coolness, steady and withholding.

The coolness, the distancing ends this weekend, I'm sure. Why else invite me all the way the hell up here?

A towering pile of stripped logs lies to one side of an industrial building to our left like Paul Bunyan's cast-off toothpicks. The sign flies by: BOUCHARD TIMBER OUTFIT. The buildings on-site are done up as log cabins. Quaint.

I reach down and dig in my leather satchel for a stick of gum to help me freshen up. Audra holds her hand out, and I give her one, too.

"Thanks," she says.

I run my hand through my hair and roll my head around on my neck, feeling cooped up. I take my glasses off and polish the lenses with my T-shirt then return them to my face and take in Audra's shoulder-length auburn hair. That heavenly nest that crowns her brilliant head and looks like it's never brushed or combed and yet somehow remains so beautiful, effervescent. I look at the gentle, fine slopes of her skull, her arcs and parabolas sweet and harmonious. I look at her smooth skin dotted all over with faint constellations of freckles, she a galaxy unto herself. I look at the thick but never brutish auburn eyebrows that frame those deep, mysterious eyes. She must sense me studying her, because she turns her head to look at me, and there is a smile on her face, the gap between her front teeth beguiling.

Her ease and warmth draw a smile out of me. Me and Audra, away together, enrobed in layer upon layer of color and beauty. She turns back to the road, but I keep looking at her. At her long, elegant neck. I imagine a sinewy, luxuriant body. I have imagined, but

I have never been allowed to look, and I have never been allowed to touch. I have a prayer in my heart, in my mind, in my body.

I have little doubt that my prayer will be answered. It always is.

But with Audra, even my desire is different than with the others. In her I see the potential for true greatness, the potential to rise up in the art world and *become* someone. Someone like me. I wish to consume, yes. But I also wish to uplift. To steward and build the greatness that already exists within her that reminds me so much of myself. There is so much I could do for her. So much I could show her. So much I could teach her if Audra would only be willing to take what is hers. Courage is what's needed to become great. I learned that very early on.

And now this invitation. I'm like a vampire over the threshold.

"Professor Durant!" She laughs, the sound round and loud and hearty, like carved wooden orbs tossed in the air. "You're nothing but a crystal-clear drinking glass, sir. I can see right into you."

I laugh, hearing in her voice that we both understand everything about this weekend. That the game is afoot. She has the preternatural ability to see me better than most. Sometimes to my delight. Often to my chagrin. She brushes some hair behind her ear, revealing a bright-yellow enamel bird earring pressed to her lobe.

"Where in the hell are we, anyway, Colfax?" I ask with a smile of my own, relaxing into my seat, hands clasped in my lap, some quiet, hidden gears of desire switched on, counting down. I gaze back through the windshield as we rise farther and farther uphill, the road seemingly cut straight through an ancient, sprawling wood.

"The forest primeval. The last best place. My heart of darkness," she incants, that round laugh bounding out of her again. "Greenville, Maine. The Moosehead Lake Region, bub." *Greenville, Maine. Moosehead Lake.*

My pulse quickens in a stab. My gaze is suddenly keen, eyes skipping from one random object to another as if something out there will reverse the truth of it. As if some radical difference in the terrain will reveal my memory as false. But no. Greenville, Maine. I have been there before. *Here* before. My brow creases like paper. My heart seems to be working harder and faster than the car itself, like it might leave my body and arrive before the rest of me.

As we climb to the top of the hill, two things emerge: to the right is a small shopping center with a large sign at the road announcing it as the Dirigo Hill Trading Post, and out beyond the apex of the hill is a grand, brochure-ready vista—sprawling miles of trees broken up by thin, snaking roads and the vast, interconnected mirror rounds of a giant lake.

Holy shit.

Audra is saying something, but I don't really hear her. I swallow and work to silently manage my breathing, calm my nerves. I think of my yoga training. I think of my breath. I count. I center.

One, two, three.

One, two, three.

"Is that Moosehead Lake down there, the one you just said?" I swallow, putting on a smile. "Of the *Moosehead Lake Region?*" I ask this in my best chamber-of-commerce voice as she flips on her right turn signal and pulls us into the parking lot of the Dirigo Hill Trading Post. But I already know the answer. I feel like I'm inside a dream; but I can't tell if it's mine or somebody else's.

"It is indeed." She smiles her crooked Colfax smile. My god. My prayer for her, the baser one, is like a nervous, struggling bird in my hands, fighting to be set free. But my shock at being back in *this* place threatens to squeeze that nervous, struggling bird to death. "So, yeah. We're in Greenville, now." Her eyes pass back and forth quickly across the parking lot, watching for any cars coming toward us from funny angles. I take three quiet, meditative breaths. "About an hour and a half northwest of where I picked you up in Bangor. So, *driving*, you're about…five and a half, six hours from Boston right now. But only about an hour and a half from the Canadian border," she tells me as the car crackles over the broken asphalt and pulls into a parking space near the supermarket part of the trading post. "Does that help to orient you a little?" Her hinky smile returns. "I bet you didn't even google it before you came," she says, throwing the wagon into park. I lean forward and peer out at the structure of the place.

"I'm…not sure how it would have helped me if I did," I say, leaning back, taking it all in. My eyes stay glued on the buildings. "Why worry about such things when traveling with a native?" I take off my seatbelt and swipe my hands through my hair, once, twice, three times in quick succession. Audra cuts the engine and pulls the keys from the ignition.

A need pulses through me. To touch her. As if feeling her body might ground me, might save me. But I don't touch her. Not yet. No.

"You have the faith of an altar boy."

"When Audra Colfax is your god, a man's faith can be boundless," I reply with a slight delay. I lean forward toward the sloped glass of the windshield. She tosses her head back and laughs again, that big, unaffected laugh. I look over at her, my gaze ungluing from the trading post.

"Now tell me, Professor Durant," she says, her voice almost a whisper. "Am I a cruel god or a benevolent god?" I want to bite those pretty lips of hers, nick them with my teeth, speckle them with blood. *Hold fast to the prayer, Max.*

"You are a creature of kindness," I say, low and slow, leading her down my primrose path. Something about looking at her steadies me a bit. Her eyes brood with energy. I can feel it. I know the look well: I have seen it on the faces of so many lovers and soon-to-be lovers. She draws away from me, laughing to herself, and pulls her purse onto her lap from the back seat.

"I have the house stocked with just about anything and everything we could ever need. But I have to use the restroom. You stay here. I'll be right back."

"Audra—" I say and find I'm not sure what to follow it with. She turns and looks at me. Those milk-chocolate eyes of hers drip into me, her lips slightly parted—perfect little raspberries. Hesitation rises and makes me stop, knowing that if I go much further, I won't have any choice.

"How far to your place?" It's almost a plea.

"Forty minutes," she says. Can I bear forty minutes? I sit back in my seat, taking a few breaths, trying to reverse biology. *Think of cold showers, the Queen of England, that disemboweled porcupine on the road twenty miles ago. Fresh and slick with balloon-like organs spilling from its belly.* She laughs gently. "I know," she says, her voice seeming to understand. I look at her and wonder if she does. If she really understands. Her eyes scan all around my face, her own a mosaic of compassion, heat, tenderness, agitation, and impatience; it seems to mirror mine. She sits back in her seat, and we both look forward out the windshield, trying to cool off. She sighs, and it is like a lonely, historic wind sweeping across a great western plain. Desolation and desire; that's my Audra. I swallow and take another breath, looking at shoppers moving in and out of the front entrance of the supermarket. Many a man and woman is wearing flannel, thermals, puffy jackets.

"Hunting season?" I ask, looking at a man wearing a camouflage sweatshirt and a bright-orange knit cap. There are others, I realize, plenty of others in similar garb.

"Oh, yes," Audra says. "Bear, deer, moose right now. This is a very popular area for hunting."

How bizarre to be here once again. The scene conjures itself before me like a terrible magic trick, a palimpsest. There had been fewer cars. The lot wasn't paved then. The supermarket had been smaller, less modern, and named something else. But the general angles, the spatial arrangements, the site at the top of the hill: *yes*. Déjà vu ripples through me like a bad lunch beginning to announce itself hours before the final disaster. My stomach twists, and I feel an unease settle. I never thought I would return. I told myself I never would.

I gaze at Audra, the brightness of the lemon-yellow birds at her ears pinging in the air.

It was many years ago, yes. I force my shoulders to release their tension. So many years. Such a very long time ago that it may as well not even be the same place. The same life.

Audra

I'm exiting the trading post bathroom, leather wallet in hand, when I catch sight of him. He's moving away from a set of cash registers with a green plastic shopping bag. He's a tall tree trunk of a man, strong and sturdy and almost heavyset, with a day's scruff, a handsome, boyish face, and good, unkempt hair. Lance Peters. I look around me, thrown off-balance at seeing him and feeling relieved I was able to convince Max to stay in the car while I made this pit stop. I pause not far from the bathroom, unsure of what to do.

He looks surprised when he notices me. I bet I do, too. Lance and I go way back. We met in seventh grade, Trapper Keepers and all. As teenagers, we shot guns on my family's property, went skinny-dipping with our friends in Moosehead Lake, got drunk and a little handsy with each other up in the long-abandoned cabins at Lupine Valley. And recently, we've reconnected between my trips to Boston.

"I can say with complete honesty that I did not expect to see you in the camouflage walkie-talkie section of Dirigo Hill today," he says as he comes to greet me. His eyes are warm, but there's also something else in them. Like he wants to ask me if I'm okay but can't bring himself to do it out loud. It's been a little while since we've seen each other. Longer than either of us would like, I think.

"Me neither," I acknowledge. "Just in the last leg of driving up from Bangor. Had to take a break."

"But back on the road now?" He turns his head in the direction of the exit, the parking lot. Like he's trying to catch a glimpse of someone.

"Back on the road now." I nod and touch his arm gently, bringing his attention back to me, away from my car, from Max.

"I take it your professor or advisor guy or whatever-he-is is somewhere here?"

A fine, silken web of nerves flares white-hot in my body. He may try to play it cool, but Lance knows his name. Lance knows he's with me. I nod.

He takes a breath and places a hand softly against my ear and hair.

"Been able to sleep?"

"As much as I can," I sigh, looking around us. "A bit." I know I should go. I know I should speed this along and send Lance on his way so I can get on mine. But being with him is bracing. I need it.

"Shotgun ammo?" I ask, trying to squint and see some box markings through the bag.

"Yep. And plenty of it," he says, hands working the plastic bag to show me. I count at least five or six boxes. "Anyway. I should head on. My buddies and Uncle Marc are waiting for me in the truck."

Marc?

"You're hanging with Marc?" I ask, rattled. I swallow and steady myself.

24

"I know, I know—he's a tool," he says with a sigh.

"He's a violent, drunken maniac," I correct, my blood boiling. I *cannot* believe he's hanging out with Marc. Lance and the rest of his family have been estranged from him for years. And with damn good reason.

"I know—but he's my dad's brother, and Dad asked me to check in on the guy. My dad's been on me about it for a month. I guess he's been a wreck since Minnie left him." We're both quite sure Marc used to hit Minnie, his long-term, live-in girlfriend, but I don't say it now. "I guess the guy is doing the Twelve Steps."

"Really? He's doing AA?" My voice is filled with skepticism.

"That's what he says. Well, that's what my dad says. Heading toward making amends, I guess." Blood flows hot into my neck and cheeks. "I know, I know—he has a lot to make amends for. But he's trying."

"I'm sure we don't know the half of it," I reply, surprised at just how shaken I am, at how easily it's edging into anger.

"Well, if he keeps at it, we just might." Lance sounds apologetic, somber. I look at him and know that he is sincerely torn. "If he does or says anything out of line, today will be the end of me extending myself, that's for sure. I promise."

I really don't want them hanging out. Reconnecting. That would not be for the best. "Don't tell him you saw me. I want nothing to do with that guy." I cross my arms in front of my chest.

"I won't, I won't. I promise," he assures me, seeing that I'm upset. I take a breath. *Settle down. Recalibrate. You're fine.*

"Hunting today?" I say, changing the subject.

"No," he replies simply. "Not today." I nod, and we just look at each other for a moment. "Anyway, I should go. I'll see you soon." Then he hugs me tight. And I hug him tighter, shutting my eyes for a moment. He smells like wood chips and faint cologne and the faraway whisper of woodsmoke. I wish he didn't have to go.

"I will see you soon," I say firmly. We release each other, and he looks down at me from his six-two vantage.

"I'm around. Let me know if you need me, okay?" His hazel eyes are bright and alert.

"Will do." I nod. "See you later."

"See you," he says, and then he turns and goes. I watch him walk out of the store.

He's hanging with Uncle Marc. Now. He hasn't seen or talked to the guy in six, maybe eight months.

I take a breath, rub my eyes, get my bearings. *Deep breaths. Keep your head.*

When I look up, I see him.

The other him.

Max.

When did he come in? How did I miss him?

I wonder if he saw me talking to Lance. I weave behind a rack of rabbit-fur snow hats. Max is gazing around almost watchfully, then he wanders to the far side of the room, to the modest self-serve coffee bar named JOE—I can see he's tempted—but he ultimately turns away, his face showing his disapproval at the offerings. Only the best will do for him. Unlike Lance, who will drink any coffee put in front of him as long as it's hot enough to hurt. But Max? He's a fine-tuned machine, particular and demanding. There is no denying this. He is not to be denied.

In Boston, Max is an urbane little Newbury Street prince: self-important, handsome, fashionable. In the Dirigo Hill Trading Post in Greenville, Maine, he's just another overdressed flatlander. And it's clear he doesn't understand his difference; it doesn't even register with him. He's not the most self-aware guy. The man is wearing a fitted black tee that I know cost him seventy-five dollars. He has on slick but exaggerated black frames. His dark-wash jeans, easily a couple hundred dollars, are bespoke. He's *crisp*. Deep-brown leather Chelsea boots on his feet. Designer. Everything about him is designer. *Designed.* His clothing, his home, his reputation, his life. He has crafted it all with an almost religious egotism with himself at its center, his own god, his own theology. He is *that* pretentious a figure in a sea of large, thick men wearing slouched, faded jeans and layered workman's flannels stained with the proof of real labor. Motor oil, tree sap, soil.

But even I have to admit that for a man circling fifty, Max is exquisitely lean and youthful-looking. Smooth and strong; nothing wasted. You can see it in the way he carries himself like a lynx through the wood-paneled showroom. I had been immediately reminded of his…*vitality* in the most visceral of ways when we reunited at the airport this morning. I was embarrassed by it. I hated myself desperately for it.

I glance around, not recognizing anyone else in the store, for which I am grateful. Max walks with his hands clasped behind his back, wondering at the cramped but tidy goods stocked all around him.

I do my best to push Lance from my mind. Marc, too.

Max moves toward a display of hand-carved walking sticks. I make a casual beeline to him, forcing myself to clasp his arm gently, warmly, like a lover or a girlfriend or a naive hanger-on is supposed to do. He brushes his hand across the box tops of some of the game cameras on display.

"Hey, sorry—there was a wait for the women's bathroom," I lie.

"I got bored. Thought I'd check the place out." He shoves his hands into his jeans pockets, shoulders high and tense. His eyes zip around us like a man being watched. I wonder if he didn't want to be alone in the car without me. Maybe he has made a talisman of me in these unknown territories.

"Ready to go?"

"Just about—but there is one thing I wanted to..." He wanders off ahead of me, deeper into the store. He says over his shoulder, "I was looking at them while you were in the bathroom."

Maybe he didn't see me talking to anyone; if he did, he doesn't let on.

Max walks hastily to a case of gleaming knives hugging the eastern side of the room as I follow behind him through a cookstove display. In the case, I know, are knives for gutting. Knives for skinning. Knives for deboning. Knives for butchering, caping, hunting, camping. There will be knives with clip points and drop points and trailing points. Knives with gut hooks. I know the arsenal intimately. If you weren't doing something in the woods or on the lake, especially as a kid and a teenager, there never was much to do in these parts besides drive around Greenville or go up to the trading post and look around. I'd look at rifles, duck calls, GPS devices, game cameras, survival guides, and—of course—knives. I have hovered over this knife case many times in my life, from the time I was a girl.

The employee behind the display is farther down the case consulting a tattered *Maine Gazetteer*, giving directional advice to some out-of-towner wearing a stiff, expensive-looking parka that may as well still have the tags on it. I don't recognize the trading post employee; he must have started here within the past year or two, since I've been mostly away in Boston working on my MFA. I pull my hands up into the sleeves of my wool sweater, continuing to follow Max, mindlessly investigating a shotgun displayed on the wall as I go. I look to the far end of the knife case and see that the salesman has finished with his out-of-towner and is moving toward mine. Max, to my surprise, lingers. He's taking in the array as the salesman comes to lean his palms on top of the case opposite him. Also to my surprise, Max points to a few of the knives on display and begins to engage the man in conversation about them. I can't quite hear what they're saying over the chatter of other shoppers and the Bob Seger being piped in from overhead. I go over and join him.

"Doing a little browsing?" I ask, looking between Max and the thirty-something man behind the counter. He's wearing a battered New England Patriots ball cap with a fishhook attached to the severely curled bill.

"Getting into the spirit." For the ten-thousandth time, I am made to look at Max's too-white teeth—his dazzlers. The same immaculate teeth that I know want to pinch at my nipples as soon as we get through the goddamned door of my house. He wants me. That's why he's here, after all. I'm not oblivious. "What do you think? I like these two." I look at him and see he is speaking in earnest. A knife. The pacifist Bostonian artist. The liberal academic. I realize now he's not just admiring the lines, the craftsmanship. He means to buy one of these things. I'm irritated; maybe a little alarmed. I want to leave. I want to get him out of here. I have a timetable to keep to.

"You're going to buy a knife?" My brow creases as my gentle laugh tails off.

"Souvenir," he says. I look at him, into him, and see he's serious. A slow creep of something like anxiety or excitement ripples through my body—I can't tell which. It travels from my toes to my scalp. I search his face, calculating what he may be sensing—in this trip, in this place, in me. *Why do you want a knife, Professor Durant?* "You'll have to mail it to me when I leave since I can't take it on the plane."

"Gonna use it for anything in particular?" the salesman asks, dragging his large hand down the side of his scruffy face, looking at Max without enthusiasm, ignoring me. The question seems to take Max by surprise.

"Maybe just for the basics. If I ever got in a pinch and needed to cut rope or brush or something." I want to laugh at this. I can't imagine any situation in which Max Durant would use any sort of knife like this, in a pinch or otherwise. He's never done anything remotely handy or outdoorsy as long as I've known him. "But mostly, it's just to have. Mark the occasion."

"Ayuh, okay," the man says, seemingly satisfied. He looks at me with tired, hangdog eyes, and then he looks at Max. "Up from Portland?"

"Boston," Max replies.

The man nods almost smugly, as if he's heard everything he needs to hear. He turns his gaze back to Max after letting his eyes linger on me with some curiosity. He is trying to place me, trying to tell if I might be a local. I do not answer the tacit question. "Well, so you like these two heah?" The man brings his face closer to the display glass and considers the contents of the brightly illuminated box. "Then, of those two—I'd go with this one right theya." He points to a beautiful switchblade knife with a drop point. The handwritten tag has *Fallkniven* scrawled on it. The blade is flawless, silver stainless steel, and the handle is sturdy and immaculate, banded with what appears to be oxhide. It's a handsome knife, almost like a sports car: the lines sensual; the purpose utilitarian; the potential deadly.

You sly, woodsy little bastard, is all I can think. I start to laugh. Both men look at me.

"Forget that," I say, unable to watch the fleecing of America. "That's a three-hundred-dollar knife. You don't need any god-damned three-hundred-dollar knife." Max looks over at me, his face quizzical, as if surprised he's being interrupted. I look at the man behind the counter then down at the knives. "Your other choice was the better bet. The Buck Knives 279. It's versatile; it's sharp. It folds like the other one. It's fifty bucks. It'll cut whatever *rope* you want." The knife is mean and sturdy and strong-looking. It has a black handle with an all-metal edging. Max looks at me with wonder and subterranean annoyance. I look to the salesman. "Am I right on those price points?"

"Well, I'd have to check," he says, feigning uncertainty as he pulls the knives out and turns over the tags. Scrawled on the Fallkniven tag is $349. Scrawled on the Buck Knives tag is $59.

"He's been in Boston too long, bub, not me." I beam as I clap Max on the back, looking at the salesman. Max seems displeased.

"I'll take that one." He points through the glass at the expensive one. The one that costs three hundred forty-nine dollars. The one, it must be admitted, that is more beautiful. The sports car. He looks over at me, and in his eyes is something like spite. Is something telling me I had better never do anything like that to him again. I've embarrassed him. "I want that one. And I'll have it."

"You got it, man," the salesman says. "Want a carrying case or anything like that?"

"No," Max tells him, looking back at the clerk. "I intend to keep it close." I look at Max's profile. He won't meet my gaze, but his neck has flushed red.

"I'll ring you up right over heah." The man gestures at the cash register down at the end of the case, and Max walks away without looking at me. I push the sleeves of my sweater up to my elbows. I'm too warm. Max is buying a knife. A beautiful, sharp knife. I'm sweating. The way he looked at me. That barely contained contempt.

As he leaves the register with his knife inside a paper bag, he gives me a big, smug smirk. It says, *Look at me, being a man. I'll have whatever I want. Despite you.*

I fuel up my car at the gas station outside, and we get back on the road. I'm incredibly relieved to be putting distance between us and one of the region's biggest gathering places. For the rest of our secluded weekend away, the odds of us running into anyone at all, let alone anyone who would know me, is mighty slim. I watch Max's eyes look intently at Dirigo Hill in his side mirror as I pull away. Maybe it's good we stopped there, despite the knife. He seems a little lost in himself again.

Good.

I study him and wonder more than anything what he's thinking.

He studied me with great interest while in *his* natural habitat in Boston this past year; me, who still feels like a sketch of a person down there, not quite filled out, run ragged against the city's kinetics. I like the dark and the quiet. Boston was neither of these things. But now I'm back in Maine, in the woods, heading toward Rockveil, and everything in and of my body feels more substantial somehow, more three-dimensional and real. And I have extracted Max and transmuted both of us so that *he* is the one fading into the background while *I* am the living being of flesh and bone, fully rendered. He will drift and be drained without the city's swarm of safe, glittering lights. He will be tied to me with no quick exits on underground or road-splitting trains, on planes or in Lyfts. It makes me feel witchy. Dastardly.

As we cruise through downtown Greenville, I point out signs for the Katahdin Cruises steamboat tours of Moosehead Lake. Max asks if we could do one this weekend, and I tell him sure, we could try. The foliage is always pretty in mid-October. Max pulls the paper bag from his pocket then pulls the knife free. He turns it over, admiring it approvingly.

"What a thing," he says then whistles. "I used to do a little whittling back in the day, you know. Folksy little pieces." He's in a good mood again.

"Did you?" I laugh gently, genuinely tickled by the thought. It's just so…*down-market* for him. He flips it open and nods, smiling at me.

"Just little things. For myself. My friends," he says. I look over at him and then down at the razor-sharp blade in his hands.

We arc out around Moosehead Lake, leaving Greenville center for the rural outskirts. "Do you see many animals around here?" Max peers into the quaking pines sentried along the road. He flicks the knife open and closed, open and closed, *snick, snick*, not even looking at it. Just something to do with his hands. The more he does it, the more anxious I become. Honestly, I wish he'd just put it away. And it's not the knife in and of itself that makes me nervous. I've been adept with knives from a young age. But a man like Max with a knife like that—*that* makes me nervous. The scale between predator and prey tipping out of my favor. I can't have that, not this weekend. Not now.

"From time to time," I tell him. "A lot of deer. Rabbits. Turkey. That sort of thing. But there's so much land that sightings aren't as common as you'd think. No reason to come near a road if they can help it." The openness of Greenville has left us. The trees now creep close to the roadway and block most of the sunlight, like we're in some natural timber tunnel. *Snick, snick.* He flips the knife open and closed again. Then again. I look over at him and at the knife. Part of me still can't believe he bought it.

"Maybe by the end of the weekend?" he asks hopefully.

"Maybe," I reply. "We'll take a ride tonight at dusk along some of the logging roads and see what happens. I know a great spot." The drive is quiet for the next several minutes, the only sounds the hum of the car over the asphalt and the *snick, snick* of his blade. He's like a boy who's just discovered his own dick.

"Way out here, huh?" he asks. "You grew up *way* out here." He says this last part as if he can't quite believe it. He is putting me in one of his paintings. Inside a frame. He is making me a cameo, not quite real. *Snick, snick.* I look over at him, but he's looking out his window with intensity and focus. "I see you," Max sighs. "I see it all in you. This wildness. This beauty." The more he talks, the more he tells me what I am, the more my muscles tense like poured concrete hardening up. I look over at his fidgeting hands, at the blade being unveiled and hidden, over and over, the sleek, sliding sound it makes, again and again and again, worming into my ears. *Snick, snick.* "My woman from the woods. Halo of myrtle green, foliage, wilderness. No wood nymph, no." He laughs gently, deep inside his own mind. "An archer enrobed in her forest. Sap green, viridian, lime, teal, turquoise highlights. Parchment, to define and brighten. Tendrils. A small, glowing heart—outside of the chest, like Kahlo, as if pinned—in shades of violet; a prism, deep blue." My fingers are tense around the steering wheel. He has made me what he wishes. But I know it's not what I am. It's only in his mind. Only ever in his mind.

A Subaru with two kayaks strapped on top passes us going in the opposite direction. *Snick, snick. Snick, snick.*

"Such a surprise to get an invitation up here. To your world." *My world.* Max runs a hand through his hair then scratches his jaw, vaguely pensive again. Some buried unrest seems underscored by the incessant flicking of that knife open and closed, open and closed—a weapon that could gut me like an animal. "What a weekend this will be."

"Yes."

"What a place." *Snick, snick.* I look over at him. He gazes introspectively out the window. *Fuck you, Professor Max Durant. Fuck. You.* There are several long moments of quiet, and then:

Snick, snick.

"Would you keep that damned thing closed?" I snap. "It's flashing the sun in my eyes, Max." We're both surprised at my tone. I didn't expect to be testy with him this early on. Maybe the stress of this weekend is getting to me. Of what I must do. But it's also that he has that knife. I had not anticipated it. I look over at him. He folds it closed. Puts it in his pocket. His eyes appraise me. He's trying to sort out who he's in this car with. I've so rarely snapped at him.

Quiet settles upon us, and I can feel him growing agitated. His face is set, and I know he wants the uncomplicated fantasy back. His verdant archer. His wilderness goddess. I do not oblige immediately; I do not return his dream to him just yet, because I don't want to. But after a few minutes, I'll relent. I don't want him to be miserable or, worse yet, to spiral into one of his moods. Not yet. The weekend is so young, and there is so much promise for what it could hold.

"Sorry about that, Audie," he says, his voice strained with the effort of playing nice with me. I don't like that nickname—*Audie*. In fact, I hate it. He's the only one who calls me that. I let another solid minute or two pass in silence.

"Sorry I snapped at you, Professor. I am—that was...out of line." I look over at him, my face seeming to plead for absolution. His face brightens, bit by bit, as my hardness recedes, as he pulls the apology and angst from me. He thinks he's regaining the upper hand. He looks satisfied. "I'm probably just a little tired. And... well, I dunno—*wound up*." My voice is gentle and cryptic and maybe mildly flirtatious. I let him have it. This gift. A bit of that wolfishness from before creeps back into the lines of his face, the glint of his teeth. I relax. There he is. The predator I'm fully prepared to face.

"How far to your place?" he asks, shifting in his seat.

"Not long, now."

THESIS
Her Dark Things by Audra Colfax

Piece #1: *I Remember It Stark*
Oil and mixed media on canvas. 36" x 24".

[Close-up of a brown enamel lantern, chipped and shining. The metal curves in a never-ending arc off the edges of the canvas. The bulb in the glass center is half burnt out, eggshell, heavy cream, white, its light dusky. Found objects incorporated throughout by layering.]

Note on torn graph paper found under the drawer liner in the downstairs bathroom of the Dunn residence.

> *I cut myself again. Deep this time.*
> *Mom said come NOW to the*
> *hospital or I'll call the cops, Cindy. I stayed shut up and bled all*
> *over*
> *the floor*
> *a ruby Jackson Pollock on white tile*
> *the cops came*
> *an ambulance came lights came everything came. AT me.*
> *Brady*
> *came to visit me at the hospital*
> *the next day. held my hand.*
> *it's like a sludge*
> *builds up in me, thick and oily. inside my veins and bones and*
> *lungs and eyes and brain.*

Leaves me no ROOM.
Some die-cast mold getting drowned with liquid metal.
TRY explaining that when they ask.
They gave me new pills and a therapist. Again.

—Nov87. CD.

Note on a yellow sticky note found pressed between the pages of the family cookbook in the Dunn kitchen.

will anyone EVER find
my HAUNTY little scrawlslip in with the beef wellington?

—Jan88. CD.

Note on ripped-out paper from a spiral-bound notebook with faint food stains found in the birdhouse on the Dunn property.

Got my GED today, a year late a year later
than graduation
than Brady.
Mom and dad and Brady were real proud.
Had little starty-stoppies here and there and there
cutting and trying to kill myself and cutting and cutting again
disruptive disruptions eruptions irruptions
all along the way
in middle school disrupting in high school so many
disruptions distractions marks all over my body
but I did it

I am better
somehow
mostly intact

—Jan88. CD.

Note in tiny handwriting on a scrap of note paper found inside an empty Kleenex box in the attic of the Dunn residence.

All I've ever wanted is to go to college
for art
application deadline is coming right up, I told them
they say Cindy wait hold your horses stick around a whole year
see how you feel in a year (we worry you'll stop taking your pills)
think on it (we worry you'll stop trying, remember November?)
save up some money (let us watch watch watch you to make sure
    your heart still beats beats beats)
Get a steady job (close by, let us help you stay alive)
I see them and I hear them and I see into them and I hear
    through them and I appreciate the thought but I'll die here of
    stasis if not of my own hand
I have dreams, aspirations
bigger than this place
they said if you still want to study art after a year, fine, fine art
    study fine want to study fine art fine
but you're on your own
if you want to study business and you wait we'll pay for it
think dad wants me to work for him
dunn & daughter he'd like that not sure I would

waiting a year taking my meds going to therapy
I'm doing well now, so
we'll see
don't know if I can stand it
here
another whole year, though

—Jan88. CD.

Note on Lisa Frank stationery found in the landscaped rock wall outside the Dunn residence.

I baked a cake today
it came out really good
dad was wild for it mom was
crazy about it
which felt good
to make them feel good
like maybe I could be okay
like maybe we could

—Jan88. CD.

Note in tiny handwriting on scratch paper with red ink doodles found folded in Cindy Dunn's bedroom side table.

I sketched today but it wasn't really
a sketch.
I sat in my room with my old

brown lantern
with the sticker from that class trip to
Bar Harbor.
I remember it stark.
I drew
in the orb of its light
in the dark of my bed
a circle
over
and over
again with my pen until it cut through the paper.
It was a slick oily
black smear. Shiny like a beetle's eye.
Brady took me out to
dinner at Thelma's Landing.
I wore my favorite summer dress despite the frigid cold
I felt like an electric spark
a sunflower.
We fucked after
at his place.
He likes my crazy ass a good bit but I don't know why.
He'd say he's my boyfriend
I bet.
He'd say he loves me but
but.

—Jan88. CD.

Note on yellow legal paper found crumpled in the crawl space
beyond Cindy Dunn's bedroom closet in the Dunn residence.

Dad caved, paid the application fee for college so
art.
I saw a tiny smile in him when he said don't
tell mom.

—Jan88. CD.

Juniper

MAY 4, 1988

It's just past midnight, and I've still only driven as far as Greenville. The streets are dark, and everything is closed. Nowhere to stop for a quick bite. Nowhere to pick up a pack of smokes. I haven't eaten since Kittery. I haven't had a cigarette since Bangor. I glance down at the ashtray in the console and see the litter of butts sticking up like gnarled fingers. It's a long drive from Washington, DC, to King City, Maine. Eleven hours and change if you don't have to stop for *anything* and you avoid major traffic. A naive map calculation. In reality, it's maybe thirteen, fourteen hours total when you factor in reasonable breaks to gas up, eat, piss, stretch your legs, and smoke.

Add two more hours to that if your girlfriend of four months, Rita, breaks up with you just before you leave. Morning of. No warning. Two added hours in which you try to figure out what the fuck is happening, and why. Two hours to reach the conclusion that she was never *really* okay with you going away for a job for four months.

That she had no interest in trying long-distance. To realize she didn't love you enough to hold on that long. Two hours to cry, then rage, then plead, then promise, then rage again, then storm out, finally, at around eight thirty a.m. instead of six a.m. like you planned.

I was speeding through New Jersey before it registered that I have no home to go back to once the job is over. I lived in her apartment.

Zero fucking cigarettes left.

The farther past Greenville I get, the darker and stiller the world seems. No streetlamps. Barely a car on the road. The sky is indecipherable from the crowding pines that strike up like walls from the sides of the road. I'm tired. Hungry. By the time I finally find my way into King City and to the sneaky little dirt road that will take me up to Lupine Valley, I'm moments away from wondering if I've gotten myself lost. But King City—which is no city at all, but more of a village or territory—is like that. It's a surprise when you find it. Some of the depression and agitation begins to lift as I realize I've made it. Back here, to this special place where I've always felt most myself.

The marker at the end of the rutted dirt road is understated: a small flag hanging limp from a pole affixed to a tree. My headlights catch the flag's familiar image as I turn up the drive—three craning stems of sun-faded, purple lupine flowers.

I bump my way up the winding road, which is more like a glorified dirt path, moving slowly, carefully through the dark, the big WELCOME TO THE LUPINE VALLEY ARTS COLLECTIVE sign seeming to spring toward the road halfway up. I feel greeted. Taken in by the classic periwinkle- and cornflower-blue lettering, the painting of lupine stalks on a green hillside. After the day I've had, I almost want to cry. It's my seventh such return to this place, and every time, it forms a lump in my throat.

The farther I go, the more the place reveals itself to me: the sandy horseshoe pitch on the right; a piece of fencing emblazoned with a black stallion mural to its rear; the path on the left that leads to the ropes course high in the boughs of the trees; up and on the left again, the pottery studio with a kiln, the chimney at rest for the night.

At the tail end of the snaking road, the tunnel of trees opens, dilating wider and wider, and I feel like Alice falling through the rabbit hole, ending up somewhere decidedly more magical than the place I'd just been. The Lupine Valley Arts Collective. A thirty-acre patch of wilderness at the center of which thrives a beating, uniquely humane heart—a collection of tidy, utilitarian cabins and outbuildings sprinkled among the trees at the base of Little Chickadee Mountain. A place filled with potters, painters, sculptors, crafters, woodworkers, fiber artists. *Artists.* Making and collaborating. The well-worn paths between buildings are like blood vessels linking cabin to cabin to mess hall to latrine to studios.

Even in the dark, I can make out the colorful handmade flags sentried around the village, some tied into the branches of trees, some hung from poles off cabins, stitched with the seasons and years of their making. From a tree on my left hangs a blue-and-orange flag with a purple planet in the middle: Saturn with all her rings. Ahead, on a pole near the communal fire, is a limp flag in black and white stitched with words I can't quite make out. Hanging from a pole off the side of one of the nearer cabins is a flag embroidered with complicated pink, red, and purple flowers that proclaims in big, block stitching, ART OUTLASTS ALL.

A giddy smile overtakes my face. I'm back.

Art in the form of lawn ornaments is sprinkled everywhere: rock piles painted and stacked into little temples, fairy houses, druidic walls; thin birch limbs bent, gathered, and lashed together into creeping, living archways inside of which are sculptures glittering with broken shards of colored glass; welded and sculpted metal birds flocking in the grass as if pecking for seed, others perching on tree branches in fantastical nests made of steel wool and glass beads. Large, ever-evolving landscape murals of Little Chickadee Mountain cover the side of the mess hall. Everything is infused with a childlike freedom and whimsy, from the ROY G. BIV markers staking out the paths in every direction to the prettily threaded hammocks that hang under so many of the trees, waiting for a body or two to crawl inside and sleep under the stars.

The glow of candle and lantern light inside cabins punches the darkness out in perfect squares. The ever-present central bonfire in the Village Commons is aflame, a polestar around which all the cabins radiate. We gather at the fire after supper almost nightly for drinks and discussion, to talk art, to socialize, to seek advice.

Well, I think you truncated the annealing process just a bit too much. That's why you didn't get the hairpin bend you wanted in that section of your iron fence.

I knew Picasso, you know. We were nearly lovers once.

My work was put on display at the Met in 1968, but by then it was long overdue; I just didn't appreciate it the way I should have.

I see a few people moving between the buildings. Could be other staff like me, here a few days before the new cohort arrives, or it could be students staying on from the last session.

I crackle up the drive toward the heart of things and finally see him, the closest thing to a mascot a place like this might have: Old Gus. He's standing out front of the main office cabin, face turned upward to the speckled sky, his trusty camera around his neck. Seeing the way the campfire light splashes the surrounding tree trunks and cabins sparks a sense of wholeness and belonging in me. Unfathomable when I set out this morning, after Rita. Unfathomable on the New Jersey Turnpike as I thought about my homelessness. But of course, I was wrong about that. I realize this now. And with such clarity. *This* is home. Has been home since I first started coming in the summer of 1983. Everywhere else—the colleges and universities I've attended, the apartments I've rented, Rita's loft in DC, even my parents' house in Pittston, Pennsylvania, are auxiliary locations. *This* is my home. I found Lupine Valley back in '83. Lupine Valley found me.

When I get out of the car, Old Gus—the camp's longtime managing director—looks at me appraisingly, and I can't stop the first smile of the day from cracking my face. He doesn't talk for several long beats as I approach him.

"You look older," he says, his voice worn and chapped. I shove my hands in my jeans pockets and stand next to him, looking up into the sky at his shoulder.

"I was here only four or five months ago. The fall term, Gus," I laugh.

"Nevertheless," he says. "Nevertheless." We're quiet for a while, the only sounds the snaps of the fire, a muffled voice or two in far-flung cabins, and the rustle of the wind in the trees. "It's late," he says.

"Hope I didn't keep you up."

"Aw, no. I'm not much of a sleeper. Not with these boys and girls up here." He points at the stars in the sky. "Gotta keep an eye."

"It's been a long day, Gus," I say, rubbing my neck. "Where are you sticking me?"

He turns to look at me, his face rumpled but delighted. "No getting stuck for you." He smiles, a few teeth missing. "Come along."

To my astonishment, praise be to Old Gus, I'm assigned one of the nicer private cabins. It's called Motif. All of the cabins here are named after art terminology. Motif. Tone. Shade. Texture. I think it's a little joke Gus must have come up with, because when people describe where they're staying, they're forced to say things like: I'm in Focus; I'm in Symmetry; I'm in Shape. Motif is set slightly back from the Village Commons, tucked under an ancient pine.

"You've earned it," he says, igniting an oil lamp for me as I sling my things down in relief. "You've either taken or taught one term here each year for the past five years. Sometimes more than that."

Motif is an 8' by 8' square with a thin single mattress on an iron frame to the left side, a mini potbellied stove set in the back right corner with some metal flashing behind it, a petite wooden desk and chairs set under the front-wall window to the right of the door, and an oversize, well-worn trunk set at the foot of the bed. The cabin is ascetically clean, but years' worth of paint and dye splatters flecks the place regardless. A kind of nostalgic kaleidoscope.

He takes photos of me setting my things down haphazardly in the cabin. Then he takes pictures of the haphazard things: my hiking pack, sleeping bag, sketchbook, duffel of paint supplies, tin coffee cup. Gus is always taking photos. He likely thinks of himself mostly as a documentarian, capturing the camp's seasons and generations, but every once in a while, one of his photos is truly compelling, not just descriptive. He usually manages to sell those photos to a dealer down in Portland or at art fairs in Greenville.

"Who's here?" I ask.

"Three cooks, two maintenance, two cleaners. Now, counting you, six instructors. You're the last to arrive. Seven students. Will be twenty-three when the rest show up this weekend." He adjusts the camera strap around his neck.

"So seven carry-over artists are here from the spring term," I say. "Pretty good."

"Yes, indeed. Two sculptors, three painters, a metalworker, and a mixed-media artist. All very good." Gus buffs the lens of his camera. "Can't remember if you know any of 'em."

"And how many fresh faces?"

"Ten brand-new to Lupine, six who have been here before at some other point. You may recognize a few—maybe you over-lapped at one time or another. Hard to say. My mind ain't the steel trap it used to be."

I nod and think about the cohorts I've worked with in the past. Most students who come to Lupine Valley are in their twenties or thirties, with some talented young outliers coming in their late teens. Every once in a while, we get older students, people in their sixties or seventies. I even once had an eighty-three-year-old lady in one of my sessions. Some of the people who come here are bona fide professional artists able to sell their stuff and live on what they make. Lupine Valley is a respite from the world, a place to get back to basics for them. Some are weekend-warrior types or retirees who want to have An Experience. But most of the people who choose Lupine Valley are like me—holding some sort of formalized train-ing in their specialty and wanting to indulge in largely unstructured time away to simply create and develop and challenge ourselves in nature and in the company of other like-minded souls. Most of the instructors are in their forties or fifties. I'm twenty-eight. A little bit of an outlier there.

"We just can't stay away, Gus." I smile, shoving my hands into the pockets of my hoodie.

"Ah, Juniper—don't I know it." Juniper. *Juniper*. I'd been at Lupine Valley for three days when I was first christened. I'd been told by LV veterans that Gus granted every student a nickname. In the first few days, all he seems to do is study the new faces, trying to sort them out. Name them. Make them part of Lupine Valley's universe. On that third day, it came out of him: *Help Falcon get some more firewood, Juniper.* He'd looked right at me, and I felt reborn. He took a picture of me as he spoke it, and that photo is now part of a collage in his office cabin—hundreds of intimate, close-up portraits filled with wonder, honor, good humor, confusion, sometimes annoyance or relief. He caught us all in our newness. Trying on a new skin. The collage, Gus's pride and joy, extends back years and feels almost painfully private to look at. Like a priest opening up the door to the confessional booth.

To come back to Juniper is to feel reborn once again. *Jordana* is far away now. *Jordana* lives out there, beyond the boundaries of the Lupine Valley Arts Collective. Beyond King City, Maine. She exists in a modest, dysfunctional home in Pittston, Pennsylvania. *Jordana*, then deeply into cocaine, exists in the squalid apartment I shared with my ex-girlfriend Chloe while doing undergrad at Hunter College in Manhattan. *Jordana*, condescending and performative, exists in the overcrowded house I rented with my fellow MFA candidates in Providence, Rhode Island, near the RISD campus. She exists back in Rita's yuppie loft in Washington, DC, unemployed, sexually ravenous, pathologically into cigarettes. *Jordana* lives elsewhere, in the mundane, ugly, ordinariness of life.

Jordana got broken up with this morning.

But *Juniper* is finally home.

MAY 5, 1988

In the bright morning, I put on my flip-flops and carry my shower caddy across the pine-needle-padded earth to take a chilly shower and get dressed in the shared bathroom facilities. I feel like a new woman when I emerge. I return my toiletries to Motif and then head toward the mess, where they are serving breakfast alfresco on the collection of picnic tables outside. I'm excited to see who's already here and just as excited to see the fresh meat.

Old Gus prowls around the far edges of the outdoor dining spot in a hitching, lumbering way that indicates a bad hip, taking pictures of all the introductions and reunions taking place around the picnic tables. The place is abuzz with chatter. I recognize River, a cook who's been here at least since I started coming in 1983. He's a heavyset, bald man in his fifties with a lilting tenor voice; he wraps me in a crushing hug when he sees me and tells me he's been waiting on my return. I also recognize Lotus, a dark-haired cleaner in her early twenties who was here during my last term. She gives me a warm smile when she sees me, clearing her plate into compost and moving off to start her work for the day.

I meet a few new-to-me folks as I fuel up with strong campfire coffee, beans, and eggs—Hillock, a stately, gray waif of a woman who advises on weaving and all manner of fiber arts; Toad, a plump metalworking student in his forties; Ash, a seventeen-year-old painter new to LV who asks me all about my MFA experience at RISD before he takes his breakfast back to his cabin. His were the wired eyes of an artist up all night, creating. When he leaves, I start leafing through one of the worn, dog-eared novels left on the table. Books of all sorts and conditions are scattered around the community, shared, passed along, enjoyed. I brought a few this time to add to the mix.

"Junebug—dude. I didn't know you were coming back this term!" I know the voice immediately, even as I lift my eyes from my beans and eggs and copy of *Miss Lonelyhearts*. Moss. And then I see my friend. A smile spreads to my lips even as I try to swallow a mouthful of beans. About a year ago, Moss was a baby-faced, neatly trimmed Midwestern boy. Now he is thin and lean, as if stretched out and solidified, with a dark mop of hair and a wildly growing beard and mustache, espresso black. He must only be scarcely into his twenties now, but a handsome man has replaced the scraggly boy. I feel dazzled at the transformation in the five months since we were last together back in December. The Maine winter has winnowed his body into something utilitarian and refined for solitude and the elements. He walks toward me, barefoot, a bright smile showing through his mane. "So good to see you!"

I stand and we hug heartily, taking each other in. "Good to see you, too, man," I reply, wiping my mouth with my hand. It *is* good to see him. To see everyone. He sits down with me and pours himself some coffee, pours me a refill. "You seem like a man who has been here all winter. Are you on carry-over?"

"Yes, indeed. On carry-over, my friend. Three sessions in a row. Can you believe it?"

"Wow—three in a row? That's a solid year!"

"At cruising altitude now, Junebug. Why come down to earth?" He winks and spears some sausage links from the communal platter onto his tin dish then scoops some beans. We catch up. He tells me about the projects he's been working on, some of the students he's become friends with, the dawn meditation sessions he's started doing out on the Ledge in the nude. The Ledge, as we call it, is through the woods about a half mile up a steep trail from the Village Commons—a rock face in the side of Little Chickadee that looks out across the wilderness of King City and beyond. It's a spectacular view.

"I'm talking to a man who's got it all figured out, if you ask me," I say, brushing an ant off the picnic table and onto the soft ground.

"Ah, well. When the mood strikes me, I'd be tempted to say that's true. But what about you?"

"Not as figured out."

"Not even when the mood strikes you?" He pushes his chopped, black hair back from his face.

"Was living in Washington, DC, with my girlfriend. Who was beautiful. Smart. Redheaded." Moss whistles his approval. "Funny, articulate. And it felt like when she looked at me, she really *saw* me, you know?" Moss nods as he scoops up some beans with a triangle of toast. "Even kind of rich." I sigh.

"A patron of the arts?" He holds up his fork to punctuate his question, asking me if she was a meal ticket.

"She did buy one of my paintings for a thousand dollars. *A thousand dollars.* That's how in love with me she was."

"Nah, that's how good the painting was. A steal at a thousand. A lover's bargain."

I take a breath and run my hand down my face. "She broke it off right before I came here." I push my dish back and forth the space of an inch or so with my forefinger, looking down into the wood grain of the table. Moss makes a sound of deep contemplation but says nothing. I frown.

I look away from him, feeling judged somehow, and see another one of my friends—Mantis, a local on staff. He's emerging from the mess hall with sausage and toast to add to the family-style array on the large serving tables. We became close my last session over a bummed cigarette behind the mess, both of us bonding over our blue-collar upbringing and Motorhead. He catches sight of me as he steps back from the table and gives me a nod. I wave at him, a smile growing on my face as he starts making his way over. He's a tall, square man. Built like a football player. Or at least a man who *used* to play football (which he did, and never lets you forget it). Mantis is probably twenty-five, twenty-six years old, about six foot three. The scaffolding of the relentlessly cut, muscled high school star he must have been is very much still there, it's clear—but time and beer have thickened him, softened him slightly. His hair is buzzed close to his skull for summer. I can see a small scar on his scalp now I've never noticed before, an L shape where hair doesn't grow.

"Mantis, hey, man." I smile and stand as he comes to greet me. Moss looks over his shoulder, and when he turns back in my direction, his lips are pursed.

"Gus said you were coming back, but I had my doubts." Mantis's voice rings sure, loud, and gravelly. He smiles, putting his chipped front tooth on full display.

"Well, doubt no more," I say as we hug heartily.

"I thought you were outta here. Done with this place." He claps my back firmly. "Washington, DC, I mean—come on. Seat of power."

"Not for artists," I say as we withdraw from the embrace.

"Even so. I got your couple of letters. You have that pretty red-head down there," he says.

"Now you've stepped in it," Moss says, mischief in his eyes. "The redhead is no more."

"Dead?" Mantis asks with worry, his eyes flashing to me.

"Jesus, no—" I laugh. "Just broken up. She broke up with me yesterday morning. Right before I drove here."

"Well, sorry to hear it all the same, J," Mantis says, giving Moss the eye for a second. "It's Bark, right?" Mantis says to him. An unexpectedly tense silence erupts between us. I look between the two. Moss's face is a tense, borderline pout. Mantis looks smug.

Oh, so this is a thing.

I can't say I'm *surprised* these two don't like each other—Mantis hates pretention, Moss loves putting on airs—and even when we were all here together last time, during the small moments they would cross paths, I could tell they grated on each other. But this seems elevated now. Like it's been simmering while I've been away. Mantis knows Moss's nickname is not Bark, of course. They've been here, together—one working in the kitchen, one painting as a student—during the whole continuous year.

"Moss," he replies, annoyance on his face as he looks up at Mantis, who towers over him from his seat. My gut tightens.

"Right. Moss." A smile curls on Mantis's lips. He pulls a pack of cigarettes from his jeans pocket and smacks the end of it against his palm, still staring down at Moss like they're playing a game of chicken. Moss caves first, looking away, sheepish. He goes back to his breakfast, ears burning red. Mantis turns his gaze on me and pulls a face. I shrug and smile; I'm not sure what else to do. I like them both. They're both my friends.

Mantis slips a cigarette between his lips.

Cigarettes. I have to get cigarettes.

"I'll get you back, but I could use an emergency cigarette or two. I'm totally out," I tell Mantis. He raises an eyebrow at me then tips the mouth of the pack toward himself, close to his body, so only he can see the contents, as if wanting to keep his supply level a secret. His eyes flit from me to the pack, me to the pack, as if weighing us up.

"Come on, man!" I laugh anxiously, pushing his arm.

"Two," he says, withdrawing the cigarettes and handing them over.

"I'm good for it."

"I know you are." He fidgets with the pack and looks around

at the other campers clustered here and there. Then he looks down at Moss, who's flipping through *Miss Lonelyhearts* and eating his breakfast like we're not here and never were. "Anyway, I gotta get back to it. But let's hang soon." He looks from me down to Moss again.

"Absolutely," I tell him. "See you soon." He gives me a nod and then playfully raps his knuckles against Moss's shoulder, making him jump.

Mantis smiles, that chipped tooth flashing again. "See ya's around." And then he's gone, weaving through the picnic tables and off behind the mess hall, presumably for a smoke break. I look down at Moss, who's holding the novel limply in his hand, eyes squinting in thought. Here we go. He's going to go on some tirade about Mantis. I brace myself.

"Does she still have the painting?" It takes me a moment to figure out what the hell he's talking about. Rita. The painting she bought for a thousand dollars. He's scratching his beard mindlessly with the tines of his fork, looking off into the middle distance, thinking. It's like Mantis was never here, like we'd never been interrupted.

"Yes. As far as I know. I mean, I left yesterday." I look at him, and he just nods and nods. He eats the last few scoops of his breakfast, still nodding, and downs the rest of his coffee. He wipes his face with the back of his hand, then rinses his dish at the water pump, shakes it out, tucks it under his arm. I just watch him do all this, unsure if we're still in a conversation, as other people move in and out of the scene, say hello to me, introduce themselves to me for the first time. He starts to walk away, deep in thought. "I'm in Motif!" I call out to him. A long pause stretches between us.

"Focus," he calls back, already twenty yards away. Focus is

another nice private cabin across the Village Commons from Motif. I guess staying on a year solid—and *paying* a year solid—will win Old Gus's kindness, too.

MAY 19, 1988

It's unseasonably hot today. Into the eighties. The late-afternoon sun is baking me as I lie on the hood and windshield of my Jeep Grand Wagoneer, white with wood paneling. I feel broiled and light-headed and about fifteen feet off the ground. My jeans and dirty Keds are in the car. I'm wearing just underwear and a David Bowie tee, both wet with lake water from the dip I took fifteen minutes ago with Trillium, Zephyr—painting students new to LV this session—Moss, and Mantis six miles from here. Mantis's dad has a nice lakefront hunting camp, and Mantis will invite Lupine Valley people he likes there from time to time. I'd had to do some real convincing to get him to include Moss. I'd felt like some sort of elementary school negotiator. *But he's so condescending. And entitled, June.* I'd assured Mantis he just needed to give Moss a chance. That he was a good guy once you got to know him; insecurity made him the way that he was. *Please? For me?* I'd said. Mantis had eventually relented. And things had gone quite well, even if I did catch a few eye rolls and scowls throughout the afternoon.

After the dip, Mantis, Zephyr, and Trillium had gone back to Lupine Valley, Mantis needing to get back to work, the other two wanting to return to their painting. So here we are, just me and Moss, at Stoneham Bog. I pass the joint we've been sharing back to him. He's stretched out next to me in cut-off jean shorts, chest gleaming.

"I love this fucking truck," I say, adamant. "Perfect recline." I hear him inhale and hold. I smell the smoke come from him. We stay like this for seconds, minutes, back and forth, back and forth. Now I'm thirty feet off the ground, and the dirt logging road below us is like a white-hot stripe through a green carpet.

"You got any beers in this fucking truck with perfect recline?" He hands the joint back to me, and I hold the little nubbin, look at it.

"Paper bag. Back seat." He slides off the hood like water. I look out across the bog, deep and wet with marshland, fallen trees, bracken. *Stoned 'Em Bog*. Clever, no? At sunset, over weird, dead-seeming ground, the colors morph and transfigure. With weed, even better. Moss and I find it inspiring. The others think it's ugly. I always say to them: Why can't it be both?

Moss returns with a warm can of Genesee for each of us. I drink it like I'm dying of thirst.

"Maybe I'll stay at Lupine forever," Moss says then burps. I laugh, rolling my skull back and forth on the hot glass of the windshield.

"You'll be Old Moss. Running the place." I take a few smaller sips of the flat, warm beer.

"Fuck, no. Old Gus will never die. He'll just keep on being Old Gus. And I'll be Old Moss. It's a tier of living. A state of being. To be Old." Moss pushes his sunglasses up into his hair and raises his beer can toward me, squinting into the sun as he looks my way. "To being Old," he toasts. We cheers and drink. "Anything left on that joint?" I hand the tiny nib back to him.

"That Ash is pretty good," I say. Ash, the pale, endlessly toiling wunderkind who'd been so eager to hear about my MFA experience that first morning at breakfast. I close my eyes, letting the sunbeams create strange shapes in the membranes of my eyelids. Everything tinged red. Oxblood.

"He's technical. Has no vision," Moss replies, dismissive. I think of Ash, then of Moss and Ash, then of the three of us together until finally my whole beautiful flock has conjured itself before me. Moss (the charming and ambitious chameleon from South Bend, Indiana), Ash (the serious-eyed and gifted teen from Tallahassee, Florida), Zephyr (the gorgeous and mellow natural, originally from Senegal), Barley (the young assistant professor of philosophy from India, now teaching at Colby College), and Trillium (the soft-spoken, soon-to-be Brooklyn College freshman from San Juan). We're thick as thieves now, the painters. Intensely close. Aware of each other's art, aspirations, bodies, histories in ways it's hard to imagine. Hard to separate. And this in two weeks. But living together like we are—secluded, focused, way out in the woods—it binds you fast. Especially us; we spend more time together than most at camp because we genuinely like each other.

The first time we all hung out, Moss had managed to gather everyone with the lightest of touches. They gravitated toward him, and he drew them to me and to each other. We sat packed in my cabin drinking bourbon, declaring our artistic manifestos with bombast. Ash and Moss fought over who's influenced more by Eric Fischl. Barley told us that if he could sell one painting in his life, he'd be happy. Trillium listened with bated breath to everything Moss had to say, eyelashes batting in his direction. The small cabin stewed us in our body warmth, our physical proximity, our bourbon breath, the tinkle of glasses, our bounding voices.

Zephyr watched in shyness and delight, casting gazes at me that seemed to ask, gleefully: *Is this what it's like here? Is this how we play together? Work together?* And I drew her into the playful, performative half argument, half statement-of-purpose discussion to show her that *yes*, we are family and you are safe here. Squabbling is part of it. Then the conversation devolved (or evolved, depending on who you ask) into Who'd You Do: Outside the Painter's Circle Edition. Ash listened, his face set into something hard. He seemed to find it all very silly, beneath him, which only goaded Moss to razz him more. The longer Ash refused to play, the more narrow and outlandish Moss's guesses for Ash got.

"So, okay, then—you'd either like to fuck Toad or Old Gus. Who will it be?" We were all quiet, knowing that this would either tip into laughter or into a full-blown schism. I was about to stop the whole thing when Trillium, to my utter surprise and delight, defused the whole thing for me.

"To be honest, Toad or Gus would probably be my two Fuck Finalists," she said, tipping her glass of bourbon into her mouth. She saved us, like a pilot able to pull a crashing plane up from a fatal nosedive at the last moment. An explosive giddiness erupted from us then, doubling us over in laughter, in relief. Even Ash. "I'm serious."

"We know. And you're wonderful for it." Moss had laughed. Ash's face had been filled with warmth I'd rarely seen in him as he watched Moss crawl across the circle to give Trillium a kiss on the cheek, his seriousness momentarily forgotten. Trillium had lit up like a sparkler.

I adjust my sticky back against the windshield. "But he's seventeen; vision can come." I drain the last few sips of my Genesee, crumple the can in my hand.

"I disagree. Technical prowess you can cultivate. Vision you must have innately."

"And you at seventeen?" I turn to look at Moss, opening my eyes, the world too bright. Too hot.

"Vision far beyond Ash. Obviously." He gives me a toothy smile, as if challenging me to tell him otherwise. "Technical…lagging *just* behind Ash."

"I think your technical still lags behind Ash now." I close my eyes momentarily and let the sun fire me like a piece of delicate pottery, a smile on my face just big enough to irritate Moss.

"Don't be a bitch." His eyes are pink, irritated. I laugh at him, his ridiculous, stoned face. "I'd say you lag behind the teeny-bopper now, on both counts. What are you, like, forty?"

"You shit stain." It's his turn to laugh at me, but I can still sense how I've stung him. The dope has me speaking too freely. And it was a joke. Mostly. The thing is, I think we both know that what he's been up to so far this summer is, well, disappointing. And he's also shown me the myriad paintings he's done over the past year he's been secluded at Lupine Valley. And that's all a little boring and unexceptional, too. Moss is incredibly talented, and he has a deep hunger for greatness. But his work hasn't caught up. He seems stalled to me. Stuck.

We settle into silence and close our eyes. Horseflies and bees buzz in the atmosphere. I think of my own work, iterations of a woman with red hair. Unreachable. Disconnected. She drowns in her hair in one. Her hair is a house in another. It's where we live. Together.

"You could stay on at Lupine forever, too," Moss says, his voice tired and lazy. An olive branch. "Old June. Old June and Old Moss. And Old Gus." I smile. My skin must be lobster red. The insides of my eyelids are shape-shifting, oxblood prairies. The sky, above me, beyond me, must be a fuchsia prickling, aching to turn itself black.

Two

A Rising Tide

Max

When Audra parks the car at her house and we get out, I am singularly focused. I am a wolf. I am vile. Wicked. My baser prayer has been activated. All I want is for Audra to yield to me. I heard her say words about how the house had been designed and built and tweaked by her grandfather over the years as we drove up the long, snaking driveway and pulled up in front of the garage, but I couldn't stay with it. All I can think about is Audra and her genius works, which I know are locked away somewhere here. The paintings that show me the inside of her brain, her heart, her soul. The spark inside of these works that show a piece of the brilliance I had at her age. I am ravenous for it. I am ravenous for her. Her art, her body—they have grown knotted into one concept within me. One demand: show me.

She leads me up onto the porch, each of us carrying a bag or two. I want to press myself against her as she unlocks the door, so tight, there is no daylight between us. I want to kiss the backs of her ears and the back of her neck. But I don't. I control myself. She points out something about the door knocker—a dove, gleaming and brassy—and then finally the door swings in, and her home is open to me. We enter the foyer; the delicate scent of lavender and fresh linen comes to me. Maybe rosemary, too. I look to Audra. I am mad with expectation. I want us to drop our bags to the floor as if pulled from us by magnets. I want us to disappear into a bedroom together, finally, mercifully—but she doesn't immediately turn to face me. Instead she heads directly into a large kitchen and sets her purse and her mail on the marble countertop. She looks at me and smiles, but it's an innocent one. She is calm, collected, under complete control. Infuriating.

"Welcome to my home, Max." She gestures hospitably. "I'm super glad you were able to come for a visit." She heads toward the large, stainless-steel fridge. "Do you want some water?" She opens one of the fridge doors and looks over her shoulder at me. I stay standing dumbly in the foyer, door open behind me, luggage still in my hand. I look around the nice entryway like it will provide some sort of answer. I need to get my bearings. I'm in a new world. Her world. She grabs two bottles out of the fridge when I don't answer, sets one on the counter, and brings one to me. "Let me help you with your bag." She comes toward me and takes the small suitcase from my hand. She hands me the water.

"Thanks." The ordinariness. The lack of charge or passion or blatant desire. I look at her and want to grab her by the arms, shake her, scream that I know exactly why I'm here, exactly what she wants; that I am more than happy to give it to her. But I manage to stay my hand. Again. Maybe she feels shy. Maybe she's feeling nervous, now that we're so totally alone together. Way out here in her home. No watchers, no boundaries.

"I'll show you to your room. You can rest or wash up or just take a few minutes to settle in if you'd like. Take as much time as you need." A spark of hope. A room. Which will undoubtedly have a bed. She hauls my bag through the foyer and up the wide staircase, so I close the front door behind us and follow her. I take in the expansive hallways and meticulously clean, comfortable rooms we walk by. This is a nice house. A big house.

My room is a large guest suite on the second floor, handsome in shades of light blue and rich brown. Pristine picture windows look out across an expansive, green field swelling with wavelike hills and dales, crisscrossed with low, stone walls. Floor-to-ceiling bookshelves packed with volumes line one wall.

"So, there are various towels and basic toiletries in the bathroom." She moves to the darkened doorway and flips on the light. "Extra stuff in the closet in there." She then moves out of the bathroom and toward a door on the other side of the bedroom, opens it up. "You can hang your clothes in here if you'd like, plenty of room. And there's the dresser of course."

"This is great, Audra—thank you," I tell her, piqued by the niceness of everything. I look at her as she gazes out across the beautiful field to the tree line a quarter mile or so away. The trunks of a few of those trees are banded in a couple bright streaks of yellow, maybe some sort of ribbon or tape, tails fluttering in the breeze.

"I have so many things to show you, Max," she says as she approaches me, a twinkle in her eye. "I have such plans for us." The ember of wickedness always just under my surface glows redder, hotter.

"You're in charge, boss." I stroke my thumb gently across her cheek, and I see she is mildly surprised but not displeased with the gesture. "Had a little something there. Eyelash or something." We both know it's a lie.

"Should have let me make a wish," she says, the two of us standing painfully close.

"What would you have wished for?" I ask, voice gentle. The gap-toothed smile returns to her face.

"Oh, Max," she sighs. "You know I can't say that out loud." She squeezes my forearm as she walks past me toward the door. "Then it might not come true." Her hand lingers on the doorframe. "Let me know if you need anything. I'll be downstairs putting together a little nosh. I'm starving. You must be, too."

"Ravenous," I say; we look into each other. We are in the borderlands now, the dangerous place where we know no one is looking. I watch her swallow, a glint of something darker, unreadable in her eyes.

I watch her go.

I run a hand down my face and take a big, silent breath.

A bracing shower would do me good.

In the first few minutes, I deal in cold water, trying to banish my hardness, trying to slow down to the simmering pace at which Audra apparently wants to move. After a while, I turn the hot water up, feeling regulated. Feeling vaguely cleansed. I turn it up so it's almost unbearably hot. But my solitude in the shower, the quiet patter of the water falling to the tile, the heat conjures Audra back into my mind.

I was on the admissions committee when she applied to the program more than two years ago, and her application had struck all of us; her written materials and portfolio had been instantaneously arresting. We've accepted our fair share students from the University of Maine's flagship campus in Orono over the years, in addition to places like Bowdoin College, the University of Southern Maine, and Colby College. But the letters of recommendation in Audra's packet had been particularly interesting, prophetic. Each of her professors and advisors had praised Audra's work with awe, insisting we'd be mad not to take her based on her portfolio alone (about which they were correct; her pieces had been incredible—tear-your-hair-out incredible) but said they'd found her a challenge to interact with as a person. It was a consistent thread. She had never availed herself of most of the department's resources. She returned to her house on some rural lake often and never really described what—or, perhaps more importantly, who—kept drawing her back. She would pause her studies for entire semesters and then return as if nothing had happened. She was quiet, they said. Completely present for classes, instruction, mentorship when it came to her work, but an absolutely closed book when it came to the rest of her life.

Some artists, especially those with real raw talent, have their quirks. We on the admissions committee knew this. Hell, I'm one of them. I've been called brilliant, eccentric, gifted, a divine vessel in the various write-ups and introductions and articles and talks that have been created for me, about me, with me. But I have my quirks. We assumed Audra was one of those types, too. She seemed born from the froth of the ocean or from Zeus's own head, a goddess, a revelation. We admitted her, and she has been a feather in our collective cap ever since.

She didn't appear much at all during her first semester. I began noticing her at parties and soirees in the spring of her first year. She was a mirage: you would see her, but it was hard to get close. She'd disappear. I would feel her eyes on me during these shindigs. And she would continue to look, even after our gazes met. She was not cowed. Her confidence and her silence reminded me of myself when I was younger. She seemed to show up to these events primarily to drink deeply of the unfolding scene and its improbable people and its hyperbolic talk and then retreat to her own inner world, as if the whole thing was an exercise in reconnaissance. But she never approached me, and I never really approached her, though I wanted to. On the few occasions that I tried to get near this gorgeous, mysterious woman, she'd vanished again. I knew I would get my chance soon enough, so I just bided my time. Fate and bureaucracy would funnel her to me.

Every studio painting student must take my Theory of Form class in the fall of their second year, and that's when I finally met her. She did not disappoint. She was laser focused and passionate when it came to discussing the work, the theory, the techniques we worked on in class. She engaged with the other students. She engaged with me. But she never brought anything biographical, as so many of the other students naturally did. Audra would smile and laugh and empathize with everyone as they exposed themselves, but she never would. She showed only what she wanted to show. When pressed by other students, or by me, she would say some sneaky, jokey thing. She would deflect, and people would move on; her mysteriousness became her hallmark, until no one much tried to crack her anymore. She is a mirror, reflecting back only yourself. It began to drive me nuts. I wanted to know more about her. I *needed* to know. Her mind. Her body. Talent like that—secrecy like that—comes from somewhere.

In the evenings, after my heady seminars, the students and I, including Audra, would often go out to a bar near campus, and I would be the charming, witty life of the party. Most of them listened hungrily to every word I said or over-laughed at every lightly amusing anecdote I told, but Audra was a tougher crowd, giving me almost nothing. As the night wore on, students would fall off, some grudgingly so, until it was just she and I. She would say little but give off the vibe that she was thinking, *Well, the party seems to be over, doesn't it? Maybe I ought to be going.* I would draw her out then, not wanting to lose her. I would ask her to stay until I finished my drink. This is when she would finally, truly talk.

This happened on numerous occasions, the little game we would play. Soon, we started making plans, just the two of us. I would take her to interesting, hole-in-the-wall bars in Chinatown or Dorchester, or extravagant artist's parties on the Cape or in Cambridge, or to underground art showings in New York, even, sometimes on a weekend. I would tease her that the standard artist/lover differential always involved a couple of decades, that some things are just written in the stars. She would laugh with me, but that was all. Even on these field trips, even on occasions when there would be overnights, she would never spend them with me. She found some way to beg off, to crash with a friend or get a hotel or something. I would be sure right until the moment she abandoned me that *this* was the time. This was the moment. But I was always wrong.

It all teetered on the edge of something intimate, special, but never got there. And I can see that this was purposeful. That she is the conductor of her own silent score, the beats and movements of which I am unable to hear. I have simply been led. Conducted. Curated. It's a novel position to be in, one I recognize only from the other side. And so I've decided to let it happen. An experiment, an indulgence of sorts. To follow. To wait. And here I wait still. Naked, in her remote home, two hundred and fifty miles from anyone I know.

I step out of the shower to the entire bathroom shimmering with steam. I turn on the fan and grab a big, fluffy towel from under a large double vanity. This is quite a nice bathroom. Large. Finely appointed. Nothing about it is woodsy or rustic. There are a few small, black-and-white landscape photographs on one of the walls, framed professionally with title cards. *Birch Trees in Spring*, then *Scavenger Hunt*, then finally *Boat in the Rough*. I look back at the second photograph, *Scavenger Hunt* by Rowan Augustus McCue. The backs of a woman in baggy overalls and a man in a T-shirt, short jean shorts, and sandals stand close together next to a camp-fire, heads lowered over something as if reading. Some distant bell sounds unmistakably within me, a muffled death knell trapped in the soft marrow of my bones.

I turn away.

I look out the windows that frame the soaker tub. The view is breathtaking. Pure.

I can see the driveway, part of the garage, and a large hill that slopes up toward a stand of apple trees. One of the trees toward the center of the orchard is strung up with countless flowing ribbons in a shocking yellow. I look toward the tree line and see those others with the same ribbon tied around them. I squint, trying to divine the exact shade. It's a desperate color, attention seeking. A color of warning; or a color of triumph. *Goldenrod*. I feel myself frowning. It's like some sort of pagan maypole, that tree. The wind tears and lulls the ribbons about. There's the taste of something sour in my mouth.

I wrap the towel around my waist as I open the door and enter the bedroom, which is also impressive. There's a king-size, four-poster bed. Large, cherrywood furniture, all with classic lines. There's a wall of built-in bookshelves filled with hundreds of volumes—novels, biographies, poetry collections, art books. I notice a book on the right side of the wall, at about eye level, with which I am intimately familiar. It was published ten years ago by a colleague at Brown. I'd written the introduction. *Edward Hopper: Thoughts and Essays*, by Joan Mary Jenkins. It's a little hard to find these days. Where had my sweet Audra gotten it? And when? I take it from the shelf and flip through the first twenty or so pages. It looks like it's been read, or at least my introduction has. I place it back on the shelf, feeling a boyish sense of pride.

I turn to the bedside table. On it I find one purple lupine stem in a tall, thin glass of water, a tidy little envelope, and the brand-new pocket knife I just bought at the trading post. The array pleases me. There's something artful to it all. My overnight bag is on the floor nearby. I walk over to the table, just barely able to hear Audra's movements down in the kitchen. The outside of the envelope reads *Max*. I sit down on the edge of the bed, wearing only the towel, the remaining droplets of water growing cold on my skin. I slit the envelope open with my knife to find an artisanal greeting card inside, made from good, thick, textured paper.

I'm so glad you're here.

The message on the front of the card is in a pretty, scripted type. A single red rose blossom is on the lower left corner. It's like a blot of paint or blood. I open it up. In Audra's own hand:

You're always saying you want to find me, Max. Get to me. Now you have. Thank you for coming to my home, to where my truest self resides. Thank you for finding me. It feels like I found you, too. Against all odds. -A

I swallow. *Thank you for finding me.* It is something I say to her often. *I know you, Audie, I'm with you, Audie, but I don't think I've found you yet. I don't think you've quite let me. I haven't made it all the way in there, but I will.*

So she's ready to let me find her. Finally.

Excitement ignites like wildfire inside my body.

Audra, the closed fist, ready to open up. It's wild how unlike my most recent ex she is. Misha was willing to be undone and remade from the very start. Unsteady. Easily shaken. It's like she craved it, what I got from her, what I did to her. Misha with her silken, blond hair and light-gray eyes, her whole self a spectrum of airiness and pliability. I opened her right up like a glistening wound. I saw her deep reds and pinks and blacks over the years. Years of toil. I think of my languid, tonal *Builder* portraits—which are of Misha, ultimately, an architect—and feel an almost erotic shiver. I, the consummate synesthete, see them all, these women, these muses, in pure color—sunbursts, fireworks.

I think of grabbing Misha—cornflower, navy, steel, powder-blue Misha—by her smooth, flaxen locks, pulling her toward me like a shaking sheep.

Francesca—spunky little *Chess*—was a student I had a few years ago. Fire engine, chili, ruby red. Stubborn and needful, overflowing with body, Rubenesque, unquenchable. Looking for a father. Finding me. I think of sinking my fingers into her deep-brown curls and squeezing like a bear trap.

My muses. Misha and Francesca and many more besides. Their pain, their love, their trust has been everything, has given me everything in my life.

But Audra is more like me than she is like them. Audra is not a passive resource. Not something to simply be broken down and drawn from. She's an active engine of genesis. A maker. Like me. Audra is rich plum, eggplant, mauve, always—indicative of passion but two ticks off-center. My job with Audra is not to dismember her and put her back together again. It's not to break and then remake as I have with so many others—lovers and students alike. It's to show her how to climb up here with me. To find her own

Mishas and Chesses. To take from these sources what was never really *theirs* but was actually always rightfully *hers*—and make it something worth looking at. Something greater than themselves. Something that can live on forever.

A rising tide raises all ships. As Audra rises, so will I.

Audra

Right about now Max will be discovering the little note I snuck on his table while he was showering. I wonder what he might be thinking as he reads the words inside. Is he lost in a whirlwind of want and possibility as he sees and understands that I am finally ready to *let him in?*

What a joke.

Max does not care much for opacity, which is a bit of an irony, of course. I know he finds me difficult, impenetrable, and that it irks him to his core. But other students, past partners, lovers, friends—they have always given all of themselves to Max. Because Max makes giving feel *good*.

Last semester, a fellow painting student, Tanya, who had always been talkative and bright, seemed to change midterm. Max recognized the shift before the rest of us did—certainly before I did. What I noticed first was how *his* interactions with her evolved, subtly; he engaged with her more frequently but more gently, and he put himself close to her, bodily, when he asked a question or responded to her comments. He drew her out, encouraged her to open up, his eyes never leaving her while they interacted, his questions not always academic but haltingly personal. It was like watching a hangnail get slowly and painfully peeled back. Once or twice he put a hand on her shoulder and gave her a generous smile, which Tanya absorbed into her tense body like a muscle relaxer. Poke by poke. Nudge by nudge. He brought forth the pain and then became the salve. Max would call it catharsis. I would call it coercion. And then one day at the tail end of class, he strategically shed his obtuseness and went straight at her.

"Something is trampled in you. Deadened. A loss of will, of self," he said, a hand on her back as she sat at her desk. The rest of us just watched, transfixed. "It is so lovely and fragile, to relinquish one's power in this way. To be so broken and to try to shoulder it in silence. But we can all see you. I see you, Tanya." He nodded his head like a therapist. "Beautiful." Tanya started crying. It was desperate, broken-levee kind of crying. She croaked out that her father, who had adopted her as his own when she was three, was on his deathbed, about to die of colon cancer back home in Montana. "Ah, yes—loss begets pain begets beauty," Max said, retreating from her. While the other students crowded around Tanya to comfort her, I watched Max, who leaned against the whiteboard at the front of the room and studied Tanya and the collection of bodies that swarmed her. His expression was alive with hunger. His eyes glittered with stimulation. I wanted to dig my nails into his flesh then, draw blood. Because he was making a cameo of her in his mind then, too. I was sure he would go home that night, remembering every detail, and paint what he'd pulled out.

Tanya's father died the next week. When she returned to class a couple weeks later, tired-looking, Max had no more interest in her. It was like he'd forgotten the whole thing.

But it doesn't always take a few weeks, like it did with Tanya. He has a similar bewitching effect on people he meets in passing: clerks at the grocery store, ticket takers at the theater, tourists asking for directions. Their faces open up, and they turn to him, willing to give or receive anything, even if only for a few moments. He has this way of taking that turns you into a kind of undeniable truth, if not a beauty. You are suddenly power, loss, innocence made substantial. Simply because he says it is so. Oftentimes he does this through literal art. I have, to my great alarm and more than once, found sheets of paper covered in delicate and not-so-delicate likenesses of myself sketched, drawn, painted in watercolor, sleeping, worn-looking, prone, supine. In his work satchel, wide open, waiting for me to peer inside. In his large Beacon Hill apartment, poorly hidden away. He has wanted me to find them, to understand that he is trying to see even what I hide. Despite me. And I have *seen* myself in these snapshots. I have. They rattled me. His pointed perception, his watchful eyes seeing, undoing. He has gotten close, too close sometimes.

God knows what he's taken from others.

I know, too.

But in me he senses an instinct for withholding, and to withhold anything from Max is a sin. I think this is why he has sketched and then eventually painted me only when I was otherwise unaware: resting on a train to New York once, or concentrating on driving us from Boston to the Cape, or working on a painting of my own in one of his classes. He wants to catch the hidden glitch between frames, between heartbeats.

But in him I also sense a desire to mentor me beyond my thesis. To make me his apprentice of sorts; to make me like *him*. If only he could see the truth of what this weekend will be. Of what I will be. Then he'd finally realize.

I will *never* be like him.

I finish brushing a light egg wash on the chilled puff pastry dough I've wrapped with care around a wheel of fresh brie and jalapeño jam. I put it in the oven and set a timer on my phone. The room smells of garlic salt, oregano, and butter. I clean up then pour myself a glass of wine, a big one. A pinot noir I brought from Boston three weeks ago. "Yo La Tengo" plays from the smart speaker on the other side of the kitchen. The midafternoon light slanting in through the floor-to-ceiling windows turns the room golden and a little wistful, perfect with the music.

In the middle of October, in Maine, midafternoon feels like early evening; you can tell the sun is leaving you. The angles and registers of light feel like they're escaping, running away. This kind of light always brings to mind memories from when I was a kid. Hot apple cider and raking the yard in my grandpa's oversize flannel shirts. Pulling as many crunchy leaves together as I could into a larger-than-life heap then designating a runway and jumping into the pile with abandon. Coming inside and warming my hands by the fire, feeling cold and tingly and perfect.

I look at the clock on the microwave. 2:38 p.m. It will be full dark by six. I drink deeply from my glass.

Faint sounds of a man dressing and walking around upstairs finally reach my consciousness. Is what I'm hearing the normal amblings of a man putting himself together, or is what I'm hearing pacing? I listen to the creaks and can't quite tell. Pacing means worry. But what has Max to be worried about? He's made it to the

Promised Land. Far from the city's frenetic streets and the department's relentless gossip. He's drying his perfect body with expensive,
high-thread-count Egyptian cotton towels. I'm cooking for him. It
does not make me feel good to think that Max is on edge. It would
not be for the best. The image of the knife he bought just hours ago
flashes into my mind. The knife he'd *snicked* open and closed, open
and closed. The knife I'd placed at the side of his bed—to show him
I'm not afraid of him. Even though maybe I am, a little bit.

I think of the last man who was upstairs in this house. Lance.
Just over a month ago. It was the last time I'd seen him in person at
all before today. It feels much longer than four weeks since we made
love upstairs in my bed. Since he ran his calloused hands over my
shoulders, my breasts, my hips. Since he kissed the hollow of my
throat and said, *At a time like this a man might be made to do anything for a woman like you.*

But now Max is here because I am nothing if not dedicated
to the cause. And Lance knows that. Lance knows all about Max.
About the books I placed on the shelves. The art I hung on the
walls. The minute touches. Each moment, each detail. Just for Max.

I take out a long, crusty baguette, a cutting board, and a newly
sharpened knife. I cut the bread up into little discs so that they're
ready when the brie is done. Max must be starving. I know I am. I
get out some crackers. I take from the fridge a platter of vegetables
I cut this morning, grab a few appetizer plates from the cabinets,
some utensils from the drawer.

"There's the girl." Max's voice rises from my left as I stand at the
large granite island arranging our repast. I look over at him and put
on a smile. His look is bright and relaxed. My guess is, in addition
to the shower, he also had a cigarette on the bedroom balcony. I can
smell it faintly on him. He's Max. Rebalanced.

"There's the guy," I respond with my half of our usual playful greeting.

"Something smells good."

"Baked brie with jalapeño jam."

"Heavenly," he says, his eyes dancing around the kitchen. "This is quite the place, Audra. It's a chef's kitchen in here! And that view from the bedroom." His eyes fall upon the spread hungrily.

"I'm so glad you like it. I knew you'd be comfortable here. You just had to trust me." I rub his back with the flat of my palm. I withdraw my hand almost a little too quickly, feeling his hunger for my touch flare in the sudden tension of his muscles. We look at each other in silence for a long moment. He is wearing an ocean-blue, button-up shirt—untucked, a few buttons undone, revealing the first bit of his taut chest—and a pair of handsome gray khakis, cuffed at the ankle. His feet are bare. His hair is drying, slightly messy, and divine. I look away, clearing my throat.

"Faith of an altar boy, remember?" he says, voice mostly level, trying to make eye contact with me, which I avoid. "And thanks for that card. It was very sweet of you."

"You're welcome," I say, eyes down on my work at the sink. Max strolls around the front of the island, looking at the features of the kitchen, a couple crackers in his hand. He takes in the six-burner Viking stove; the massive stainless-steel fridge; the double ovens; the handsome copper pots and pans hanging from the rack above the island. "Would you like a glass of wine?"

"More than anything."

"I'm drinking the pinot from that wine shop on Charles."

"Oh, yes, please, if you don't mind."

I fetch another glass and pour him a healthy portion. I hand it to him as he runs his fingers along the spines of a few of the cookbooks displayed on a nearby shelf. "You have the Edward Hopper book Joan Mary wrote," he says, the books spurring something in him. "The one I wrote the introduction for." He turns to face me, taking a sip of his wine. I think, *A narcissist can always find himself in any room.* I want to laugh, but I don't.

"I do," I reply, returning to my preparations.

"How long have you had it?"

"After I was admitted to the program, I picked it up. It'd been on my list for a while, and once I got the good news, I allowed myself the indulgence." This is a lie. I bought it long before I'd even applied to the program.

"Well, I'm flattered." He raises his glass to me, and we toast. We drink. "I'm starting to think this whole trip was an elaborate ruse to get me up here and sign it for you." He winks.

"Ha. You got me." I hold my hands up in surrender. He laughs and takes another long draught of wine as he circles around the kitchen.

"We have about fifteen minutes before the brie comes out. Would you like a quick tour of the place?"

He's looking at a built-in china cabinet. "Yes—that would be wonderful." The expression on his face shows me he's impressed.

"Excellent. So, this is the kitchen, obviously. Which I love. It's one of my favorite parts of the house. My grandmother was a talented cook, and so my grandfather renovated and updated everything for her, right before they retired." I gesture around to the appliances and the subway-tile backsplash and the sleek, chrome light fixtures.

"So this was your grandparents' house, yes? They left it to you?"

"They did," I reply as I lead him through to the attached living room. "Pops died about seven years ago. Gram about five."

"I'm so sorry, Audra."

"Thanks," I say, feeling the back of my neck grow red and hot. The things some men feel sorry for. The things Max feels sorry for. Hilarious.

"Did you grow up near them?"

"I grew up in this house, actually," I tell him. "With them."

We enter the living room, which has a few sofas and easy chairs grouped around a square, leather ottoman. They face a fireplace, above which sits a TV. It has a similar feel to the guest bedroom and even to my own master bedroom; Persian rugs, wide-plank floors, handmade furniture. "I've refreshed the house even more in the last few years. The bones and rooms were all pretty much to my taste, but I changed out a lot of the furniture—except for anything that was an antique or had major sentimental value. Changed the curtains and things like that, too. Finally put in a garbage disposal. It's starting to feel like mine. Which I know is what they wanted for me."

"I can only imagine," Max agrees, running a hand along the back of one of the comfy sectionals I bought about two years ago. "And good for you for making it your own. I'm sure they're so happy, wherever they are, that you've settled in." He turns toward the large fireplace. He rests his arm on the stone mantle and looks at the antique wooden clock sitting up there. It was my great-grandfather's. I've been telling the time by that clock my whole life. Next to it is a framed charcoal sketch of a bird that looks like a raven, hanging upside down from a branch, wings spread wide open.

"I'll put on a fire a little later." I watch Max closely as his gaze drifts lazily across the drawing, and then it stays. He looks at it and looks at it. I let him. I put it there for a reason. I want him to see. I want him to look. "I'll need to bring in the grill in the next week or two, before snow comes. The same with the patio furniture." He doesn't respond, just keeps looking at the bird drawing. I hold in my breath, watching.

"Snow," he finally murmurs at an extraordinary delay. He takes a breath and straightens out his posture. "Where—did you draw this?"

"No, I didn't," I say with something like apology in my voice. "I inherited it from my grandparents." I wait to see if there's more. There isn't. He moves away from the mantle, joining me at the pair of French doors that lead to the patio.

"Another extraordinary view," he says, taking a sip of his wine. "What's with the ribbons?" Max points toward the rise of the hill, the plush apple orchard perched on top. We see the yellow ribbons flagging in the wind.

"The ribbons I put up for hunting season. To warn hunters that there's a house here. The official color to use during hunting season is 'blaze orange,' technically, but I suppose it's the artist in me." I feel myself flush as we both look at the ribbons. "I prefer this yellow. It's bright. It gets your attention. And it sends the right message: don't kill me." I chuckle. "It's also more beautiful than blaze orange." I look at him. Max nods, sipping his wine, seemingly satisfied. I feel almost giddy. It's too easy.

"What did your grandfather do? As his job, I mean?" I have told Max this very thing before, more than once, but of course he doesn't remember. I knew he wouldn't.

"He started out in carpentry," I say as I lead him back out of the living room toward the hallway. I point out a powder room, for his general information. "He was a carpenter's apprentice in Jackman—not far from here—when he was a young man. Fifteen, sixteen. He eventually became a carpenter in his own right. Met my grandmother at a dance being held in an old VFW hall in

Greenville. They fell in love. He started his own carpentry business a few years after they married." I pause when we reach the study and lead him in. There's Pops's heavy artisan desk at the center, a leather chair behind it, two tufted leather chairs in front of it. Two walls are filled with expertly made shelving carrying books and family doodads and photos. The other walls have several large, framed paintings, which I did as a teenager. "This was my grandfather's desk. Walnut. The guys at his company built it and stained it for him upon his retirement."

"It's beautiful," Max says as he runs his fingers over the surface. "Real quality." I nod and take a sip of my wine. "So, he had his own company?"

"Yes, eventually. What was a carpentry outfit became a cabinet-making outfit became a full-on building contracting company over the years. He was very successful locally. No Mr. Moneybags, but he did well, invested well. Sold the business for a nice sum when it was time to retire." He places a gentle hand on my back, strokes it. I am painfully aware of every gentle brush of his fingertips on my shirt, on my back. His hand. My body. I swallow a rising queasiness.

"You miss them, don't you," he says more than asks, his voice gentle.

"Very much. Every day." I can feel his eyes drinking me in. Gathering material.

"It's quite a loss, Audra. How horrible it must have been as each of them was taken from you." There he goes, doing what he does best. But it won't work on me. I swallow down my genuine pangs of sadness. I steel myself.

"C'est la vie," I reply and sip. Max looks at me, and I look at him. He removes his hand from my back.

"And these paintings—they must be yours. They can be no

one's but yours," he says, regaining himself. He goes over to stare wonderingly at one of them.

"They are." I laugh. "I did them in high school. Maybe one after high school, but just after." His nose is inches from the surface of one now. He's looking. Really looking. The majority of them are mine, but one isn't, though the styles are similar. I see mostly appreciation in him, only a sprinkle of jealousy. But the jealousy is there. Oh, yes.

"The early works of Audra Colfax," he breathes, almost to himself. "Wow." I stand there quietly and realize he's really having a moment. He moves from the first to the second, and then to the third. He spends a full minute looking at each one, his eyes studying fixedly and casting about for details, brush strokes. He looks at the illegible jumble of letters making up my signature in the lower right corner of one. All three are paintings of the lake, of a nearby shore my family always visited.

"These will be worth something one day," he murmurs. He looks at me then turns back to the paintings. We are silent for a few moments. "Your grandfather must have been very proud of you." Max nods. "I bet he insisted on framing these, putting them in a place of honor. You would have been too humble." He laughs, eyes hungry on the canvases. I look over at him, struck and a little unnerved. Because he's right. Pops begged me to let him get these professionally framed, to let them be in his office where he sometimes conducted business with clients. I'd felt silly and unworthy, a mere amateur, but Pops was determined. He believed in me long before I did. And here they are. Still. "My god, Audra. These are wonderful." I feel an unexpected stab of gratitude toward Max then, watching him admiring my work. It is a weak moment for me, a sliver of appreciation for which I feel ashamed. I sensed from the beginning with Max that he thought my work—maybe even me—a wonder.

Not that I care what he thinks, ultimately. I can't afford to.

"Thank you, Max." He comes to me. He takes my hand and squeezes it. Then I lead him out of the study and show him two guest rooms down the hall.

"I feel embarrassed to say this," Max says as I show him the sunroom full of plush furniture and verdant ferns, "but I don't think I know very much about your parents. I don't know that you've ever offered it, and I don't know that I've ever asked." He looks out through the glass wall at the rough, hilly field beyond.

"Yeah, I've not really talked about them much. I haven't with anyone, really, mostly because I don't know a lot about them myself," I say. I touch the waxy leaf of the palm plant to my right. "Come." I guide him from the sunroom and into the hall. "My dad was young and flaked not long after I was born. My mom died when I was just a baby. Like one year old or something. So I never knew them. Her parents, my grandparents, raised me." Max is quiet. I start climbing the stairs, him behind me, toward his bedroom. There are more rooms up here, more I could show him while I talk. "It was tough. Tough on my grandparents, too. I mean, they lost their daughter and suddenly became parents all over again." I grasp the railing on the stairs tightly as we ascend.

"God, I am so sorry, Audra. That is so sad. So tragic."

"Yes," I reply. "It is. It was. But my grandparents were wonderful, amazing people. They were kind to me. Loved me like their own daughter. I was very lucky." We turn to face each other in the wide, carpeted hallway. Sun glow filters in through the octagonal, stained-glass window at the end of the hall. It gives Max a gold-dusted look. His eyes are tender, gentle as he takes this in. "When they passed, they left everything to me." I laugh now, shaking my head. "Sorry. I know *assets* are kind of a douchey thing to talk about."

"No, not at all," Max says. "It's okay to be well taken care of."

"It's not like I'm set for life or anything, but it's definitely softened the blow of getting through school. And I'm a homeowner." I raise my arms to gesture at the house.

"Well, amen and god bless. Probably had enough cushion to do whatever you wanted, and you came to us." He holds up his glass to me as if to cheers. I gulp down the last of my wine. It was a gift to be able to go to the institute to work on my art. But the reputation of the school itself is not why I applied there or ended up there. Max is. I came for Max. He may not know it, but I do.

Because there are some things a man just can't outrun.

The timer I'd set on my phone hums from my pocket.

"The brie," I say hungrily, starting to head back down the stairs, dismissing the timer with the flick of my thumb. "I can show you the other rooms later, and the finished basement. Come, now. Food!" Max descends behind me. I can feel his eyes on my back, I can feel him thinking about my land, my house, my life. The paintings on the walls. The books on my shelves. My abandoning father. My dead mother. How much more expansive I am getting. That large raven hanging, dark, proud, wings spread wide open. Croaking prophecies only I can hear.

You are alone. You are abandoned.

You are mine.

THESIS
Her Dark Things by Audra Colfax

Piece #2: *Like Stardust on Me*
Oil and mixed media on canvas. 36" x 48".

[Image of giant, golden swoops evocative of thick wings given dimension with slate-gray, midnight-black, olive-green shading. Found objects incorporated throughout by layering.]

Note on loose-leaf paper found under the drawer liner in the laundry room of the Dunn residence.

> *I dunno*
> *about Brady*
> *he's just alright*
> *safe boring traditional*
> *has no real goals no big ideas for himself*
> *he does stay though*
> *and he thinks I'm really talented*
> *pretty nice of him*
> *that is*
> *staying and saying these nice things*
> *I need to hear*
> *I dunno*
> *we've liked each other in some kinda way since sophomore year*
> *I think he likes that I'm not afraid of anything*
> *not afraid to hurt—*
> *myself, mostly*
> *he says I'm brave*

with my past
with my cutting and bruises and cigarette burns
like
bravery
has anything the fuck to do with it.
if it does:
I'm the bravest cunt north of Boston.

—Mar88. CD.

Note on Lisa Frank stationery found folded in Cindy Dunn's bed-side table.

Thelma said maybe she can help me with
a job she says
her old pal Gus runs this
wild place
the Lupine Valley Arts Collective in King City
he needs a girl
to clean and guess what she said you can be around art and artists
and fresh air make money
I said
yeah okay I need a job
it would be good
I need money for school

—May88. CD.

Note on torn graph paper found in an envelope filled with turkey feathers in a desk drawer at the Dunn residence.

A little something
to celebrate this new chapter
it's a dove
doves are supposed to bring
peace
mom told me this and gave me a
meaningful look
we hugged for a long time
for longer than we have hugged in a long time
she touched
my cheek and pulled my fancy tasseled scarf—
she calls it yellow
I call it butterscotch—
(she says that's the ARTEEST in you)
around me better
I've been wearing the necklace the
gold little
necklace like stardust on me
ever since.

—May88. CD.

Note on pink scratch paper found folded and tucked under a floorboard at the Dunn residence.

I started at Lupine Valley I use my
body I work my
body I use my
hands in this different way on
pounds and pounds of laundry and on scrub brushes against

floors and my hands are in a shock about it a shock about it
  but
Gus is a nice enough man and a photographer, an artist too
I move between the cabins
a ghost
silent
cleaning and rectifying and saving all manner of things
and I watch them all
move in and out of classroom sessions and workshops
and someday I will be them and
some days I am them

—May88. CD.

Note on pink scratch paper found pressed inside *Watership Down* by Richard Adams in the den of the Dunn residence.

Me and Brady are fighting
ever just want to hurt?

—May88. CD.

Note on pink scratch paper found taped inside a tissue box cover in the Dunn residence.

Brady won't talk to me
right now
because I slipped he said
I stopped taking my meds which made
the sex real good for a while

which I thought he'd like
which I did for him
but it made me worse
I threw a ROCK through his passenger
window when he tried to drive AWAY from me
like he was scared

—May88. CD.

Three

Go On, Torture Yourself

Juniper

MAY 25, 1988

Ash, Barley, and Trillium are already with Zephyr in her cabin drinking beer by the time Moss and I get there. Zephyr has little candles burning everywhere, dripping wax onto wood, their flames flickering in the gentle cross-breeze of the open windows. It's like we're about to hold a séance.

We crack open some beers and immediately begin to gossip about the only thing there is to gossip about in our little community right now: the newly hired staff. Pretty Lotus ran off with a man from Kokadjo who's easily twice her age almost two weeks ago now, so they had to find a new cleaner. And one of the cooks broke his femur in a four-wheeling accident and *also* had to be replaced. We're all really hoping Mantis will come hang tonight and give us the full lowdown. Mantis has become our man on the inside for all things staff drama and camp gossip. When Mantis isn't around, Moss refers to his stories as the Townie Chronicles, which usually gets a snicker out of the group. But it makes me uncomfortable. Like the locals are some sort of soap opera built for our own amusement, and that feels wrong. But Mantis seems to like the attention and gravitas it gives him. In this, he's the expert, and we're *his* students, and you can tell he relishes it. He explains the politics between Gus and the senior staff or the past sexual histories that entwine the winter snowplow guy with a string of lovers from sessions gone by, and we all are rapt. And he is in his glory.

So after we've exhausted our sans Mantis capacity for projecting about the newbies, our focus turns to—what else—ourselves. Our work.

Zephyr shows us a few examples of her latest, which are meticulously complex abstract paintings done on 4" by 4" white bathroom tiles. She's unsure if they will ultimately make up some larger mosaic or if they will each be individual pieces unto themselves.

"I keep needing to buy new tiles." Zephyr laughs. "I come stomping in here in my tennis shoes after one of our classes and forget I have them all over the floor. Crack, crack, crack." Her smile is broad, sparkling white. She shakes her head, her skin deep and smooth, an onyx goddess. I feel a flutter in my chest when she turns her brown eyes on me, full of warmth. "Clumsy girl."

I smile back, unable to do anything else under her gaze.

About an hour in, Moss is regaling the group with one of his grand tales, arms flourishing, pushing his hair back again and again in his soliloquy, drawing all eyes on him, when Mantis shows up with a six-pack. The crowd cheers as he enters.

"This is the last cabin I checked, of course," he grumbles.

"Glad you were able to make it. We missed you last time," I tell him as he settles in next to me. I pat him on the back then crack one open for Mantis and me to share, seeing as how the six-pack won't cover all of us without a little selflessness. Moss has turned notably quiet. His story forgotten.

"Yeah, we really did!" Trillium chimes in, cracking her own beer open.

"Just the one," Mantis tells her, and seventeen-year-old Trillium nods sheepishly.

"You have to tell us about this new cook. And the four-wheeler crash. We want details," Barley says now. Mantis smiles, feeling the power balance shift his way. Us, rapt. He takes his turn with our shared beer and holds court.

ॐ

Hours later, after our group's social séance has disbanded, Moss and I stumble our way back to Focus. It's almost three in the morning, my flashlight guiding us along in our bouncing two-person parade, laughing too loudly, whispering like we have real secrets to keep.

When we get inside his cabin, he lights his oil lantern, and I tell him how impressed I am with Zephyr's tile pieces and how funny it is that she keeps accidentally breaking them. He offers me a nightcap—absinthe in a tin cup—before I have the chance to take my leave. I take it in my hands and start sipping, still talking, laughing, half-pained for the poor broken-legged cook Mantis told us about.

Moss gathers a mass of sketch paper from the bed and dumps it on his desk. He seems to be looking for something under all the mess but eventually gives up, giving me boring answers in return to my questions about Zephyr's tiles, Zephyr's cabin décor, Zephyr's warmth and kindness.

His place is a wreck, per usual. Covered in canvases, sketch pads, crumpled pieces of paper, food scraps, empty wine bottles.

I pad around the small space as he takes a seat on his bed, looking at the explosion of stuff. I find and look at some of his work. I see multiple iterations of the Ledge in daybreak colors, from different vantage points, in different palettes, on different-size canvases and pieces of sketch paper. Then another series, the Ledge with a man—probably Moss—conflated into equal, magnificent sizes. Interesting primary color juxtapositions.

"Lots of Ledge," I say as I thumb through some more, lift corners of sketch paper on the floor, my tin cup in the other hand. The paintings are just okay.

"I think it's out of me now," he says, throwing his oversize canvas jacket and leather moccasins in a corner.

"Something new moving in?"

"Oh, yeah." He grins, setting down his notebook, pencil, and multi-tool on the desk. "Some*one*." We catch each other's eyes, a sudden panic stirring in me. He smiles, and at first there's a note of cruelty in it. Then it softens. "Not Zephyr, I promise. I know you love her or what-the-fuck-ever." I throw a crumpled piece of paper at his head, which he ducks. He laughs hard and loud, like a bully on a playground.

Zephyr. A forty-something abstract impressionist with buzzed pink hair. Breaker of tiles. And sure—I think I might be in love with her.

"No, no, it's good." He smiles his real dickish smile. "Glad to see you're ready to *love again*." I roll my eyes at him and down the rest of my absinthe, which immediately makes me nauseous. I toss the tin cup on his bed.

"Goodnight, M," I say, annoyed.

"J, come *on*. I'm just playing. I'm honestly a little offended you don't think I could have my *own* girl. That I'd be brought so low as to have to fight you over the same one." He plops down on the edge of his bed.

"Trillium?" I ask him.

"Not Trillium," he says thoughtfully. "But not *not* Trillium. I mean, maybe. She's incredibly beautiful." He says this last part as if it's only just occurred to him. "Maybe her."

"That easy, huh?"

He waves me off. "Trillium isn't who's captured my attention at any rate. No, I've found someone a bit more…inspired. And if it means anything at all to you, I think she's into you, too. Zephyr, I mean." I look over at him, unsure if he's fucking with me. His face is earnest.

"She's my student," I say. Moss shrugs.

"She's like ten years older than you. It balances it out."

I want her. I do. She's all I've been thinking about lately. I scratch my head, unsure. I think of my chances. I think of the ethics. I think through repercussions if I make a move and find out I've read it all wrong.

He knows before I do that I won't do it.

"You coward." He flops back on his bed and laughs, turns over on his side so his back is to me. "Go on, torture yourself." He yawns. "For now. But you'll come around." I watch his ribs expand and deflate, expand and deflate in the yellow light of the lantern. Watching it is soothing, steadying.

"Moss?" I whisper. Only deep, rhythmic breathing comes from him. I watch his ribs some more. I sigh and go over to his desk, blow out the oil lantern. I leave his cabin, closing the door behind me. The commons are empty and lit by stars and a weak middle-of-the-night central bonfire. I go over to it, stoke it, throw another piece or two of wood in from the pile nearby, knowing Old Gus's nocturnal amblings will probably bring him by at some point. I look past the flames into the distance, where Zephyr's cabin is hidden by darkness. I want nothing more than to go to her. To be unafraid.

But Moss is ultimately right, which annoys me to no end. I'm a coward. Because when I leave the bonfire, I go to my cabin for the night. Not hers.

THESIS
Her Dark Things by Audra Colfax

Piece #3: *Alive with Creation*
Oil and mixed media on canvas. 36" x 48".

[Image of a chickadee's head expanded to be overlarge, the color blocking transforming into a gaping hallway, white and narrowing, with towering black walls on the sides. The eye, a hidden glitter, peers out from the blackness. Found objects incorporated throughout by layering.]

Note in tiny handwriting on Holiday Inn notepad paper found in Cindy Dunn sketchbook #2 in the basement of the Dunn residence.

> *I went back with Brady as a way to apologize*
> *for how I have been*
> *that slip slip slip*
> *for lying about applying to school*
> *for stopping the meds and*
> *skipping therapy*
> *I am trying to make things RIGHT*
>
> *—June88. CD.*

Note on torn, half-width graph paper found tucked in Cindy Dunn sketchbook #1 in the sewing room of the Dunn residence.

> *little IMPS with red blotchy cheeks*
> *like a good-time devil has just been there*

the devil's LIPS have been there
and they look so alive
the artists at Lupine Valley
alive with creation
and with each other's bodies
and they say hello
do you want to come in?
I see it
I see ALL of it
their red BLOOD splotchy cheeks after emerging
from cabins with potbelly fires from
cabins with too many bodies pressed inside
hidden away nooks
their limbs entwined like the
TWISTED old birches
little DEVILS they are
running between the cabins
aflame
I look at them and feel perfectly alive
I want a devil to kiss me
I want this King City devil to redden me
to KISS me too

—June88. CD.

Note on folded watercolor paper found in one of the toolboxes in
the shed on the Dunn property.

the devil in King City is just
a man and a man

men
beautiful
One like a PARENTHESIS mark
(M)
made of platinum
a tensile WISP
or claw
Then like a craggy MOUNTAIN
(M)
made of blue granite
unyielding earth
or leviathan
he brings his COLOR to
so many of them
there in
King City
I have SEEN it myself and he and he
has seen me
seeing

—June88. CD.

Note on yellow legal paper found folded inside a birdhouse on the Dunn property.

I did some sketching in Brady's room
I showed
BRADY a new drawing of a
chickadee he said it was
good he said he wants to FRAME it and put it UP at

his
place he wants me to sign it before it goes under GLASS
he is so proud of how well I am doing
I made love to BRADY
and did everything he has ever wanted
as a way
to say sorry
for going off the meds but now I'm back on
but on my own terms
trying to stay on
and be happy
with myself with my art
and I'm sorry for
lying I keep
lying to him I don't know why
he doesn't know that I want to leave him
for school or
what
I have done and want to do
in King City

—June88. CD.

Note on Lisa Frank stationery found in the living room wall of the Dunn residence.

M says I will call
you C

—June88. CD.

Juniper

"Can I get two? I'm bringing one to Moss." I give Mantis my warmest, kindliest smile. "Please?" His dark, heavy brows are drawn together unhappily.

"He can't bring his lazy ass in here?" His voice is deep and gruff. He sits on a wooden stool behind the food counter. We're inside the mess hall, my back turned to the large windows that overlook the Village Commons. His trusty rag is slung over his shoulder, his meaty arms folded in front of him.

"He's working," I tell him.

"Nah, he ain't working. *I'm* working. He's playing."

"Well, that *play* is what he and every other paying artist come here for, Mantis. The art is their work."

"You know how I feel about these stupid fucking nicknames," he growls. "Mantis is—is nothing but a fucking bug," he sputters, tossing the towel from his shoulder onto the counter before him. "Might as well call me Bug!" I frown, surprised at this outburst.

Mantis suffers, just a bit, from Doth I Protest Too Much syndrome. While it is true that he has always found the camp's nickname thing silly, since falling in with my flock this summer, he's eased that cynicism a bit.

We use his name affectionately, and he knows that. He knows it's a way of making him one of us, one of the members of our group. And ultimately, he does mean more to us than the gossip he's able to provide. Of course he does. To Ash, Mantis is his mentor in all things fix-it and utilitarian, and Ash wants to be self-sufficient. He looks up to Mantis. To Zephyr, Mantis is a thick-skinned and brooding little brother to look after with gentleness. To Trillium, Mantis is a cool guy who will sneak her booze, with only a mini lecture first. To Moss, Mantis is another alpha, a playful rival for whom he holds a tenuous respect. To me, Mantis is a grouchy bear who just needs a friend not frightened off by every roar that comes out of him. And I'm not frightened by his general grumpiness because I understand him better than most. We both grew up poor. I'm estranged from my sister, he doesn't get along with his brother. His dad has a drinking problem. My mom struggled with pill addiction for a while after she hurt her back on the job. There is, for better or worse, a kinship in all of this. We're both outsiders—outsiders who somehow found our way to the inside.

"Jesus, what's eating you?"

"Nothing," he grumbles, his eyes flitting over my shoulder. He gets to his feet and impatiently holds out his hand for my dish. I give it to him.

"I know I still need to pay you back for the new battery in my car, but we said by Monday—"

"It ain't that, okay, J? Just leave it." He fills my plate generously, covers it with tinfoil, and then hands it back to me, not even looking my way. He grabs a spare dish from off the shelf behind him. He loads it with eggs, fruit, bacon, buckwheat flapjacks. He covers it with tinfoil and slides it across the counter to me. His jaw is set, and his eyes are again lingering over my shoulder. I turn and look behind me, squinting out into the brightness of the day. There are a few people walking through the commons, a few hanging by the firepit, talking. Thrush, a fiber artist, is sitting on the ground playing a set of bongo drums that are nestled in his lap. But in the middle of it all is the new cleaner. Coral. She's holding a notebook to her side and talking with Trillium. They're both smiling and laughing. Coral's hair is long and flaxen, her build thin and lithe. I turn back to Mantis, whose eyes are still on her.

"We know each other outside of here," he finally says, his voice an agitated grumble. "She's a townie like me, and just out of high school." He scratches his eyebrow. "We're friends. And I don't like this for her. Cleaning up after artists in her own goddamned backyard. I've done it for years now, and it just…" He shakes his head. "She wants to *be* one of you. She draws and shit." He looks at me, his eyes squinted. He looks down at the counter and flicks a crumb away. "And she follows Moss around like a puppy, getting chummy with him and then still having to scrub the floors he walks on. It's embarrassing." He's genuinely upset. For my part, I didn't even know Moss was friendly with Coral—and he usually tells me everything. I tuck that bit of information away. I watch Mantis wring out the dishrag in his hands over and over again.

Old Gus introduced Coral to us at the beginning of May when she came in to replace Lotus. He'd rung the dinner bell one midafternoon, the signal for announcements, and we'd all convened at the firepit in the center of the commons for introductions. Since then I've seen her gliding through camp with her mops, cleaning sprays, buckets, and sponges, going from building to building at various hours, but I haven't really gotten to know her too much yet. She keeps to herself.

"Well, I'm sure Coral knows what's best for her," I try. Mantis sniffs. "It's honest work, decent pay, and she gets to be around other artists—like herself." Mantis is listening begrudgingly. "If you're so worried, why don't we make an effort to include her in our hang-outs more? There's no shame in working here and learning a bit more about art on the side. It could be a great starting place for her. Everyone's gotta work. You do. I do. At least she's getting some fringe benefits from it."

Mantis looks up at me, less aggrieved. "Will you try to help her? Invite her to stuff?"

"Sure, I'm happy to. From what I can tell, she seems kind of… quiet. Private. But maybe if she sees that we're all friends—you and me, too—she'd be more comfortable," I say, my words visibly soothing him. He nods.

"Thanks, Junie," he says, making a point to use my Lupine Valley name. I smile. His eyes drift back behind me once more.

"No problem, *Mantis*," I reply, and he allows himself a Mona Lisa grin. "So, listen. You're still taking me shooting tomorrow, right?" I take one dish in each hand.

"Sure, yeah," he says, lightening up a little. "I mean, we can't be friends otherwise. It's embarrassing to me to associate myself with someone who's never even shot so much as a BB gun before. I mean, Jesus Christ."

"There he is," I say, smiling. But just as quickly, his attention is again behind me, and there is no smile on his face. Sensing the conversation is over, I let out a "see you tomorrow," to which he doesn't respond, already lost in his thoughts. I turn away slowly, exiting the mess hall and heading toward Focus, Moss's cabin. But as I do, I see that Coral has left Trillium and is now standing on Moss's front steps. Knocking on his door. I pause in my progress and watch. Moss opens the door, and his face beams. He looks genuinely happy to see her. Unsurprised at her being there. Welcoming. He puts his hand lightly on her back as she says something I can't hear and steps inside. The door closes behind them. I just stand there for a moment, holding the two breakfast plates. Mantis was right. *Chummy.* Should I still go? Should I leave them alone? I think of Mantis and his protectiveness of this girl, of how I made a promise to him to include her, and I decide it's time to introduce myself properly.

When I get to Moss's door, I tap it a few times with my boot and call, "Coming in!" I balance one dish on the other and swing the door open.

"Just call me Mother Theresa, brother, because look at this," I say with jovial innocence. Coral is sitting on Moss's bed, cross-legged. Moss is sitting on top of his desk, legs dangling down. I squint into the relative darkness of the cabin, my eyes adjusting rapidly. Both are fully clothed, but it feels like I've walked into something impossibly private. I feel my cheeks going red.

"Juniper," Moss says, hopping down from his desk. He only uses my full nickname when annoyed, like a mother using their kid's first and middle. "Wasn't expecting you."

"Yeah, sorry, I just figured I'd bring you breakfast," I say, looking between the two. "You haven't been eating much lately. And I saw Coral here come in, so I thought I'd bring her breakfast, too." Not exactly true, but I'm willing to sacrifice my own flapjacks for group unity. I hand a plate to Coral and the other plate to Moss. His face is tight, his eyes telling me to leave. But Coral looks grateful. She smiles at me.

"Thank you so much," she says, peeling the tinfoil back. "That was thoughtful of you. Wasn't it, Moss?" She looks over at him, and his face rearranges itself into something less standoffish.

"So thoughtful. Thanks, June," he allows. I look at her long, sandy-blond hair, her trim build, her narrow rib cage.

Her eyes are pale, penetrating. Somehow too full. Too active, even in their stillness. She has a gaze that's hard to meet. To match. I look away.

"You've met Coral," Moss says, looking between the two of us.

"Yes, of course—hi, Coral. Nice to see you again!" I go for extra warmth, wanting to keep things light and uphold my promise to Mantis to make her feel welcome. I go and shake Coral's little hand made of little bones. "Juniper. Or June," I say warmly.

"Or Junie," she says. "Or Junebug." Her voice is a little lower than I would have thought given her diminutive stature, a kind of singsong contralto, quiet but kind.

"Y-yes," I say.

"Moss talks about you a lot. Hunter, RISD. Rita. Your time in Washington, DC." Her eyes remain firmly on me, scrolling around my face like it's a topographic map, a friendly, if slight, smile on her lips. "Moss really admires you." I look over at Moss, who looks pained. "He's also told me a lot about the painters." Her eyes brighten and sharpen when she says this. "Zephyr's tiles. Ash's photorealism." She's eager, interested. "It's wonderful what you all are doing. I think everyone around here sort of envies your group." She looks at Moss now, finally breaking her gaze with me, which feels like a relief. "You're so close, and together so much. Having fun. Talking about the Big Things." She looks back at me now. "I see the others—the potters, the metalworkers. Some of them only see each other in class. I watch. I pay attention. It's not the same with you all." And I believe her. She does watch. She brims with intensity.

"We've been so fortunate," I tell her. "Our little group has been extraordinary." She nods, hanging on to every word I say. "Mantis tells me you're an artist, too." A quick flush overtakes her face and then recedes.

"Yeah, she *is* an artist," Moss jumps in. "Just happens to be on staff as a cleaner right now." He's defensive, like I might be secretly judging her. Judging him for fraternizing with her because she's a townie, because she's non-teaching staff. But I'm not, of course. I'm friends with Mantis, who is also both.

"Oh, lovely. What kinds of things do you do?"

"Drawings, mostly." Her eyes swim around my face once more, as if reading instructions. There are dark circles smeared under them. "Charcoal or pencil." I watch her begin to fuss with the cuffs of her sweater, pulling them up and down, up and down, up and down over her thin wrists. I catch sight of raised white scars with each anxious yank of her sleeve, a morbid stage curtain. I still at the sight. "I'm just an amateur of course. Nowhere near where you guys are," she adds quickly, in painful earnest. "But—but Moss is going to teach me." She gazes up at him warmly. "He's been so kind. He's going to show me how to do great work. How to be great."

I nod at her, internally thinking that Moss has to get there himself before he can bring anyone else along. But it's a nice sentiment—and, honestly, very unlike Moss. To want to help anyone. Maybe they could be good for each other.

"I'd love to take a look some time," I offer, pulling myself back from distraction, drawing my eyes away from her wrists.

"Would you?" Her face illuminates with eagerness.

"I really would. And listen, any time you want to pop in and join us during the instruction periods or just hang, please do. We'd love that." Coral nods appreciatively then looks over at Moss, a big smile on her face. His expression when he looks at her is gentle. Earnest.

That sense of palpable intimacy fills the cabin again. Something that's not for me.

"Anyway—just came to bring you breakfast, is all. I'll leave you guys alone." I give them one last look. "One of those dishes comes back to me. And please, if you care about me at all, bring the other back to Mantis in the kitchen. He was in a sour mood when I asked to borrow it for you."

"Mantis saw me come in here?" Coral looks at me intently, her hands stilling. Her features have returned to their steady state: somehow both empty and electric. The girl brings out something motherly in me. I want to ask her: *Are you okay? Have you been eating? Can I hold you?*

"Yeah," I reply. "Working all day today. But is off tomorrow." She starts pulling on and worrying a strand of her hair. I look over at Moss. "The plate goes back. Alright?"

"Will do, Mom," Moss teases. I roll my eyes and leave Focus, shutting the door behind me, leaving those two to whatever world they were building between them before I arrived. I squint against the sunlight drenching the pines and dense underbrush at the periphery of the commons as I make my way toward Motif. I think of the plates of food I left them. I think of Coral and her tiny body, her deep voice, her pale eyes. The scars on her wrist, deliberate but clearly long since healed. I think about the fact that usually the cleaners don't work the weekends. Coral must be here, on a Saturday, on her own. For Moss.

Audra

"Up for doing a loop in the field before it gets too dark? It's probably about a half-mile circuit." We're standing out in front of the house, sated for now by our brie-and-veggies snack. The light grows ever sandier the deeper into late afternoon we get, a gentle sleepiness cast over everything.

"Sure. Let's get this old man's heart pumping." He is good humored as we get going, and I find myself smiling, thinking, *Yes, Max, go on ahead and enjoy yourself; enjoy this time.* After a couple silent minutes of walking through the dense grass, down slopes and over rough furrows, looking carefully in the lowering light, Max speaks again. "When do I get to review your thesis work, by the way? I'm so anxious to see," he says with genuine excitement.

"You've only just gotten here!" I smile.

"I know—I'm a kid at Christmas."

"Well, keep in mind it's not done, of course. But how about

tomorrow? I want you to see it in the natural light. Maybe toward midafternoon? The light is best then. I'll make sure to have you full of delicious food, and you'll have nothing but praise and assurances that the committee will pass me with the highest honors and accolades." I grin over at him, and he returns the look as he loops his arm through mine, the two of us tromping along side by side like there are no other people in the world. I look over at my favorite scarf, the one I've leant Max, wrapped around his neck to save him from the chill. I think about what it would be like to pull on the ends of it tight, then tighter, and watch the air squeeze out of him.

"One of the smartest students I've ever had. Wise beyond your years, Colfax." He laughs.

"I think you'll be pleased. What I proposed and discussed with you right before summer, I've kept pretty faithful to that. They're landscapes of a sort—my 'moody landscapes' as you call them—and I'm finding there's something sort of, I don't know, spectral in them. Like there was something there, already, that comes forward the more I paint. A history. A phantom or something." My breath is just the tiniest bit short as we walk over the somewhat challenging terrain in the cooling weather. It's nearly five p.m. "I'm taking these objects, these images that feel very close and familiar to me, and blowing them up into a size that makes them a terrain of their own. In doing that, I'm finding out new things about them. And I'm incorporating some outside media."

"This sounds promising." His voice is serious, genuine. "You're conjuring now. That's a good sign. Mysteries and images are emerging within you, without you. You're a conductor, the electricity is coming. Let it strike and move through you."

"Watch your step," I warn. I point down at the narrow but deep gash in the earth beneath us, a rivulet of runoff water that has snagged more than a few feet and ankles in its day. We both step carefully over the gash. An owl hoots, long and low, from somewhere off to our right; we both look to see if we can spy it but can't.

"How does it feel being in your penultimate semester?" He squeezes my arm bracingly, supportively.

"It feels good. I feel confident. I think my production pace is right."

"And what about the artist's statement? The critical introduction to your work?"

"I'll admit, Professor Durant"—I laugh—"I haven't quite broken ground on that end of it."

"Mind yourself, now. That's sixty-five pages of polished, thoughtful, well-sourced, and supported writing needed by your full committee sometime in March so you can have your defense in April and your graduation in May."

"Yes, sir," I say and salute him. "You can count on it. I'm definitely thinking on it as I do the work; I just haven't started the writing process."

"Well, when you get some done, email it to me if you want comments and all that." Max scratches an itch just under his nose. "I'd aim for the winter break to have some preliminary prospectus done for me to look at."

"Okay," I reply. "Will I see you over the break?" I ask, tentative. His eyes are focused on the ground, minding his step.

"I don't know," he says, his voice simple, unemotional. I sense a pause in him, a hesitation that surprises me. Is it possible for a person to know something before they *know* it? To know what I have planned? Tonight, showing him my home, my woods, the places and pieces meant to haunt and remind. Tomorrow, showing something more. A calculated game of connect the dots. "Let's worry about that then. We're here now, together." He looks over at me then reaches down and squeezes my cold hand. I clasp back, pause, and swing him toward me so we are facing each other. I reach up and place my hands gently on the ends of the honey-bronze scarf, looped loosely around his neck. I pull on the ends. I pull him closer to me, gently, a kind of lasso.

"Alright, Max. Alright," I say in just over a whisper. I look in his oceanic eyes, blue and choppy and stirring. My breath fogs up his glasses, and I laugh. He smiles. He leans into my personal space ever so slightly, his lips just barely parting. I feel a flash of disgust scrawl my face, there and gone, pure reaction. I turn away slightly, trying to cover, faking a sneeze. Pretending he didn't try to kiss me. "Oof—excuse me." I playact a sniff. "Let's finish our walk, and then I'll take you on that sunset drive." His face flashes from embarrassment to anger to suspicion to composure in milliseconds. He looks again like a man in complete control of himself.

We are both very good at our respective games.

"Sounds good to me, Audie," he says. I grant him a warm look because I must. We set off again, and as we do, our arms hooking together again, more for balance than out of intimacy, he drones on about tedious department politics, but what I think about is the fact that he seems to have some doubt about whether we will see each other over the winter break between semesters. And I think about how funny it is that Max is uncertain, that he doesn't know for sure whether he will see me, like he has any control over it. But still, his hesitation is curious. Have I grown boring to him? Have I not given him enough?

Before I'm done with him, he'll have more than he can handle. He can count on it. Because I know for certain what is going to happen. There's no doubt in my mind. I will certainly not be seeing Max in

December. Max will certainly not be seeing me. Max will not be seeing *anyone* anymore.

Not after this weekend.

We make the final turn around the edge of the field, Max talking about some new art installation at his favorite gallery on Cape Cod.

"Mm-hmm," I say, barely paying attention.

Then a sudden snag-jolt. His arm rips from mine, almost throwing me entirely off balance. Max is down on the ground before I know it.

"Ah, fuck—!"

"Max, you alright?" I ask, my human instinct kicking in as I kneel beside him, worried he might be injured. Which is laughable. Considering my plans for this weekend. The whole reason I invited him up here in the first place.

He's on all fours. Vulnerable. Pathetic.

"I—my foot got caught on some root or, or something." His whole face is wincing, his voice strained. "My ankle—I think I twisted it." He settles back on his knees and looks at each of his hands in turn, finding some scrapes on each one. A small amount of blood.

"Looks like you caught some rocks." I look at Max and he looks at me and I can tell he's wondering why in the world I'm not touching him. No hand on the shoulder, no bracing squeeze of the arm, no soothing pat or rub of the back. I can see it in his face. *Why won't you touch me? Why won't you comfort me, even now?* But he is a coward and does not say these words out loud, even though I can see them bloom in his face. Soon, I'm sure, they will burn in him. He will be angry with me. I've seen it before, though he tries to hide it.

Why won't you just give yourself to me, you condescending bitch?

"Let's get you up and inside. I'll treat your hands and take a look at your ankle." I pull his arm over by shoulder and brace him up to a standing position. "We'll take it nice and slow."

"It really hurts."

"We can do it. Probably just a twist. Maybe a sprain."

"Maybe it's broken."

"I doubt it." But as I say it, a thrill of possibility runs through me. Could it be this easy? A break in Max Durant, and so fast? And with so much more to come. I try to keep the rise of satisfaction down. "Come now. Little at a time. I've got you."

I've got you.

Max

The fading light of dusk and the headlights of Audra's car mingle into a vague mash ahead of us. Everything is just barely illuminated, like something could appear at any moment, unbidden, unexpected. The road unrolls like an asphalt tongue. The dark, silent trees zipper closed behind, giving the impression that we can never go back.

I wanted to stay at the house, relax, ice my ankle—which feels like murder right about now. Every bump over these rough back roads sends a jolt of pain through me. But she insisted. She wouldn't hear of it. She wants me to see the wilds at night. To give me my chance to see some animals at this juncture in between times while the sun is falling away but true night has not yet arrived. I feel half-powered in this light, half-real. Like I could do anything inside this veiled suffusion and get away with it. Like she could.

Audra slows and takes a right onto a dirt road. "More apt to see something interesting down here. There are lots of potholes, but I'll take it slow. I promise—look!" And there, just for a moment, springing forth along the shoulder of the road ahead of us is a red fox, small, fuzzy, and then it disappears into the forest. "We're on our way, Max!" she says excitedly. "Already seeing cool stuff."

Despite my discomfort, Audra's unguarded delight is refreshing, like a window opened on a spring day. I cherish it.

"Out here is one of the best places to see deer, moose. Sometimes even bears."

"Kinda hope we don't run into any bears, I have to say." I chuckle gently.

"Did you bring your knife?"

"No." I look over at her. She clucks her tongue in disappointment.

"Too bad. Never know when you might need something like that in a place like this. If not now, when? You know?" She looks out the windshield, leans forward a little over the wheel. She's serious. I suddenly feel naked without it, like right now that knife in my hand would feel like a sword, a shield. But against what? Audra's beautiful home filled with her beautiful paintings? The plush towels? The decadent brie? The joyous smiles Audra flashes me? It is all so comfortable and comforting. And yet. I find myself prickling with anxiety. Teeth set on edge. As if the whole thing could crumble in an instant. Like I might be looking at everything from the wrong angle. The only thing I can possibly attribute this to is the unresolved tension between Audra and me. The unspoken tease of it all. It electrifies the air around us.

"When I was maybe nine or ten"—Audra's voice cuts through the repetitive rhythms of the car, the crunch of the dirt and gravel beneath the tires and the low whisper of the heater—"I went out on a hike through the property. By myself. It was summertime. Pops was at work, Gram was up at the house working on the garden." Audra eases down and through a major rut. I brace my hand against the door, teeth gritted. "Sorry," she says quickly. "So, on this hike, I brought my backpack, I brought some water, I brought a compass, I brought my knife, I wore good shoes. I took it all very seriously." She laughs. "I figured I'd be gone an hour, two, tops. Well, I got all turned around at a certain point, dropped the compass without knowing it somewhere along the way. One hour turned into two turned into four turned into six. Because I panicked. I kept moving in the direction I assumed was correct, but I was in so deep that everything looked the same. The trees, the clearings I passed through, the patches of sky I saw above me. I kept moving and moving, getting more and more lost."

As she speaks, I look out into the dense forest surrounding us. To be lost somewhere in there. To be small, to be Audra, with her mane of auburn hair and her backpack. What a thing.

"I couldn't hear or find any water to follow anywhere," she continues. The road feels like a continuous rumble strip, my ankle sparkling with sharp jabs. Audra seems not to notice. "Nothing to give me any direction. I tried using the sun, to sort out which way our house was, but I just didn't know. I couldn't figure it out. So, as late afternoon set in, I did the only thing I could think of. I got out my knife and started cutting down brush, looking for the driest stuff to start with, piled it on a bald patch in a clearing. Luckily I had a lighter. I started a fire." The road smooths out a bit, and I take three deep breaths, light sweat on my brow. "As it got going, I found wetter stuff so it would smoke. I kept the fire going and going, terrified I wouldn't be able to contain it and I'd burn down the whole forest around me. But I didn't, I managed to keep it pretty safe and good and smoky. On my, like, fourth round of cutting brush, I was rushing. I got careless, my hands were tired, and the sun was sinking, and I cut the palm of my left hand open." She holds out her hand and shows me the white scar line that cuts across her palm.

"Jesus, Audra," I hiss. She pauses in the story here and looks at me. She sees my wince. But she also sees my interest. I swallow, realizing that she knows I am imagining the colors in all this. She waits, her eyes turning back to the vacant road. "The gray-black smoke. The proud, brown tree trunks. The evergreens. The trailing, failing light." She nods at my words. "And then, in all of this, the bright-red blood, like a cardinal through the trees." My voice is almost a whisper, like the last remnants of light outside: barely there, hardly anything at all.

It's so vivid in my mind, coming at me all at once, that I know it will be my next piece, that I must work on it once home. Maybe even sketch it out somewhere tonight, before we go to bed, so I don't lose it. I can see the heavy daubs of paint creating topographies of foliage in seaweeds, basils, pines; a pale, young hand with a slash of ruby currant that splits the peace and the piece wide open.

"That's right." Her voice is gentle. A deep ripple of heat runs through my body. "So I grabbed the spare pair of hiking socks I'd packed in my bag and tied one as tightly around my hand as I could, to help staunch the bleeding. But it kept on bleeding, and it burned under the wool." Audra raises her arm suddenly and points through the windshield—I catch the blaze of tiny, brown-and-white back legs as a rabbit vanishes into the depths of the woods on the left. "About thirty or forty-five minutes after I cut myself, I heard someone or something coming. Then I heard my name being called. It's Pops. He found me because of the smoke. I was three miles deep into our neighbor's land. Only about three-quarters of a mile from a proper road, the one our driveway is on." She shakes her head at her younger self. "If I'd gotten to the road, I could have sorted myself out easily. Pops took me to the hospital, I got stitches, I learned my lesson: don't lose your bearings and always bring a knife. The knife saved me."

"It also harmed you."

"Two evils, one is always the lesser." Her voice is quiet and sure. "Most of the time, anyway. And I chalk that up to user error."

I think of her left palm, that hand that has painted so many incredible things. That hand that rests so close to me in this car. I would like to grab it, seize it, kiss my way down the length of the scar. I would like to press on it, imagine the rawness of it that day, the cardinal blood, a vivid flutter added to young Audra's panic.

The car slams down into a pothole.

"Fuck!" I bark, gritting my teeth.

"That's a bad one," and there's almost the hint of a laugh in her voice as the car rises back up with a *thunk*. "Snuck up on me." She eases around the next rut, saves me from another jolt.

The forest on the left is opening into a low, wet marsh area. It's like seeing the opening of a familiar movie from long ago. The marshy vista expands and widens, like curtains opening on a stage. The sky is painted in smeared marmalades. That feeling I had in the parking lot of the trading post leaps upon me—that I might be a man reliving the same moment twice: a double exposure. I stare out across the scenery and the dirt road, momentarily paralyzed, beleaguered with a kind of deranged sentimentality, wondering if it's a feeling that could possibly belong to me.

"You alright, Max?" Audra is giving me a funny look. I nod.

"Fine," I say, making myself smile.

"I'll pull over here. Famous local spot for seeing moose. Out-of-towners always want to see moose." She pulls over onto the side with the marsh, hugging as close to the edge as she dares. We look out at the purpling, bruised sky, the marsh grass pressed down and springing up in various lumps, pools of water lit as if from underneath. Broken husks and trunks of trees lean this way and that—tired, wounded soldiers. "Yeah, this is good." We sit in silence for a few long moments, taking in the expanse, both beautiful and eerie in its desolation. Worry has crept into my bones, hazy and unnameable.

"Common sightseeing spot, huh?" I ask her, my throat constricting like a finger trap.

"Very. It's not a guarantee to see something, but pretty close." Okay. I swallow and take a breath. It's a common place to go. Everyone goes here. Especially with out-of-towners. I was then. I am now. I devour the uncanny scenery, a memory arriving: In the daylight, the road had seemed almost white under the glaring sun. We drank warm, skunky beer. We talked about art. We talked about each other. We smiled, and we laughed and had not a care in the world.

Now, laughing is the furthest thing from my mind.

Audra suddenly turns her head and looks behind us out the rear windshield. I turn my head to follow her gaze but see only the empty dirt road slithering off into the darkened tree line. She keeps looking, her eyes squinting.

"What is it?" The silence all around us feels material, like my eardrums have burst. She looks this way and that behind us for another moment or two.

"You ever get the feeling you're being watched?" She turns her brown eyes on me. I look out the rear windshield, seeing nothing but trees, grass, a potholed dirt road. But there is so much darkness out there, so much density. I feel surrounded by the unseen.

By that which wishes to remain concealed. By that which I wish to remain concealed. "Probably just some animal. I can sense them sometimes," she says, turning back around. "Hunter's instincts."

"Do you really think something's there?"

"Hard to say." She shrugs. "Unless you want to go look." That hinky Colfax smile breaks on her lips; a dare.

"Not particularly," I reply, her beauty and magnetism distracting me from my low-level paranoia, my tender ankle. We are so alone out here. No one, it seems, for miles. Just the sunset. The blank forest. "I'd rather stay right here. With you. In your car."

"Suit yourself." Audra laughs. Her eyes fall upon the open marsh. They rest on the landscape lightly, as if the whole scene might be in soft focus for her. Quiet gathers between us. We're both eased back in our seats, looking out onto the cragged, spooky land. She, perhaps, really is looking for moose, deer, bear, rabbits, foxes. All I am doing is looking out into the rough landscape, the scene registering as an indiscriminate wash of colors and shapes, a melted watercolor, aware that I was a player on just such a stage before. But not inside of a Volvo. On the hood of a truck. But a woman, yes. A sunset, yes.

I feel Audra's body heat, hear her quiet breaths, smell her faint perfume. The rosemary from her kitchen. I want nothing more than to take her, to feel grounded in *her*. She is a vitalizing violet shock in the near dark. I have been holding my prayer for so long, for too long.

"Audra—"

"Do you hear that?" Audra's eyes are suddenly keen on me. My eyes search her face, wanting to see a flicker of desire for me, but instead I find she is simply alert, ear tilted up.

"Maybe we could—" I slip my hand on top her hers.

"Shh," she says, but she does not pull her hand away. We are both quiet. I listen with her, the sun all but gone now. Then I hear it. "There!" she whispers, her fingers intertwining with mine, squeezing. It comes again, a low, bass sound, fading from blaring to weak. It comes again, lasting for four solid seconds.

"It—it sounds like a moan," I whisper. She bites her lip in mild anxiety and looks at me, nods her head a little. She turns the key in the ignition, flicks the headlights on. The road illuminates before us. Low brush borders the narrow dirt road ribboned out, bog on the left, dense tree line on the right. The insistent moaning sound—a lowing almost—is more urgent now.

"It's ahead of us, I think, whatever it is," she whispers, leaning toward the glass of the windshield, straining to pin down the source of the noise.

"Perhaps we should head back."

"I'll pull forward, slowly, a few yards at a time," she says, ignoring me.

"Are you sure?"

"Yes." She laughs gently. "Are you scared?" The knowing smile, the closing darkness, the mystery of the desperate sound, the centerless sense of kinship with this road, this view—I feel myself growing aroused.

"Never. I'm with my local."

She smiles bigger and eases us ahead cautiously, dipping through a few potholes, weaving slowly around some errant rocks. We scan the road and the ditches alongside as we inch forward, the sound lower, more tired. Our tension and my growing desire for Audra are almost unbearable to me now, as if the two are linked, intertwined; they are muddled up, the moaning out there somehow my own moaning: desperate, pathetic, visceral, iris mulberry. These desolate woods are manifesting my need for her, drawing us on, haunting us. A sudden, short gasp-shriek from Audra, a sudden, unsteady shape in the road. She hits the brakes, the red taillights flaring behind us.

An impossibly gangly, young moose calf has stumbled into the road. Its improbably long legs shake. It stands there dumbly, before us, not knowing what to do.

"Ah, shit," Audra sighs. "Look. In the ditch." Audra points down and to the left. At the very edge of the range of the headlights lies a hulking brown mass, fur thick and bristly. A full-grown moose. It groans and snorts and moves its lanky front legs, agitated, unable to stand, its back legs seemingly still, dead. Audra turns the wheel as far left as she can and inches forward as slowly as she dares so she can set the headlights more squarely on the injured animal. It is huge. Monstrous. Eyes watery and exhausted. Audra puts her window down. The pained lowing of the moose in the ditch is loud now, aggressive.

"Audra, maybe we should go." We sit there for a moment, transfixed. I look at the calf. I can feel Audra thinking hard beside me. She leans over me, her hand reaching down between my legs. My breath catches in my throat, but my eyes stay trained. I hear her pull the glove box open in front of me, and her door opens a moment later.

"Stay here." She gets out of the car, holding something, and shuts the door behind her.

"Audra—Jesus—" I lean over her seat, grasping the now-driverless wheel. "What are you doing? Where are you going?" A spike of genuine fear flashes through me.

That giant, brown animal. The empty black road. Her squall of copper hair. The jagged red line on her young palm. The bog, mocking me, welcoming me back.

She approaches the calf, who chirps and *squonk-squonks* like a wooden door creaking open and closed. It stumbles dumbly backward into the ditch beside its mother, who emits guttural groans and honks angry, chapped, chesty noises. "Fuck. Fuck," I whisper. Though I fear for Audra, I do not get out of the car. I do not go to pull her back to safety. It is beyond me. She is beyond me.

All of this is.

I can see Audra speaking gently to the animals, but I can't make out what she's saying over the *squonks* of the baby and the frantic groaning of the mother. The sounds assault my ears nearly nonstop now. Audra is looking down hard at the grown moose, who keeps trying to use its front legs to stand, but the effort is horrific and desperate to behold. It digs and collapses, digs and collapses. The beast is full of pain and fear. Terror.

It's so quick, what happens. It's unfolding already before I understand that Audra has even raised her arm.

BANG.

BANG.

BANG.

BANG.

BANG.

My hands fly to my ears. I am cowering.

Audra's arm still raised. A powerful black pistol in her hand. Her body steady as a stone totem. The moose in the ditch is silent. Still. Dark-red blood soaks the area around the ear and eye facing us. The calf has scrambled frantically down the side of the road. It picks its way down into the ditch. Audra fluidly lowers the gun, flicks the safety on. She approaches the edge of the road and the shape of her name starts to form in my throat, but it never arrives. I just watch. She carefully takes the slope down into the ditch, standing not three feet from the enormous animal. She looks at it with fondness. With sadness. I look at it, too. Its once heaving chest is still. I watch Audra swipe her hand under one of her eyes. She takes a deep breath and puffs out her cheeks in release.

At the edge of audibility, the calf cries out half-heartedly. Once, then twice. Audra turns to face it, sees it is just standing in the ditch down the road twenty yards or so. It doesn't know what to do. Audra stands there and looks at it, her back to me, for a long minute. I imagine she and the orphaned baby are looking at each other, but it's too dark to see clearly.

Audra climbs up the embankment, her face completely composed now. She makes her way to the car. With her gun. She gets in and closes the door, opens the glove box. She places the gun in a case, closes the case, then closes the glove box. It's been there this whole time, I realize. From the time she picked me up in Bangor to this very moment. Audra has had a gun.

"My guess is a logging truck clipped it." Audra sniffs, then takes a deep breath, gathering herself. "The hip, the back legs. To do that kind of damage on an animal that big—had to be a huge truck. One leg was completely snapped. The other was covered in blood. God knows how long it was there suffering." We sit in the car, heat on, headlights grotesquely bright on the dead moose. The baby has come a few yards closer but still stands in the darkened ditch. It makes no sound.

I want to shut my eyes tight against this, as if that might obliterate what I've just seen. I want to remember the bog as it was, as I had known it. Not like this. *Not this place, too. Christ.*

"And the calf?" My voice sounds separate from myself. Audra is quiet. We look at the calf, which looks at us, too afraid of the car and the lights to come nearer to its dead mother. How long had they been there like that, together? "You did what you had to do. It was a kindness, Audra." My eyes feast on the stark, horrible form of the moose. The brown coat, the blood, the emptiness of it now. Then the calf, down the road, so vulnerable, alone, already nearly consumed by the dark, by its fate.

Four

She Can Speak for Herself

Juniper

JUNE 9, 1988

"So, gang—what did you think of Old Gus's annual scavenger hunt?" I look around at Moss, Zephyr, Ash, Barley, Trillium, Coral, and Mantis. I hear grumbles. I see scowls or the sheepish rolling of eyes. We're sitting around a campfire in an idyllic clearing deep in the uninhabited part of the Lupine Valley property. Coral's pick. She showed us this spot, which sits about halfway between the Lupine Valley Village and the lake, with such pride the first time she brought us all down here. She was beaming, veritably twirling around the clearing as she pointed out the arcing birch trees and scattered boulders left behind from when Ice Age glaciers dragged, melted, and scored the earth. She asked us if we thought it was beautiful. We told her we did. She asked us didn't we think it would be a great place to paint, sketch, carve—make art of any kind? We told her we did. And this seemed to make her so happy, to have that genuine approval, to be giving something so beautiful to us.

Right now the clearing is crowded with wild, jumping shadows in the firelight. Dusk is falling, and we are back to our core group, away from the other artists and instructors we've spent the better part of the day with. I get the sense that most of the group prefers it this way, just us. I'm always saying how much like a family we feel. Mantis always jokes that we're more of a cult.

"Oh, come on," Trillium says. "It wasn't that bad! I thought it was kind of fun. And clever, too—asking us to focus on our senses, which are so important to our art. See a spider web. Smell a blooming flower. Touch a muddy rock. Hear splashing water." She genially nudges Moss, who shakes his head like a true grouch.

"Wasn't a big fan of my partner," Moss jabs.

"Toad is a nice person." I sigh, tired of his day-long pout. "And thank you, Trill. Bless you, Trill," I say, appreciative, exasperated, trying to hold on to the positivity. "Gus only puts one together for the summer session, so you should really all consider yourselves lucky."

"What I'm taking from this is only come in fall or winter. Got it," Barley jokes as he lets his stick-skewered marshmallow brown over the flames.

"Sticks. In. The. Mud." Trillium points at each of them in turn. I look around at the group, all of whom are animated with begrudging smiles except for Coral and Mantis. Who did not participate in the scavenger hunt. Staff usually doesn't.

I am stilled when I look at Coral as she sits hunched and small, apart from the rest of us just a little. Blank. Everyone else is sitting right next to at least one other person. But Coral is a small island, alone on the forest floor. She looks…miserable. But at least she's up and about. It had taken some real doing to get her to come with us for even this little get-together. I wasn't sure she would. She could barely muster the will to join Mantis on the front steps of Focus earlier to watch the scavenger hunt unfold.

When I went to Focus to gather Moss for the day's activities early this morning, Coral was in his bed, fast asleep, in layers of clothing and blankets. Her little oval face had looked spectral hanging in the relative dark of his cabin. It seemed like Moss had been awake for a while. Wired, hair disheveled. When I looked over his shoulder, the painting on his easel was of a woman. Dark shades of maroon, ochre, brown. Drooped. Deflated. Her face a wash of tear tracks. I was struck by how good it was, despite my horror. He grudgingly let me in when he saw the concern in my face.

"She's in one of her bad ways," Moss whispered to me as we hovered over the bed. "She's usually fine, you know. But she gets like this sometimes." He shrugged. "She drove out here at, like, three this morning."

"Is she hurt?" I whispered, brimming with worry. I'd never seen her like this. Most of the time Coral is a busy-brained humming-bird, intense in her cleaning work, intense in her art, intense in her revelry with us, teeth and beer bottles gleaming in the summer sun.

"No, nothing like that. Just—sad." I looked over at his easel then at the messy bunches of paper and canvases on his desk. Fractions of Coral visible. "She just came here and cried and went to sleep." Moss looked at her intensely as she rested. I studied my friend, thinking about him painting her in these moments that had clearly been so full of difficulty. The canvas was her, evocative of her even though there was something …ghastly and mashed about it. I didn't know how to feel. But I did have to concede, it was striking.

When it was time to leave for the scavenger hunt, Coral was awake but not talking. She just looked at us with tired, empty eyes. Tracking back and forth slowly between the two of us. It had been startling for me. Then Mantis arrived and took over. Told us to get on with our *stupid fucking game*. Moss and I checked in on her throughout the day, tried to get her to have some water or eat some crackers. She just shook her head no. I tried. Moss tried. Mantis tried.

At the end of the day, she and Mantis were still sitting outside on the front steps of Focus, Coral looking out of it, Mantis looking stony. We convinced her to come hang with us. We told her she could even pick the spot. And so here we are.

"I had a nice time, too," Zephyr admits. I swallow and look away from Coral, catch eyes with Zephyr. She smiles at me slyly. We were, fortuitously, paired together by the luck of the draw. Out of the view of others, while I worried over a scavenger item, she kissed me down by the lake. I'd looked at her, stunned at my luck, grateful that she was not the coward I am. And then kissing was about all we did the rest of the afternoon.

"And Barley, you're such a liar." Trillium laughs, pulling her curly hair up in a bun. "You were *loving* ticking the little boxes off! I saw you dragging your poor partner all over creation, for Christ's sake." She snorts, which gets almost all of us laughing. Coral even smiles a little.

"Fine, fine." Barley holds his hands up in defeat.

We soon start talking about our various painting projects, and Mantis, clearly bored, gets up to gather some more downed brush for the fire. I keep an eye on Coral, and relief floods me as the artsy chatter seems to bring her back into herself bit by bit. Twenty minutes in, she still looks tired, but her eyes are alert, and she's leaning in toward the circle as everyone talks through their progress.

"And Coral," I say, "what about you?" Mantis grows still at the fire's edge, only his hands breaking small branches in half and tossing them into the pit. He's listening. Intently. Moss looks at Coral gently but with concentration. If she speaks now, it would be the first time all day. Coral blushes under the group's gaze. She swallows then clears her throat. We wait for several long moments, and I worry she isn't going to speak after all.

"Well, I—I wouldn't say that I have a *project*, exactly." Her low voice sounds scratchy, like smoked cardboard. Less than confident. But still, I feel like I can breathe again when I hear it.

"Sure you do," Moss encourages her. "You've organically been circling around birds. Drawings of birds. Sketches of birds."

"Birds are fantastic subjects," Ash affirms, jumping in quickly to try to help. Coral looks strengthened by their words. She has a small twig in her hands and is gently tracing the top of her foot with it.

"Oh, well—then, yeah. I—I've been drawing a lot of birds." She nods, lifting her eyes to us and then dropping them again. "Pencil and charcoal mostly."

"Blackbirds. Crows. Lots of dark-shaded birds, right, Cor?" Moss says. She nods. "She's a real natural and can draw on anything, with anything. And wings—I would say the wings—"

"Yes, with a special focus on the wings," Coral picks up the thread gratefully, her voice slow and methodical, like someone relearning how to hold a conversation. "Very…fine-tuned things, wings. So, I'm…playing with the idea of, like—what do you call them? Schematics. Engineering schematics in some of them." She swallows, a dreaminess to her voice. "While still working to—to show the delicate natural textures. Moss has been helping me so much." She smiles over at him, her eyes lifting with confidence to his. Moss smiles back an earnest, unjaded, unironic smile. Rare for him.

"We have fun in old Focus," he says. I think of the state of her this morning, the types of drawings that fill Focus as we speak, and I feel a stone in my stomach. "Coral will bring these great big sketch pads—thick—like portfolio size, but she'll also bring small little notebooks, like the kind you see detectives in movies carry around—" Moss is energized.

"Yeah, so I'll bring those, big and small—" Coral is beginning to get her feet under her, which is heartening.

"And I also got her a Moleskine to sketch in," Moss cuts her off.

"Right, and the Moleskine, which I love." She picks up the Moleskine from her lap and presses it to her chest. "So I have all of these different paper surfaces I've been working with. All of these different types of pencils—"

"I keep telling her that a person has to try various tools," Moss breaks in, steamrolling her. I watch Mantis's eyes flash to him, supremely irked, the last of his twigs snapped and out of his hands. "Various qualities. You never know how it will impact your output." Coral shrivels a little beneath his magnetism, just sits back and listens. Nods. "And with the Moleskine, I just let her know that's a classic. A classic. Those little books can make anyone feel professional. Just carry around one of those, write in it from time to time, and watch—"

"Take a fucking breath, Bark. She can speak for herself," Mantis snaps, cutting the clearing down to silence. His eyes bore down into Moss's skull. Trillium looks around the group nervously. Moss's face betrays fear for a split second, but then he regains himself.

"I know that. *Bug*." Moss's voice is defiant, venomous.

"Call me that again, you pencil-dicked twerp." Mantis bounds up to Moss in a flash, that old athleticism exploding to the fore. Moss flinches from his seat down on the ground, as if preparing for a blow.

"Guys—" I start to say, springing to my feet. Moss's jaw tenses, but he says nothing. Neither of them moves. We all hang in tense suspension.

"He's just helping me explain, that's all," Coral says, rising to her feet and coming to stand between them, her voice gentle but wary. She places a hand lightly against Mantis's chest, her eyes searching his face for a way to diffuse this. Then she looks down at Moss, who doesn't look back at her. His face is locked in an embarrassed snarl.

"It's okay to stand up for yourself, you know," Mantis hollers at her. She flinches and looks down into the dirt. I flinch, too, not expecting the sharpness to turn her way. "Don't let this asshole speak for you. You don't need that much help explaining yourself." He looks down on her. "Do you hear me?" Coral swallows and nods. "Speak," he commands her. Coral bites her lip, her neck and cheeks red with embarrassment. The discomfort in the air is suffocating.

"I hear you," she finally says, lifting her eyes. Her voice betrays no fear. Just agitation. A desire to end this scene. I look at Moss, who stays silent. Seemingly relieved Mantis is no longer yelling at *him*. "Come," Coral says, holding out her hand to Mantis, beginning to walk toward the edge of the clearing. Mantis drags his eyes away from Moss and follows her, putting his hand in hers at a delay. I look at the two of them—Mantis and Coral—and sense a deep and abiding kinship between them, despite his outburst. The way she offered her hand. The way he accepted it and followed her, without a word. And of course they would feel this quiet closeness; they grew up in the same small town. Have overlapping friend and family circles. Went to the same schools. They know each other in a way none of us could ever know them.

We watch as she takes him just beyond the sphere of light cast by the fire. They look like mere silhouettes. Paper dolls in the night.

She has her arms wrapped around her slim body for warmth, looking like a curled blade of dry grass. He is standing over her, bearlike at this distance, so she tilts her head back to look up at him. I watch their bodies shift positions around each other like magnets simultaneously attracting and repelling. I watch Mantis place a hand on Coral's shoulder, slide it to the side of her arm. I watch Coral move her body toward his just the littlest bit. There's a kitten. There's a wolf.

"What do you think is up with them?" Moss's words startle me—he's suddenly sitting right beside me on the downed log we dragged over when we first arrived. I was so focused on watching the Mantis-Coral shadow box that I didn't realize Moss had made his way to me. Ash is getting up to stretch his legs. I watch Trillium and Barley pop up to go join him. Soon they are standing in a little triangle whispering among themselves at the far side of the clearing. Zephyr is tending the fire. Moss draws his knees up and rests his arms on them. I keep watching the two bodies in the forest, darkness on top of darkness. The heady smell of smoke threads through my hair. Once in a while, one of their voices pokes through on the wind, but I can't make out any words.

"I dunno," I respond, and that's the truth. "They know each other, though. From town. They're…*close*, maybe. Friends, anyway," I say, not totally able to read their dynamic either. But there's something. Something. "He's protective of her, I think. He doesn't completely trust us, our intentions with her, or something."

Maybe it's the outsider status. While they pass in and out of Lupine Valley daily, back and forth from home to camp, camp to home, living their larger lives and dealing with people besides us, the rest of us stay put in King City. Wake here, work here, learn here, eat here, shit here, fuck here, sleep here, and do it all again. It's a closed system. Coral and Mantis are our free radicals. I imagine there's a bond in that, too.

"It's his ego. He's insecure. He doesn't believe any of the people who pay to be here could actually be friends with the people who get paid to be here. It's very, like, reverse-classist, really," Moss says.

"Well, maybe he has a point. We all come and go. They stay."

"Coral doesn't want to stay," Moss says.

"Maybe Mantis didn't either. Yet here he is," I reply. Silence falls between us. "Do you. You know." I sniff, my nose suddenly runny. "Like her."

"I don't know yet." He pushes his hand back though his black mop of hair. "But I do need her." He sighs.

I feel a frown tugging at my face. Before I can try to understand, Coral and Mantis return to the campfire. Coral sits next to Mantis, rubbing his back in encouragement.

"Uh, so, Mantis would just like to say he is sorry for his…outburst," Coral says, a tight, faint smile on her face. She looks down at him and waits for him to continue, and I can tell she's nervous that he won't. She leans down and whispers something in his ear. He sighs heavily.

"Been a long day." Mantis sounds like an oak log. "Watching grown adults play kiddie games doesn't do a lot for me." His eyes peer around at us all, hard; I feel shamed. "And Coral wasn't feeling well all day…" He shakes his head, kneading the back of his neck. "And she's just so talented in her own right. And smart. Just wanted her voice to be heard," he says, looking into the fire. "So, I apologize, Moss." He looks across at Moss, who's still sitting next to me. Moss gives him a nod. "And I apologize, C. I got cranky with you, and I shouldn't have."

"I appreciate that," Coral says and gives him a side hug.

Things settle down and get back to normal from there, Barley entertaining us with stories from the world of dopey college co-eds, and Trillium capturing our imaginations with lush descriptions of her life in Puerto Rico. We let the fire die way down as we continue to talk, all of us leaning against each other in fatigue by night's end.

"Time to go, kiddos," Mantis tells us when even our conversations have burned out. He gets up and dampens the remaining ember ashes with the gallon jug of water he brought, turning over the soil with a sharp branch. We all rise to our feet, creaky and ready for bed. But we still have the mile trek back through the woods to our cabins. I walk with Moss and Zephyr. Coral walks beside Mantis. Trillium, Ash, and Barley walk in their own little group. Our disparate flashlight beams bob and scatter in the trees, as if the light itself is breaking apart.

JUNE 11, 1988

I went into Greenville today to re-up on supplies at the Dirigo Hill Trading Post and the local art supply shop, a well-stocked but over-priced boutique place called Maker. I offered to pick up supplies for my painting posse if they gave me cash up front, and everyone was more than happy to let me be the Sherpa for the hour-and-a-quarter trek each way. I felt half pack mule, half soccer mom, just trying to remember and haul everything my charges might need.

Ash needed a bar of soap, nail clippers, and four canvases. Moss needed scissors for cutting his hair, trail mix, wine, and some indan-throne blue. Barley needed toothpaste, pencils, and canned soup. Zephyr needed a travel sewing kit and more 4" by 4" tiles for her project. I also bought her a bouquet of flowers because I'm pretty sure we're a thing now. When I asked Trillium what she wanted, she simply turned her light-brown lookers on me and said she had everything she could ever need. Her cabin looked bare. Austere. Well, then.

I get back at around three o'clock and deliver everyone's items to their cabins, though Ash is the only one actually home at the time to receive me. He thanks me profusely but clearly wants me to leave. He's lying on his bed with his forearm thrown over his eyes. He sighs. He says he doesn't want to talk about it. It's all terribly dramatic. So I wish him the best, tell him he can seek me out any time to talk, and leave him to his sulking. I get to Perspective and see Zephyr's left a note on her door letting everyone know she's down knitting with Hillock in her cabin. I leave her things and a sweet note paired with the flowers on the tidy desk. Barley's cabin is also empty, but the door is left ajar, propped open by a boot. I surmise he's airing it out—it smells strongly like he spilled some oil from his lantern. I leave his things just inside his door. Moss's cabin is empty, no note, door closed, but I get the sense he hasn't gone far: his paints are out and open. I set his stuff on the bed, since his desk is awash in paper and socks.

I decide to wait, now done with my delivery service, to see if he wants to take a walk with me. Maybe out to the Ledge. While I wait, I stroll the few paces around the cabin and look at the painting on his easel. It's a striking swipe of a thing done in bright, cheery colors, mostly yellows, a woman's form ecstatically and vibrantly tangled in its lines and arcs. I can't know for sure, but I know it anyhow, because I know him. It's Coral. It's arresting, compelling to look at. Better than anything he did before I got here in May. Not great, but very strong indeed. I go to his desk and flip through some of the sketches and paintings there to find more iterations of Coral. There are dozens. Most of them not so bright and cheery as the one up on the easel, and yet most of them even *better* in quality than the one displayed. In these, a darkness and brokenness haunt every line, every stroke. A cold shiver permeates my body. I set down the sheets of paper and back away, wondering how often this lovely, birdlike girl gets in *one of her bad ways*.

I wait another minute or two for him then leave, impatient to stretch my legs, impatient to get away from the versions of Coral with her dead doll's eyes, where her mouth seems open in an agonized wail. I assure myself that it doesn't mean she necessarily modeled for him in distress, just that she as a subject is fruitful for him. That he can envision her in many states. There's nothing wrong with that. And it's none of my business anyway.

I take a looping arc toward the Ledge, everything feeling warm and pliable and yielding: the air, the earth, the trees. A few birds chirp and trill and hop between high branches far above, the pines creaking in their slow, gentle sway. Fifteen minutes on, the forest begins to thin and open, a hard-packed trail winding up and to the left, revealing itself. As I take the familiar path past bare, wind-weathered trunks, the view out over the Ledge rises before me. But there's something else, too. Or, I should say, someone else.

Two of them. Embracing lovingly, kissing deeply. I halt to turn and leave them to it, but my step crunches some small stones as I do. The woman turns to look, but the man looks only at her, entranced, his eyes soft and loving. It's Coral. And someone I don't recognize; a man of about her age—nineteen? twenty?—with shaggy, brown hair tucked inside a blaze-orange beanie that reads *Bouchard Timber Outfit*.

"Hey, June," Coral calls. She looks happy to see me. Solid and assured in the man's arms.

"Hey, there, C," I reply, forging my way toward them; no sense turning away now.

"This is June. Or, well, Juniper," Coral says, hugging into the young man's side as I make it the last several yards. "She is one of the instructor-mentors here, in painting." I come up and shake his hand.

"Juniper, huh? Real name, or Lupine Valley name?" He smiles warmly.

"Lupine Valley name," I reply with a laugh.

"What it means to be baptized twice." Coral's lips curl into a sleepy smile. "June, this is Brady—my boyfriend." I try not to let surprise reach my face. But all I can think about are the numerous times I've watched her leaving Moss's cabin—flushed and alive, only occasionally cold-eyed and scraped bare. Or the numerous times I've seen her and Mantis off on their own, some unreadable tempest between them. I feel suddenly very warm. Exposed. Coral manages to seem at ease in her body, despite her vaguely harried eyes. As if everything I know about how she spends her time is mine alone to shoulder. I wonder if Brady knows how much time she spends alone with Moss, with Mantis. I wonder if she tells him Moss paints her ceaselessly. I wonder if she tells him that Mantis hovers with her always. But something tells me he doesn't know. His face is too wide-open. He has the look of a high school sweetheart.

"So tell me the story." I smile. "How did you two meet?"

"In school. Probably really started getting to know each other sophomore year," Brady says, looking down at Coral for reassurance. She nods. "Been together ever since. Football player, artsy girl. Match made in heaven, right?" He smiles.

"Oh, football—so you must know Mantis?" I ask him.

"He does," Coral replies. "Brady and Mantis are friends. That's how I got to know Mantis—through Brady." Coral shoves her hands in her jeans pockets.

"*Mantis*," Brady scoffs good-naturedly, shakes his head a little. "He hates that—you know that, right?" Coral just shrugs.

"Oh, so you all are pals," I say, pointing vaguely in the air.

"Yeah, kinda." Brady rubs the back of his neck, looking uncertain. "He was one of the volunteer assistant coaches for football when I was on the team in high school."

"Brady was the quarterback," Coral tells me with some pride. "Mantis was a defensive lineman, in his day."

"He was…an interesting character. A little too much of a wild man for me." Brady's chuckle is tinged with weariness.

"Brady thinks Mantis is a dick," Coral says simply, her long hair fluttering in the mild breeze. Her fingers comb through the strands, running over and through some snarls.

"Oh, yeah?" I ask, surprised at her candor. I look between the two, not sure what else to say.

"Yeah. You get to know a guy," Brady says. "Parties with the whole football team, girls who don't know any better, him kind of wanting to show off. Relive his glory days." Brady shakes his head. "Anyway, we don't pal around so much anymore." He looks down at Coral. "Try to keep our distance, right, Cindy?" He hugs her closer to his side, tight, and kisses her on top of the head. Her eyes flash to me for a split second, mischief in her face.

"That's right," she says. An awkward silence falls. Brady, like Mantis, is a big guy. Football players. I think of bookends, Brady and Mantis. Little Coral being held between them.

"Cindy?" My brain jump-starts, looking to Coral for confirmation, grasping on to this piece of information hungrily.

"Cynthia." She nods.

"I prefer Cindy myself, but I can let her have her fun. Let her come out to the willy-wags and traipse around with you artist types. Part of the job, I guess. But thank god you go home to the real world at the end of the day, right?" Brady runs his hand up and down her arm, voice jolly. Coral's face strains.

"What's so real about the world out there?" I ask him, wanting to stand up for us but also wanting to make sure it comes off as playful. I think it does.

"People…can pretend to be whoever they want to be out here," he says, very serious. "Like their pasts don't matter. But they do." He nods then looks down at Coral. "Gus likes to give people second chances. Sometimes to people who don't deserve them." He strokes Coral's arm again. "Besides—I'd get the life beat outta me if I went in to work asking to be called Boomerang or something." He laughs, shrugs.

"That's a problem with *out there*," I say. "Not Lupine Valley."

"Maybe so, maybe so." He nods politely.

"And what do you do, Brady?" I ask. He points to his hat.

"Work for Bouchard Timber Outfit. Brady Bouchard, at your service," he says. "We supply wood to lumberyards. It's my dad's business." He stands up straighter. I take in his flannel shirt and plain, forgettable handsomeness.

"You're out of an L.L. Bean catalog," I say.

"He's even got the Bean boots." Coral gestures down at his feet.

"Well, shit," I say, looking down at the rubber-toed duck boots, and Brady smiles.

"Anyway—we were just about to head out," Coral says, her eyes locking with mine. "I'll see you around, okay, June?"

"Absolutely," I tell her.

"Maybe I can sneak into one of your cohort powwows this week?" she asks hopefully, a small smile creeping onto her lips. A genuine one. She comes to almost all of them now, our painting group gatherings. We both know there's no sneaking about it and no need to ask permission. She's one of us now. Which makes me wonder if Brady doesn't understand the extent of her involvement with us. Which makes me worry that it would be a problem for her if he did.

"Sure, we'll see what we can do." I nod, playing along.

"Nice to meet you, Juniper," Brady says to me, sincere enough.

"You, too," I reply. As they head off down the trail, Coral turns around to look at me for a moment, but I can't read her expression. Maybe I never could. Soon, they disappear, hand in hand, and I am alone. I take a breath.

Why has Coral never mentioned Brady?

Why doesn't Brady like Mantis?

I need to talk to Moss.

I walk up onto the Ledge, gathering myself, the wind pulling higher the more exposed I get. The endless sea of green forest and slender stripes of road beyond and beneath me are spread out like a child's playset. The great puddle Moosehead Lake makes down below has me feeling bigger than big. Smaller than small.

I turn to go a few minutes later, the clouds and sky starting to rapidly darken toward gray, and pass Lovers' Tree, emblazoned with rough, archaic initials. I look for a C+B or a B+C but don't find them.

"Yeah, of course I know. They've been dating for, like, two or three years," Moss says to me, totally unfazed, bored almost as he wolfs down his stew. He's sitting cross-legged on top of his desk. I'm sitting on the edge of his bed with my own bowl of cooling supper. Rain is pelting against the windows, the outside steel gray but for the glowing windows of other cabins in the distance.

"You knew Coral had a boyfriend?"

"Yes."

"Named Brady Bouchard?"

"Yes," he says, mouth full, flipping through some used sketch paper under his thigh. I'm deflated.

"Damn—I really thought I was bringing some good intel, here," I admit.

"I totally appreciate you," he says, tipping the bowl against his lips and draining the last of his stew, wiping his face with his wrist. He puts the bowl down beside him on the desk. "But—yeah. We talk about everything. She tells me *everything*, Junie. It's like—wild. Her family, her school days, her past. Like, did you know she has manic depression?" He looks elated. Astonished. I have never seen Moss so *into* something. Like he's telling me the trading card stats of his favorite baseball player. My appetite has left me.

"I mean…I sensed *something* was up the day of the scavenger hunt. But—I didn't *know* know," I say, pushing the stew around in my bowl.

"She tried slitting her fucking wrists in November. This past November." His eyes sparkle. He thrusts his own wrists out toward me and slashes a finger across each in turn. "Think of how much blood there must have been. Think of how, even after she felt the pain on her first wrist, she *kept going* on her second!"

"Jesus, Moss." I wince, holding my hand up as if to say *easy*. I think of the snowy, papery skin under the cuffs of her sweater. It's fragile enough as it is.

151

"Yeah, dude. Brady and her parents were, like, down the hall. Having a grand old time, a lovely dinner, licking each other's assholes for all I know." He laughs. "Meanwhile, she's over in the bathroom, doing that. Ruining her mom's towels." The image makes me queasy. His ease with all of it makes me queasy. I set my bowl down on the wood-plank floor. "And there's more where that came from."

I can feel my brow is creased. I press my hands between my knees and look down into the floor. It's so hot in here. It's always so goddamned hot in here.

"There is?" I ask him. "More?" He nods solemnly.

"She's been through a lot. Put herself through a lot," he says. "She tells me about it."

"But she doesn't still...you know. Hurt herself?" I ask, wondering if it's something I'll have to go to Gus about. Moss hesitates.

"No," he says, pushing his bowl around on his desk. "Not so much anymore. She's got a whole regimen. Therapy. Pills." I swallow and nod, feeling relieved. "She doesn't like the pills too much." He laughs gently. His eyes wander to a stack of sketches and paintings on his desk.

"But if they help." I shrug.

"Right," he says, pinching his lip between his fingers, looking down at the floor. "But stuff like that only helps in a certain way, you know? They don't just fix a person. And not everything—not everybody—needs to be *fixed*. But anyway, she's okay, Junie. She has peaks and valleys, she told me. But she knows how to cope and deal with it. She's been dealing with it for a long time. Trust me."

I nod, breathe in deeply through my nose. Beautiful, brilliant Rita fills my mind. My ex doesn't believe in much, but she sure as hell believes in modern medicine. She was always really open about how grateful she was for the little white antidepressant tablets she took every day.

But that's Rita. I guess Moss would know better than me how Coral is. "In other news: Brady does not seem to like Mantis."

"Who does?" Moss replies, dismissive.

"Brady, like, purposefully keeps his distance, though. And I think he'd prefer it if Coral did, too." His eyes flick to me, suddenly invested again.

"Oh, yeah?" he asks. I nod. "Interesting," he murmurs.

Silence settles between us. We're lost in our own thoughts.

"Are you okay?" I ask after a while. "You look tense."

"I'm fine." He waves me off. He's biting his thumbnail.

"You're sure?"

He looks at me like his square, fretting older sister who just doesn't *get* it. He shakes his head and sighs, smiling just the littlest bit. He unfolds himself off the top of his desk and stretches.

"Gonna eat that stew or what?"

I look down at it. It's starting to congeal. I shake my head no, a little nauseous. He ruffles my hair as he walks past and takes the bowl for himself, unaffected. Ravenous.

JUNE 23, 1988

The distance from our two large canoes to shore is probably about a quarter mile. Zephyr is sitting in the middle seat between me and Mantis, cradling a boom box that's screaming out X-Ray Spex across the water. Mantis is on one paddle, I'm on the other. We're in the canoe closer to Kress Beach, the sandy bit of shoreline that's part of the thirty-acre Lupine Valley property. No one is on shore even though the temperatures have finally started to climb. It's far enough away from the village—a mile and a half through the woods—that students venture down on only the hottest days of the year. Mantis had said, *This place is wasted on you people*, and so we wanted to show him it wasn't. So we're here. Well, not all of us. Trillium, Ash, and Barley are on a side quest of their own to Quebec City. Gone for a few days.

Coral and Moss trail behind us by fifteen or twenty yards, each of them with a paddle. They've been bickering for the last five minutes, their voices echoey and indistinct on the water, sometimes totally smudged out by the boom box just in front of me. Each time I turn my head back to look at them, it's like a new frame in a comic strip:

Coral trying to direct Moss on the paddle.

Moss snapping at her as they begin turning their canoe in a circle.

Moss crossing his arms over his chest huffily when she tells him he's not doing it right.

Coral half standing in the canoe as she tries to reach for his paddle, frustrated.

Moss on his paddle again, but sullen and silent.

All of this underscored by Poly Styrene's deeply English voice shouting about bondage.

Eventually we're all settled into our paddling rhythms, heading nowhere in particular. Mantis gestures and narrates points of interest around the lake. An eagle's nest. The rough site of the largest fish he's ever caught. A few minutes later, I look behind us and see that Coral and Moss have fallen way behind. They're not even paddling. They're talking. A good half football field away from us.

"I've got to keep my eye on the prize here, Zeph. But do some spying for me." I smile. "What is going on in the mighty vessel behind us?" Zephyr turns herself completely around on the middle bench so she's facing me in the stern, her eyes looking over my shoulder.

"They're not even moving." She chuckles, her nose stud glinting in the sunlight. "They're…talking. They look mad, maybe?" I see Mantis in the prow turn to look over his shoulder for a moment, trying to see what Zephyr is seeing. "Yes, they look mad. I think they're arguing."

"About the canoe, you think? I don't think Moss is exactly the outdoorsy type," I say. Zephyr's face squints, relaxes, smiles, then grows more serious, and I can tell she's watching something nasty unfold between Moss and Coral. Then, as if on cue, I can hear the faint, angry lilt of explosive voices over the water, but I can't make out what's being said. Zephyr turns off the boom box, sets it down by her feet. Mantis stops paddling and turns around. So do I.

They're yelling at each other—Moss's face emanating something savage, Coral's face reflecting hurt. Their voices are raised, their arms gesticulating. Then Coral stands up and points down at Moss.

A silence.

Moss barks, furious, but doesn't dare stand up in the canoe with her.

"Cindy!" Mantis calls. I turn forward to see his hands cupped around his mouth, his face pissed. I rotate back to look at Coral and Moss, but they don't seem to have registered Mantis. They're back to screaming at each other, their bodies on fire.

"Cindy! Everything alright back there?" Mantis shouts again, getting antsy, our canoe rocking as he shifts inside it. I brace my arms on the sides, almost dropping my paddle. I grab it and pull it inside with us. Suddenly, a silence has fallen over the lake. I turn to look back once more.

Coral is still and quiet, her arms at her sides, staring Moss dead in the eyes. The fight out of her. Moss is coiled like an animal ready to strike. His lips move, speaking in a lower voice that we cannot hear.

Coral goes slack. A cornstalk gone to seed. Pale, gray-yellow. Leaning.

And then I realize she really *is* leaning. Too far. She's falling backward. *Letting* herself fall backward. My mouth opens to cry out, but no sound comes, all the muscles in my body seizing. Zephyr lets out a little shriek. Mantis lurches in the canoe.

Coral falls over the side of the canoe into the water, arms spread out like a child trying to make a snow angel. The splash is barely audible from where we are. Moss's face is wide open in shock. He clutches the canoe as it rocks wildly from her departure. She floats on her back in the wake of the canoe like Ophelia for several long moments. And then she goes under. The flutter of her pale hair is the last thing we see.

"Cindy!" Mantis cries, paddle digging desperately into the water, turning us around at a painfully slow rate. I finally come to my senses and take up my paddle and begin to help him, the cold water slapping up at us. I look out over the blue-green ripples beside Moss and his canoe and don't see her. Moss peers over the edge of the canoe but does not jump in after her. He doesn't even reach his arm down into the depths so that he might try to grasp some trailing piece of her clothing.

A terrible thought crosses my mind. *Did he push her?*

I shake it away. No. I would have seen that. I would have seen his hand on her. We were looking. We were all looking. Why would I think that? The questions ball in my throat, but I cannot speak them. Mantis and I paddle, all of us oddly silent in the shock of it, in our mission to get back to Coral, the canoe. Moss is still looking over the edge.

"Do you see her?" Mantis shouts to him. "Do you see her, Moss?"

Moss lifts his head, as if waking from a dream. He doesn't speak. He doesn't shake his head or nod his head or duck his head in any way that indicates anything.

"Moss, you son of a bitch!" Mantis shouts, and it's furious now, not just panicked. "Get in there! Get the fuck in there! Do you see her?"

My heart is racing, my arms on fire. The lake looks so still all around Moss's boat. Around Moss. Still, baffled, alone.

And then she breaches. Coral. Her head pops up maybe ten yards away from the canoe Moss sits in. She gasps, her arms grappling with the surface of the lake, sopping and heavy in her gray hoodie.

"Jesus, fuck," Mantis breathes, a new kind of vigor in his paddling.

"Oh, thank goodness." Zephyr's voice is shaky. Coral seems to gather herself as we draw ever nearer, her arms treading water in wide circles. She looks at Moss in his boat. Then at us approaching. She looks tired. She keeps looking between the two canoes—Moss near but unmoving. Mantis closing in but furious.

Between the devil and the deep, blue sea. The line springs to mind, unbidden.

She seems to sigh. As if disappointed. As if exhausted. Her eye tics.

She closes her eyes, and her lips.

She lets her arms go still, and she begins to sink.

She doesn't fight it.

She slides back beneath the surface of the water.

"What the hell is she doing?" An acidic edge of panic is buried in Zephyr's cry.

"Coral, we're coming for you!" I call out, useless, pathetic. She can't hear me under there. I think of her heavy clothes, her Bean boots, so like Brady's. She doesn't appear; there's barely a trace of her. Just the bubbles percolating on the surface above her. I keep paddling. Mantis is stripping off his boots.

"When I get out, get this canoe up alongside the other one. Having both together will stabilize things better for when we get back in." I nod at Mantis and then he's over the side of the canoe, almost taking us with him. Zephyr and I hold on for dear life as the canoe struggles to find its equilibrium. Zephyr takes up Mantis's paddle, and we make our way over the final fifteen or twenty yards to Moss, who just sits, dumbstruck.

Mantis dives under. Zephyr clutches my hand, on the edge of tears. My eyes scan the ripples madly, and phantom shapes reveal themselves, not one of them Mantis or Coral.

It must only be seconds that pass—long, eerie seconds—but it feels like an eternity before their water-warped shapes start to billow and bloat toward the surface, pale skin and dark clothes conjuring something not quite human. They breach in a frantic spray, gasping, arms flailing. Mantis shakes Coral to rouse her, slams his hand against her back hard as she chokes out water. I extend my paddle out to them, and Mantis grabs it immediately, holding on to Coral, and I pull them in. He instructs us on how to balance and brace the neighboring canoes so they can get in. He tells Zephyr to get in with Moss, voice gruff, breaths straining. He pushes and I pull Coral's rag doll body inside. Then I help him in. They both sprawl awkwardly in the bottom of the canoe, drenched, at my feet. Coral's chest is heaving, her eyes lightly closed, her skin a sickly white. But she's alive and breathing. Mantis leaves his forearm draped over his eyes for a few moments, catching his breath.

"Moss—you little—fuck!" he gasps. "What is—the matter with you?" Mantis tears his arm away from his face and pushes himself up in the canoe to sit, his bulk jostling us again. Moss looks truly cowed for the first time since I've known him.

"I'm not a great swimmer—" Moss tries, but the line and his voice are feeble.

"You would have let her die, you shit." Mantis's face is cragged in fury, eyes scorching. "You understand that, Cindy? He would have let you fucking die." He glares at Coral now, but she's looking unwaveringly into the sky from the floor of the canoe, detached, removed, heaving. "How stupid can you be? I mean, truly?" He digs a finger into his ear and flicks some water out.

"Why don't we go easy—" My words are shaky, my heart in my throat.

"Go easy? Go easy?" Mantis barks. "She's been pulling this shit for years!" His voice echoes around us. I swallow, silenced. "I've *gone* easy, that's what you all don't understand. This whole fucking town has, and look who is still fucking here, driving me fucking crazy. Isn't that right, Cindy?" His eyes fall back on her sprawled, sopping form. I can't tell if some of the droplets on her face are tears now; her eyes look pink. "If you're going to do it, then just get it fucking over with, because I can't—" He shakes his head, fuming. Voice clipped. "You don't die without my say-so, got it?" Silence settles on all of us, bound tautly together in our congealed fear and shock at what just happened.

"Alright—maybe we should—" I start, anxious to diffuse Mantis and get us to shore in one piece. Mantis's eyes clear as if he realizes what he just said, and they ping across our expressions,

Cindy's blank face. Something releases in him, the tension loosening into something wrung out.

"She's the only person on the planet who can get me so worked the fuck up. Shit." Mantis runs his hands up and down his face. Zephyr and I look at each other worriedly. "Look—I'm sorry, C. I'm sorry. You just scared me so much. And I care about you so much. I didn't mean it at all, I'm sorry." He's looking off into the water as he speaks, as if unable to bear looking at her. Coral says nothing.

"Why don't we just focus on getting back to the beach?" Zephyr says now, her voice managing to sound both authoritative and calm.

"Yeah, why don't we," Mantis rumbles, taking up a paddle from beside Coral's body, almost accidentally hitting her with it. She's still looking straight up into the sky, which is soft and gentle as blue hydrangea. I turn to Moss and see he's looking at her. His face chalky and still.

Twenty or so minutes later, we've made it to Kress Beach and Mantis has started a fire on its shore. Coral's down to her underwear, bra, and camisole, standing right next to the flames. Almost too close. So close, I'm afraid a stray ember will land on her thin, birch-like arms or her wing-like clavicles and singe holes right into the very center of her. That one ember is all it would take. I'm shaken looking at her. Bruised color blooms on her naked legs, prints her upper arms, a map of pain. I have never seen so much of her body before.

"What's with all the bruises, Cor?" Zephyr asks her, as if we are processing the visual in tandem. Alarm etches my love's face, but she keeps her voice calm and level. Mantis and I are wringing Coral's clothes out and hanging them on rocks and pieces of driftwood near the fire to dry. My eyes skitter between my work and Coral, heart thudding in my chest.

"Aren't the colors something?" Coral says hazily, almost lovingly, like she has worked so hard, like they are achievements. Mantis strips down to his boxers, wringing and setting out his own clothes alongside Coral's. His chest is broad and strong. His arms and legs thick as tree limbs.

"Those look pretty tough, honey. How did you get them?" Zephyr's question is a gentle press, a light touch. But Coral is looking up into the sky again, then out onto the water, then up into the boughs of the trees farther up the shoreline.

"Oh, little of this, little of that. I just bruise easily," she says, voice quiet and disjointed. Unconcerned. Silence falls over the group. Mantis looks at her with agitation, hands on his hips.

"I didn't push her," Moss says, his voice steady. "I know that's what you're all fucking thinking," he says, defensive. He runs his hand through his hair once, twice, three times. I look at Mantis, whose face has turned hard. Coral giggles, shivering despite her proximity to the fire, despite the June warmth. We all look at her.

"Of course you didn't," she says, looking deep into the flames.

"Are you sure, Cindy?" Mantis asks, looking like he wants to kill Moss. Mantis moves toward her, and Coral tucks herself into his side, her cheek against his rib cage.

"More sure than sure," she says dreamily.

"Why didn't you help her?" Mantis's jaw is set, his eyes burning into Moss.

"I froze," Moss replies, maddeningly placid and guiltless. Neither Zephyr nor I know what to say. I swallow. I can tell that Mantis would like to snap Moss's skinny little neck.

"You're a cowardly piece of shit," Mantis growls.

"Don't fight now, boys. Not on such a day of celebration." Coral's eyes are unfocused on the fire. She sounds...disconnected.

Not like herself. We all look at her, noting the strangeness in her voice. Then she starts to laugh. But then the laugh fades into a woeful sob—as if the two emotions are linked, one and the same. She slaps her hands over her eyes and then grinds the heels of her palms into the sockets. We're all silent. Scared. At least I am. This is a Coral I have not seen before. Not even on scavenger hunt day. "He didn't push me," Coral reiterates, almost angry, pulling her hands from her eyes and wrapping her arms around her body for warmth. "He wouldn't do that."

"Did you lose your balance?" Zephyr asks, ever the optimist, standing close to my side.

"No," Coral replies simply. "Felt like it might've been okay to drown just then." I look over at Mantis, who does not seem surprised at or alarmed by this statement, but I am. I look over at Moss. A strange expression has overtaken his face. Wide-eyed fascination. I think of what Moss told me about Coral in his cabin almost two weeks ago. About how she'd cut her wrists back in November. How she had a tendency toward self-harm. Was even suicidal. Moss had been astonished by it. Almost enlivened by it. I look at her collarbone above the sagging line of her damp camisole. The delicate skin stretched there. I feel the urge to pull her into a hug, pull her away from the fire.

"You two were fighting," Zephyr says. Mantis is focused on Coral now like a laser beam.

"Oh, sure," she replies, her inscrutable face breaking into a giggle that passes away as quickly as it erupted. Almost a shudder. "That'll happen. I fight with everyone, don't I?" The muscles in her face tic once more. "With you," she says, gesturing to Mantis. "With Moss. With Brady." A flicker of something like mischief is in her eye. Or is it terror? Glee? Panic? I feel so inexplicably nervous, I can't stand to speak. I cannot read her. Her face, her voice, her mannerisms are mingling into a mixed-up language I cannot understand.

Mantis's face reveals nothing.

"Get out the beer and all that," Coral says, her hand extending toward the fire, farther and farther, so close to the flames that I almost scream. "We must have a toast to celebrate."

"What the hell are you talking about, C?" Mantis's voice is almost pleading. "Are you alright? I mean, truly? Are you okay?"

She giggles, her fingers close enough to the fire that the heat must be excruciating.

"Coral—" I breathe, stepping forward, terror in my chest, about to snatch her away bodily from the flames.

"I'm pregnant," she says, drawing her hand back suddenly, pressing the hot fingers to her chest, balling her hand into a fist.

Pregnant?

Zephyr sits down at this, on a driftwood log, as if unable to stand any longer. Maybe, like me, Zephyr is unable to completely process the dissonance of the two salient points before us: Coral is a woman who tried to drown herself in this lake only minutes ago. Coral is a woman who would like, now, to toast to her pregnancy.

"Are—are you fucking with us?" Mantis breathes, looking shaken, licking his lips.

"No," Coral replies, earnest. "It's true. And growing."

Mantis runs his hand back over his buzzed skull and turns away toward the water. I look to Moss like he might be able to anchor me somehow, but his expression only further unmoors me. He looks pissed. His arms are crossed in front of his chest. I think of how close he and Coral have gotten, and I think of Brady. It occurs to me that Moss must be jealous. Of Brady. Of this claim on her that Brady now has. I look over at Coral and wonder if she'll even stay on at Lupine Valley. I wonder if this is also what's bothering Moss. What will he do with his little muse gone?

"And you—are, are we happy about this?" Zephyr asks delicately. Coral smiles at Zephyr, those pale, harried eyes looking so tired to me now—then she laughs. And once more, her laughs bleed into sobs.

"We're so happy!" she cries, shivering. And it's like she's drowning in thin air.

THESIS
Her Dark Things by Audra Colfax

Piece #4: *Look What It Can Do*
Oil and mixed media on canvas. 24" x 12".

[Close-up of a fat, round apple in nuanced and complicated shades of dusky red and pink. Found objects incorporated throughout by layering.]

Note on Lisa Frank stationery found in a purple-and-pink caboodle in Cindy Dunn's bedroom-closet crawl space in the Dunn residence.

> *The Dunn girl is pregnant*
> *unmarried*
> *and PREGNANT*
> *just out of high school*
> *what a shame*
> *Brady convinced me to keep it*
>
> *—June88. CD.*

Note on Lisa Frank stationery found in a purple-and-pink caboodle in Cindy Dunn's bedroom-closet crawl space in the Dunn residence.

> *It's like the two things*
> *were living in separate WORLDS before*
> *the world where I was going off to*

school in August
where I was working on my art fine art
my fine art
and the world where I would be having a BABY
in the middle of the school year
that RIPPED OPEN place inside me, that new one
the tar pit
is bubbling and OOZING and I feel like I am
burning up from the inside out like I want to JUMP
out of a moving car
off a cliff
into the ocean
into nothingness
what a shame
BRADY convinced me to keep it

—*June88. CD.*

Note on yellow legal paper folded and found in *Nightwood* by Djuna Barnes on a bookshelf in the den of the Dunn residence.

Look at what LIFE can do mom said
with a marveling
contented sigh
she looks at my
TUMMY
she looks at the
GOLDEN DOVE
at my throat
peace peace peace be with me

I think of
the CUTS I just
made in the skin of my
upper arms
with a STEAK KNIFE
from the butcher block
she and dad got for me and
Brady since now we moved in
together
for the BABY
the cut skin that
touches my ribs
yeah
look
what it
can do

—*June88. CD.*

Drawing on water-stained sketchbook paper found in a clear, yellow, plastic trinket box in a birdhouse on Lupine Valley property.

[A large, sprawling crow or raven, feathers minutely rendered across its wide, robust chest. The black of its perfect, intricate feathers is deep, rich. Its expansive wings spread across the entire width of the sheet of paper, which is given a grid effect by its fold lines. Charcoal pencil.]

—*June88. CD.*

Note on torn scratch paper found in a seventh-grade report card belonging to Cindy Dunn in the Dunn residence.

> BRADY *told my therapist that I have been*
> *"obsessively"*
> *reading my college* ACCEPTANCE *packet*
> *that it is making me worse*
> MAKING *me depressed*
> *that he'd like to take it from me, burn it*
> *I drew Brady a picture a picture just a little picture to show a*
>   *show and tell*
> ILLUSTRATIVE
> *after the most recent appointment I told him*
> *he could*
> *frame it like a real* SWEETIE PIE
> *he looked at me like I was*
> *disgusting*
> *it is called* MAMA & BABY
>
> —*July88. CD.*

Note on coffee-stained graph paper found folded inside a 1988 edition of the *Farmer's Almanac* inside the Dunn residence.

> *I showed M*
> *in his little cabin*
> *at Lupine Valley*
> *my new drawing Mama & Baby*
> *he thought it was hilarious he*
> *laughed at me and he also said*

it was really good that I had gotten it
just right
that it was perfect and true
don't I feel better he asked
and would I let him
draw me
he asked
with my face all tired and sad like that
and with my hands clenched up in fists like that
and with the tears on my cheeks like that
and the cuts on my ribs like that
in the glow of my old brown enamel lantern
with the Bar Harbor
sticker
he loves the light of so much
and I said
yes
but when I showed M out behind the mess hall
when I showed M the cuts on my ribs like that
he just looked at me like I might be
a monster he said
this is an abomination
he said what is wrong
with you

—July88. CD.

Drawing on ripped loose-leaf paper found folded inside a volume
of poems by Nikki Giovanni in the den of the Dunn residence.

[Pencil sketch of a thin, tired fox lying curled up prettily, fur coat rendered so finely, she looks three-dimensional. There is a baby fox, a kit, eating its way out of the mother fox, its nose and sharp little teeth pressing up and out from under her rib cage through the soft belly. The face of the precious kit is covered in slick gore. The precious kit is very healthy.]

Title: *Mama & Baby*.

—*July88. CD.*

Five

What Do You Call This?

Max

Today will be better. I have to believe that.

Even in the bright light of a new morning, however, I am hounded by last night.

Audra's gun, the jarring blasts of the shots, the guttural groans of the moose, the sharp pain in my ankle, confronting Stone 'Em Bog in such a grim way—all of it mixed into a bodily repugnance inside me as we drove away from the bog, and it stayed on to roost when we arrived back at her house. She had me settled on the couch, socks off, calf propped up on a pillow on top of her coffee table. While I chewed Tums, she took another look at my scraped hands and assured me the cuts were only superficial. She told me we were wound twins now, and she showed me the scar on her palm again. A broad smile spread across her face. I was not amused.

"And I think your ankle's just sprained," she reiterated as she held ice on it. "You were able to put some weight on it, obviously, getting back and forth to the car, so that's a good sign."

"It really hurts now," I told her, voice hard.

"We'll keep it iced and elevated and see how you are in the morning," she said, unfazed.

I looked down at my swelling ankle with worry and disgust. Something about this—maybe my expression, maybe my overt concern—made Audra laugh.

"What's so funny?" My voice bit with anger.

"Oh, nothing—what a night we've had." She shook her head. "Leg injuries abound. I just hope I don't have to do to you what I had to do to that moose." And she'd started laughing again. The strong urge to recoil from her touch swelled within me, which is something I never expected to feel toward her.

After a while Audra had helped get me up into my room, and I felt only a dangerous, angry form of attraction to her then. The kind that could only manifest in hate-fucking, the kind that comes out of a seedling of fear. And I did feel fear. I realize that now, in the morning light. I feared her. Something about her. I felt like an old man, and like she was my nurse with far too much control. Annie Wilkes in *Misery*.

As I lay in bed last night, all I could think about was that gun.

I just hope I don't have to do to you what I had to do to that moose. Ha Ha Ha.

The flash of the gun was the flash of the yellow ribbons in her apple tree, the flash of the lemon enamel birds on her ears. I had closed my eyes against it in some pathetic attempt to banish them, to fall asleep.

She never even said she was sorry. That stands out to me, too. There was no *I'm so sorry, I should never have suggested we take that walk in the growing dark like that. On such rough terrain. I feel so bad.*

Oh, Max, I'm sorry. I shouldn't have driven through all those potholes. Shown you the gun in the glove box. Oh, Max. I could have worked with guilt. *You know, there are a few things you could do to make me feel better, Audra.* A lesser woman might have smiled sheepishly, bitten her lip, asked what she could do, that she would do whatever I wanted if I would only feel better. No, there was no apology in Audra, no pity. She went to her own room. We slept apart. She touched me as little as was necessary to get me set up for rest. And by then, that's all I wanted to do anyway—rest—and I hated her for that, too. A bait and switch, all her fault.

Maybe it's a test. Maybe that's what it's been all along, over this whole last year. One big fucking terrible test. But of what? For what?

Or maybe it's just some standard-issue misfortune. Hard luck in the wildlands. If I take a breath and think for a second, it is likely the latter. Animals get hit by cars. People who live in remote areas often have guns. Walking on rugged terrain can result in injuries. So what that Audra literally lives in the place that is the epicenter of my longest-held secret? So what that there are goldenrod ribbons dangling from her tree? So what that she took me to the bog? So what that she shot an animal to death before my eyes? So what that I am here less than twenty-four hours and already injured? So what?

The images threaten to rise—weathered picnic tables, tin cups, papery-white skin, so much gold—I push them all back where I have kept them all this time. I shut my eyes against my own frenzy.

Keep it together, Max. Hold to the prayer, man. Hold it.

My mind conjures blue Misha's silky, blond hair, red Francesca's deep curls, purple Audra's wild, auburn mane. In my grasp. Holding. Held.

Today will be better. It has to be. It can't get much worse than yesterday.

I manage to get myself into the shower, taking my time, meditating under the hot water and trying to rinse away the negativity. *Hold to the prayer, Max. The prayer still abides.* I get out of the shower, testing my ankle—it chirps at me, bright, sharp, acid yellow in its clarity. I lean one way to dry myself then recover.

She's probably right, it's probably not broken. But it still fucking hurts.

I make my way downstairs to find Audra cooking us brunch. I see some of my favorites—poached eggs, French toast, black coffee. Maybe it's a peace offering.

"Morning, professor." She smiles from across the kitchen. "How are you feeling?"

"Sore, you know. But I'll survive." I pour myself some coffee and orange juice.

"Good. Because today is thesis day. Studio day." She flips the toast in her frying pan. I stare into her taut back, the black tank top she's wearing clingy and thin. She wears black leggings with it. Bare feet. "And I know you said you have some work to do—for school. I'll make sure you have time to do what you need."

"You're the boss," I reply, and I realize how true that is. I'm hundreds of miles from anything that has even the semblance of being mine. My apartment. My car. My office at the institute. The places I shop. The streets and routes I know backward and forward. This is Audra's turf. Audra's rules. I have no choice but to follow the leader. Usually I am the one calling the shots. "As it turns out, a professor's weekend is often not much of a weekend at all, my dear." I sigh, thinking of the letters of recommendation I have to write over the coming weeks and months, the independent studies I'm directing, the ever-present grading and prepping.

I start scrolling through the *Boston Globe* on my phone. Then

I go to the institute faculty website to see if the department admin has updated my page with the news of my latest publication credit. It's an essay in a collection about historical censorship in art coming out in the spring from the New York University Press. Not yet. I'll have to nudge them. Again.

By the time we finish our late brunch—my mood much improved by the food and coffee and a cigarette or two out in the sunshine and bracing autumn chill—it's nearly one in the afternoon. We've taken our time, luxuriating in the meal, in our conversation about the institute, her thesis project, my theories about what has made a successful thesis in past years, even some chatter about awards and recognitions and gallery showings I've achieved in the past. Audra is patient as I prattle on about myself, and then she opens up about her own process. It has fully brought me back to myself, back to why I'm so attracted to her in the first place.

"The idea is to harness these voices, women's voices, in a chorus that reaches through time. Through these mixed-media collage pieces I've pulled together. A kind of chant or a siren song drawing the looker farther and farther into the world of the pieces, of the thesis, into its message and truth." She taps the tines of her fork against her bottom lip, looking off into the distance as she tries to describe her work to me. Her mind. Her eye. Her talent. Electrifying, maddening, incredible. She blushes and laughs at herself gently. "That's a lot of talk, I know. But that's what I'm *trying* to do. I'll show you this afternoon, and you can tell me if I'm even close."

"If there was ever an artist I thought could pull off exactly what they imagined they could, it's you." I let my napkin fall onto my plate. I smile at her because there's nothing else I can do. Smile, and wait for her genius to bludgeon me. "Alright," I say, feeling full and somehow already sleepy again. "Let me go do my homework before

I lose all motivation. And then studio. Thesis." She smiles when I say *homework*.

"Feel free to use Pops's office down the hall. Or your room. Wherever you'd like."

"Thanks," I tell her and head off. I climb the stairs on my pulsing ankle and grab my laptop, bring it back downstairs to her grandfather's plush office. I close the door, and over the next two hours, I respond to the emails I'm most overdue in responding to; I proofread a grant proposal a few colleagues and I have put together on behalf of the department; I grade a few short response papers by a student from my Art & Critical Theory class. When I'm getting ready to shut it all down, I hear a new email ping through. I close my other windows and go back to my inbox.

TO: mdurant@biva.edu
FROM: thedevil@kingcity.me
SUBJECT: Hi, Moss

Everything seems to slow down. Tunnel down into one point of light. I can hear my heart in my ears, as if the rhythm lives there. My finger hovers over the track pad. I look down and see it's shaking. My hand. My finger. It acts as if outside of me and clicks.

who are you drawing these days
who are you painting

A strangled yelp erupts in my throat, and I stand up so fast, the chair falls over behind me. The clatter it makes startles me again, my shoulders high and tense as a spooked cat. Then the room is still again. Just my breathing. The silent screen. I reread the words over and over again. It's like worrying the shell of a scab. I read it and read it. It stings each time.

I force myself to look away from the screen. I inhale more than breathe.

I push my eyes onto objects around the room, struck with a creeping vertigo. The solid wood desk. I press my hand onto it. A photo of Audra and her grandfather on the sideboard. The window behind me. Sunlight. The nice Persian rug under my bare feet. I curl my toes into its fibers. I breathe in and smell furniture polish. I focus on these things, these real things I can touch and sense, like a dreamer wanting to banish away horror with a pinch.

Moss.

When I look down at the screen, the email is still there. I feel sick.

I slam the laptop down hard. Hard enough that, for a split second, I worry I may have broken it.

I stand up too fast and cry out when my ankle angrily protests, a hot spike driven in sideways. The bite of it is jagged and clarifying. My astonishment that became fear has now become anger.

Who did this to me? Who would do this to me? Who *could* do this to me?

I pace around the room like an animal, trying to get a hold of myself.

Maybe I didn't see what I saw.

I did.

Maybe it doesn't mean what it meant.

It does.

I lean against the desk and force myself to take three deep breaths.

I turn my gaze out the window. The light is pushing from clear and lemony into veiled and golden. This must be the light Audra was talking about yesterday. Our light for looking.

I glance over at my laptop and feel only terror. I can't open it. Not now. Later. I'll look at it again later. Maybe I didn't see what I saw. The room feels too quiet now. The laptop too menacing. I flee the room.

Audra is on her couch, legs tucked up under her. She's reading *Trout Fishing in America* by Richard Brautigan. She looks up at me, expectant, happy.

"Were you able to get—"

"The ankle," I say by way of reintroduction, my voice terser than I want it to be; Audra is cut off. She looks sheepish. "It kills."

"Advil?" she offers. I nod. "How about a drink?"

"How about several," I say. I watch her get up to go fetch me these things. I stand in the living room, dazed.

Someone knows what I did. And someone knows that I'm back.

Audra

He emerged at around half past three, asked me to fix us some drinks, and then immediately chain-smoked three cigarettes outside in succession. I watched him smoke and limp back and forth across the patio, jacket pulled around him, body looking tight. It's rare for him to smoke three in a row.

How bad could work have been?

He's agitated. Maybe more than agitated. Maybe worse than agitated. When he comes back in, he gratefully accepts his gin and tonic.

"Got anything stronger than Advil?"

I offer him a half a Vicodin from a small cache I still have from dental work several months ago. He takes it down with the drink, ignoring the Advil. I say nothing.

We sit down in the living room, Max rolling his head around on his shoulders like everything in his body is kinked up. I'm trying to tell him a little bit about the Brautigan book, but he's disinterested.

Distracted. So I start talking about my thesis work again. Where in the process I am. The goals he and I had developed together. Max is on his third drink of the afternoon, and, very uncharacteristically, he has nothing to add. No pearls of wisdom to bestow. No anecdotes about his own incredible triumphs as a graduate student. I see him eyeing everything rather baldly. The furniture. The art on the walls. The family keepsakes. It's like he's trying to discern a coded message. His face is serious, the hint of dark circles under his gently glassed eyes. His lip twitches.

"I came all the way up here to see your portfolio. Let's have it, then," he finally says, taking a final swig of his drink, placing the empty glass down on the coffee table roughly.

"Oh, yes, of course—I suppose the time has arrived."

"I only have one more full day, and I imagine there will be quite a lot of…work for you to do." His tone is borderline nasty. "So much talk, Audra, so much confidence, and I haven't even seen it." He rubs an eye socket with the palm of his hand. "I'm here to look at your work. Critique it. Then leave you to see what can be made of it." He's on edge. He looks dreadfully worn, as if this afternoon has become impossibly heavy on him.

"No, yes—you're right. Let's do that." I lead him out of the living room and down the long hallway to the attached garage. I wonder, as he follows closely behind me, if he still has that knife in his pocket. The knife he flicked open and closed mindlessly yesterday in the car. The knife I told him it was handy to have on him in these parts. I feel every vertebra in my spine, every expansion of my rib cage, my intact lungs. We cross the garage, moving past my white Volvo wagon and my Gram's old red Toyota Tacoma. I take him up the unfinished staircase to the loft above the garage, which is half-finished with plywood but has plush area rugs, raw outlets but expensive curtains, rough shelving but top-notch art supplies, an open, roughed-in bathroom but a divine, pink velvet couch, a darling, squat, potbellied wood-burning stove. My canvases of various sizes lean about the space, three different easels with three different works in various stages of completion particularly displayed. My paints cover various table and shelf surfaces, my brushes and tools in large coffee cans, jam jars and supply organizers. Smocks hang from pegs, lovingly paint-splattered.

"Just about everything you see here is—is part of the thesis collection, or a draft of something that will be in the thesis collection. There will likely be eight to ten total—I know there are more than that here. I promise to choose carefully." I scratch the back of my head, nervous, waiting. Ready. His face manages to be a disconcerting mix of slack and stony; soft with drink, tense with anger or fear—or something. God knows what is in his mind now. Does he understand his position? He's a rabbit caught in a snare. I look at a vein straining in his neck and the wear in his face and think he is beginning to.

I watch him mindlessly pat, pat, pat his jeans pocket; the knife is surely there. He's prowling around. He looks hunched and predatory. He pauses in front of a series leaning against a workbench. He studies deeply. It is a golden wing, sensual, brave, loud on the canvas. Small, rough wafers of paper are suspended in layers of paint, sloping letters and language and charcoal pencil drawings barely visible as they peek out of the landscape here and there.

Max is a frozen man. A statue.

What has he seen in my work? What has he read?

"You—did these?" he asks, voice taut. He turns so half his face is toward me. His teeth are just bared.

"Yes, it's what I've been working on all these months."

His eyes climb to my face, then look away, moving over to a hyper-alive, bursting, erotic apple painting, layered similarly with scraps of paper. The edges tapered into a veiled, dusty rose. Primal. Sleepy. Some subconscious carnal core. Magnified to a sexual redness. Max steps back and then seems to take in the myriad other paintings. He is surrounded by them. It's an assault. A series based on the bark of a birch tree, composed in similar fashion. A coiled, bone-colored rope. A butterscotch scarf. A russet lantern. Magnified, all magnified to a shocking visibility. Sub-sketches and sub-notes layered and collaged inside folds, smears, veils of color. A sketch of a woman's bare chest, clavicles elongated.

"What—what do you call this?" he asks.

"*Her Dark Things,*" I reply. He mumbles the words as he brings his face close to the lantern painting again.

"There is so much paint in these. So much paper—so much *subject.* Where does the eye rest? Where does the viewer get to rest?" He is upset. "These *your* little macabre doodles? I can't even read this chicken scratch. There's so much paint globbed over these notes. So much matter. Too much," he spits. My jaw clenches. *You're so brave now, Max. So dismissive. Let's see how long that lasts.* He is leaning in toward a scrap of paper inside the lantern image.

"No, those are the found objects I was telling you about. The intermedia component. Interesting, right? The interplay? The texturing?" A heat and thrill run through my body as I watch him devour my work. As I watch it get into him. As I watch it push inside. His right fist clenches and unclenches. It feels like a long time before either of us speaks again.

"You do not know," he begins, voice low, almost creaky, "what it's like to be around someone like you, Audra." He turns to face me. His hair is a nest in disarray. From the incessant running of his hand through it while we sat and drank and he tried desperately to read my walls, my belongings, my life—much of which I have curated for this very visit. For his eyes only. It becomes clear to me, in this moment—the faraway glassiness of his eyes, the hunched, harmed posture—that I might be in for a very bad time. The kind of time I have only ever seen intimations of, heard tell of. Max, out of control. My gut lurches. "How impossible it is. How impossible you are. The very—the very fact of you." He gestures at me in a way that indicates both disgust and exaltation. I swallow and steel myself, gazing out the large picture windows onto my field in the goldening, late-afternoon light. He turns to me. His glasses frame his troubled expression.

"Max, I—"

"And, and I'm sorry if my...my *worship* of you has become tedious, Ms. Colfax." There are storm clouds in his eyes; they hang heavy on his brow, creasing it.

"Worship? Max—what is this? What's happening?"

"Oh, would you quit it with this act? Like you don't know. Like you don't know of your own brilliance. Of the shadow you cast. Not only upon your classmates but upon—upon me as well. Your *mentor.*" He limps on to the next easel to find a midnight-black crow, elongated and abstracted, the eye oversize, overwhelming, glinting. "You don't know what it's like." He is rubbing his hands up and down his face as he turns away from the crow, as if trying to expel it. He limps a few paces over to one of my workbenches and absentmindedly picks up a half-finished bottle of Barbera and takes a swig straight from it. It's been sitting there for days. It must taste awful. "You don't know what it's like. To teach someone like you, to want to celebrate someone like you, to want to mentor someone like you—who already shines so brightly and at such a young age. To want to *be* with someone like you," he mumbles, anger and despair mixing in equal measure. I feel overwhelmed by his sudden honesty. He has been careful up to now, cryptic, sly, quiet, veiled but persistent. This is something else. I'm undoing him. "I mean, Jesus. You come to the work, to the craft fully formed. And so young. So goddamned young." He looks at me, and his eyes look hurt, burgeoning into bloodshot. "It's so *easy* for you." He's teetering on the edge of implosion—and yet it's not out of fear, exactly. Or at least, it's fear of the wrong thing. Fear of my excellence, fear of his own obsolescence is breaking him down. Mere jealousy. Pathetic insecurity. It's unbelievable, maddening, that *that's* what he's taking from the work. Even in *this* he manages to put himself at the center.

"Max, you—maybe you want to—" I shake my head, trying to think of something to say to redirect him, gesturing back at the paintings.

"I'm old, and my best production is, is six, seven years behind me."

"You're spiraling." Perhaps it's a challenge, the way I've said it. Or a taunt. A reprimand. An observation. It's the truth.

"Name the last work of mine that you've loved. Really loved. Name it." We are playing a dangerous game now. He has produced precious little in the months we've known each other. Most of what I have seen has been almost brilliant. But only almost. We both know that the peak of his career is a decade behind him. He's in the business of collecting now—collecting mentees, his shiny show-and-tell girls. He's become the definition of the old phrase *those who cannot do, teach.* He senses my hesitation. "You have always been a cruel one, Audie. Always a cruel streak in you." He takes another swig from the Barbera. The deep-red color on his lips and teeth is grotesque. *Rancid.*

"Your *Builder* series," I finally relent. He looks at me then, fixated, almost frozen. "Those were…excellent," I admit. It pains me to admit it. There were three or four of them. His ex-girlfriend paintings. Haunted, dastardly, compelling, and rhapsodic in impossible shades of blue. His face softens a bit, and I see his eyes go distant for a moment; he is thinking of them. I swallow. I'm sure he knows how good they are, despite their utter darkness. Not his best ever, not the kind of work that launched his career, but strong nonetheless.

"But just those few, huh?" He comes back into himself, something deep inside of him hunched and demonic, hidden under his handsome exterior. He's taken over again. By jealousy. "And what I had to do to, to get those—you have no idea." He shakes his head, a meanness in the shape and curve of his mouth. But I do know. All too well. I have more of a sense of his process than he can begin to imagine.

"That's enough, Max."

"Your work…it has made me weep, you know." He stabs himself in the chest with his index finger, the rest of the fingers on that hand clutching the wine. "I mean, Christ. *Christ*, Audie. Look at this! Scores of them!" He slams his fist down on the table, making a dormant candleholder topple over. I jump, my pulse up.

"You are overreacting."

"Am I? Am I? Or has the time finally come," he says gravely, a bit dramatically, "when the master comes upon the protégé"—the word is garbled in his mouth—"who will make him obsolete?"

I want to howl with laughter. He drinks deeply again from the olive-green bottle. Some of the liquid dribbles pathetically down his chin.

I want to scream.

"Give that to me," I demand. "No more of this. Of any of this.

Professor Durant—" I stalk over to him and am about to swipe the bottle from his hand when he seizes it by the neck, spins to the work-table at his hip, and smashes it down with shocking force directly into one of my paintings resting on a workbench. The sound is a startling thud and crack as it contacts the canvas; glass shards fly up at us. I shield my face, hearing the glass scatter to the floor.

I slowly lower my arms. I look at the table, then him. My mouth falls open; he is red-faced, sweating, maniacal. Wine is splashed all over the table, the floor, pooled in the stretched divot in the painting the impact of the bottle has made. A winged cardinal/red apple orchard hybrid painting I had high hopes for.

"Jesus—" I breathe almost involuntarily. I look at Max, who now wields a jagged, deadly piece of glass. *Easy now.* He stares me down, heaving. He raises the knifelike shard and drives it through my cardinal/apple canvas with obliterating force. He grabs the wooden frame and wrenches his weapon-wielding fist through it, rending it repeatedly, grunting, growling in fury. He leaves scores and gashes in the table in his violence, he topples paint cans, water cups, rattles and sprays trays and sketch paper everywhere. He suddenly stops clawing and ripping. He just holds the bottleneck inches above his handiwork, heaving. I stay frozen still, right where I am. Within slashing distance, I realize with a flinch. I almost dare not breathe.

Finally, he lets the neck of the bottle go. It drops limply into the mess. His hand is white from the death grip he had on it. I look at him, shocked and not shocked, stunned and not stunned. But something gives way inside of me, and the words come before I know what's happening.

"You fuck," I heave, furious. He can see it. For the first time since we've entered my studio, he smiles. A vague, deranged smile. A mean smile. Glee at my weakness. My emotion. At his ability to pull this from me like stitches from flesh. He snatches up the bottleneck again and holds the jagged, glinting point about a centimeter from his own jugular.

"I ought to, huh?" he cries. "Give everybody a little relief? Huh?" *Everybody?* I just look at him, dumbfounded. The scene feels surreal. Hyperreal. The light from the fixture above the table is suddenly too bright. The broken bottle in his hand too green. The wine splashed here and there too red. Bloodred. He has never been quite like this before. "All of this is wrong, Audra," he says suddenly, a small droplet of red wine clinging to his cheek. Several icy seconds of silence pass between us as I just look at him, his throat, the bottle, barely breathing. He is gently listing to the left, eyes devil red, lips stained.

"You listen here, you self-obsessed piece of shit. Get it together. You're acting like a child. Throwing a fit over your own insecurity," I hiss. "You disgust me." Every ounce of derision that's been burbling in me inflects the words, makes them blades. His face slackens. He swallows. "Now," I say in my full voice. "What are you going to do with that thing in your hand?" He looks at it. It takes him a few moments to bring it into focus, I can tell. It's like he's realizing it's sharp for the first time. My heart thuds in my chest.

Is this the moment?

His arm drops. Slowly. I watch every millimeter of motion. Then he tosses the broken bottleneck onto the table. His shoulders relax. I swallow. He *isn't* going to do it. Not right now. He brings his hands to his face and rubs up and down again under his glasses, then his hands drop. He looks transformed. What had just been tense, taut, and primed for destruction is now flaccid, exhausted, and drained. The high color fades from his face, neck, chest. Like a light switch. A flash flood. Here and then gone.

"I deem your progress sufficient." His voice is a little spiteful and cragged but jarring in its normalcy. "I'm going back downstairs." He turns and makes his way across the creaking floor then heads down the staircase into the garage and out of sight.

I stand there, in the same spot in my studio, for a few minutes, eyes resting in the pooled mash of shredded canvas, burgundy wine, and emerald glass. I realize my adrenaline had been up, up, up in those few, intense minutes—and now it is coming back down. My knees feel like jelly. I want to sit but don't. Max came the closest he's ever come to hurting himself in front of me. I've heard through the grapevine that he's teetered on such an edge with clandestine lovers behind the door of his Beacon Hill apartment. I've heard of the seeming thrill it gives him to manipulate someone with the threat of hurting himself, what a release it is for him to see them jump as high as he asks to get him to keep from following through. *You can't tell the institute about us, you can't tell Switzer. Do you understand what that would do to me? To us?* But this crescendo had ultimately crashed. Like all the other ones apparently had. But the way he looked just now…it felt close.

I finally lift my eyes from the mess on the table. I take out my phone and snap pictures of the destruction. Then I take a video, slowly circling around the room, quietly narrating what has just transpired, my voice sincerely trembling from time to time. I had always meant to have evidence of his explosive behavior. I hadn't expected it to look like this. So terrible, so perfect.

Then I pick up every shard of glass Max shattered all over my tables, my rugs. I sop up all the red wine. I look down at my destroyed canvas. Max's sudden moods are some of the reasons why I made multiples. An apple *series*. A wing *series*. A rope *series*. There was more than enough intermedia ephemera to work with.

There was no way he could destroy it all in one go, no matter how out-of-control he became. No matter how much he understood by the time we got here.

The worktable has a few faint, red splotches soaked into the wood. Worse are the scrapes and gashes from Max's hatchet job, but I've cleaned it up as best I can.

I stand there for several long minutes. I know I have to go downstairs, but I'm afraid of what I'll walk into. I always knew it would get intense. That I would have to press on his weaknesses, his faults, his pressure points. That doing so might have consequences before I could finally remove him from my life. But being inside of it, inside of his unpredictable reactions, his jealousy, his fury, his aggression—dark memories pushing to the surface—it's different than just imagining it, anticipating it. I've set something in motion, and I must keep a handle on it. I must see it through.

Max Durant must die.

THESIS
Her Dark Things by Audra Colfax

Piece #5: *Anything for the Baby*
Oil and mixed media on canvas. 48" x 24".

[Close-up of a rippled swath of copper-honey fabric, draped like warm butterscotch in countless folds, with fine, black tassels spilling off the left edge of the canvas. Found objects incorporated throughout by layering.]

Note on graph paper found folded in a *Ladies' Home Journal* at the Dunn residence.

> *I kind of miss my parents.*
> *the apartment me and Brady have is a little dingy and small and*
> *it doesn't get the best light in the daytime and I'm finding that the*
> *   lack*
> *of light is not helping my moods.*
> *I'm trying the meds again*
> *to be better for*
> *the baby*
> *not drown for the baby.*
> *I want to be good for the baby but feel like*
> *wilting fern*
> *dying grass*
> *a sunflower stalk with a broken neck, halved on itself that's us in*
> *   here*
> *or me, anyway.*
> *Brady seems alright*

the baby, I don't know
I wonder if it can feel
the lack of light too, somehow.
But I'm trying
healthy meals, long walks, therapy
shoulder rubs from Brady, gentle music.
I hope
the baby can feel that.
That I'm trying.

—July88. CD.

Note on yellow legal paper found folded under a drawer liner in Cindy Dunn's dresser at the Dunn residence.

I just cry ALL the time now
even with
(M) even
when I take them to my
FAVORITE place to my boulder and birch
through the WOODS
to my clearing
even then it's not enough
our secret treks our
clandestine expeditions
even then I cannot be
an artist without my mind
free I cannot be an artist
but I am not one of them M says
so he sketches me like that

he loves it
crying
again and again and again
because what else can we
do

—*July88. CD.*

Note in tiny handwriting on food-stained scratch paper found tucked behind a photo of Cindy Dunn and her mother in a picture frame at the Dunn residence.

My body is changing and feels
odd and ALIEN to me alien to me outside of me BEYOND ME
   and gets
odder and more alien with each passing day
there's a DENSITY inside of me I feel like I don't have
access
to anymore this pocket of space where
the baby the baby the baby the baby the baby the baby
is like a black hole HEAVY inescapable
a place inside of me that doesn't even belong to me anymore
and instead of feeling GRACIOUS about it viewing it as an
expansion of my temple for a new sacred room
it feels like I'm being SIPHONED
reappropriated
CUT away
leaving me with less
the FOX and her KIT
gnawing glistening little TEETH

to get myself back I'm pausing the meds
I need myself back I NEED NEED NEED
to feel a different better kind of way
I'll try ANYTHING for the baby for me
for us
M thinks it's a good idea
M thinks I've got it just right

—Aug88. CD.

Entry in a journal found hidden inside Cindy Dunn's suitcase in the Dunn residence.

Brady says I can draw my
DOODLES right here he sometimes calls them
doodles
and I fucking HATE that
he tells me to use that energy to draw
YOU things, baby
to draw you little pictures and frame them for your nursery
or do a MURAL on your bedroom wall and then I sit down and
TRY to do that while he's out, while he's
away from me, and they start off as sweet, rounded, cartoonish
and THEN

—Aug88. CD.

Drawing on sketchbook paper found in a plastic pencil box under the steps of a cabin at Lupine Valley.

[A parade of animals. Hippopotamuses and giraffes, squeaky and shiny and bright and in pairs. These are mommy and baby animals. A rough sketch in charcoal pencil.]

Title: *For Baby*.

—*Aug88*. *CD*.

Drawing on water-stained sketchbook paper found in a plastic pencil box under the porch at the Dunn residence.

[A parade of animals. Hippopotamuses and giraffes, alligators, kangaroos, bears, snakes, rhinos. Shaded toward black and in pairs. Each pair grows more and more gruesome and evil and dark as you look down the page. Any visible teeth are emphasized, sharp. Any visible nails or claws are emphasized, sharp. These are mommy and baby animals. The baby animals look meaner than the mommy animals. A croc biting through its mother's neck. A joey kicking its mommy the wrong way, right in her organs. A bear cub opening up its mother's stomach and eating from it like a pot of honey. A polished drawing in charcoal and colored pencil.]

Title: *For Baby*.

—*Aug88*. *CD*.

Six

The Forest Swallowed Her

Juniper

"Shit," Zephyr coughs, laughing. The sound of her laugh is somehow like wind chimes ringing inside a rainbow. I smile and squeeze her thigh, just once, then twice, now rhythmically. I shut my eyes and breathe in the night air. I smell pine. Woodsmoke. Pot smoke. Zephyr's citrusy perfume. The bonfire crackles and spits. I hear Mantis laughing now, across the clearing, beyond the bonfire. A deeper wind chime inside a silver fog. The laugh-chatter chases itself 'round and 'round, creating a dulcet harmony, a swirling, prismatic fog. I open my eyes. Zephyr and I are sitting on a log near the fire. Directly across from us sit Mantis and Coral on another log. To my right sit Ash, Barley, Trillium, and Moss on a wool blanket spread out on the ground. Barley is eating a charred, red-snapper hot dog off a stick, and Ash is watching him with disgust. Moss and Trill talk, close. I watch Moss pass a glowing blunt over to her. He watches her breathe, hold, puff. He smiles.

We're back in Coral's Clearing, with its birches that go silver in the moonlight. It's become the official unofficial hang spot for us. Away from the rest of Lupine Valley and the artists with eyes trained on us as we pack together at picnic tables and laugh over black coffees. Eyes trained on Moss as he draws us nearer. Mantis and his broad shoulders. Coral and her electric eyes. The Painters. It feels like a little room, this clearing. Hemmed in by living walls. A bonfire spot tattooed in the earth.

We've been out here for a few hours and have spoken of many things, but I can't remember them all just now. New York City. Past lovers. How the fading light over the lake at sunset is like a strawberry-and-orange marmalade smear.

"Bitch, you're fucked," Zephyr says, her voice full of joy. I look over at her, realizing I've been looking through the licking flames at Coral. I think about her a lot, when we're together, when we're not.

It was a blow to her to learn of the baby. The first several days after the announcement, she was *in one of her bad ways*. She told me she was terrified of what it might mean for school that same day, after the lake, as she was heading home. And then a few days later, she came to me crying, saying that school would not be happening. Not right now. So I held her and let her cry it out. And then I drove us both into town for a good meal at Thelma's Landing. But since those first rocky days, I've seen her smile. And laugh. And sing to her tummy. She's come to me with some of her sketches, eyes earnest, asking for notes. She's sat in with Zeph as she works on her tiles, sipping green tea and asking thoughtful questions. She's asked Trillium to meditate with her when she starts to feel down. She has her tools, and she's using them. I'm proud of her.

And she and Brady have moved in together. She and Brady are building a family, and I think that could be good for her. She sometimes ditches shifts, which she never did before, and Gus warns and scolds, but mostly she's okay, and mostly she's here. In fact, sometimes she comes to Lupine Valley when she's not scheduled to work. In Focus, with Moss. To work on her art. Moss is helping her grow. In Mantis's old pickup truck as they carpool back and forth from town, blasting AC/DC and singing loudly as they rumble up the road. She's settling into something, a new rhythm, a new normal. Good for her.

My face must do something funny. Zephyr cackles. I feel her soft fingers pull through my curly, tangled bob like a harp. I close my eyes again.

"I'm out. My joint is gone," Moss croaks.

"*Our* joint is gone," Trillium corrects him, her voice a flirtatious pink ribbon curling in the wind, brushing against a cheek.

"Me, too, kiddos," Mantis says, tipping the last of his beer into his mouth, eyes glassier than I've seen before. I lift my can of Genesee from the dirt and take a big gulp. Coral has been supremely good tonight, despite our bad behaviors. She's had nothing to drink but tea from her thermos. Hasn't smoked even a little.

Moss stands up, spears a hot dog on a stick, and stands near the fire to roast it. He looks over at Coral, who is drawing in her sketchbook, which is tucked up on her lap. Her arm is around it protectively.

"Does Old Gus eat anything other than beans and red snappers, by the way?" Trillium laughs as she watches Moss roast his hot dog. "Red snappers and beans for breakfast, lunch, and dinner, it seems like sometimes. Makes me sick to think about." I smile, knowing she's basically right. He eats them all the time.

A peaceful quiet settles on us like a blanket. My eyes go blurry looking into the fire.

"You all know the story of Old Gus's brother, right?" Mantis is picking his teeth with the nail of his pinky finger. I blink my eyes back into focus.

"Gus has a brother?" Ash asks.

"Had," Mantis says, wiping his hand off on his jeans. Orange-yellow light leaps and jitters on our faces and the surrounding trees.

"I didn't know that," I say, somehow feeling hurt that I didn't know this about him after all these years.

"Randall McCue." Mantis braces his hands on the log and slides on his butt off into the dirt so he can use the log as a back rest. He grunts like a sore old man as he does it, the beer making him move slower. Coral has paused in her drawing. She looks down at Mantis, face warm and interested, sketchbook open. "About ten years older than Gus. Went off to Stanford for college, got into investing, became really successful. Rich." Crickets purr sweetly around us. "Got married to this woman named Autumn Francis, a Californian. A sculptor. Beautiful woman." Mantis scratches his jaw, eyes in the fire. "Randall did so well, he was able to basically retire in his fifties. He and Autumn visited Maine several times in the meantime, and Autumn fell in love with it here. So they moved to Maine when he 'retired.' Randall bought this land we're sitting on."

"Lupine Valley?" Moss asks.

Mantis nods. "Bought it for his wife. She had this vision, you see. An arts retreat in the woods of Maine." He holds up his hand and squints one eye as if framing the scene. "They got going on it, Gus helping them square it all away, being the jack-of-all-trades that he is. They graded the driveway, cleared the brush, built the cabins. It took a couple of years, mostly just Gus and Autumn working on it, figuring out who to hire, all this. Gus has all the local connections, of course, and Randall is more hands-off. He knows this makes his wife happy, so that's good enough for him. Plus, he gets to be the good guy by throwing a financial lifeline to his brother, who'd been this lost journeyman all his days. Everyone was happy. So Gus and Autumn started spending all this time together out here, working, getting to know each other. They both believed in Lupine Valley so much, in what it could mean to people, what an amazing place it could be." Moss is sitting back on the blanket with Ash, Trillium, and Barley, red snapper going cold on his stick as he listens, rapt. "They fell in love. Started having an affair."

"What? *Old Gus?*" Trillium gasps, her face delighted and scandalized. "No way."

"Oh, yeah, bub. Oh, yeah." Mantis nods, looking across at her. I think of wiry, aging, grizzled Gus. I realize I've never thought too much about whether he has a family or a life outside of Lupine Valley; he's always made us feel like we were his family, his life. "Gus had never been happier. They got away with it for a while. And then Randall found out, and all hell broke loose. Randall and Gus fought bitterly. It got physical, even—tore them apart." Mantis draws his knees up and rests his forearms on them. Coral looks tenderly down at Mantis's head. I wonder if she's looking at the little scar on his scalp. "Randall made Autumn choose: him or Gus. And she chose Randall, leaving Gus alone and devastated. For the next few years, Gus tucked himself away on the Lupine Valley property, just sort of living. Then, one day, about four years later, Autumn just reappeared. Told him that Randall was dead. Pancreatic cancer." Zephyr leans into me, and I can feel what she's thinking: the brothers never got to reconcile. How sad. "Autumn moved in with Gus at Lupine Valley, and they resumed their work on the property, trying to make it into what Autumn always wanted it to be."

"Did they ever get married?" Coral asks, voice soft as the summer air around us.

"No," Mantis says, leaning into the side of Coral's knee. The gesture warms me. It's gentle. Intimate. "As they were completing their work on the land about two years later, almost ready to open up to campers, strange things started to happen with Autumn. Small things at first, like taking a few beats too long to remember certain words in conversations or coming up blank on someone's name. Mood swings." The air is alive with lightning bugs. "Autumn was eventually diagnosed with early onset dementia. Then it progressed, and it got bad fast. Scary fast. Gus would sometimes find her in the morning, half-clothed. Out of it. She was forgetting her own name. Gus's name. Who they were to each other."

Ash sprawls out on his back on the blanket, looking up into the stars.

"She forgot about Randall, that she had even been married to him or that he was Gus's brother. She forgot about their earlier affair, what brought them together in the first place. Gus did the best he could to take care of her." Mantis clasps Coral's knee gently. "He showed her tons of pictures, old pictures, and took tons more. Started putting together these albums explaining her life back to her. Trying to document everything so he could help her to remember. *This is the Ledge, this is the first field we ever cleared, this is your late husband Randall, here at Lupine Valley.*" A lump forms in my throat. Gus and that camera of his. Always taking pictures. "Word is he took countless pictures of her. That he has them stashed away somewhere in his cabin." A chill rolls through me. "Looking back, he probably should have sought more help. But I guess part of him thought he was the only one who might be able to help her, bring her back to herself. Here in this place she loved most in the world."

Mantis looks up into the trees above us, and then one by one, we all do. We listen to the crickets, the pops of the bonfire, the hushed whistle of the wind through the trees above us.

"So...what happened?" I ask and find my voice is almost a whisper.

"One bitterly cold January night, Autumn took her cane and went outside. No one knows what for or why. The truth is, there probably wasn't a real, clear reason. She was so far gone by then. In the morning, Gus found she was gone and went out to look for her. He found her less than a hundred yards from their cabin, cold and blue. Dead." Mantis rubs his palms against his knees.

"Jesus," Coral breathes.

"How fucking sad," Trillium coos, leaning into Moss. I watch him stiffen, like he doesn't want to be touched.

"God—and the pictures. Still," Barley murmurs, eyes far away, chewing his lip.

"Old habits," Mantis acknowledges. "Seeing someone lose themselves like that, lose their history. Probably does something to a man." We all sit with this for a few long moments. The fire is dying down. "And you all do understand that's why he gives out those nature names, right? Because her name was Autumn. It's for her." Something within me seizes up, and I feel rooted to the earth. Zephyr clutches on to my arm.

Someone starts to cry.

I look over at Trillium, but it's not her. It's Coral.

"Not so cute and fun now, huh?" Mantis says, looking around at us. Coral continues to cry, and Mantis makes no move to comfort her. His eyes rest on the weak fire between us. "I've heard stories," he says, voice low. "People seeing her in these woods. Seeing Autumn. Cold. Alone." Coral cries harder.

"You're making this shit up," Moss says, looking at Coral with concern.

"Like hell I am. I've heard it from a bunch of people. The story about Gus, Randall, and Autumn. Lots of people who have worked here over the years know," Mantis says, talking over Coral's sobs.

"But the whole, like, Autumn wandering the woods thing," Trillium says meekly. "That's just a ghost story. Summer camps are full of them."

"Every word of what I've said to you is stuff I've heard from multiple people. Dead-serious motherfuckers. But you can believe what you wanna believe," Mantis says gruffly. "I always felt like something wasn't quite right here. And when I heard all that, I realized I was on to something." Coral is holding her face in her hands, starting to calm down, her sobs growing gentler. She sniffs, wipes her nose with the back of her hand. Mantis and Moss look at her intently. Quiet settles over the clearing. The mood is low, now. Reflective. Confessional. All too intense.

"I'm calling it a night," Trillium says with a sigh, getting up off the ground. "I'm too bummed. I want to get out of these woods."

"I'll go with you," Barley says, and he gains his feet beside her, reaches his arms to the sky, stretching. Ash gets up as well, looking eager to leave.

"I'd be good to go, too, love," Zephyr says in my ear, quiet. "I'm tired."

"Yeah, alright." I nod, helping Zephyr to her feet. "What about you three? Wanna call it?"

"You guys can go on ahead if you want," Coral says, the last of her sniffles leaving her. "I want to stay out a little longer. Nights out will soon be a thing of the past for me." She pats her belly. "Have to enjoy myself while I can." Her face is wistful. We're all quiet for a moment. The air heavy around us, a blanket of remembrance and calm, and something more, darker at the edges.

"I'll stay, too," Moss says.

"Yea, I'll wait," Mantis says.

"Okay." She nods. She looks over at me and Zephyr. I feel rooted, something prickling up my spine, whispering at me to stay. Coral's eyes find mine. "You guys go on ahead. Really." She gives me an assuring look. I look at them there together, their faces painted golden in the firelight. Coral has stopped crying, and there are hot dogs on sticks, and stars, and the last vestiges of summer nights. Someone can get her something to eat. She's okay. They'll take care of her.

Zephyr takes me by the hand, and her touch is all I need to tip me over the edge to leave. Mantis cracks open what must be his fifth or sixth Genesee of the night and gives us a salute as we go.

"Good night, gals," Moss says.

"'Night," we call back. Zephyr takes up my lantern, and we leave them in Coral's Clearing, firelight dancing behind us, growing fainter and fainter, until there's no sign of them, the three, at all.

THESIS
Her Dark Things by Audra Colfax

Piece #6: *The Covenant*
Oil and mixed media on canvas. 12" x 24".

[Globular and curvaceous smears of orange, red, yellow paint in the cathedral-like shape of flames, azure and midnight blue skimming along edges and depths for contour. Found objects incorporated throughout.]

Note on torn sketchbook paper found in Cindy's red backpack in the attic of the Dunn residence.

The things people will say
when they are
alone
in the heart of the forest
with just a fire
with just
each other
and some
alcohol
and some
weed
with some pain pressing out
that they can't contain
like a fairytale their hearts just speaking for them in the night
M said I would do
anything to be great

anything
and the forest swallowed his desperation
C said as soon as this baby
is born as soon as it is
out of me
I will die,
and the forest swallowed her darkest fear
M said it was no accident
what happened
that woman I loved and then grew to
hate
and the forest swallowed his polluted confession
and I said I can help you M
I can help you M
And M said I can help you C
I can help you C
but then the spell was broken
and we remembered
and the air grew heavy with our words
and M said you look scared C
of me, C
better work on your forgetting, C
and the forest swallowed them up
one two three

—July88. CD.

Seven

Lunatic

Max

I see Audra standing out in the blackening October evening, just in front of the garage, no jacket on, hugging her arms to her body. The warm light from the open garage door cuts a perfect amber square all around her. I peel myself away from the bay window in the living room and sit down on the nearby couch. That drawing of the upside-down raven looms above me. Painstakingly rendered. Fine pencil strokes. Impossible. I could swear I've seen this before. I look at it and look at it until my vision glazes over.

I turn my head and look back out the window. In the time between first going up to Audra's studio and now, it's like a shade has been dropped on the whole world, as if opaque, chewy molasses has seeped into the air. Late afternoon slipped into evening; too soon it will be night. I get up and go to the kitchen, splash some cold water on my face in the deep, white sink, and dry it with a clean linen hand towel. I go sit down in the living room again. My prayers have left me. There are no prayers left to hold on to.

I hear the door from the garage open and then close. I clear my throat quietly and sit up straight, wanting to look alert, back to my usual composed self. Audra pauses at the entrance to the den. She looks at me. I cannot read her. The skin of her face is awake and vibrant, every pore alive and singing, red splotches on her cheeks and the tip of her nose. Her coppery hair is wild, a little frizzed, a little windblown. And perfect. Her eyes are bright, keen, communicative of something—but I can't read what. What are you thinking, Audra Colfax? What will you do with me?

"Audra—I cannot tell you how very sorry I am," I say in my gentlest, most acquiescent voice. "I was a maniac back there. I apologize for it. I'm—I'm not normally like this. You know that."

"I've seen hints of it, Max," she admits in a small voice, as if it pains her. We look at each other. "When—when you feel threatened. When you don't get your way." I am stunned by her gall.

Bitch.

"I'm not threatened by you," I snap. Audra tips her chin up as if to say, *Clearly.* She looks a little afraid for once. But also defiant. Could it be any other way with her? "It's just—it's been an intense time. And then my ankle—and I drank too much with the Vicodin," I shake my head. "And, and being here. With you. Alone." Audra watches me impassively. "You know how I...admire you." She is made of stone. Of marble. Hard. Immovable. I want to bash her so I can see if she'd crack, chip, break. Anything but this unyielding facade.

"You want to sleep with me," she says plainly. The world seems entirely silent and still. I swallow but say nothing. "I've always known this." The seconds pass in terrible slowness. There is nothing to do but to face it now. Denying it would do no good.

"But I'm not imagining our...chemistry. Our connection." Every word is an effort. A heavy silence falls between us. She breathes in through her nose and exhales deeply.

"I'm cold," she says, "I'll light a fire." She walks toward the kitchen. "Why don't you get cleaned up for dinner." A child being sent away. I can't tell if it's a mercy or a punishment. I watch her leave.

Back in my room, I've changed my shirt and rinsed my face again in cold water. I've combed my hair. I look like a reasonable middle-aged man now. Not a maniac. I pad out into the bedroom and look down at my laptop on the bed. I grabbed it before I beat my retreat upstairs, the thing feeling like a ticking bomb waiting alone in her grandfather's office. I work up my courage, sit down, and open it. The screen glows to life before me. My inbox is still there on the screen. It takes a moment to refresh. A few new student emails populate. Some spam. I scroll down to find the email from earlier—the one addressed to Moss.

It's not here.

But it has to be. I saw it. I didn't delete it. I don't remember deleting it. I scan the inbox backward and forward. I check trash. I check the spam folder. Nothing. I type in the keyword *moss* into the search bar at the top. A few things pop up. A read email from three years ago that mentions an art theorist named Rochelle Mossier-Bard. A read email from eight months ago hyping a new installation at the Museum of Fine Arts called "In Conversation with Moss & Lichen." An unread email advertising the Mosso luxury apartments in San Francisco. But that's it. I close the email window and shut down the laptop entirely. I sit there for several long moments. I saw it. Didn't I? I feel like I'm losing it.

I go down into the kitchen where Audra is starting a fire in a small, devastatingly charming fireplace set in the rock wall with some matches and kindling and a small ball of lint from the laundry. When it catches to her satisfaction, she turns to me, ties up her hair, and says that I'm in charge of keeping it going. There is a little alcove built into the stone beside the hearth holding kindling and smaller split logs. My outpost. I work in silence, and she does, too, preparing dinner. The fact that she will not condemn me or absolve me for what I have done, for what she knows I want, does not soothe. It only heightens my sense of danger. This woman who holds my career, my life in her hands. This woman who wants me completely at her mercy, it seems. The silence is gutting.

"Can you handle a glass of wine, or are you going to be a lunatic?" She looks up at me from her work tearing apart a head of lettuce. Her voice teeters on coldness, but her face is neutral. Imagine a student speaking to a professor that way. Imagine it.

"Yes, I—I can handle it," I say dumbly. She leaves her immediate work, wipes her hands on the dish towel slung over her shoulder, and opens a new bottle of wine. The faint, crackling smell of smoke from the fire and the deeper, more savory scents of the meal she's making for us fill my nose. It is intoxicating. The sensory stimulation pulls at my mind as I watch Audra move fluidly around her kitchen. She pours me a glass of merlot but does not bring it to me. She leaves it at the very edge of the countertop nearest me. The extension of half an olive branch only. I stand up from my stool, get the glass, then return to my post. She returns to her salad.

The wood-burning smell evokes memories in me I would rather not contemplate. Romantic evenings with Misha in Cambridge. All the times we made love in front of her fireplace. The way she so often yielded to me. I see her body. I see her face. But now, in my mind, her eyes fill with tears. Her face is wrought in fury, in disbelief. Not ecstasy. I'm remembering when she figured out that I'd

216

thrown the latest draft of a building plan—a proposed children's museum in Amherst she'd been working on for months—into an early-morning fire. This was four Januarys ago. We'd been fighting about having a child. She wanted one. I didn't. I look into Audie's fire now and see no curls of paper, no geometric lines, no dimensions, no room names. Misha's pain from that experience helped me create one of my best works that year—a long, languid, purposefully two-dimensional woman draped almost like tissue paper on a hook. Lots of blues, whites, and browns. That's what Misha was like right after that. Flattened. Punctured. Blue. Stuck. I named it *The Draft*. It sold from the gallery in twenty-six days. At a nice price, too. I bought Misha a bracelet with part of the proceeds.

And there were other fires. The butter-ginger flicker of fire from a potbellied stove in a small, dark cabin. Sheltering a girl made of the very air at Lupine Valley. When she couldn't stand to go home. When she couldn't stand anything. She came to me. She always seemed to me a sickly swipe of ochre, fire, harvest corn just gone to mush. She would weep and weep these diamond tears—I would have her go over everything with me again and again—until those heavy tears made trenches in her face. Then, when she was ready for me, I would draw her. Paint her. Capture her. In her truth. In her cracking, diseased amber, in her misery, a spiritual jaundice.

I prod the logs, whose embers are lava orange, melting, deconstructing.

Hi, Moss

I poke at the logs aggressively, desperate to banish my darkened memory.

Focus. I need to focus.

Focus was my home at Lupine Valley.

I shiver despite the heat and take a breath.

But no one knows of my time there. No one knows.

One crisis at a time.

I need to engage Audra, try to soften the tone of the room, which feels hard and icy. I have broken something between us. I need to fix it. I have to. I think of my colleagues at the institute. Of what they would say if they knew about this. About how I just behaved. What it could mean for my job. For the reception of my work, past and present.

"Don't tell me you cut your own wood, too?" I say, trying for exasperated-impressed.

A tense silence extends during which I grow sure that Audra is not going to reply. She is not going to grant me a modicum of grace.

Finally, she concedes. "I have it delivered by the cord in the spring so I can stack and season it in the garage over the summer, little by little," she says, half sighing. She clears her throat, breathes in through her nose again. "Then in the fall I cut the pieces down into kindling and smaller logs." She's chewing on something now, testing for flavor. "So, I do need to do some legwork, actually, yeah." I look at her, that kitchen towel draped over her shoulder, her hair pulled back. She's wearing a white bodysuit with her beat-up old jeans. She looks a little sweaty and a little feline and completely divine. A shiny flicker at her collarbone. Some delicate pendant or other. She licks Italian dressing off her thumb then sets out two gorgeous-looking garden salads in front of her on the cool marble island; verdant, crisp spinach, arugula, and escarole with crunchy, cold, red onion rings, candy-red cherry tomatoes, and a scattering of homemade croutons. The salads are in wide, white ceramic bowls. "Come. Eat." She gains a stool at the island herself, picking her fork up hungrily. She pats the stool beside her. An invitation. I hang the fire poker and join her, stowing away the knowledge of its presence. My knife, the poker—items in an imagined arsenal against a danger that doesn't exist.

"God, is this good," I say after my first harried bites. I may never have had a better salad. The crisp coolness of it against the swelling, humid warmth of the kitchen is delectable. She nods and continues munching along herself. After a few more bites, she goes over to the cooktop and stirs the chopped potatoes—Maine grown—in the oversize boiling pot and opens the door of the lower double oven to check on the dinner rolls. "Almost time to start the filet." Filet mignon. She's gone all out for us. "Oh—and the asparagus." She hurries over to the fridge to grab it while I happily eat, an anxious rabbit.

"It smells amazing in here," I tell her, watching her every movement. She nods, coming back to the counter and standing beside me, finishing up her own bowl of greens. We are quiet as we finish eating, my anxiety growing with every empty moment. I close my eyes, finding our avoidance of the topic unbearable. My outburst. Her correct assumption about my motives and agenda. What is this? What do I do?

Audra just continues to work.

My phone buzzes an alert from my pocket. I hesitate and then check. A new email. Sweat that's not from the heat of the room breaks out on my skin like a rash.

To: mdurant@biva.edu
From: thedevil@kingcity.me
Subject: M + M

Mantis is nothing but the name of a bug.

Audra

It's nice and warm in here, like flannel just out of the dryer. The kind of warmth that can send you into a nap. The sleek ovens baking; two of the gas burners aflame; the fire in the kitchen hearth. Our two bodies. There is a fine sheen of perspiration on my brow, between my breasts, at my lower back. Max is red-faced and sweating like a hog.

"Head into the dining room," I tell him. He shoves his phone, which he's been fidgeting with since the salad course, in his pocket and continues to lean by the fireplace. He's looking down into the flames, lost. Off somewhere. But this is not unusual. Max loses himself sometimes. When he gets drunk enough, he's basically in another dimension. And we've taken care of a bottle of wine between us. "And no more wood in that fire for now." My voice is gentle. An extraordinary expanse of time passes before he responds.

"A little hot I guess, huh?"

"Just a little."

Max pushes off from the wall, comes to the island and pours himself more wine. *Yes, please go ahead. Enjoy yourself.* Max's cheeks are red with the pressing warmth of the room and the flow of drink. His limp is considerable. He looks feverish. So many forces acting on and within that man right now. I've outed him to both of us. What he wants from me stands like a third person in the room with us. I think of my beautiful painting, meant to provoke, destroyed by a wine bottle. Not one woman at work, but two. I think of Max, unable to contain his jealousy. Unable to contain his ghost.

"Through here?" He gestures down the hallway as he turns for it.

"That's right. Right out there. I'll bring the plates—and here—" I wipe my hands off on the towel slung over my shoulder, turn, and rummage in a cupboard for a box of matches. I fetch them and hand them to Max, who's come back over. "Light the candle that's on the table."

"How very…uhm, romantic, Audie." He seems charmed by this detail, sheepish that he has used this word. There's nothing else to do so I smile. His eyes grasp on to it. He looks down at my throat. My necklace. Then he looks up at me and tries the smile again, but he doesn't quite manage it. Satisfaction ripples through me. He heads out of the room with his glass and the matches. The silverware, napkins, water glasses, and water pitcher are already on the table. I set those out while the filets were resting. I watch Max go. I watch every painful step. Until he is out of my sight.

My hands grip the edge of the cool marble island. It is bracing. It grounds me. I shut my eyes and take some breaths. Then I contemplate the licking flames in the hearth.

The image of an old, rusted-out oil drum springs to mind, fire burning out the top. Pops used to burn garbage in one of those. Had a barrel out at the edge of the driveway and would do a burn every Sunday afternoon, no matter the weather. No trash pickup around here and the dump is ten miles away. Burning was just easier, even if it wasn't very ecofriendly. I know some people around here who still do that. Take their cast-off trash and burn it to high heaven. It makes me wonder about the letters. My letters. The ones I've sent over the past year, postmarked from Boston. I wonder if the man I sent them to kept them or if he ended up tossing them in a fire much like this one. Maybe they were relegated to his burn barrel, not wanting even the ash of them inside the place he lives. I could understand him wanting to be rid of those letters. Wanting the letters to be completely erased from the face of the earth. They're terrible little reminders. Of a terrible thing he did. *Haunty scrawlslips* sent by USPS. Just a few. Enough to get his attention. To make him understand. Just enough.

But that is for another day. I look down at the plates. It's time to go face Max. Time to feed him his last supper.

Juniper

"This is the first time a TV has ever been here, I assume?" Zephyr asks, her eyes trained on the two guys up front getting everything hooked up. They're having some trouble with the AV.

"Yeah. People have been asking for a TV and VCR for a few years," I reply, trying to talk over the riot of voices that bounce and bang off the concrete floor and high ceiling of the mess hall. "Gus always said too expensive, too distracting, beside the point of Lupine Valley. But he got a deal on these and caved. I doubt this will be more than a once-a-week indulgence, though. And after this we'll have to buy our own tapes, too, I bet." I snicker.

"Where are they? I can't believe they're going to miss this," Trillium says, almost anxiously, craning her neck around to look for them. Coral, Moss, and Mantis. "Gus gets us a TV *and* VCR—"

"And a copy of *Fatal Attraction*—" Barley adds.

"And these clowns are nowhere to be found?" Trillium can't

believe it. She's been starved for TV since she's been here, I know. She mentions at least twice a week that she has to call her girlfriends back home to find out what happened on *Days of Our Lives* each week. And then she tells us, in exhaustive detail, what happened on *Days of Our Lives* each week. She seems personally offended that our friends are not here to enjoy this.

I look around, too, in case she's somehow missed them, but I don't see them. Not tucked in a far-off corner, not scattered throughout the crowd. Not that they would be scattered. They never seem to be apart these days.

"I'm sure the Holy Trinity has better things to do," Zephyr says sarcastically. "They always seem to, lately. Don't you think?" Zephyr has a point. Moss and Mantis are pretty chummy these days, and I can't tell what it is exactly that binds them. If it's an attraction or repulsion at work. Sometimes they seem like buddies, dicking around under the hood of Mantis's truck or sharing ciggies. Sometimes they seem like two tomcats squaring off in an alley, not trusting the other enough to turn their backs. Coral hasn't come to a painters hang in at least a week or two. Since the night we all sat around the bonfire and Mantis told us about Autumn Francis. Something has been…off since then.

"When was the last time the whole gang was together?" I ask Zephyr suddenly. The room erupts in cheers as the TV and VCR start getting along and the VHS goes in.

"Like, us plus the Holy Trinity?" Zephyr slides down in her folding chair into a more comfortable position. She crosses her legs. "The last time we were in Coral's Clearing, I guess. Right? Has it been that long?"

I bite my thumbnail. "I think it has."

Mantis has been keeping his distance, I realize. He has popped in to a painters hang once, maybe twice since then. But he didn't bring his usual six-pack either of those times. And he didn't bring anything from the Townie Chronicles. That spigot has been shut off. In fact, he listens more than he talks lately. Circumspect, almost. And when he does talk, he's always asking about Coral. *Where's Coral? Is Coral with Moss? Did Coral go home already? How has Coral seemed today? What did she say?*

And lately, the answers to those questions have been:

In Moss's cabin.

Yes, of course she is.

No, she's still here.

Not great.

Nothing.

The mess hall plunges into darkness. Someone yelps in surprise and a few others laugh in response. Zephyr reaches over and holds my hand.

The glow of the TV melts over our bodies.

THESIS
Her Dark Things by Audra Colfax

Piece #7: *Spread Wide Open*
Oil and mixed media on canvas. 24" x 36".

[Close-up of the head and breast of a raven upside down. The found objects are incorporated into the black feathers strategically to create a kind of sheen with the notes' relative whiteness against the black.]

Note on torn graph paper found at the bottom of a produce crate in the Dunn family pantry.

M says stay close now
Do not stray
Keep quiet C, hush C
Who can I trust C, so
M encourages me
he is the only one who understands (M)
I do very small things to EASE the pressure so
so very small
just little things, but they help so much and M thinks it's GOOD
  it's good he says
KEEP GOING
You crazy fuck
a sewing NEEDLE—I prick my big toe with it
PULL nails off my fingers
painful and RED and angry
in the open air but just one finger, so it looks like it could have been

an ACCIDENT
M tells me to put on some white gloves
to cover them
and he laughs at me
cocks his finger
and shoots
a BURN with my curling iron
it's like it's nothing
it's nothing C, don't speak C, quiet quiet quiet C
M likes me for all of this he says I am making a CANVAS of
  myself
he draws and paints ME a lot now when I take breaks from
  cleaning
he says I'm more
interesting
these days
then SENDS me on my way
tying my butterscotch scarf
around my NECK
to hide
the hurts
we put there

—Sep88. CD.

Note on coffee-stained yellow legal paper found behind the
baseboard in Cindy Dunn's room at the Dunn residence.

I've been DRAWING with M drawing with M I've been drawing
  with

M I've been drawing
and drawing drawing drawing and drawing BIRDS with M
with (M)
with (M)
in his cabin I've been drawing birds and birds and birds and birds
   with M
in with M in with M in
drawing and drawing with M M
Brady always wonders
where I am I disappear so that
I can breathe so I can feel a little better
it doesn't last
PROLIFIC M said
Good job good job good job not taking your meds that POISON
   look how
you are without them
look at these BIRDS and BIRDS and BIRDS look
they are so good
too good
look what your clean brain can do
I was doing good, so good
I am doing good, I am alone I am not alone
There is M there is baby there is ME
I've been drawing
I've been drawing with M it's like I can't STOP drawing with M
   and he can't stop drawing won't stop drawing
ME

—Sep88. CD.

Drawing on sketchbook paper found in an old metal tea tin in an armoire in the attic of the Dunn residence.

[Paper is creased with fold lines. The bottom right corner is torn. At the far upper left corner is a disembodied bird's beak. The beak is cracked. The detail and shading are obsessively fine.]

Untitled.

—Sep88. CD.

Drawing on sketchbook paper found in an old metal tea tin in an armoire in the attic of the Dunn residence.

[Paper is creased with fold lines. Inadvertent brown stains— maybe coffee, maybe food—mark and blotch the page. A dis-embodied bird's wing, snapped in the middle and angled grotesquely, fills the page. The detail and shading are obses-sively fine.]

Untitled.

—Sep88. CD.

Drawing on sketchbook paper found in an old metal tea tin in an armoire in the attic of the Dunn residence.

[Paper is creased with fold lines. The page is filled with hundreds of disembodied bird eyes and the fine, tiny feathers just surrounding them. Some are as large as quarters. Others are as small as the head of a nail. Some overlap others. There are clusters in some areas of the page, like tumors, masses. The detail and shading are obsessively fine.]

Title: *M Sees.*

—*Sep88. CD.*

Note on loose-leaf paper found inside the wall of the living room after accidental damage was done in the Dunn residence during renovation.

so many birds feathers beaks beady little eyes CLAWS TALONS sometimes all together on one bird a full picture sometimes apart and a part sometimes the birds are HURT or MANGLED like they've flown into the windshield of a SPEEDING car sometimes an EYE has been scratched out or large swaths of feathers are MISSING sometimes the eyes are so BLACK that I think I might fall into the pinprick of them and drown in their TAR and never get back out there are all of these BIRDS I have drawn so many of them they are MEAN or BROKEN and it's like I can't stop drawing them there's this one bird some kind of made up bird from my imagination black and terrible who I keep drawing hanging upside down from a branch by its talons WINGS SPREAD WIDE OPEN I keep drawing him over and over again his expression looks different each time but he's some sort of angel of DEATH I think how I angle his head and

eyes makes him different the way his wings sprawl and dangle
there are ten of him fifteen of him FIFTY of him I don't know
M loves him M thinks he's good he thinks I'm good he draws
ME even when I tell him NO when I just want to cry and melt
into the floor he says you look your BEST in these moments look
what you have wrought through me through me through me
I spent three hours just working on a feather or two I need to get
more paper I NEED so much more paper my hand is cramped
all of this is RUINING me

—Oct88. CD.

Juniper

Mantis parks his red Ford pickup at the end of the access road we use when we want to drive up as close as we can to Coral's Clearing. We get out of the truck, and I survey the area around us as Mantis takes his two handguns from their case under his seat. The woods are more tangled and dense here, less visited than other areas of the property that trails run through.

We walk down through the sprawling, buggy field and then push into the merciful shade of the forest. Cold cans of beer tap against each other in my backpack as we follow the gentle, natural slope down deeper into the woods. Twenty minutes later, we make it to the familiar birch trees and large, prehistoric-looking rocks of Coral's Clearing.

We gather some branches, moss, and sticks and use twine to wrap these bundles in classic, red bull's-eye papers we got from Dirigo Hill last time we went shooting. We prop them against trees about ten or fifteen yards ahead of us. He watches me go through the process of safety-checking and then loading the pistol.

"You're getting good at this." He smiles, holding up his can of Coors to me.

"Not embarrassed to be my friend anymore?" I ask.

"Not anymore, no." He laughs. It's good to see him laugh. I'm so relieved to be hanging with him again, to have him acting more normally. He's been so distant lately, and I've missed him. I suggested we go shooting sometime soon, and something in my face must have softened him. So here we are.

We shoot for about fifteen minutes—Mantis's target array much tighter than mine—and then take a beer break in the peace of the green forest. We talk about the guns, then we talk about Dirigo Hill, then the characters Mantis knows from Dirigo Hill, then Old Gus, who knows some of the same Dirigo Hill characters, then, finally, Lupine Valley.

"What made you come work at Lupine Valley anyway? No offense, but you seem to find the whole thing kind of hokey," I say, sitting against the base of a pine tree.

"I dunno," he sighs. "How does anyone come to be here? If you ask me, it kind of has a way of collecting lost souls."

"You think so?" I ask, considering this. "I've always seen it as a place of—of, I dunno—transcendence." He gives me a look that seems to say, *Honey, please.* It makes me hesitate. I think of his story of Autumn Francis—how she lost herself here, literally, then lost her life. According to Mantis anyway. I've asked around with some of the old-timer staff, and they admit that have heard similar versions, but no one dares ask Old Gus what is or is not true.

"Maybe for the ones who use it for what it's meant for." One heavy eyebrow cocks. "For a term or two. The ones who move on." He takes a big gulp of his beer, standing out in front of me. "Transcendent for the ones who make it out of here, maybe. But it *collects* the lost souls. Like me. Like you." My face indicates protest, and he just laughs.

"You've told me yourself: you've never felt comfortable, not like your true self, until you got here. Here. King City. Lupine Valley. A place where there is no real life and people don't even use their real names." He crunches the empty can in his fist and tosses it lazily toward my backpack. "You can pretend to be someone else for a while. Except some people need to pretend for more than just a little while. Exhibit A." He points to me. "Exhibit B." He points to himself.

"I don't think that's fair." I shake my head.

"No?"

"No." I laugh a little. He looks at me like he's deciding on something.

"Moss stays because he loves that everyone licks his ass here," he says. "He can't stand not being beloved out there in the so-called art world immediately. And he's what? Like, twenty? Twenty and an egomaniac. He wants to be a fully formed wunderkind." My mouth falls open. Mantis's words are swift, succinct. Cutting. "He thinks if he stays here long enough, he'll somehow magically earn respect. Like he's some sort of monk sacrificing something. He's not sacrificing shit. This is playtime. Summer camp. He has a total cocoon/butterfly fantasy situation going on. He can't *do* the real world." Mantis, a man of few words these last many weeks, is suddenly psychoanalyzing.

I think about fragile, cocky Moss.

Mantis is not necessarily wrong.

"Zephyr's been very clear about *her* situation," he barrels on, whatever has been stuck in his craw about Lupine Valley suddenly coming loose. "Hasn't lived in any one place longer than a few months since she left Senegal six years ago. She's a nomad. A wanderer without a home. And now suddenly she's here and says she plans on staying for at least another term or two? In fact, I heard her talking to Old Gus about what it would take for her to become an instructor. Like you." He gestures at me. I'm surprised. *She wants to stay on as faculty?*

"God, and then there's Cindy." He laughs. "She's crazy, of course. Batshit, that girl. Has been as long as I've known her." He shakes his head, pacing a little. I frown, hurt by this. Coral is *not* crazy. I'm surprised to hear him—her close friend—frame her that way. "But has always been obsessed with drawing. And she's good, too. You've seen her stuff." He points at me, as if I am evidence. "All she's ever wanted to do is get out of this Podunk town and become something. Someone. But her brain was born on the fritz." He says this last part sadly, stabbing his finger into his temple. "Jumping into the goddamned lake—that's who she is, June. Cutting her wrists. She purposefully burns herself on stovetops. Two years ago, her dad tweaked his back on the job, and she overdosed on his muscle relaxers."

I gaze into the brown, verdant earth, unable to look at him. "Coral has her stuff, yes. But she is not a constant wreck. And she was doing well for a long time, there—"

"But not anymore," he challenges, and I can't tell if it's a question or a statement. I finally look at him. I swallow.

"Not anymore," I concede. The uptick in good health and spirit we saw in her in the several weeks after the baby announcement— her tea with Zephyr, meditation with Trillium, walks and cooking with Brady—it has all turned the other way. It's true. She's retreated into herself. She looks unkempt. Exhausted. She's missed a lot of work shifts, tucked away with Moss, refusing to come out. Gus has had to reprimand her many times. But I've held out hope, and I've waited for the upswing. But it hasn't come.

"Lupine Valley is as far as she will ever get into the 'art world.'" Mantis kicks a pine cone away from him. "You know that, and I know that. She had these dreams of going off to college, but now there's this baby coming along, and Brady—Brady!" Mantis laughs loud, his head thrown back so his face looks into the canopy above. "Brady wants to settle her down. Was getting her to do it there, even, for a little while. So that's over. That dream—school? art?— that's dead, my friend. She'll raise that goddamned baby, and she'll heat up Dinty Moore for Brady after his long days of logging, and she'll clean cabins at Lupine Valley for the rest of her miserable life. Having to make do with being in *proximity* to real artists." He says this like there's a bad taste in his mouth. "Cleaning up after talent who will eventually—if they have any sense at all"—his gaze is blistering, and I feel cracked open, burnt up—"get the fuck out of here like they're supposed to." I can feel his eyes on me, on my flushed cheeks. "Lupine Valley is a stopover, Junie. Not a life."

I think of all the students who have passed through and left. I think of how Barley and Trillium, both having obligations that coincide with the academic calendar, will be leaving in a week's time. Barley to go teach at Colby, Trillium to go learn at Brooklyn College. And Ash has secured himself an internship at a gallery in Miami. He'll be leaving us, too. So it'll be me, Moss, and Zephyr staying on, and we'll see who joins us new in the fall term. Plus Coral.

"Well, and what about you, then? Why are you at Lupine? You never answered my question," I say, upset. "Who are you on our little island of misfit toys?" He takes a breath and takes a turn around our beautiful little clubhouse clearing. He climbs up on top of an enormous boulder. A large birch tree is nestled against its side, almost romantic. He leans against the tree, standing high above me.

"I've been in some trouble before," he says.

"You're going to have to do better than that, M. I feel eviscerated." He smiles down on me, and I feel so small. I look up at him as if he's on a pulpit.

"When I was eighteen, I had some troubles. Let's leave it at that," he says firmly, and I don't press him. "An accident, but even so."

His eyes rapidly dart around my face, looking for some tell. Some undesirable expression. I don't move. It feels like the oxygen content of the air has depleted. Like I might not be able to move, even if I tried.

"This place is like some sort of confessional." I laugh, but it's papery.

"Ha." He looks around and considers this, smiling. "It kinda is," he agrees. He looks above and around us. "And isn't it gorgeous? Me and C really love it here." I think of tiny little Coral and big, overwhelming Mantis here in this place. Alone.

Moss comes here with her, too. He's told me about their little treks. He's told me about how Coral becomes a more fragile, gentle person when she's here. More vulnerable, more wide-open. *More clear* is what he always says. *The static goes away, Junie.* I've seen the drawings he's done of her here. Dozens of them. Dozens and dozens. Some show her as a beacon of perfect creation. Radiance if not joy. Peace if not giddy abandon. Other drawings show deep, gulch-like tear streaks on her face. Ghastly, spreading marks of violence on her body. Her thin frame collapsing in on itself as if the weight of her own skull is too much to bear. The drawings have caused me jealousy—they are excellent. The best stuff I've ever seen out of Moss—but they have also caused me pain. Anxiety. Caution. Worry. For Coral. For what Coral is doing to herself now. For what she is giving to Moss. And why.

She must come here with them both.

"Anyway," Mantis sighs, sliding down off the boulder, "suffice it to say that it's good that Gus is a forgiving man." I come back to myself. "A man who will let you remake yourself. Isn't that right?" I nod at him, and he smiles at me like we understand each other completely. Like we are the same. He walks across the clearing to me until he is standing over me. He is very big. Like the trunk of a tree. He could fall on me, and I'd be crushed.

"Thought you might be here." A low, subtle voice punctures the space. Mantis and I both turn to see Coral standing at the edge of the clearing, slight and fragile. I haven't been near her in so long. She's wearing her bright-yellow, spaghetti-strap summer dress— her hallmark. It drapes down to the ground. Her bare toes peek out the bottom. No shoes. The dress makes her look soft. Like a black-eyed Susan. Like the feather of a goldfinch.

"Guilty." Mantis smiles toothily at her then me. He reaches his hand down to me, and I flinch. He's offering to help me up. I take his hand and stand up. "We were just finishing up, C. Weren't we, June?" I nod blankly.

"Can I take a shot or two?" Coral says, her voice quiet, low. Her body barely moving. Just a stalk of wheat, swaying infinitesimally. The breeze presses her dress against her body for a moment, and I can see the faintest shape of her three-months-pregnant belly—a teeny, tiny pooch against her thin frame that was never there before. I can feel Mantis's hesitation.

"Sure you can," he finally tells her. I want to protest, but what would I say? I know you've been shooting guns since you were twelve but it makes me uncomfortable? You're too sad to hold a gun? So I say nothing. He sets her up with the gun and then guides her toward one of the targets. I watch her squeeze off a few shots into the heart of the target. She's a good shot. A really good shot. Mantis stands just behind her, over her shoulder like a spirit. A father. Saying quiet things to her I can't quite hear.

But soon it's like static growing in the air, a signal going haywire.

Their voices volley back and forth, the sound escalating. I look at the two of them, their bodies seeming to be bent and angled around each other, talking their secret, inflamed talk to each other. Bursting with strained secrecy. Passion. Energy that borders on a kind of violence.

Suddenly her arm is pointing straight up into the sky, and she pulls the trigger and screams. I shudder and bring my hands to my ears.

Mantis reaches up to grab her hand, more pissed than scared, like a parent looking to take away a toy from a bad child, but she wrenches her arm down and lurches back a step. She points the gun at him, her arm bent and half-hearted. I gasp.

"Ohhh." She laughs, a smile brightening her face as she looks at Mantis, who is frozen. "So you're the only one allowed to point guns at people, huh?" she taunts. I look between them, terrified, confused.

"I have *never* pointed a gun at you," Mantis barks. "I have never pointed a gun at her, June—" He turns to me, and his voice is softer, more pleading.

"Me? Me! I never said you pointed it at *me*!" Coral chuckles. "But gosh—if I'd been at the wrong place, wrong time, who knows what might have happened! Just a white glove in the trees, who knows!" Mantis's face is ashen. Hard.

"What—what does that mean?" I choke out, my voice strangled.

"Who in god's name knows!" Mantis roars, regaining himself.

"I heard it with my own ears—" Coral shouts.

"I bet you hear a lot of things!" Mantis snaps, poisonous, circling his finger around his ear in the universal *loco* gesture. "You're a nutjob and a liar! What a great combo, Cindy! Lucky kid you're about to have!" His voice is bearlike and consuming. It frightens us both. Coral shrinks and shivers, tears coming to her eyes. The clearing plunges into silence. "You're not even taking your meds—are you?" His tone is soft now, gentle. I feel whiplashed. He sounds concerned. "And be honest, now." He starts to edge toward her. The gun is still pointed directly at his chest. Coral's face has lost its wild giddiness.

"I—" she says then she shuts her eyes tight, shakes her head hard. "They make me fuzzy," she says, forlorn.

"I know it, Cindy. I do. But you and I know you've got to take them. Otherwise *this* happens." He gestures at the current predicament: a gun in her hand aimed at his chest. He's so close to her. He inches forward a little more, the gun almost touching his sternum.

"Jesus—Coral, please—" I whisper, feeling like I'm about to have a panic attack, knowing I'm going to see my friend get shot.

"Come on now, C. We had a deal," Mantis says, coaxing. Coral swallows. They seem to look at each other for a very long time. "Don't you want to be good? You don't want to hurt me. You won't hurt me."

She releases a whistled breath. A thin, parchment smile breaks on her face.

"Oh, Junie!" She laughs, and the high, bursting sound jumps me. "Oh, *Junie!*" As if I am on the outside of a terrific joke. Like she can't believe how scared I look. But I look to Mantis, and his face is anything but amused. He looks scared. His jaw is set. His stance coiled like a spring. There is no joke here. No prank.

Her arm swings up and to the sky with the quickness of a rattler, and she squeezes off three shots. I hear screaming and realize it's coming from me. When I force my eyes open, hands over my ears, she's still laughing. Mantis and I are cowering.

Coral lowers her arms and wipes her eyes of tears from laughing, sighing and catching her breath. I feel like I might have a heart attack. I can't take this. I can't. Mantis starts to straighten up, tentative, and a hard look overtakes his face.

"You dizzy bitch," he growls, fear lashing. I startle, but Coral is solid as stone. "Give me that. Now," he says, each word spoken deliberately. Coral looks right at him, positions the gun in her palms so that the grip is facing Mantis, the barrel squeezed hard between her hands like a prayer, facing her. She holds it out to him in this way. Panic rips through me, seeing that if the gun were to go off, she'd be hit right in the chest. Her eyes are steady on the opening of the gun, as if daring it to go off.

"Christ, Cindy!" Mantis darts his hand forward in a fleet, unthinking movement and grabs it from her—then slows while he moves it away from her and angles the barrel away from our bodies. "What the fuck is the matter with you?" He flicks the safety on and then takes the magazine out of it. Coral looks down at her hands and then looks up at Mantis. Her eyes are lucid. Her face calm.

"Just old Coral. Being crazy," she says. Her face is hard. "Crazy Coral." She says it pointedly, right at him. She's as steely and clear as I've ever seen her. "That could have been a real bad accident." She nods, a taunt. They stand there for a long moment in a standoff.

Then Mantis tears his gaze from her, grabs the other gun from across the clearing, puts the safety on, and relieves it of its magazine. He puts both guns and all the ammo in his pack.

"Are your h-hands okay?" I manage to ask Coral as I take a

step or two toward her. I feel shaky. Like I need to sit. She holds them out and shows the burn marks. Mantis stomps over and grabs her wrists hard, trying to get a good look at her hands. "Be gentle, Mantis—" I say, but my voice is weak.

"Don't call me that stupid fucking name!" he hollers at me. I jump, his voice echoing around us. He twists her hands and wrists this way and that so fast and so hard, I'm afraid he might break her.

"Isn't that what you wanted me to do? Give you the gun?" Coral asks him, her face hard. He studies her palm, hisses at the burn, frazzled. "Isn't that what you wanted me to do?" She is demanding he answer, not asking. "Didn't I do what you wanted me to do?" Her voice grows louder, more out-of-control. I want to bury my head in the earth. I don't want to look upon these two anymore. It's too painful. They are too frantic together, too rabid and reactive. "Don't I always do what you want?" She's screaming now. She keeps asking these questions of him over and over again, her voice having transformed from a cool, languid mist—disconnected and challenging—to a torrential, furious rain. Mantis releases her, barks at her to calm down. To stop this right now. That they need to clean and ice and wrap her hands. I watch him talk her down—first he's yelling, then eventually he's speaking softly to her like she's a wounded animal. Easily frightened.

Mantis finally looks over at me. It's like they've forgotten all about me.

"Jesus—why are *you* crying?" He groans, his patience thin. I shake my head, not understanding. Then I touch my face and realize that I am.

The walk back to the access road is tense and distressing. Mantis and Coral walk ahead of me, in a pair. They lead by about ten yards. I see the underside of one of Coral's bare, dirty feet with each stride. Mantis's large hand grips her shoulder almost the entire time, as if afraid she might collapse into dust. Or like she might run. They look like the birch and the boulder from my vantage; his body hangs over her inexplicable immovability. His voice is an indecipherable baritone, a soothing hypnosis as we pad through the forest. I can't make out what he's saying, but I can hear that he's saying a lot. Coral is silent. She just lets his voice pour into her ear. I feel sick to my stomach.

As we break the tree line, the field looks as still as ever, but on the access road next to Mantis's pickup is Coral's little Chevette. Mantis turns to me as we make it to the road.

"Why don't you take Cindy's car back to the village," he tells me, his mood seeming to have completely regulated again. He appears more tired than anything. I watch Coral keep on moving, never breaking stride even as Mantis pauses with me. He holds her keys out to me. "Me and C are gonna hang back for a bit. Gotta deal with her hands." He sighs. "I have a first aid kit in my truck and ice in the cooler. I'll drive her back after."

I look over at Coral, who's now standing next to the hood of his truck, her fingers playing delicately with strands of her hair. I see the first color of bruises blooming where Mantis grabbed her wrists. I feel her pale eyes on me. I look for some sign in them. Some signal that she would like me to stay here with her. Some sign that she would like me to tell Mantis to leave. Some sign that she would like me to rescue her, take her away in her car. *Tell me what to do, Coral. I'll do whatever you want me to do.* But her eyes remain impassive. If anything, I get the feeling that she wants me to leave.

And I'm too afraid to speak my heart, my conscience out loud. I think of the way her legs looked at the lake, the explosive marks. I think of the way he grabbed her arms just now. Hard. Ruthless.

Could Mantis be hurting her?

I shove this thought away. He was scared just now. That was all. Panicked. I was panicked, too.

"Alright," I say and take the keys from his hand. In a fog.

And then I leave her. There, with him.

I stay out on the commons, in view of the dirt parking lot, when I get back to Lupine Valley. After all that has happened, after all that was said, I want to make sure she gets back alright. I try to seem casual, leafing through a book I can't concentrate on enough to truly read.

I'm chatting distractedly with Old Gus when I see the red pickup pull into the lot. I watch Mantis and Coral talk for a few minutes in the front seats. Then Coral gets out, her hands bandaged. Mantis calls something out to her as she leaves the truck, but she doesn't turn back or answer him. His face turns angry as he watches her go. He slams his hand on the steering wheel then peels out backward, kicking up a cloud of dirt, and rumbles off back down the dirt road. Old Gus turns his camera on Coral as she climbs the hill toward the commons. He snaps photo after photo. I try to tell him gently not to do that, to leave her be today, but he keeps on. She just keeps on walking, pays us no mind.

"Gus—I need to talk to you," I tell him when she's out of earshot.

"Ayuh, okay," he says, camera directed down at my feet.

I lift my eyes to see Coral arriving at Moss's cabin. I watch him appear in the doorway and greet her warmly. I watch him take her inside and close the door.

AUGUST 24, 1988

Mantis got fired yesterday.

When I got back to LV that afternoon, after the incident in the woods with Mantis and Coral, I told Gus about the volatile dynamic I had witnessed between the two of them. I told him how scary it had been. I told him about the bruises on Coral's body. The way he had grabbed her. Gus looked at me very seriously as I told him these things. I didn't outright say that Mantis gave her those marks—but Gus drew his own conclusions, and quickly. Like he'd been waiting for something like this all along. When Mantis showed up for work the next day, Gus was waiting for him in the Village Commons. He fired him, right then and there, in front of everyone, in the heart of the community. He wanted everyone to know, to see. Mantis erupted. He shouted at Old Gus, who, with infinite patience, simply held up his hand, closed his eyes, and sighed into the onslaught. When Old Gus refused to take it back, Mantis pushed the old man hard enough that he fell on his ass. River, Toad, and a few of the other guys had to rush in to help Old Gus up and to run Mantis off. Coral clung to Moss, crying, screaming that she was sorry. Moss stood by stoically. Maybe even smugly. I tried to approach Mantis to apologize, to help him exit with whatever grace he could, but he turned his gnashing teeth and frigid gaze on me in a way that made me pull up short.

"This is a bunch of bullshit!" Mantis bellowed over his shoulder as he was escorted, bodily, down to the parking lot. Everyone clustered in the commons, watching in frightened amazement. "This fucking town can never forget and let a man fucking live! I didn't *do* anything! Not now! Not then!"

When they got him to his truck, he threw their arms off and

got in as fast as he could. He gunned it so hard out of here that he kicked up some rocks that hit River, which made a small nick in his forehead that started to bleed.

Coral was inconsolable and refused to see me. It felt desperate, her anguish. Like there was something calamitous in what I had set in motion.

"It's just a job, Cor," I'd tried to call to her as Moss pushed me, gently, out of Focus. "He'll be alright!" She kept on wailing, telling me I didn't understand. That I would never understand. She kept wailing, *Why did you have to say anything? Why did you open your mouth?*

And that's when Moss closed the door in my face.

SEPTEMBER 10, 1988

The scraps of paper come from many different sources. Hotel notepads. The Yellow Pages. Notebooks. Bill envelopes with the little plastic window. Takeout menus from Thelma's Landing. Roughly ripped from their original contexts, they take on the look and texture of feathers, especially at a distance, especially when gathered in a clutch. Coral's notes. This is mostly how she communicates now. She won't speak, at least not with me. It's unnerving, watching her float around the grounds, a slip of a girl with a baby belly, all paleness and blondness, like she could fade into the ether, like she's made of nothing at all. She steers clear, mostly. Keeps to herself. Keeps to Moss. She'll sometimes look at me from across the commons, but there is nothing in her expression for me to latch on to. Sometimes it's like she doesn't even recognize me. Even see me.

Everything has splintered. Ash left us for Miami as we knew he would, Barley and Trillium for school as we knew they would. The one new painting recruit this term, a guy in his forties from Santa Fe dubbed Thorn, doesn't much like to hang with the rest of us. I think he finds us frivolous. Too young. Something. He comes to class three times per week as scheduled, but there is no more playful cadre of painters. No more group hangs around the bonfire. No more sharing bourbon and gin and ghost stories. There is no more spiritual clubhouse.

What there is, is me and Zeph. Hopefully always.

What there is, is Moss and Coral. Constant.

What there is, is me and Moss. Uneasy siblings, doing our best by each other.

Broken-down, half-hearted triangulations.

And Mantis? He's gone from Lupine Valley, but I can still sometimes feel him here, like an enormous oak tree whose massive branches and consuming leaves blot out the sun. I have this terrible feeling that Coral still sees him outside these grounds, so it's like it was all for nothing, ultimately. At least when he was here, I could check in on him. On her. On them, together. Moss neither confirms nor denies what he knows on the subject. He has become a priest with her these days, self-righteous, almost Hippocratic. What he and Coral speak about is between them and them alone. I fear what was once a confessional is now an echo chamber. But I don't know. I never know. And that is the problem. I'm not alone in this.

Brady started casually showing up to "surprise" Coral with flowers or lunch once or twice a week. But I can tell in his eyes it's done out of anxiety. A fear. That he may be watching his partner crumble before him. His face betrays his real intentions: *Are you alive? Are you alright? Do you promise to come back to me at the end of the day?* I watch him leave and wish I had the courage to say, *I understand. What can we do? What should we do?* But I don't.

Moss found Coral's first note pinned to his door with a tack about two weeks ago. A message was written on it:

Moss a verdant kind of softness

—Sep88. CD.

Then the next day I found one pinned on my door with a nail:

Juniper galled by cedar apple rust

—Sep88. CD.

Compared to Moss's, I didn't know what to think. But it didn't seem entirely neighborly.

Since those first instances, the volume of notes has ballooned, and their territory has expanded like a fungus. Gus now finds them stabbed into the front of his cabin like Martin Luther's theses. Zephyr, too. Students are finding them in kilns, ready to be burned up before they're even read; folded and tied into the limbs of trees like Christmas ornaments; staked into latrine doors with fishhooks that are straightened to look like tiny harpoons. Random slips meant for no one, meant for everyone. Cryptic little things no one knows quite what to make of. Are they poems? Prophecies?

Playful nothings? Worrying somethings?

Bough down the earth's knee tree's knee down bow

—Sep88. CD.

Weave your own waiver or never get out

—*Sep88. CD.*

Imagine having it grow inside you just imagine

—*Sep88. CD.*

Not one not one is bigger than this idea

—*Sep88. CD.*

Curtain calls the curtain when the last one makes the time dear

—*Sep88. CD.*

No one ever really disappears; no one is erased

—*Sep88. CD.*

Cretin creation creator you are a disemboweler of hearts

—*Sep88. CD.*

And on and on.

OCTOBER 22, 1988

The Lupine Valley grounds are aflame with autumn leaves, the boughs above me buoyant sprays of Skittles that drop and embed themselves into the moist, forgiving soil. I breathe in the living, earthy midday air as I make my way back from the mess hall with a cup of fire-roasted cinnamon apple slices. Some of the artists went out and got cornstalk bundles and pumpkins from the local farmer's market yesterday, so those are set up outside some of the cabins and studios, giving everything a festive, small-town air. We all seem to carry around thermoses filled with black coffee now, our little woodstoves getting seasoned a few hours a day in the run-up to deep fall and winter. The air is cool, dry, and delicious. The whole scene is so idyllic here that it might as well be a paint-by-number.

Zephyr is on a Greenville Sherpa run for me and her and Moss and should be back any minute. I had such a breakthrough this morning on an abstract painting I've been working on that I feel lighter than air. The pressure lifted, the skies cleared, and suddenly the confident, vibrant strokes came from me with surety. I can't wait to show Zeph. I can't wait to get back into Motif and smell the oil paint. It's been a while since I've felt this way.

As I pass through the commons, I watch a Rubenesque woman paint directly on a nearly nude middle-aged man's body. Orange Crush. Midnight black. She's making a tiger of him.

As I approach Motif, I see a little square is pinned to the door. I walk up onto the steps and look at the thing. And then I keep looking at it. I take it down from the door, turn, and sit down on the steps. I put my rapidly cooling cup of apples down.

I'm holding a Polaroid in my hands, one that Zephyr had taken of me down on Kress Beach in July. It's usually tacked up above my desk. In it, my short, curly hair is frothing, my freckles pronounced. My Coors Light muscle tee is wet with lake water and hangs down to cut across my upper thighs. My legs are naked. I'm pointing at the camera and smiling, mouth half open in playful protest. It's one of my favorite pictures from the summer, one of the few of me I've ever liked. I think I like it so much because Zephyr excised and immortalized this moment in which I felt so happy just to be looking at her.

But my eyes have been scratched out. Where they should be are ragged white gouges. I can see angry scratch marks in the plastic, grooves made as if with a sewing needle or an inkless pen tip. On the white part that you hold at the bottom, a note has been scrawled:

He's coming. He's here. But do you see?

—Sep88, CD.

A hard lump forms in my throat.

OCTOBER 27, 1988

"I'm not sure she even really *works* here anymore, if you know what I mean." Moss laughs gently. He's sitting cross-legged on the floor of his cabin, gathering up sheaf after sheaf of drawing paper. Most of the drawings are of Coral. His *muse*.

"Coral got *fired?*" I ask, lying on my side in his bed, smoking a joint. For a moment the idea of Coral being gone is a relief. It's almost one in the morning, and I should really go home to Zephyr.

"Nah, nothing like that. She's still technically employed, you know. But she doesn't exactly...*work*. She comes in and everything. Is at Lupine Valley all day most days. Not really on time, but she does ramble in at some point each morning. Makes her appearance before Old Gus. Sometimes she just walks around the grounds for hours. I've found her down in the clearing. I've found her out on the Ledge a few times. A little too close to the edge, if you want to know the truth. A little too curious about it." He gives me a knowing look. "But mostly she comes here." He shrugs. I nod.

"And you all do what exactly?" I can feel myself growing agitated despite my buzz.

"Art mostly. And talk. We both—"

"So she does deign to speak to you?" I interrupt. Moss looks over at me.

"Of course she does. We understand each other," he says. "And I didn't get her friend fired."

"I really thought at the time that he might have been hurting her! What was I supposed to do?" I spit.

"But you didn't know for sure," he says. We just look at each other. "And Coral never said he did—"

"It's not always easy to admit—"

"Right," he says dismissively.

"Based on what I could see, the evidence I had—"

"Evidence," he mocks. "Fucking Nancy Drew over here. On the case."

"Fuck off," I tell him.

"Fuck you," he replies, smirking. We settle into a simmering silence. I'm pissed off. Moss just looks amused. "We talk and we sketch a lot," he goes on, like we never raised our voices. "She's been sketching like a fiend lately. Birds. All these fucking birds. Still with the birds." He shakes his head and crawls across the floor to a stack of notepads under his desk. He pulls the pads toward him and then tosses them across the floor to me. "This is her stuff." He sets down an enamel lantern near me. I sit up reluctantly, feeling pretty spaced, pretty tired. I slide off the bed and rest my back against its side, dropping the tiny remaining blunt into a stagnant glass of water nearby. I pick up the brown lantern and look at the spiffy bumper sticker on it. WELCOME TO BAH HAHBAH.

"What the fuck is bah habah? Bahhabah? Bah—what the fuck is this?" I cough.

"You gotta ease up on them doobies, bro." He laughs at me. "It's a Mainer joke. That half-touristy, half-hoity-toity coastal town, Bar Harbor? Think of the accent." I read it over and over again.

"Ha, that is funny," I cackle. Moss looks at me dubiously.

"It's Coral's. She leaves it here sometimes. She likes the light it gives for sketching," he says. The lantern somehow feels ominous to me now, knowing it's hers. Coral the Silent. Coral the Defacer of Polaroids. I start looking. At these birds in these books. Coral's birds. There are hundreds of them. Mostly in black or gray shades. Pen or charcoal or pencil.

Some of the black birds are hyperrealistic. Astonishingly done. Others are jagged, rough, done in an addled hand. Some of the drawings are of parts of birds—a head, a wing, a taloned foot. I flip the pages of the sketchpad and see that both sides of the paper are covered with iteration upon iteration of birds. Horrid, dark, evil-looking birds. I flip and I flip, the black marks on the pages becoming a blur.

"There's…more of these?" I ask him, a muted, buried alarm clanging somewhere deep within me.

"Oh, yes." He points at four or five thick sketchpads.

"All—all of these?" My mouth is cottony and slow.

"All of them. All birds. Birds and birds and birds and birds." Moss watches me pull the pads to me. Watches me work my way through them.

"Moss," I say, my voice quiet. "Is she okay?" I look up at him. He sighs and shrugs.

"What do you think, Junebug?" His tone says: We both know Coral is not ever really "okay." Never has been.

"But doesn't she seem worse to you?"

"Oh, sure," he agrees. "Getting pregnant did it. Not being able to leave here, go to school."

I run my fingers across the sheets of paper softly. I swallow. "She went into my cabin when I was gone, Moss. Defaced a picture and then pinned it up outside for me to find. I mean, what the fuck is that?" I shake my head, pushing her drawings away from me. "And all these notes. Those—those little poems or whatever everywhere."

"A little acting out, I guess." He shrugs. My jaw tightens. Moss crawls under his desk and withdraws an empty wine bottle, puts it on top of his desk. He turns to look at me, back against his desk drawers. I glower at him. He just crosses his arms over his chest, looking entertained.

"Do they still hang out?" I ask.

"Who?"

"Coral and Mantis."

"Yes," he says, his tone flat. I sigh and rub my hands up and down my face.

"Mantis probably hates me," I say.

"Probably," Moss says, in no way trying to comfort me.

"Do you think she takes her medications?" I lift my face from my hands. "Do you think she still goes to therapy?" I close the sketchpad resting in my lap, chew on my lip. Moss pulls at his beard gently, over and over, and looks away.

"I think that she's doing what works for her. I think she's doing what she needs to do," he tells me.

"Brady has certainly been making his presence known since all that went down," I murmur, my eyes half focused on the steady flame of the lantern. Moss makes an annoyed, scoffing sound.

"No shit," he says. "He comes here every day during lunch to check up on her."

"Not *every* day."

"Just about."

"Maybe he's right to do that," I reply, biting my thumbnail. "She's not exactly the most stable right now. And she is carrying his child." Maybe Brady was right about Mantis, about not trusting him, trying to keep his distance. Wanting Coral to do the same. Maybe Brady is good for her. Straightforward. Steady. Moss is neurotic, self-involved. Mantis is overbearing, calculating, possibly violent. I'm—I dunno what I am. A coward? And here Coral is, surrounding herself with all of us. Us and our fake names. Our drinking problems and desperate desires for validation.

"You really don't think Baby Bouchard is up here a little too much?" Moss challenges me. "I mean, give the girl some fucking room to breathe. I know she hates going home after work. She tells me so, Junie." Moss is worked up. "She hates their shitty little apartment and going home just to cook and clean some more. First for us, then for him. Dinner, dishes, all of it. And he's constantly asking how she's feeling—except Coral sees through that and sees that he's really asking about the baby. Not Coral so much. And then he falls asleep in front of the TV at eight forty-five. And she's alone again."

"I'm just worried about her," I admit.

"Oh, like I'm not? Like I don't care about her, June? Jesus, come on! You're not even *friends*. Like you know any-fucking-thing."

I feel contrite for a moment, because, honestly, it's true. I don't have evidence of anything. But then I let my eyes trail across the various drawings tacked up, easels half filled. Coral's tears, ragged down a canvas. Coral screaming, lit up by firelight. Coral, spectral, otherworldly, dredged up from the lake beside a bobbing canoe. Rage bubbles up from deep within my belly. I point at the image.

"And is that what you are? Friends?" I growl. "Look at this shit. Look at her, Moss! Coral, Coral, Coral, Coral. Fucked-up Coral. Sad Coral. Hurt Coral. Fucking *drowned* Coral. She is not your friend, she is your *subject*. And when she gets better, guess what? Your paintings get worse." Moss is shaking his head, huffing, barely able to listen. "Everything you've done this past year has been shit except for your sad Coral paintings. You're *using* her!"

"Wow, you really don't understand anything, do you, June?" He's laughing at me now. And that's what finally gets me. That condescending, wheedling laugh that makes me feel so small.

"And the kicker is, Coral was doing just fine before you started monopolizing her," I hiss. Moss's face twitches in anger. "She was fine when she came here. A little quiet, a little shy, but perfectly happy. Perfectly well! Managing her ups and downs when they came for her. But then you got your needful little claws on her, and you started creating the first *truly good* paintings I've ever seen you make. Meanwhile, she's a fucking wreck. Worse by the week." I'm heaving. "You need *her*. She doesn't need you!" I look right at him, down the barrel of a gun. "And you urge her on, don't you?" His face is crimson. He's furious. "What do you say, Moss? Huh? That the meds will dull her *sparkle?* That therapy is indulgent? Some messed-up bullshit like that?"

"You don't understand a fucking *thing*." His voice is a serrated blade. "It's what she wants. It's what she needs."

"I bet that's what Mantis says."

"Hey. *Hey*," he snaps, grabbing my arm. I gasp, shocked by the strength of his grip. "We are not the same." I yank my arm from him, breathing hard. He looks at me with wonder. Like he can't believe I would—what?—*disobey* him? "Well." A mean smile cuts his lips. "If you feel so sure, if you care so much, if you're so close with her—you fucking psychology genius—well, go right on ahead, action hero!" he mocks. My breaths shake as I try to master them. "No, yeah—go ahead." He pushes my shoulder. "Go save Coral! From *me*. From *him*. From *herself*. Go on."

"Moss, stop it," I breathe, but he's on his feet and pulling on my shoulder, on my arm, pulling me onto my feet with him. "Stop it," I bark, my sob crystallizing back into anger. But I'm wobbly on my legs.

"No, go on, you coward. You enabler. We're all so bad, the rest of us, huh?" His face is sweaty and very close to mine. "But just so you know, *Junie*, if Mantis and I are the same, then Christ, you and I are the same, too."

Eight

No Hard Feelings

Max

Audra was right. This is perking me up.

We're ascending an easy, well-kept hiking trail through the forest about thirty-five minutes from her house. The air sings in its cool clarity, the sun dappling through the confetti-bright canopy. We left Audra's car down at the trailhead of the Moosehead Lake Scenic Byway and have passed some other casual hikers in our progress. Mostly white-haired birder-types with sensible shoes and pressed trousers. We've smiled at each other, commenting on the glorious day.

But we haven't seen anyone for the last half hour. We got a late start, and the afternoon light is already starting to fade into something dimmer, more amber. I'm sure Audra blames me for that—I woke this morning with the worst hangover of my life and couldn't pry myself from bed until about noon. The throbbing in my skull was excruciating. And with the pain came undesirable mental set pieces: the horrible emails. Black type. The gin and tonics. Diamond. The Vicodin. White. The stale Barbera in her studio. Burgundy. Broken glass. Green.

My brain was torn up; a jagged kaleidoscope of colors pulsing with every cranial throb.

But she made me good, strong coffee, sunny-side-up eggs, and toast. I smoked a cigarette.

I've got just the thing for you. A nice, easy walk. Fresh air. I felt I couldn't say no.

"We're nearly there now," she says, turning back to look at me, smiling. "It's worth it—I promise!"

"I hope so. My ankle is really getting on top of me again," I tell her, puffing just a little. *Too many cigarettes, Max.*

A few minutes later, when we make it through the parting of the forest at the end of the path, a windblown rocky sill materializes. The elevation we've achieved is clear now; we're tucked into the notch of a small mountain. The notch looks out over an expanse of blazing foliage, fire colors flickering over the earth. And there, the lake. The most dazzling blue I've ever seen, the sky above it seeming to meld with and mimic it, as if the lake has poured itself out up there. The clouds are pure white, voluminous, buoyant. My stomach plummets.

I know this view.

I know this frame of pine and granite. I understand the particular diffuse autumn light of a late afternoon in October from this precise vantage. A sour tickle skewers my middle. We've stopped walking, but it's harder to breathe.

"The Ledge," Audra says, gesturing at a little sign affixed to a nearby tree that says the same. I feel ripped back in time thirty years. "Pretty good, right?" She is smiling, beaming; proud that she has been able to hand me this gift of expansive, obliterating beauty. She looks over at me and squeezes my hand. In the setting sunlight, in my squinting, her hair looks almost white for a moment, white-blond, the angles of her face sharper and thinner, and it shocks me. The resemblance.

I blink, and it is Audra again, rosy-cheeked with that squall of reddish-brown hair, healthy, vivacious, gap-toothed, beaming—a woman beyond belief. I smile back at her, terrified of what my face might be doing, might be telling. I squeeze her hand in return. The deep scrape in the flesh of my palm stings me, like she's been hiding a wasp in her hand. She looks at me and seems to take my silence for awe. She smiles and then pats me on the back, walking closer to the edge. She puts her hand over her eyes like a visor and takes it all in.

I don't move. I just stand there. Looking at the rock beneath my feet. Where I led meditation sessions with other young, supple bodies. Yoga sessions to center and ground. Where I painted in the nascent, too-early morning, hauling an easel, canvas, paint kit. I look at the framing trees, the tenor of the light. It's the same. Like I never left. The images, the memories flock and amass now like a murmuration of sky-blotting starlings.

I feel swallowed whole. I don't want to be here any longer. Here at the Ledge. Here in Maine, in King City. Oh, god, King City. The name gives rise to something like terror. Terror at this terrible, this wonderful, this Hadean, this divine place. The urge to flee curls in me, coils at my feet. But I can't move. I am possessed, haunted.

"Shall we?" Audra's face is open, welcoming. Without shadow. She holds out her arm, and I take it.

A few steps down the path that leads out the other side of the Ledge clearing stands a fat, old tree with naked patches, the bark torn and worn away by years of wind and passersby. There are initials and hearts and plus signs gouged and carved all over it. It's Lover's Tree.

KAF + MKL 4EVR

KEN + MARY SO MOTE IT BE

CHRIS + MEG '09

1998 EVAN + BETH + DREW 1998

WORKMAN POWERS 4 FUN TIME

On and on and on. So many initials. So many names. So many dates. So many people carving an imagined fate at various times over the years, all likely broken up by now. Audra must see me looking. Eyes tracing for something specific.

"Cute, right?" she says. "Do you have your knife?" I pause and look at her then pull the beautiful thing from my pocket. "Well, make your mark, Durant." That Colfax smile springs forth. I step up to the tree and run my hand over the surface, feeling the cuts and gouges like a primitive braille. The surface is surprisingly smooth. Older carvings have faded and receded into near illegibility. Others are clearly much fresher.

MIKE + BEC WERE HERE 08-17-2018

I start to carve my initials, somewhat surprised at the force it takes to make the cuts deep enough. MFD. Maxwell Fiore Durant.

I add the plus sign.

I add Audra's initials. AGC. Audra Genevieve Colfax.

And there we are: MFD + AGC

And I leave it at that. Audra comes close, running her finger along the marks I made. Her fingers then trail elsewhere, following some invisible, wandering, subterranean logic. She takes in all the names and dates and promises.

"Hey, look," she points. "Another MFD. 1989."

And sure enough, there it is. MFD + CCD 1989 ART OUTLASTS ALL.

My pulse surges to a gallop.

"Looks like another moony artist type." She laughs. Audra's intense brown eyes are on me. She holds out her hand. "Come." I look at her hand for a long moment, immobile. I look past her and see a narrow, less manicured path beyond her tunneling into the forest. A path you might miss if you didn't know what it was. I take her hand. Wherever we are going, we're going together.

We make our way down the narrow path, barely speaking now. I'm afraid that if I open my mouth, I might scream.

"This next thing I'm going to show you—just wait. It's wild." She turns her head, her gap-toothed smile winking at me. She turns back around and keeps walking. But I already know. I am a sentenced man walking to the block. She doesn't have to say another word. What lies before us swells inside of me in picture-perfect clarity—monstrous, miraculous. "Most people just know the Moosehead Scenic Byway, and they don't know the Ledge also connects to this *other* super cool place. It used to be like a—like a rental cabin place, a camp," she says, voice easy. But there is nothing easy here. "Tourists rented them. Went out of business in, oh, I'd say…2007?" My ankle throbs. Sweat beads my brow, even in the chill air. Audra's steps are so sure. So practiced. Like she's walked this as many times as I have. "Before that the land and the cabins were used for this little arts community. Isn't that neat?" she tries brightly. "It was a thing from the mid-seventies until about…1996?"

We're not far now. I can feel it. I can feel the place calling me, a siren song, pulling me into its embrace. Just as it did then.

"I thought I'd get bonus points for showing you some beautiful scenery *and* a piece of property way out here in the sticks with an arts ethos. No?" She pauses just ahead of me, puts her hands on her hips and looks back, sparks of mirth in her eyes. But my face must be set with a horrid mix of things. Terror. Sentimentality. Shock. Nostalgia. "No? Have I misstepped?" She chuckles almost anxiously, eyes ping-ponging from me back down the path. "Too remote?" she asks. But then she keeps on walking. I do the only thing I can do. I follow her, each step taking us closer to my past. To a dread long buried.

The leaves blaze and flare tangerine, scarlet, goldenrod. I close my eyes, and the ribbons in her trees spring to mind. I have to open my eyes to banish them.

"You alright, Max?" she calls back.

"Fine. I'm fine," I assure her, but my voice sounds disconnected from me.

Pieces of myself from a time I have long put in the rearview mirror are resurfacing through the muck, resurrecting against my will.

The big, brown mess hall rises and looms first. A shudder seizes me.

We're here. I'm back.

It's at this far back edge, set into the tree line. Mess. It was always the first thing you saw when you came back down from the Ledge. It still is. The brown paint is cheap looking, chipping and cruddy. The mural of Little Chickadee has been painted over entirely. Only innocuous graffiti breaks up the massive brown mothership now. My mouth opens, as if to gulp down the air, as if there could never be enough to save me.

In what feels like the space of a blink, we're in the nucleus of the place.

The Village Commons.

I feel stony. Hardened. My face must be a mask of illegibility. My jaw set in tension. What must Audra be thinking? I can't tell her now that I've been *here*—I can't admit I've been lying to her this whole time.

But I'm terrified. And afraid that she will see it.

It's Lupine Valley. *Lupine Valley.*

I look around me, feeling surreal. The air smells just the same: sweet and wide-open. The cabins sprinkled around the periphery of the communal field are ragged, the grass everywhere wild and overgrown.

The ornamental metal birds are gone from the grass.

The cobbled rock structures are disappeared or toppled.

The flags are nowhere to be seen.

The cabins—ah, it's gutting—they're each painted a different Rainbow Brite color now. But it's a sad, deranged feeling it gives you, not light and playful. The paint is chipping, peeling, and some of it is water and dirt stained. Oh, what a shame it is. It used to be so pristine. So natural looking. So *of* the forest, one with nature. Back then, the cabins were tidy and puritanically clean and well kept. The outsides natural wood, unpainted. The grass was clipped. And Old Gus was here to greet us. *Gus McCue.* He captained this place. He ran it. Anxiety flares in my chest, hotter than a kiln.

The kiln.

I remember the dying heat of that room in the evening, the flash of smiling teeth, flaxen hair covering thin ribs. I shake myself from these thoughts and look at Audra, who is all placidity and softness and awe at seeing the height of the ancient pines.

The photo from the guest room bathroom drops into my consciousness like a slide in a viewfinder. A man and a woman from behind, looking down at something. *Scavenger Hunt.*

Rowan Augustus McCue.

Gus.

I *knew* I knew that fucking photographer's name. Gus McCue. Old Gus.

Fuck.

His photo in her house, in the bathroom I've been using this whole time. I place my hand against a cabin—what was once, ironically, Balance—to brace myself. My system is utterly overwhelmed. I need to breathe. I need to catch my breath. I'm drowning in thin air.

I look over at Audra, who is toeing a rock in the dirt drive, looking toward the Pepto-pink cabin nearest to her.

What is this? What is going on here?

"How"—I swallow, working so hard to keep it together, keeping my face turned away from her—"do you know about this place?" Audra slowly rotates her body to take it all in. She's not even looking at me.

"The rental cabins went out of business in 2007, like I said. I actually can't believe it's been that long, but it has. No one has done anything with the place." She shakes her head, disappointed. "Anyway, there were commercials for it back in the day. *Stay like a king in King City. Stay at the Lupine Valley Cabins.*" She sing-songs what must have been their jingle. To hear her say the words—to hear her *say* it—rocks me. "But after that went under, it became a known teenager hang spot. Sex, drugs, and rock and roll. Fireworks. Firepits. Ghost stories. The whole nine. I remember kids in school coming up here to party—there were even a few urban legends about the place. The whole woman haunting the woods bit. Classic, right?" She chuckles. "Added to the vibe of it all. But even that bit of activity has waned, from what I can tell. People usually just come up here to get to the lake. It's a pass-through. Whoever owns the

land must not be local. I don't think anyone really looks in on it."
She turns, hands in her black jacket pockets, and smiles at me.
"Kind of cool, right?"

Old Gus always walked around with that goddamned camera
around his neck. Taking pictures when you knew it and pictures
when you didn't. I feel sick, being back here. Like the pinprick of
light down that long, dark tunnel of time has suddenly exploded
into blinding incandescence. The past. It's right here. Right now.
King City, Maine. Lupine Valley. The place where I became *me*.

I can't help it, I have to look. All I want to do is go into my
cabin, go into the mess hall, go into Motif; I want to scour and
study every square inch of this place that was my home. I want to
find my friends. I *need* my friends. A deep desire to never leave this
place consumes me. I can see it as it was: vibrant, tidy, whimsical,
alive with the bodies and minds of electric people. I can't help but
gawk. I feel like crying. Lupine Valley is welcoming me back.

I brace myself, and then I gather my bearings and find the
cabin. The one that was mine. It's right where I remember it being,
though the trees around it are bigger now, the undergrowth behind
it pushing against it more aggressively than it ever did when I was
here. It's now a moldering banana color. I walk slowly toward it,
remembering how many times I went in and out of that screen
door, the sound it made when it slammed. It now hangs half off
the hinge, the screen torn away. I was in that damned little cabin
for almost two years. Focus. The sheer volume of work I did in this
tiny, 8' by 8' cabin, Christ. The sketches, the drawings, the paintings. They had to have been the most generative years of my artistic
life. They were certainly the most pivotal. The work I created here
was what jump-started my career. In this shitty old cabin. In the
middle of nowhere.

In, apparently, Audra's backyard.

It's so quiet. I turn and find Audra staring at me. Her face is blank, just like mine. But her eyes are keen. I wonder how long she's been looking, watching. I wonder, suddenly, with a jolt of fear, what she might have been looking for. Watching for…what? What does she know? What *could* she know? A false smile comes to her face now—a smile that doesn't reach her eyes. A stage smile.

What happened here, what I did here—what *we* did here—Audra would never understand. She would not be the type to understand something like that. She is the light that cuts through the fog. She is a woman without shadow.

I look at Audra and feel I am looking at a stranger. Boston has never felt so far away. *Why are you doing this to me?* I want to grab her and shake her and make her…what? Admit something? Admit what? That she somehow knows what I—*we*—decided here all those years ago? It's ridiculous. Ludicrous.

We look at each other, and then her eyes fall to the knife in my hand. I must have taken it from my pocket. I don't know when. I'm startled to look at it. I close my eyes as a shoot of pain rifles through my ankle. I see the gun and the moose with its shattered legs, and I see the blood in the brown bristle. I see Audra. I squeeze the knife tighter. The pressure of the knife handle against the scrape in my palm is like a yellow-black sting. I see Lover's Tree. The cuts, the marks, the letters. MFD + AGC. MFD + CCD. The pinprick that expands to encompass everything.

Then in my mind I see the other tree. Her birch tree. Somewhere else, not far from here.

And then I see her. The woman haunting the woods.

CCD.

Coral.

Audra

I watch Max circle the perimeter of the field slowly, looking at the cabins that peek through the trees here and there like a paleontologist at a dig site. He can't stay away. The pull is too strong now. I It's in a trance. He's somewhere else. I'm sure every instinct is telling him to run. To get out of this place. But destiny is bigger than any of his petty desires. Much bigger.

My body is almost trembling with the electricity of the situation as the sun continues to sink in the sky. I am on the precipice. I must not fail. He is gravely shaken. Agitated. In pain. An explosive man at the culmination of a years'-long vigil. I will not fail. Not now.

When he comes to an exhausted halt in the middle of the commons after all his examining, studying, silent reminiscing— bewildered and still as a spent wind-up toy—I tell him I want to walk him nearly a mile and a half down to the lake. I tell him I want him to feel the amazing stillness, to hear the perfect silence, to see the myriad shades of blue and black that constitute the darkness, to feel the otherworldly moon glow glittering on the water as the light fails and leaves us. A tightness comes to his face.

"I'm tired, Audra," he says, voice trembling. But he looks wired. "My ankle."

We stare each other down and work out secret calculations within ourselves.

I explain that there are lights to help guide us. Every fifty yards or so is a solar-powered light on a tree on a sunset-to-sunrise timer, all the way down the rough path to the lake. Some do-gooder did it a few years ago, as a kind act for the community who uses the land, which is private, even when we technically shouldn't. I tell him there is nothing to be afraid of—that we'll just follow the lights, a straight shot. That I'll hold his hand if he's nervous. His face flushes at that, and he spits that he isn't scared. But he is.

I also promise him a warm beverage for his trouble: spiked hot cider in a thermos from my backpack, a virgin one for me. But I don't tell him mine is virgin; I don't tell him I need my wits about me more than ever.

The look on his face seems to say, *Do I really have any choice?* I don't tell him the truth. That no, there is no choice left for him anymore. And by now, I think he almost wants to go. He must know where we're heading.

Which makes me wonder when Max will stop pretending. I know he knows this place. I know he's been here before. Despite the moony, wide-eyed City Boy in the Country act he'd performed for me when we were first discussing the trip. But Stoned 'Em Bog rattled him. The paintings in my home, in my studio rattled him. The emails to Moss, sent by me, on timers from an anonymous server, rattled him. Lupine Valley, the Ledge, Lover's Tree are shaking him.

Proving that I'm right. That I've *been* right. About everything. I just wonder, what will it take to break him?

I hand him his thermos. He takes it slowly. Everything has slowed down half a beat with him since being here. I must watch that. He's thinking. Processing.

"You do know I—I…that I care for you? Despite whatever foolish things I may do?" He looks me square in the eyes. We look at each other for a long moment, trying to see each other. Figure each other out.

"Yes," I say. "I think so."

"You think so?" he says with some disappointment. He cups my jaw with his hand.

"You admire me, you care for me." I nod with acknowledgment. "In your way." His lips purse a little, but it is not in anger. It's more like regret. My favorite scarf around him. Coral's scarf. *Cindy's* scarf.

"In my way," he repeats. "How else could it be done?" But the question is hypothetical.

"Come," I say, holding out my hand to him. "Let's go."

I take special note of how he slips his knife from his pants pocket into his right-hand coat pocket as we trundle off. This will be important for me to keep track of, too. It's not a factor I had anticipated being in the mix, and so I must be supremely cautious in everything that I do, now more than ever.

In ten minutes we are deep into the tree line, my heavy, old, brown enamel lantern casting a bright orb of light around us, saving us from bursting roots and rocks cropping from the earth. I'm sure-footed as we move, and occasionally Max reaches in my direction for support, but I stay just out of his grasp. He lilts gingerly on his bum ankle.

We pause at the bases of trees, lean, rest, and drink as we go.

"You made these pretty strong, Audie." He coughs a little but does not indicate that he doesn't like it. He needs it. I think he senses that.

"It's good for you." I smile.

"Undoubtedly," he says. He finally lifts his eyes and looks at me. I look into the sky.

"Ready?"

We pick our way slowly down the well-worn path that campers and locals like me have made through the years, moving from one glowing orb of light to the next, each one seeming to reveal itself just in time, right before all light is consumed by the almost perfectly still and dark forest.

An owl hoots from somewhere off to our right. What breeze rustles in the boughs of the ancient trees is gentle and intermittent. A few minutes later, I can hear the distant yodeling call of a coyote. Max and I walk in silence for most of the way, his gloved hand now in my gloved hand as I guide him through some of the trickier terrain. The path is beginning to slope more aggressively down toward the lake. He hisses and winces and sometimes asks me to slow down, sometimes asks me to stop, but I don't relent. I tell him it will be fine, it will be worth it, keep drinking, keep walking, keep looking for the next mysterious light floating in the blackness guiding us to the glittering moonshine. He barely speaks the last quarter mile. I can tell he's pissed. In bad pain. I can tell he's thinking that he will have to do this all again on the way back.

Eventually we emerge into openness; the lake sprawls before us in navy-midnight sparkles under the light of the moon and stars that are a perfect reflection of each other. A beach lines the stretch of shore just ahead. The grass, soil, earth fades into roots, rocks, sandiness as we move from the pitch of the forest. I turn off the lamp. We don't need it now, not with this moon glow. There are a few fallen trees at the shore. There's a rowboat lying upside down on the beach, waiting to be put away for the season. I watch his eyes scan all around the further shoreline, across this cragged little inlet of Moosehead Lake.

"Isn't it something?"

"Incredible," he says, his voice tremulous with wonder or fear. "Incredible." His eyes are suddenly glassy with tears. He turns to my dormant lantern sitting by a fallen log. The ripped sticker on the lantern reads a ragged BAH HAHBAH. He looks at it for what seems like a long time. I feel jittery. On fire. I scan the shore around and across from us; no light. There are one or two camps positioned around the inlet just off the water in this little neck of the woods, but they are summer spots, owned by out-of-towners. The Penley place. The Berrigan place. The Klimas place. I listen, and there is not a sound but the gentle lapping of the lake and a feather-whisper of breeze at my ears. There may not be anyone for three or four miles. Maybe more.

Max and I stand beside each other on the shore. We drink deeply, hands wrapped around our thermoses. His hand is shaking. The hand holding the thermos. Is it cold? Is it nerves? Is it fear? Does he finally understand? He's looking up into the stars, clearly quite toasted. Somewhere dark and far away.

I tell him about memory after memory of myself down on this very beach playing, dreaming, adventuring. I take deliberate breaks as I talk to give him the chance to say something but Quiet, Pensive, Serious, Drunk Max is in full effect. He nods or grunts. He looks very sad and...something I've never seen before...remorseful? Something. Something is stirring in him. He finds his way over to the fallen tree on the beach and takes a seat, tripping a few times over rocks as he goes. He looks down at my old enamel lantern again. Just keeps looking at it.

"I used to know someone who had a lantern just like that," he says, his glassy eyes tracking up to mine. We lock on each other. My heart races in my chest. *Have we arrived? Are we ready?* I study him, but his eyes fall back down onto the beach. I swallow.

I move past him to the little rowboat, turn it over myself, barely able to look at him.

"Sit in here. More comfortable." I help him to his feet then to sit down inside the rowboat, which is by now a third in the water. Max looks relieved for the bench. I take a seat opposite him in the boat. We both look out to the lake, or up into the sky, or both. The stillness and silence are daunting.

"Had a fishhook clean through my thumb once," I tell him, my voice quiet in the freezing night.

"Jesus, Audra," he breathes. I look over at him. These are the first words he's spoken in several minutes. He looks harrowed. His voice is rough.

"Lots of blood."

"Jesus. Audra. Jesus."

"The pain was incredible," I say, turning my gaze away from him, back out toward the water. "I was young and thought of teta-nus and was afraid they'd have to clip the end of my finger off."

"Ah, Audra. Jesus." He takes a few more sips. He slides himself down off the seat to the boat floor with a wince so he's resting his sprained ankle up on the bench beside me. He pulls his coat tight-er around himself, takes out the switchblade from his pocket, and starts flicking it open and closed. *Snick, snick.* "But the color," he says now, words slurred, smeared. I turn to look at him. "Summer, was it?" he asks, *snick, snick.*

"Summer," I affirm. "Fishing with my grandfather."

"Deep, healthy blue. The water. Right?"

"That's right," I say. His eyes are on the blade almost unseeingly.

"Vibrant, lush green in the trees. At the shoreline. Something… more lime the closer to shore. Low brush. Gray and tan rocks. And the sun?" He is painting me a picture.

"Golden. Diffuse. Embedded in everything."

He nods like we are seeing the same thing. "And then the *red*," he breathes sensually.

"And then the red," I reply in a whisper.

He almost winces at the beauty of it, at the pain of it. *Snick, snick.* "Like when you were lost. Small and lost in the woods with your knife and your gash and your smoke signals." He shakes his head. "And you must have cried."

"Yes." I nod.

"Diamond on your cheeks. Salt. Tears. You must have looked so beautiful then. I would have loved to have seen that. Young Audra. Crying." My eyes are ice on him. "This pain at the very tip of you. At a literal extremity, on this young, beautiful girl. Supple and perfect and young. And *then the red*."

"And then the red."

Snick, snick. He downs the rest of his thermos. He is sloppy getting the cap back on. I hold out my hand as a way of asking for the knife. He closes it and hands it to me without question, without thinking.

It worked. I want to yelp with relief.

I look at the knife casually for a moment and then climb from the little boat. Max watches me, sleepy, slumping down farther, clutching his coat, as I kneel beside the log next to the boat and begin to carve. I carve and scratch, and Max sighs and watches me, half-awake. "Kress Beach," he murmurs, just barely audible.

A shiver runs straight through me. An electric shock. He's getting here. He's arriving. He's joining me.

I steady my hand and carve a heart shape around the letters I have just scratched out.

"Kress Beach," I whisper back, so, so soft. I nod gently at him. I move away and slip the knife into my jacket pocket, hoping he won't notice. "Look, Max," I tell him, gesturing to the spot on the log. He arches his back and neck to see, squinting, trying to move as little as possible from his cocoon.

"E—A—D and…M—F—D." He says the initials neutrally, uncomprehendingly. "EAD and MFD?" He looks up at me. "What does that mean?"

"It's us, of course," I say, and I look him right in the eyes, and for the first time, I see something, deep down and far, far away shift. Like a twig breaking underwater—the infinitesimal ripple of molecules that might occur at the surface. He almost has it. He has most of it, I think.

"I don't get it." He laughs gently, thinly as he shuts his eyes as if out of protection. "I don't…get you, sometimes, Audra," he murmurs. He breathes in through his nose and seems to settle himself. He lies in the boat. I take a seat on the stump next to it. I listen to the ripples on the water. I listen to Max breathe. At first, lying there, he rests gently. Before long, he's far from the world, deeply asleep.

Juniper

It's the shouting that leaks through the quiet space between Guns and Roses' "Night Train" and "Out ta Get Me" that makes me stop painting. I pull my Walkman headphones from my ears and listen.

Barking, enraged voices. High, keening sobbing. Words clash and overwrite each other in the air, a tangle of fury.

I stand up and go to my window, pull the curtains back. Across the commons I see three people outside of Focus—two men and a woman. The men are shouting. The woman is screaming and crying.

Moss, Brady, Coral.

Shit.

I yank on my boots and heavy sweater and go out into the frigid air.

"She belongs at home!" Brady yells. Moss yells something I can't make out. From Coral I hear shrill, panicked tatters: *No!...let me...can't...no idea...Brady!* I trudge as fast as I can toward them.

"Hey," I call. They keep shouting, oblivious of me as I draw near. "Hey!" I shout, air misting before me in my efforts through the snow. They turn to look at me, but Coral is still screaming words I can't quite make out.

"You running a fucking cult up here?" Brady demands. His ferocity surprises me; I didn't think he had it in him. Moss is barefoot in the open maw of his cabin. Coral is on the slick, snowy steps leading down from the cabin wearing canvas tennis shoes, highwater pants, and a slouchy sweatshirt. "You can't keep people here for days on end!"

"She wasn't being held captive here," Moss growls, annoyed. "She *wants* to be here!"

Brady rounds on me. "Cindy's been run off for four days, or didn't you know?" he spits, his eyes challenging. "No word. I came up here the other day and asked that old fuck Gus if he's seen her, and he was useless. I've been looking for her everywhere. I finally heard from my favorite person, *Mantis*, that your boy here probably had her stowed away in his fucking cabin." Brady is gesturing with his thumb back toward the parking lot. I can see Brady's truck; there's someone in the passenger seat. A hulking figure. Is Mantis *here*?

"He's not supposed to be anywhere near—" Moss starts, angry and pale.

I'm so stunned, it takes me a moment to figure out where to start. I turn to Coral.

"You've been here for four days?" I ask in disbelief, looking at the small, hunched girl with the growing belly.

"This is my home." Coral's face is wet with tears. The tip of her nose is red.

"Your home is with me, Cindy," Brady says, trying to control his temper, but it's barely working. "You need to be home with your boyfriend. Safe. You're six months pregnant and things are falling apart. We were doing so good, Cindy! You were doing everything right. Feeling good. Happy. What happened? What kind of spell are you under out here?" Brady's voice is almost a plea. He's scared. Exasperated. Coral starts crying again. "And you're not as slick as you think you are, honey. I find the pills stashed around the house. Like a squirrel with acorns." Her hair is wild and tangled. Her eyes are as tameless as I've ever seen them.

"Coral," I say gently, alarmed to hear this. I reach out to clasp her hand gently, but she pulls it away.

"And what the fuck are you playing at?" Brady demands of Moss. Moss flinches. "What kind of sick fuck are you? I can *see* the paintings behind you. They're of Cindy. A miserable, monster Cindy. It's horrible! Don't you understand that that's not her—she's sick, you asshole! Do you get off on that?" Brady stutter-steps toward the cabin door, and Moss jerks backward in fright. I grab Brady's arm, and Coral puts herself against his chest, screaming.

"What in the living daylights—?" Old Gus's voice wedges into the cracks between us, and suddenly he's there. He waves me back and pulls Coral gently aside and inserts himself on the first step of Moss's porch, between Brady at ground level and Moss up in the cabin. "This all has got to stop! It's got to stop, you hear!" Brady is red faced and heaving, seeming to look through Gus right into Moss.

"You listen to me," Brady growls, speaking directly to Moss. "If you don't leave her alone, I will come back here myself and mess you up. Do you understand? I don't want to see you near her ever again. If I do—I swear it—I'll kill you."

"Brady!" Coral wails, horrified.

"This is not a game, Cindy! This is your life!" Brady shouts.

"That is *enough* of that! Mr. Bouchard, please take your leave!

You're going with him, Cynthia, and that's that." It's jarring to hear Gus use her given name. Harsh. "You're done here. Let go. Fired. Whatever you want to call it. Early maternity leave—"

"Gus!" Moss cries, his face twisted in horror. He grabs at his hair. "You can't do that!"

"No!" Coral is squalling, nearly falling to her knees. Brady bears her up. "No!" She collapses into his chest, crying. My heart hammers.

"Stay away, Cynthia. Stay away for a while. Get some rest," Old Gus tells her, and Brady is nodding at this.

"This is—this is crazy! She's allowed to do whatever she wants!" Moss bellows, frantic.

"Juniper, why don't you help Mr. Bouchard get Cynthia down to his truck," Old Gus tells me, looking weary and upset. We all seem to freeze for a moment, taking this all in. Coral is in shambles. Moss looks panicked, Brady vindicated. Gus tired, quiet.

I look around the commons and see a few rubberneckers watching from a distance. I go to Coral's right side, and Brady takes her left. We hold her hands. Brady rests his hand on her back.

"Okay now," I whisper near her ear. "It's alright."

She's still crying, loudly, but she's not fighting us. We lead her away from Focus and down to the lot.

"I have to-to come b-back," Coral keens as we reach the messy lot, nodding her head, freaked as a spooked horse, eyes bulging.

"Sure, of course," I coo. "We can talk about that," I say, looking up at Brady, who finally nods his appreciation when he sees she's going to go with him without too much of a fight. We both realize we have to say whatever we need to say to get her to go home and get help.

Mantis climbs out of the truck as we approach, and I feel every muscle in my body tense up. He somehow looks bigger than I remember him. Or I feel smaller.

"Looks like we gotta keep a better eye on you," Mantis says, placing a hand on Coral's shoulder as he and Brady help her into the cab of the pickup. His hand looks so big on her small body. He looks at me with bemusement.

"You—you okay, Cor?" I ask, voice weak. She doesn't look at me as they settle her in the middle of the bench. The two men slide into the truck on either side of her.

Bookends.

Mantis pulls the passenger door shut, and suddenly Coral is behind glass.

"Thank you," Brady calls through the cab, his voice muffled.

"Sure," I reply numbly, stepping back as Brady starts the truck up and turns it around. Mantis tips a salute to me with two fingers through the window, and it somehow feels vindictive. Like he has gotten his way. I watch as they take Coral away, taillights sinking in their descent of the driveway, disappearing around the bend.

Cold shivers wrack my body, and I feel strung taut.

I eventually turn toward the commons. Toward Focus. Toward Moss.

His face, even from this distance, looks devastated. Terrified. His body trembles in the doorway, his hand clutching the frame as if for support.

A bolt of hatred radiates from his body to mine. It says, *You took her from me.*

He ducks inside and slams the door with such force, it sounds like a gun going off.

Nine

Natural Order

THESIS

***Her Dark Things* by Audra Colfax**

Piece #8: *See Me*

Oil and mixed media on canvas. 12" x 12".

[Image of a gnarled jumble of abstracted, paper-white birch trees and oversize, overlapping iron-gray boulders evocative of a bird's nest. Found objects incorporated throughout by layering]

Note on a sticky note found tucked under laminate flooring in the laundry room during a renovation of the Dunn residence.

> *the baby is here it*
> *came early.*
>
> *—Jan89. CD.*

Note on yellow legal paper found folded inside a copy of *Slouching Toward Bethlehem* by Joan Didion in the den at the Dunn residence.

the baby is MINE is the
baby the baby is Eveline
mine
is my baby Eveline
my DAUGHTER and Brady
is gone he left he's
done with me with us says I'm too much now
that I'm off the MEDS
he can TELL even though
I lie and tell him I still take them
he REFUSED to be what she needs
a FATHER
I said haven't I been BETTER since
we learned about her
about Evie
he said yeah he said for a WHILE
but that ended a while ago
when you ABANDONED your plan
your treatment
which feels like he's blaming M
who he doesn't even really know
so I hate him for that because
M (M) sees me is the only one who
sees me

—Jan89. CD.

Note on Lisa Frank stationery found in a tea tin in Cindy Dunn's bedroom closet in the Dunn residence.

I've drawn some pictures of
HER
some sketches when she's been napping I should have been
napping too I KNOW but I can't it's like I CAN'T and
when she's peaceful she is so BEAUTIFUL so I sketch her when
*   I can*
the drawings are not very good somehow she is so beautiful but the
*   drawings*
are not it's like
I can't
SEE her.

—Feb89. CD.

Note on torn graph paper found in a tea tin in Cindy Dunn's bedroom closet in the Dunn residence.

I sneak sneak sneak back to King City
Like a ghost, unseen, only felt
because
M wants to draw me he wants to keep drawing me and he
*   tells me to keep drawing he says he likes me this way in this*
*   crackedwideopen way and he says it's good it's better being*
*   around him I'm better*
it's beautiful
to keep letting myself be raw and empty and keep NOT taking
*   my meds and stare blank eyed at walls and at HER and just let*
*   him*
paint

and paint and paint me and now I bring
Evie and
she has colic
she screams and SCREAMS all day and she
screams and screams all NIGHT and M hates it and he LOVES
    it and I think he hates her and I think he loves her
for the way she makes me all broken and broke down and skeletal
    and turned inside out and at least
he likes ME
some kinda way at least he still lets ME come to him when I need
    to
we exhaust ourselves and deplete and RANSACK and ruin
    ourselves
down in my clearing
all three of us
sometimes all four of us
and
M says sure okay my canarybananagoldenrodlemonyellow girl
but that's just the way I LIKE you.

—Feb89. CD.

Drawings on loose-leaf sheets found in a sandwich bag in the roughed hollow of a birch tree on Lupine Valley property.

[A rough pencil sketch, ovoid, a potato, a potato trying to be a baby, formless, blurry.]

Title: *Evie.*

—*Feb89. CD.*

[A rough pencil sketch, a baby, human, naked, with discernible hands and feet that are formed more like the claws of birds. The talon-hands reach toward a throat, a chest, a disembodied person, maybe a woman, naked. Scratches. Gashes.]

Title: *Evie.*

—*Feb89. CD.*

Note on water-stained, loose-leaf paper found in a sandwich bag in the roughed hollow of a birch tree on Lupine Valley property.

mom says there is something
MISSING
in me
I think she has
SEEN
what I have done
fingernails and pricks and burns and bruises, cuts getting bigger
she wants me to think
up
to think UP
like my necklace, the dove
but
a GHOUL

like me it could only ever be
an anchor
too heavy
to lift my head above
its shine.

—*Mar89. CD.*

Juniper

Coral's official due date is two weeks away.

But here the baby is, before me, two weeks old, two weeks out-side of Coral's body already. Coral had gone into difficult preterm labor on a Sunday evening while home with Brady. An ambu-lance had been called. All pain medications had been refused, and so Coral suffered through an agonizing, dicey, ten-hour delivery. Neither Coral nor the baby had been up to Lupine Valley to see us since the birth, and Coral had refused almost everyone from Lupine Valley from coming to see her.

But Moss? Yes. Of course.

She allowed Moss to see her. I know because I've seen the draw-ings. Found them one day, by accident, while I waited for Moss to return to Focus from a colleague's cabin; we had plans for a hike to the Ledge. He had a cache of drawings of Coral and the baby partial-ly hidden under his mattress pad. But I saw the edges of them poking out and my curiosity got the better of me. There she was. Coral. Coral's postpartum body, its soft, slack belly. Her swollen breasts. Her exhausted face. Ten, twenty of them, all in different light. Different sizes. Different emotional compositions. The baby always a small, tight ball of expression and withholding—but looking less harrowed as each drawing progressed. And they're dated. All between January fourth and January fourteenth. The baby was born on January third. Moss denies he's seen her, seen them, but I know better.

The baby is a scant thing with squinty, puffy eyes, and dark fuzz on its head. A girl. Coral has her swaddled in a beautiful blue blanket Hillock knitted for her. Gus invited her back—for a *visit*— so we could all meet the baby. He feels bad for her, I know. So we stand in a circle around her in the mess hall as she shows the baby off to all of us gathered—Moss, Gus, Thorn, River, Hillock, and Ember, the new cleaner. But no Zephyr. Zephyr is gone. She left at the end of the fall session to go be with her sister, who just moved to America from Senegal, in Austin, Texas. I understand that her sister needs Z's support. Z understands I need Lupine Valley. We made promises to find each other when I am ready to leave this place. I hope that we both remember.

"My dad thinks she looks just like Brady." Coral looks down into her daughter's face, very serious, as if trying to see who's in there. The mention of Brady freezes us all up.

"No, no—spitting image of her mother!" Hillock coos, trying to elevate the mood, trying to distract her from the fact that Brady is gone. It's hard to believe, but he left her. And the baby. Coral has not shared the details. But I'm sure Moss knows. Moss *always* knows. He just chooses what to share, and that, so far, is not one of the things he's chosen.

I study Coral, a hunched, exhausted wisp. Even wearing her

layers of winter clothes—clunky boots, sagging coat, mustard-yellow scarf, blue hat, red mittens sticking out of her pockets—Coral looks slight. Too thin. Gus claims he heard from his friend Thelma (of Thelma's Landing) that the baby came prematurely because Coral was (and is, I'd argue) underweight and was feeling incredible stress. I believe both claims.

"So, what's her name?" Old Gus asks, snapping pictures of the baby, of the group surrounding Coral and the baby, on and on. I watch Coral lift her eyes and watch Gus snap picture after picture. She looks at him like she can't quite understand what he's doing.

"Eveline. I call her Evie."

"And what about her Lupine Valley name?" Moss asks sarcastically, his expression dark, his eyes locked on the baby. Everyone laughs except for Coral. Except for me.

FEBRUARY 8, 1989

Now me and Moss and Coral share a secret. I know that Coral sneaks into Lupine Valley under the cover of darkness via the access road. Most of the time she is without Evie as she trudges through the deep, wet snow in the middle of the night, lantern in hand, backpack strapped on. Moss lets her in, and she stays tucked away with him as long as she can reasonably manage.

I knew she was back when I found one of her signature notes tacked to my door.

For now I come alone but soon the third will follow

—*Jan89. CD.*

I wondered if the note was referring to Evie, but Evie stays with Coral's parents most of the time these days. I think they are more or less the guardians, to be honest. I went straight to Focus when I found the note, and after a brief blockade at the door, he let me in. And they made me swear not to tell. What finally got me to agree was the fact that Coral seemed...*okay*. She seemed more present than she had right before the baby came. Less vacant. More at peace. Less frantic.

Not everyone is meant to be a mother, I figure. Not everyone is made to be a housewife at nineteen. So I'm leaving them to their compact. Whatever that may be.

FEBRUARY 12, 1989

My new wool socks, bottle of cranberry juice, dental floss, burnt-umber and cadmium-orange oil paints, Moss's soup and Coral's toothpaste are sitting in a paper bag in the back seat. So is Evie, in her car seat, sleeping. Coral's parents both had to work today, and Coral couldn't...handle her. So here we are. I look at Evie's perfect little face with its chubby cheeks in the rearview mirror, my hands clutched around the wheel. We're sitting in the parking lot of the Shaw Public Library in Greenville.

I grab the Coral note I found slipped under my door this morning and read it again.

With him, there are no accidents. Justice for Ashley Pelletier.

—Feb89. CD.

I shove the note in my pocket then get out of the car and open the back passenger door.

"Hey, sweet pea, hey—shh, shh," I whisper as I unstrap little Evie and cradle her against my shoulder. "Just gonna do a little research," I whisper are she gurgles. But her eyes stay closed.

Twenty minutes later she's still asleep but strapped to my chest, her little cheek pressed like a flower, some drool spilling on me. I'm sitting in front of the microfiche, heart pounding hard enough that I worry it will wake the baby.

In 1982, a local high school senior named Ashley Pelletier was shot and killed in an apparent hunting accident. She was wearing white gloves. Men's. The hunter mistook the white for the upturned tail of a deer. He shot and killed her.

"These things happen," the hunter was quoted as saying. "It's terrible, but these things happen." The hunter was sentenced to ten months in jail for manslaughter. He ended up serving about six.

Negligent. Unfortunate. Tragic. Heartbreaking. Words like these pepper all of the articles from the time.

Because worst of all, the hunter was her boyfriend.

Her boyfriend was Mantis.

FEBRUARY 13, 1989

When I came back from the Shaw Public Library yesterday, burdened with this horrid new knowledge about Mantis, I went into Focus and found just Coral there. I handed her Evie, who was swaddled in a blanket inside an innocuous wicker basket, which had been covered by another blanket. Like I might be carrying bread.

She told me Moss was at the Ledge. I told her everything I read, everything I found out. She nodded sagely as Evie began to cry.

"Your note—I figured that you were telling me to—" I started, unsure how to finish.

"Yes," she affirmed, looking worn.

"It wasn't an accident? Right? He murdered her?" I asked, my voice hushed, trembling. Her eyes locked with mine, wise, world weary. She tilted her chin, looking very, very sad, her blond hair pulled back in a loose, greasy ponytail. A nod. I swallowed, thinking of the occasions I went shooting with him, alone. Thinking of how Coral found us that day trying to tell me something. Or tell him. A warning. "But—how do you know? I mean, for sure?"

"Oh, Junie," she sighed, and she looked at me with more affection than she ever had. "I just couldn't keep it in, don't you see? Promises hurt sometimes." I searched her face as Evie's cries rose into keening wails. Coral picked up the baby, lifted her shirt, and started breastfeeding. The baby calmed and ate. "What's done is done. I thought it was important that you know. That someone would know."

"But Coral. What—"

The door creaked open behind me and frigid air struck us three women as we sat hunched together, tight as a coven. It was Moss. Coral made eyes at me that commanded: *Not a word to anyone. For me.*

Ten

Where a Bird Should Be

THESIS

Her Dark Things by Audra Colfax

Piece #9: *Dread Project*
Oil and mixed media on canvas. 8" x 8".

[Close-up of an intricately knitted, blue baby blanket, the textures almost agricultural in their shaping, ocean-like in its expanse. Found objects incorporated throughout by layering.]

Note on scratch paper found in the living room wall during a renovation for accidental damage in the Dunn residence.

> *I am the dead COAL of a*
> *ROTTEN tooth I am the tar-black MAW of hell I am his*
> *DREAD project a*
> *swollen midnight WOUND*
> *I am BOUND to him in this*
> *in his glorious ascension*
> *and I am bound to him like EVE*
> *choking on the apple*

for what I know
I am BOUND to them
in the final hour
he can make me that way KEEP me that way in my highest
form my HIGHEST
SELF forever
we PROMISED each other, C
the night the forest swallowed us whole
it's time to become the
golden sunshine starshine canary goldenrod bright bright golden
  girl
he's going to
HELP me
and he's going to help me
I'm going to let him.

—March89. CD.

Juniper

"Well, let's go to my place and take a look at the roster from last session," Gus offers. "Maybe we can get it returned to him somehow. I think I know who you mean." I'm carrying the expensive-looking watch I found this morning outside one of the cabins that have been shut up for the winter season. We trudge our way down the mucky path to his cabin, the air unseasonably mild, the temporary snowmelt conjuring swatches of fog in various surprising locations.

"Stork, maybe? From Pittsburgh?" I offer as we get to his door. "Or Heron?"

He lets us in, and as he does, he points to the new lens he just got sitting out on his workbench. I stay on the welcome mat and turn to look at it while Gus slides his muddy boots off.

"It's a beaut, huh?" he says. He creaks forward a step or two, and then he goes suddenly still. I look up, setting down the lens where I found it.

"Alright, Gus?" And then the reason for his silence becomes clear. His enormous wall collage of camper photos faces us. There are easily forty-dozen up there. At an average of sixty campers a year, that's about eight years' worth. He has previous years' pictures archived elsewhere. I've seen the wall countless times. We all have, whenever we come in to visit with Gus.

But something is terribly wrong with it.

All of the eyes in each and every photo have been scratched out to white, blank nothingness. Four hundred and eighty faces, blinded.

And they're not in their usual grid. They spell something out. I have to let my eyes settle across the massive breadth of it.

ART OUTLASTS ALL

My stomach plummets to my feet.

Gus drops into a crouch, hand over his mouth.

"Why?" he croaks. "Who?" His voice is tremulous.

But I know who. Of course I do.

MARCH 10, 1989

I'm half sitting on the stool in front of my easel. I've been sitting here with a paintbrush in my hand, stymied and distracted so long that the smears and scrapes of paint on my palette are starting to dry out.

I can't stop thinking about the photos in Old Gus's cabin.

I can't believe I didn't tell him what I suspected—what I *know*. Even when he called us all to the communal bonfire in the commons via the dinner bell and described, heartbroken, what had taken place. Even when he begged plaintively for someone to come forward if they knew anything. Even when he asked the group why this had been done to him, tears in his eyes. I stayed quiet. Because I couldn't bear it. I couldn't bear what might happen to Coral if anyone found out. What I've done is keep my distance. And pretend there's nothing to be said.

I swallow and set down my paintbrush and palette. I rub my face and eye sockets hard and deep, trying desperately to chase the tension away. I look at the pathetic canvas before me. Unbroken expanses of white with insecure swipes of black here and there. I sigh and get up, crack the window for some bracing air.

Two figures are emerging from the forest at the far side of the commons. From the direction of Coral's Clearing. I squint.

It's Moss.

And Mantis.

They keep walking, not talking to each other. Moss's eyes and face are cast down. Mantis faces forward, confident. *What the fuck is Mantis doing here? What are they doing together? Are they coming from the clearing?* My gut clenches. The Holy Trinity hasn't been down to Coral's Clearing since the night of the Autumn Francis story. Since the night that seemed to change everything.

When they're almost halfway through the commons, I suddenly break from my trance, from the feeling that I'm watching something on a TV screen, separate from me.

I stumble down my front steps in my moccasins onto the muddy pathway.

"Hey!" I cry. "Hey!" The two men pause and turn to look at me. Moss looks both nervous and relieved, somehow. Mantis looks agitated. I watch Mantis clap Moss on the shoulder, hard. Moss flinches under his touch. And then Mantis starts striding toward the parking lot like he doesn't even see me. "Mantis," I call, heading toward him, but his longer stride outpaces me easily. I start to trot after him, not sure what I'm even doing. Why I'm chasing after a man who on some deep, elemental level now terrifies me.

I slip a few times on the embankment down to the lot, and by the time I get there, he's already in his truck and starting it up. "Mantis," I say again over the noise of the engine, breathing hard. He looks at me now, hands on the wheel, and there's something like pity in his eyes. Like he finds me pathetic. "Where's Coral?" is all I can think of to say. His features turn stony. Unwelcoming. I wrap my arms around my body, shivering. It can't be more than forty degrees.

"Go ask Moss," he finally says. A small smile curls his lips. Icy, dislocated panic floods me. Then he yanks his truck into gear and speeds down the driveway. Gone.

I stalk off toward Moss's cabin at a half jog. My breath comes in quick, nervous bursts. When I get to his door, I rap on it hard three times. Silence greets me. I knock again. Then again. "Moss! I know you're in there!" Then I start slamming the side of my fist ceaselessly against the door.

The door flies open.

"Christ, June. Fucking give it a rest," Moss snarls. He rubs his forehead like a headache is splitting it wide open. He looks pale. And cold.

"What the *fuck* was Mantis doing here?" I bark, trembling. Moss just shakes his head and turns away from me. He sinks to sit on his bed like he can't hold himself up.

"Where's Coral?" I demand.

"Not here," he replies, voice impossibly weary—unlike I've ever heard it.

"Where is she, Moss? I'm serious."

"June, please." It's a plea. The desperation in him makes me pause. My eyes flicker around his face, which is wrought.

"Moss. Talk to me. Tell me right now. Where is she? Where is she?" I'm begging. Almost crying.

"She's not here anymore, okay?" he shouts, finally locking his red, watery eyes on me. He looks exhausted. Like he's been chased by the devil. His skin looks anemically white. I'm so startled by his appearance that I lose my words for a moment.

"Where is she?" I ask, nerves making my voice tremble. "Moss." I breathe. "Where is Coral?" Moss swallows and shakes his head. "Moss," I whisper, a terrified tear creeping from my eye down onto my cheek. I wipe it away.

"She's where she wants to be." His voice cracks, and that one small vocal imperfection sends a shudder of deep, nebulous terror through me.

I don't remember turning away from him or leaving his cabin. I don't remember rushing into the woods. I don't remember slipping and mudding my way down the path to Coral's Clearing. But eventually I get there, dirty, cold, trembling. I push my way past the trunks of trees, until I make it into the center of Coral's favorite place.

And in the heart of it, a shock of lemon yellow. A shock of blond against slate gray, arctic white, pearwood brown. The cragged rhinoceros boulders, the elegant arc of ballerina birch trees. Soil and bark. Mud and snow.

And Coral in the limbs. Where a bird should be. Weightless, and free, high above the ground, unburdened—

Or too terribly earthly, much heavier than air, gravity pulling her down, down.

I can't tell which.

A rope gone taut. Her body gone slack.

I shake my head no in disbelief, big and naive, like the motion might serve as an eraser.

Then I scream.

THESIS
Her Dark Things by Audra Colfax

Piece #10: *See You Later*
Oil and mixed media on canvas. 36" x 36".

[Close-up of a frayed rope, coiled, rough, animal-like. Found objects incorporated throughout by layering.]

Note on water-stained, linen-woven stationery found in the landscaped stone wall outside the Dunn residence.

> *It's all set*
> *EVELINE is still with my parents she is*
> *SAFE*
> *Brady is off living his life*
> *I think he knows I think he*
> *understands*
> *I have made the deal with M with M*
> *M took my wish*
> *Saw my deepest heart*
> *and provided a narrowness*
> *something I could not back out of*
> *a girl who could not go on knowing*
> *a kind of courage*
> *and M will make me a*
> *golden WONDER forever*
> *forever his goldenbright girl*
> *M slipped me a note it said*

MEET ME IN THE PLACE YOU SHOWED ME
  UNDER THE STARS
and so I will
(and I kept the note—special place with EE)
mom and dad, I'm SORRY
everyone, everybody, even Brady
I'm sorry
Eveline Audra
I do LOVE you I want you to
know that
I tried so HARD
I want you to
know that

—March89. CD.

Eleven

Signature Color

Max

The sound that I hear—whether in real life or in a dream—is a sharp pop. Or a bang. Or a crack. In the space of milliseconds, I see a yellow balloon snapping and giving way. I see a ninety-mile-per-hour fastball hitting the broad side of a sun-splashed barn. A golden firework exploding into an opaque blackness.

My eyes open into tar-thick darkness, the black wings of ravens, scorched and piled on me. A different kind of drowning. In the feathers of those birds. Coral's birds.

I blink and blink, trying to shake the blindness. Trying to shake Coral.

There are other suggestions of shape. Of light.

I am rocking. Swaying. Bobbing. Something. I wake in phases, it seems, rising out of a viscous swamp, disoriented. I lift my body to my elbows, feeling dense and heavy. Slow. I sit up. Ripples frosted with diamond dust from the heavens. All around me. Water.

I am in a small, wooden boat. The boat is in the lake. I am in the small boat in the lake.

"Coral?" I rasp, garbled.

Coral, falling backward. Arms spread wide, a black raven. Down, down she goes.

No. I shake my head out. I have to get it together.

This is…Audra's boat. The boat from shore. *Kress Beach.* I knew it as soon as we arrived.

I am alone. There is no Audra.

My cardiac system bursts into high gear, my sudden, clumsy movements making the boat sway and rock more violently. Straight ahead of me is more lake. Endless lake. The silence profound. The air freezing. I look around me. No oars. I twist my head all the way around, panic rising ever higher, and see that the shore I had so recently been walking on, then standing on, then sitting on inside this boat, is about a hundred yards behind me.

Coral, half-naked and shivering, standing painfully close to the flames of the fire Mantis built for us.

I blink and make myself look at it how it is now, not as it was then. *Don't get confused.* The fallen logs. The stump with those strange initials. But no Audra. What has happened? What has happened to Audra? Is she hurt? I look at my hands and wonder— with a searing shock—if I have strangled her. Had I simply blacked out? Pushed her into the lake? Killed her? Dropped her body into the depths? Bile rises inside of me.

Why would I think that? How could I think that? I peer madly around the perimeter of the boat but find no ghostly hands or faces in that black water. Not Coral's face. Not Audra's.

I didn't reach for her that day. I don't reach for her now.

Audra is simply gone.

I force my body to one side of the boat, bracing the edge of it with my left arm and dipping my other arm into the freezing water. I hiss. My coat's arm is immediately soaked from the elbow down. I start splashing and paddling the boat wildly so the prow is facing in the right direction. Toward land. Toward the beach. Toward Audra.

"Audra!" I call, but my voice is weak, rusty. I clear my throat and call again, with more success: "Audra!" But the word, her name, only echoes emptily back to me. I listen above the paddling noises of my rapidly numbing hand and forearm.

BANG!

"Fuck! Fucking Christ!" I rip my hand from the water and cover my head. A gunshot. A fucking gunshot. It sounded like a big one. Maybe like a…like a shotgun? I drop down in the boat. I lie on my belly. I listen. I wait. The sound seems to take a lifetime to finally fade from the air, from its own echo. I peer over the lip of the boat, looking all around me. But there is only water and dense, black, forested shoreline in every direction. I see no one. I hear no one. Where did that shot come from? How close is the gunman? It felt close. It sounded close. Who is firing a gun in the night? Can you hunt at night?

I swallow. I close my eyes, feeling nauseous from fear, from booze, from lying flat on my stomach. Heartburn creeps up my throat.

I'm shivering.

I take a breath.

It takes several moments to gather myself, but then I push up again and start paddling sloppily, loudly toward shore. I don't care about the noise I'm making. I have to get off this water. I have to get to shore. I have to find Audra. Get to the car, far away, down that damned trail. Get to her house. Any house. The one-armed paddling from the right side sends the boat into a left turn and then nearly a circle before I realize it's happening. I go to the left side and dunk my left arm in and course correct. I groan, both arms soaked and freezing. I imagine Coral, standing in a similarly spinning boat. Her deep voice, arguing, *I think I need to stop, M, I need to be better. Meds, therapy. Brady.* Me, refusing. Me, defensive. Me, disappointed. Me, awestruck. I want to cry out. I am still bobbing, wide open on the lake, no closer to shore. Panic and frustration seize my chest and throat and limbs—I sit there dumbly for a moment, body painfully tense and erect. A sob grips my throat, my chest.

My phone. Relief floods me in a way I have rarely felt in my life. I stab my hands into my jacket pockets, sniffing, wiping my face, feeling the familiar square shape of my wallet. But there is nothing else. No phone. I feel around more aggressively. I turn out the pockets. I shove my hands into every pocket on every article of clothing on my body. Wallet, yes. Phone? Nothing. Knife? Gone. My teeth clench in my skull. I drop to my hands and knees, struggling to see clearly the nuanced shadows in the bottom of the boat, and begin to feel around. *It just slid out of my pocket. It's here. I was lying down. It just slipped out. Stay calm. You'll find it.* But I don't find it. I scour three more times. My body. The boat. It's not here.

I sit heavily on the bench, my back hunched in cold resignation. I look up into the dazzling sky. I look out onto the shimmering lake. My breath mists before me. I think of that gunshot and force myself to go to the very farthest point of the prow, as far as I dare, the nose dipping more and more into the lake, but it stays above the waterline. I hunch low and rest my chest against the front point. I drive both arms into the water on either side of the prow and start paddling. The water soaks my coat and makes my arms heavier and heavier to move with each minute that passes. My progress is painfully slow, but there is progress.

"Yes," I whisper. "Come on. Come on." It takes, I'd guess, a solid fifteen or twenty minutes for me to travel the fifty yards or so that marks the halfway point back to shore. Maybe longer. I pull myself back up into the boat to rest my arms, which are throbbing in pain from the freezing water and exhausted from the rowing. I close my eyes, trying to catch my breath. How could this have happened?

"Audra!" I call again. Silence returns to me. "Audra!" I try harder, louder. "Someone!" I scan the shoreline, the tree line.

Nothing.

I'm alone out here. On my own. I have to make my own way back. There's nothing else to do. I resume my post at the prow. I sink my arms into the water and begin paddling. I need to get to shore and get to the car and get to somewhere I can call 911. They can help find Audra. I need to get somewhere safe. There's someone with a gun within earshot, and Audra is missing.

The cold seems to dismember me, make parts of my body not my own anymore. Every segment of my fingers is blindly, baldly numb—absent. My arms are leaden. By the time I get to be fifteen feet out from shore, I'm so eager to get to dry land that I make my way over the side and splash into freezing thigh-deep water. My ankle screams at me. I grab the boat, and I crash and struggle through the lake to pull it to shore—using it as a brace for my ankle, a crutch for my fatigue and wooziness—far enough up so it won't drift out into the lake like it did with me. I sink down onto the cold beach, flat on my back, my breath misting above me as I try to catch it. I swallow, close my eyes momentarily, then turn my head to the side. There is Audra's log. EAD & MFD inside of a heart. Did she say it was us? I certainly recognize my own initials, but EAD?

Then I notice something. On top of the log. Something small. I squint at it, then push myself onto my knees and crawl the two feet over to it. I kneel, feeling my cold, wet jeans clinging to my chilled skin, my ankle throbbing as I use it to partially prop me up. I look at the item and then bring my hand to touch it. It's a neatly folded piece of paper. It is held down at its corner with a small stone. The tidy, square parcel is wrapped up in white string, like a present. There is writing on the outside. It says *MOSS*.

Moss.

So here we are.

I look around myself, feeling more paranoid than I ever have in my entire life. But there is no one anywhere that I can see, and hardly any sound, hardly any movement. Just the lake, the trees, the beach, the sky. This place of Coral's big announcement.

My heart thuds. I touch the piece of paper very lightly, as if waiting for it to bite me or burn me. I pick it up. I untie the string with shaking hands, unfold it—one, two, three, half, and half, and half—until the inside reveals itself. Taking up most of the space on the inside is a picture. Of something. I turn my body so I can catch as much of the moon and starshine as possible. I squint. It is a printout of an image of a painting.

From side to side, corner to corner, the painting is filled with color—canary and mustard and xanthic yellows with some cedar greens and blacks for shaping and highlighting. But overwhelmingly, the image is goldenrod.

Goldenrod upon goldenrod upon goldenrod.

Like the ribbons in the trees, those damn trees.

It is a shock against the black night. Burnished and flowing; liquid and sensual. The colors undulate in a feminine drape across the canvas, but there is no woman here, really. There is an elongation. An abstract landscape from deep inside someone's heart, someone's mind. If there is a woman to be found at all, the form of a human body, it is in the shapes to the left side of the image that evoke thin shoulders, a delicate too-long neck, a head with almost no features but an elegant, enrobing swath of goldenrod "hair." A stark, black line—the most straight, geometric mark in the whole scene—cuts violently across what could be seen as a throat. The black line—jarring in its darkness, jarring in its lack of curves—eventually begins to wend and thin until it curls off the top edge of the canvas. It is evocative of vibrancy, and yet also evocative of death.

It is mine.

In a simple, nondescript font beneath:

Animus. *Max Durant. 1993.*

And then:

This is Coral, isn't it, Max? Isn't it, Moss? Isn't it, M?

I go cold. I go still. I go empty.

I cannot tell if the world is falling away from me or if I am falling away from the world.

I crumple up the sheet of paper and shove it in my pocket to take it out of sight while all the blood rushes to my face and to my heart, while a battering dismay wells up inside of me. What in the hell does it mean? Is this some sort of game? Some kind of sick joke?

How did I get out onto the lake? Where is Audra? Who left that note? Did *Audra* leave that note? My mind reels. *But how? How could she know?*

A cold, boundless terror has taken hold of me. I whip my head around, poised to see someone lurking nearby, but there is no one. There is the lake. There is the shore. The log with my initials. The boat with no oars that has, in a chipped, looping brushstroke, *Happily Eveline After* painted on the back.

Coral. Eveline. *Eveline.*

I can't think. I just move. In my wet, cold jeans and my wet, cold jacket on my throbbing, swelling ankle, I just move. Panicked. I gain the break in the trees Audra had taken me through—how long ago was it now? Who could know?—and enter a new level of darkness. I hold up right away, unable to make out anything for a moment. I try to blink the dark and the drunkenness from my eyes. The shapes in the spectrum of blackness begin to reveal themselves to me. *Where are the lights? Where are those path lights?* I shiver just inside the border of the forest. Dread dismay snatches me in the blackness.

There. To the right. A light. *A light!*

One of the lights, just like on our way down. There is the path, thank god. I start picking my way slowly, so slowly, along the path. My ears are radars in the relative silence. When I get to the tree with the light, I rest my head against the bark and try to catch my breath. In my solitude, in the quiet, I think of the words in the note from the shore, over and over and over again. I think of Lupine Valley. I think of the jarring goldenrod ribbons flowing from the branches of Audra's trees, so evocative of my painting. The yellow birds on Audra's ears.

My painting.

I am filled with sparking amber. Goldenrod.

This is Coral, isn't it, Max? Moss? M?

I circle around to the side of the tree with the light and find there is something pinned into the bark. A tiny scrap of paper.

M is going to make me beautiful
M is going to make me beautiful
M is going to make me beautiful
M is going to make me beautiful
M is going to make me beautiful

—March89. CD.

I touch the fragile, creased piece of paper, yellowed with age. Shock grips my chest.

But how? It's her. It's her handwriting.

And M. That's me.

It's *us.*

I suddenly feel watched. Stalked. I take my hand from the note and move away from the immediate glow of the light. I look around me, eyes wide and wild. I listen.

"Audra?" I whisper hopefully. "Audra—are you there?" Audra. Do I even want to find Audra? Do I truly want Audra to find me? After this?

I jump when some ancient tree towering above me creaks like rending Styrofoam. I take a breath to steady myself. *You're spooked, Max. Get it together.*

I don't know if I see the flash or hear the thunderous shot first.

The muzzle blast blooms—instantaneous, sudden, there and then gone so fast, I think I might have dreamed it—from the darkness less than eighty yards off to my right.

I scream.

I hear the violent spray of buckshot wide of me and short of me.

I vault in my skin. A croak of sheer horror leaks from me at the closeness of it.

I start to run, senseless, wild with terror. I dive into the blackness of the woods, trying to put distance between myself and the gunman—no innocent night hunter but a madman. Who the hell hunts at night? Where is Audra? Has he already gotten to her?

Or is she the one doing the hunting?

M is going to make me beautiful.

I stumble hard during the first several yards, wrenching my ankle further, whimpering like an animal, grabbing on to the rough bark of trees to find my footing. I go on like this, scrambling, desperate, for as long as I can manage, then I slow—out of necessity as well as strategy—and begin to choose my steps more carefully, try to dampen the sounds of my passage, so my hunter might not hear.

My god, my *hunter*.

I pause and try to get my bearings. I need to find another light. The lights will lead me home. To Focus. I close my eyes and force deep breaths. *But what might you find at the next light, Max?*

I open my eyes into blackness, feeling overwhelmed by it. I look and look. I shiver. I take a few steps forward and there, in the distance, is a pinprick of light, floating like some ethereal being from a fairytale. A strangled noise escapes me. It's my way out of here.

But what if there's another...?

I shake the thought off and make a beeline for the light, thinking of getting to the car, getting to safety. Twigs and leaves crackle underfoot. Audra said the lights led to the lake, that there was no reason to be afraid. That means the lights will lead back, too. I have to keep going. I squint for any shred of moonlight. As I move through the trees, stumbling over roots and rocks and rises, the image of small, lost Audra with her knife and her cardinal blood and her smoke signals rises into my mind. She was lost for hours. In the daylight. On land she grew up on.

She was also a child, Max. And you have these lights. Lights that will lead you back to safety. But my own reprimand gives me little solace.

Another gunshot booms out, but it is much farther away. Immediate fear at the sound followed by relief at the distance swells in my chest.

My teeth chatter, and I wrap my arms around myself as if in an attempt to hold in the heat, to hold myself together. My ankle is pounding with excruciating force. Keep going.

This is Coral, isn't it, Max?

M is going to make me beautiful.

Audra's glinting smile flashes in my mind.

As I get nearer the light, I see there is something posted to the tree above the fixture, and I feel my heart sink. A piece of paper pinned with a tack, just like the last one. I don't want to look. But I do. I can't help myself. As I come to the outer limit of the light's circle, I pause. It's a drawing this time. But not one of mine.

[A bird's beak is sketched in the center. A bird's taloned foot is to the right. The beak and talons, disembodied, are rendered in impossible detail. Obsessive, fine, ultra-real.]

—*Feb89. CD.*

The light pulls me in. A moth to the flame. I get very close to the drawing. My breath puffs out before me, brushes the old, fragile paper. Equal to the proportion of my sense of shriveling, collapsing under these circumstances is a sense of blossoming anger. At her. At Coral.

"No," I whisper. "Coral. No." Even as I stumble away from the spot, fists clenched, my eyes remain fixed on it. I can't look away. I finally turn, and not far ahead, I see the next light.

I can hear someone.

Moving through the terrain steady and quiet as a jaguar. It's hard to tell how far off they might be. I recede into the blackness, making disorienting angles between myself and the sound, myself and the next light, my breaths short and harried.

I focus on the light, on the next light.

It doesn't quite seem like fifty yards ahead, which I think is how far apart Audra had said the lights were, but who could tell in this darkness, on this terrain.

My mind swirls and roils with questions, with fear, and, yes, with anger. Everything that happened with Coral was so long ago. A lifetime ago. How could any of it even matter anymore?

I limp on, using trees I pass as braces to get me a few feet forward at a time. At every other tree, I stop and listen, but I don't hear my pursuer anymore. I move ahead, closer to the next light, my salvation.

I recognize the drawing without even having to step into the orb of light emanating from the tree. It's a drawing of a beautiful mother fox. Her eyes are almost feline, almost feminine. Her fur is fluffy and excruciatingly detailed, every hair lovingly drawn. The curve of her curled body, the way her puff of a tail snakes around her—both precise. She is a picture of perfection but for one thing. Erupting from her belly, just below her rib cage, is a beautiful, tiny fox kit, slick with blood and meat, its tiny teeth so sharp and glinting, they're almost sawlike. The kit is eating its way out of the mother. When you look at the mother fox's eyes more carefully, you see that they are flat, dull, empty. She is dead. But the kit is alive. Beautiful, disgusting, alive.

I find that I have a hand covering my mouth. I find that I am shaking my head no.

"You were going to give it to Brady, you said," I whisper into the night. "He wanted you to draw for—for the baby." My head is shaking back and forth, back and forth. "You drew this and said you tried to give it to Brady, but he was—mortified." I swallow, my voice a strangled whisper. "I—loved it."

BOOM!

It's one beat of my heart or the sound of a gun going off.

I run without realizing I've begun to run. The booze-wooziness and the exhaustion and the pain in my leg and my utter fear are blending my gut into a relentless, sickening mash. I want to throw up. But I keep going. I keep finding lights. *So* many lights. But the angles are wrong. The distance and pacing are wrong. It seems like there are lights everywhere. That they are leading me nowhere.

The next light.

[Yellow legal paper. Fold lines. A cracked beak, close up, hyperreal.]

—*Feb89. CD.*

The next light.

[Sketch paper. A wing. A beady little eye. A crow torn down the middle, guts spilling out.]

—*Feb89. CD.*

I want to scream, but the sound is bludgeoned in my throat, held down as if with a lump of clay, because the gunshots, like the messages from Coral, are coming faster now. Coming closer. The buckshot is nipping my heels as I limp wildly through the black trees, from light to light, orb to orb, horror to horror.

[A nebulous, horrid thing, all curves and water and insubstantial mess. The colors dark and terrible, the eyes cocked at odd angles, the nose off-center.]

Title: *Evie, v. 7*

—*March89. CD.*

I go to the drawing. I go to the light. I can't not go. My body just brings me there. I met that baby. Eveline Bouchard. Brady Bouchard. Cindy Dunn. Little Evie Bouchard. God, I knew that baby once—the creature rendered here. So unalike. What Coral was seeing—my god.

The next light.

No one sees sees sees where the marks are the marks are within
and
without but they
don't they don't see they don't see.

—*Feb89. CD*

BOOM.
BOOM.
BOOM.
BOOM.
The next light.

I tried to die today and they all stopped it and I thought what for.

—*Jul84. CD.*

BOOM.
The next light.

Who is that devil in king city who is that devil that devil in king city who hmmmmmmmm? mmmmmmmmmmmmmm

—*Feb89. CD.*

I fear them all like they are bullets with my name on them.
BOOM.
BOOM.
But then my eyes catch on something. A brighter, bigger light than all of the other lights. Hope blooms in my chest. I stand stock-still. I listen. I attempt to quiet my breathing, my heart, which both threaten to deafen me.

The gunshots have stopped.

The dogged, chasing rustling has stopped.

I focus on the light source ahead. It's steady, unmoving. Big. So bright. My heart pulses in my neck. Every muscle in my body is taut as piano wire. I fear what—or who—I might find inside that light. Some *Deliverance* maniac?

Or is Audra the one *doing* this to me?

Audra.

The lights. The drawings. *Coral's* drawings. My painting, tied up for me in a little packet on the lakeshore. Who? Who is after me?

Coral?

A creeping, slow-suffocating terror metastasizes.

No.

I close my eyes.

I have to go to the light.

But it could be a trap. I must be careful.

I begin moving forward obliquely and at a glacial pace. As I get closer, I realize the light is in a small clearing. I see the horrid, stark shadows the bright light casts around the clearing, branches creating ominous and labyrinthine shapes. No car in sight, no cabins; with sinking dread, I realize I'm still deep in the woods. I circle and pause, circle and pause, getting a better and better look at the clearing. By now, I can see clearly that there are many lights affixed to many of the trees inside the ring of the clearing. Audra's brown enamel lantern is in there, at the edge, turned over on its side. The ratty old BAH HAHBAH bumper sticker just visible. I freeze. My god.

I see no Audra. I see no madman. I sense no presence at all.

I creep to the outer ring of the light sphere, which has lit up the small, suffocating space bright as day. Inside, not quite in the middle, is a Volkswagen-size boulder into which an old, tall, fat birch tree is leaning, lilting, pressing, growing. The birch is tall and dying and swoops to the left, thick branches snaking from it. From the branches hang torn and shredded pieces of bright, goldenrod fabric. Dozens of them, in varying lengths and roughness. So like Audra's apple tree, bright ribbons flowing in the breeze. I can see that on these ribbons, though, are markings of some kind. Words. Writing. Almost without thinking, I ease into the clearing. Drawn to the boulder and the birch like it cannot be helped. Because I know them. The boulder. This birch. This clearing, now that I have my bearings. This exact place. Hallowed ground. Haunted ground. I limp onward, painfully, and I feel a crystalline, cutting, terminal fear and desperation.

THIS IS CORAL, ISN'T IT, MAX?

THIS IS CORAL, ISN'T IT, M.?

THIS IS CORAL, ISN'T IT, M.?

THIS IS CORAL, ISN'T IT, MOSS?

THIS IS CORAL, ISN'T IT, MAX?

THIS IS CORAL, ISN'T IT, MOSS?

A groan of outsize fear escapes me. The thought comes to me so quickly, too quickly that I can't stifle it before it arrives: Is Coral doing this to me? Somehow?

This is Coral, isn't it, Max?

Is it Coral?

"Coral," I say quietly, as if speaking her name might conjure her from a spell. "Is it you?" But no, it can't be—Coral is gone. Long gone. It's impossible. It was so very long ago. So, so, so long ago.

"So long ago," I whisper, shaking. "So long ago, Coral."

A different life. But this is the place.

The boulder. The birch. The boulder and the birch. Yes. Coral's Clearing. Yes.

She knows. Audra.

Somehow, some way.

The horrid goldenrod fabric is electric against the night in the myriad, dazzling lights. I am all lit up. So bright, god could see.

For almost thirty years, I've been able to keep Coral Dunn in a tiny box buried in the very back of my mental closet. Not seen, mostly forgotten. I'd moved on. Because what happened to her was not my fault. It was not my doing.

Chuk-chuk.

In the maw of the clearing opening to my left, not fifteen feet away, just at the border of invisibility stands a ski-masked man with a shotgun. A man. *Not Audra.* The gun is trained on me. *I am all lit up. So bright, god could see.* I close my eyes.

BANG!

I scream and fall to my knees, the sound deafening, waiting for the burning sensation of thousands of particles of molten-hot buckshot to explode into my skin and organs. But I feel nothing.

The gunshot echoes into the night. I open my eyes, my hands groping all around my body. I feel no blood. I feel no pain. I whip my head around to look for the man with the gun—but he's gone. The suddenness of his disappearance startles me. My heart hammers. My eyes bulge.

Then someone. To my right.

"Coral!" I cry without thinking.

"Max," Audra says in a low, almost sultry voice, a smile hinting at her lips. *Audra. It's Audra.* "Or should I call you M?" The hinky, gap-toothed Colfax smile attacks me. She is wearing a goldenrod summer dress, light, papery, with thin straps that show off her beautiful clavicles, despite the cold.

It is *the* dress.

Coral's yellow dress from that day. Coral's favorite dress in her hallmark color. The color she lived in. The dress she died in. The color in which I immortalized her. The color that has given me everything. *Animus.* Goldenrod, sparking amber, flowing to the ground. Audra, a double. Coral, returning.

Her hands are clasped behind her back. She is barefoot.

"You look as if you'd seen a ghost!"

My mouth flaps dumbly.

"Coral Dunn"—she says the name so, so carefully—"was a girl you once knew." I nod at her, unable to help myself. Her perfect body is a sharp, bright cut-out in my vision. "I want you to understand very clearly what I am about to say to you. Are you listening?" Her voice isn't even loud now. It's low and dangerous, and her eyes are lasers on me, into me. I nod, tears leaking from my eyes. I'm crying, and I'm scared. "I'm sure you've already guessed it by now, M. Coral Dunn was my mother."

It's as if every bodily function in me seizes up simultaneously— my lungs, my heart, my eyes, my bowels. I just look at her. Then it comes back in a rush, and my head might explode from the pressure.

"N-no," I manage in a whisper of a voice. I grab my head in my hands.

"*Coral Dunn was my mother, and I know what you did.*" Her voice is a snakelike hiss. Audra looks beautiful, even in her mangling fury. *Fury*, I think to myself. *The Furies. That's it. That's where we are. That is who she is.*

And then there is a gun pointing at me.

I'm going to die tonight.

Audra

The man goes white and pasty as the rind of a brie. I mean, he really looks like hell when I tell him.

Coral Dunn was my mother, and I know what you did.

I can't even imagine what I must sound like. Everything inside of me feels like it's rattling at a frequency that might kill me. My every molecule and cell shaking with rage. With adrenaline. *I will set you free, you fuck. I am the way, the truth, and the light.* His hair is in disarray from scrabbling around in the dark, in the night, running away from the shotgun, the lights, my mom's *haunty scrawlslips.* Despite the cold, sweat crawls from Max's temples and hairline and neck. He nervously swipes his hand through his hair over and over again. He looks elementally shaken. His face is blanched with a sickly sheen. His eyes glassy and sunken and far away, and I know he's terribly scared. He looks small inside his own clothes somehow. The butterscotch scarf with the black tassels wraps around his neck. His back is hunched as he sits there on the cold ground under my gaze, under my gun. He looks at me, and it's different from any other time he's ever looked at me. He's not looking at me as his Audra. As his almost lover. As his student, his wunderkind, his mentee, his competitor. He's looking at me as Coral Dunn's daughter. Probably trying to reconstruct me as a baby then fast-forward me in time to see if the whole thing holds up. He looks petrified and worn and unbelieving.

"You can't be." I leave him in silence for a long few moments. He starts shaking his head and crying again. "You *can't* be!"

"I am. I am Coral Dunn's daughter. My father is Brady Bouchard. Don't you remember him?"

"Well, I—" He's about to say something honest for once in his goddamned life, but he clams up when he realizes it. Tears stream from his eyes.

"Go on," I encourage him. "I already know all of the answers. Or most of them anyway. You're looking at the proctor giving the test, Max."

"But it can't possibly be," he says, stricken. He grabs his hair, his face wrenched in existential agony.

"Sure it can. And I'll tell you how in a minute. After you answer my question: Do you remember my dad? Brady?" I feel nervous. I've had so few people to ask about my early life. There were my grandparents of course—Cindy's parents, Buddy and Hanora— but no one else, really. Until recently.

"Yes," he relents. "I knew him." I feel my hands begin to shake.

This man *knew* my father.

It solidifies everything into a horrifying, congealed reality. The notes. The drawings. Everything I found. Everything I've ever heard about Coral/Cindy. My mother. Real. My father. Real. M. Real. It is not just a story I read somewhere, half-formed glimpses allowed by my grandparents, by a series of crumpled notes found in innumerable places across our property, our house, in the cabins and on the grounds here. Lupine Valley. The terrible knowledge isn't just inside me anymore. It's out here, too. With me. With *him*. "Th-things were not going well between them when I was here." We both look at each other cautiously.

"Between—" My voice catches for a moment, then I harden my heart. "Between my mom and my dad."

Max nods. He is stroking and worrying something in his hand. Something small and square.

"What is that?" I demand. "Give me that." I point at his hand, which had been mindlessly running over the object. He looks down, seeming to recognize it's there for the first time. He tosses it to my feet, terrified, unthinking. I carefully, anxiously retrieve it, never taking my eyes off him.

It's the folded-up print of *Animus*. The little package I left him by the lake. I swallow, shivering in gratitude that I was able to recover this part of tonight's breadcrumb trail.

"This is a prank. This, this can't be—" he says again, returns to this safer idea. He places his face in his hands. "There's no *way*." He looks up at me searchingly. "You don't even *look* like her!" He's irate.

"I know," I say. "I've seen pictures. I look like my Gram. Cindy's mom."

He looks like a dying man. "So tell me," he finally says. "Tell me how, how…any of this could be t-true." He turns his far-away eyes on me. Then he turns to look up into the branches of the birch above him, strangled in goldenrod. My mother's signature color.

"It wasn't very hard to find you, Max. It wasn't hard to put it all together. And now, it's finally time to face what you did. To face the only person left to hold you accountable. Me."

Twelve

Ascension

Max

It's not even really thinking anymore, what I'm doing. It's all sensation. I feel hot. I feel cold. I feel poisonous nausea in my gut and throat. My body feels useless, outside and in. I'm out of control of it. I'm out-of-control. Audra has placed a bottle of gin beside me and is commanding me to drink. She points her gun at me. So I drink.

Audra is standing. She is the only firm thing in the whole world. She looks intractable. A pillar of stone. Yellow. So yellow and bright, blinding. And the gun.

Coral Dunn. Jesus Christ. Coral *Dunn*. She's been coming back for me these last few days. A phantom. Fully realized. Troubled. Sad. A new mother. The baby. *Her* baby. *Evie?* Could it be Audra? I try to do the arithmetic of it, but it's really hard. I can't.

"Tell me what you remember about my mother. Tell me what you remember about Coral."

I lift my eyes from the spot on the ground I'd been absent-mindedly focused on. I look at Audra. "I can't," I breathe. "Please—I can't."

"You can, and you fucking will," she barks at me. I think I see Coral off in the distance, an expanse between us.

White snow.

Red mittens.

Dark-yellow scarf with black tassels.

I cry out like I've been stung by a wasp. I look down at the scarf around my neck. Dijon with black tassels. I rip it from my body and throw it to the ground like it's a boa constrictor.

Her throat. My throat.

Audra's looking at me with a burning hatred I have never before seen in my life from anyone. She doesn't like that I've thrown her scarf on the ground. Her *mother's* scarf.

"Are you going to kill me?" I croak.

"That's really going to be up to you," she says through gritted teeth. I look at her. She's so crisp compared to me. I am a bleary mass puddled on the earth. On all fours. A beast. But she is all architecture and geometry and surety. I can't beat her. I won't beat her. She'll end me with what she knows anyway. What I now know that she knows. I swallow—I feel so dry and thirsty. I'm shivering.

Her paintings swell into my mind. The ones that sit up in her garage studio. The ones she showed me earlier. The thick, deep strokes of umber and myrtle, or mustard, raspberry; the undulations of erotic and macabre landscapes born from simple objects, unreal, too real. The painting I destroyed. Obliterated. They come to me, and I don't know why. They fill me, fill me, fill me up. Why? Why are they in me?

Then it hits me.

Because Coral is in them.

Little bits of Coral. The small scraps of paper with the near-illegible handwriting. The little drawings. Those "found" objects painted and pasted and weaved on and under and through the brush strokes. Coral. Little slivers of Coral, come back to destroy me. She would write and draw some of them when she was with me in my cabin at Lupine Valley. These cryptic little scraps of paper. She used to hide them. She used to post them. Everywhere.

I've reached the center of the storm, ground zero. Coral's clearing. Here we are.

I realize the house I've been sleeping in, eating in, lusting in is the Dunn house.

The drawing of the upside-down raven in the living room, the one Audra said wasn't one of hers. It's a Coral Dunn. Of course.

My hands grip my face. I can feel her—Audra, Coral, both of them, somehow—looking at me.

"Coral D-Dunn," I croak, feeling wretched, "was just a girl when I knew her. Young. Nineteen, twenty, something like that. Blond hair." My eyes are zoned out on a spot on the ground again. I can't look up at Audra. I can't. I won't. I won't look at the dove. The golden bird at her throat. That necklace. Coral's necklace. Of course it is. "Down to her rib cage. Straight. Like silk. These oversize eyes. Blue gray. Slight and wiry but strong. Shorter than you." I can feel Audra's eyes penetrate me. "She was from the area. Born and raised. A sad thing, really. She—she tried really hard not to be sad. But it was in her. *It was in her.* Part of what made her."

"Not that you tried to help," Audra spits. "You destroyed her."

"Oh, no—I did try to help. I helped in my own way," I look up at Audra finally. "I helped in the only way I knew how."

"You giant piece of shit." She shakes her head, dark amusement in her growl. "Tried to help? You convinced her to go off her meds. You told her self-harm made her beautiful. You didn't tell anyone how bad she was getting. *You*." Barbs skewering me, one, two, three.

"No—no." I shake my head, adamant, old frustration burbling up into something akin to confidence. Righteousness. "They didn't understand, and you don't either." My face feels tense as stone. I can hear the bite in my voice. "I mentored her. In her interests. In her art. I let her be *exactly* who and what she wanted to be. She became a better artist with me. With my help. And through her *I* became a better artist. And we both understood that—"

"You encouraged her to destroy herself. So you could wring her dry." Audra is cold and hard as granite. She wants to do something terrible to me, I can feel it. But she doesn't let herself. Why, I don't know. She holds back, at least for now. But I can feel the violence in her. I can feel the urge to kill. To end me.

I thought I'd made it far away from all of this. From this place. From that time. From what we did, together. That's the thing Audra will never truly understand. That what happened to Coral, it wasn't just me. I didn't do anything *to* her. Not really. And I never truly forgot what we did. What my part was in it. In our art. In her end. Coral helped me become me. Max Durant. It springboarded my ascension in the art world. *Animus*. It was a metamorphosis for both of us. She knew that—Coral knew that. But I've led an expansive, interesting, big life since then. A life much bigger than the decision of some dumb kids more than twenty-five years ago.

I thought it could never catch me. That it would never catch me. That I had grown superior to it. But here I am. In King City. Under the very same boulder and birch where Coral's life ended and mine began. With Audra, the daughter. What a world.

Audra adjusts her gloves on her wrists with a primness that makes me queasy.

"I've lived here with my grandparents, without a mother or a father, my whole life," she says, lifting her eyes from her hands. "I was pretty aimless for a long time. Eventually I started taking classes down at UMaine, commuting both ways each day. Art classes, a gen ed or two. But at least I was painting. I had a gift early on, and Pops and Gram were so supportive because of what happened to my mom. They had told me she got pregnant with me, never got to live out her dream of going to college. Studying art. Becoming an artist. But I had a hard time fully committing for some reason." Audra is shivering, just the littlest bit, gun still at the ready. "Maybe I was afraid that they wanted me to be the new Cindy. They spoke of her lovingly, effusively. They spoke of her mental health issues, yes, but also her brilliance. Her skill. Her talent. Her incandescent energy at times. I worried that they wanted me to become everything she never got to be. It was a lot. But then they died. I was very sad for a very long time, Max."

She pauses now and glares at me. My whole body is trembling. "You would have loved to see me then, you sick bastard. Some of the worst months of my life. Here, alone. Mourning. You would've said I'd achieved my highest form. And then you would have gotten a goddamned easel out," she spits. Her ferocity surprises me. Her accuracy, a laser. "Take another drink, Max." It feels like my insides are full of bile and fire and shit.

"I can't."

"There are so many, many places I could hide your body on this property, Max. Drink." I swallow and grip the gin bottle with my hand and take a big swig. I immediately vomit. Hard, and heaving, and sickly. "Good boy." I am sweaty and wrenched. My stomach cramps. I swallow and shut my eyes momentarily, moaning.

"After my grandparents died, eventually I started going through the house." She holds the gun on me in those gloved hands. Her form looks warm and radiating like she was sent down from another place entirely. Or up. From hell. For me. Her face is unclear to me now. Just a mangled smear. I wish so much that I could see her clearly. Remember her exactly. The things I could do with her rage, with this explosion of feeling. The catastrophe in the lines of her face. "And I found a lot of things I didn't know about—all these notes—they were these startling little diaristic things. They intimated so much. About her mental state. About my father. Coral wanting to go to school. Her dreams, her nightmares. The Lupine Valley Arts Collective." She looks at me hard, now. My anxiety skyrockets. "The devil in King City." I feel cut wide open.

"So I started assembling a timeline. She religiously initialed and dated everything. Every scrap of paper." She shakes her head. "I'd never had anything but pictures of her, a few short home video clips. My grandparents' stories. That's it. I had no idea what she was really like. This was different. Her own account of her own life in her own words." Audra's auburn hair lifts and flutters in the breeze. "I found out so many things. Disturbing things. She was clearly bright. Clearly smart. Had ambition, wanted to be an artist. But I knew that much already. I already knew, even, that she struggled with bouts of depression, bouts of mania throughout her life. My grandparents had told me about that. They told me that after I was born, she got postpartum depression. Except—that's not quite right, is it, Max?" She smiles at me, but it's more like a wolf baring its teeth. "She didn't have postpartum depression. She was suffering abuse. By you."

"Audra—"

"Shut up!" she screams, gripping the gun tighter. Her chest rises and falls like a bellows. She doesn't understand. She *still* doesn't understand. "Eveline Audra Bouchard," she whispers. "It's the name I was born into. But then my dad split, and you killed my mom." I start to shake my head, but her ferocious eyes silence me. "So, my grandparents, my legal guardians, changed my surname legally to theirs—Dunn. Eveline Audra Dunn. EAD. That's who I was for so long. Until just a few years ago, really. Until the notes and the drawings I found. Until they led me to *you*." We are looking at each other, but I am not really seeing her. It's hard to apprehend anything—the words she is speaking, the form she makes in my field of vision.

"It was easy to find you. Max Durant of South Bend, Indiana. Born April third, 1968. Your dad, a former custodian at the University of Notre Dame. Your mom a career secretary in the History Department." My heart plummets. I can't breathe. I can't quite make out her expression; she is all streaked and blurry. I cannot fathom how my face must look. Dumbfounded. "And their son, Max Durant, acclaimed artist at the institute in Boston. Not very subtle, Max, not even trying to hide.

"And then I knew what I had to do," she whispers. "I changed my name legally to Audra Colfax—Gram's maiden name. I applied to the institute under that name. All I had to do was ask politely that my recommendation letter writers respect my change of name, so they would refer to me as Audra Colfax in their letters. I told them something about family troubles. They didn't press me. Same thing with all the other paperwork. I got new everything, legally: change of name, new social security card, new ID, all of it. And here we are. I think it's better this way. I was never a Bouchard. And Dunn has a lot of baggage." I can feel the tension of every muscle in her body radiating at me. "She was, at times, deeply troubled, my mother. But she had always figured out a way to manage. Until you. You killed her."

"I didn't kill her!" I shout, furious.

I did, didn't I?

I did it. It was me.

But it wasn't just me.

"You don't understand," I breathe, scrambling.

"I think I understand very well, *M*," she growls.

"B-but there—you have to—" I'm almost hyperventilating.
"There was another M!" She laughs at this, unbelieving.

"Another M?" Her voice drips with skepticism. She's mocking me.

"Yes," I breathe. "Yes. It wasn't just me! I—I wasn't even the worst of us! There was a third person. A man. Another M." I heave, trying to explain. "Mantis. Mantis, we called him!"

"Mantis?" she asks as if the name sounds made up to her. She's pausing. Waiting to hear more. She's going to let me tell her more. So I dive in, headfirst. Into the deep end.

"There was a group of us here. We were friends. The painters group. Y-your mom and this other local, Mantis, were like honorary members. We all palled around. But Mantis was—was a difficult guy. Had a mean streak. One night, we were down here—just the three of us. Mantis was plastered." I swallow, my breath struggling to keep up with my words. "I was high. Really, really high. Your mom was, I think, just depressed. About not getting to go to school because of—" I pull up. I gesture timidly at Audra. At Eveline. A hard silence grows between us. I continue before she pulls the fucking trigger, done with me.

"So we got to talking—and talking and talking—and in this sort of, um, vulnerable, weird state, we said some things. Some things we had been holding deep, deep down inside." My voice is trembling and scratchy. I can remember my words from that night, my confessional—so desperate, so full of pathetic *want*. Craving greatness. Even now I remember the acute feeling I had—that it was just beyond reach. God—the things I promised to do to stop the unquenchable *yearning*. I sip the gin, sick but parched. Ashamed. "Your mom confessed that she planned to take her own life once—once you were, um, born. She wanted to be done." I can hear her start to growl. "That's what she told us, okay? That is honest-to-god what she said," I emphasize, heart thudding. "And this guy—the other M, okay? The *other* M—he confessed that his girlfriend's death, which had happened when they were both still in high school, had not been an accident. He'd shot her while out hunting. She was wearing white gloves, he took her for a deer, he said. He was convicted of manslaughter. Not murder. Everyone always had their doubts around here, I guess. But he was a *murderer*. He had *planned* it. Because this Ashley had slept with his brother, and he was mad. And this stupid fuck *told* us this!" Recounting it now, I can still barely believe it. It had been a shocking thing to hear. Terrifying, really.

"Ashley..." Audra murmurs thoughtfully. "Ashley Pelletier?" Something close to joy erupts in my chest. I can hardly believe it.

"Yes! Yes! Ashley Pelletier! That was it! So, you've, uh, you've heard of the case!" Relief washes through me. She's going to understand. "Right, so—we all said this stuff. And it's—it's the kind of thing where as soon as it's out there, in the open, you know you've entered into something serious. Like a covenant. To never say a word. About any of it. But unlike me, and unlike Mantis, Coral just could not keep her mouth shut," I say, immediately regretting my phrasing. "I mean—" I hold up my hands, trying to show I understand my mistake. "She just, she had a hard time keeping it in. What she knew about Ashley burned in her. She was a good person, your mom." I let this hang in the air between us. "So once it was clear Coral was too...unpredictable to keep something like that a secret, Mantis wanted to make sure she was gone." Audra's face is serious. She's listening. I've really got her attention. "So he threatened her. Hovered. Reminded her she needed to stay quiet. Hurt her, even. And she hurt herself, too. It's important for you to understand that. But *he* actually laid his hands on her. I never did. Do you understand? I never hurt your mother."

"Oh my god," Audra says, lowering her gun thoughtlessly as she listens. I nod and nod, seizing on any glimpse of daylight.

"He wanted to make her feel trapped here. So he hurt her, and he encouraged her to hurt herself. He made her feel like there really was no way out. That the only way out was...the ultimate way out. It was his plan, it was *him*.

"So Mantis and I both had vested interests, sure." I nod vigorously, feeling like it's important to be honest now. Completely honest. "But Coral saw herself in my work. She really *saw* herself. And I knew, even as it was happening, that what she was giving would become my breakthrough. But I really did see it as a way of helping her." Coral and I spoke of it many times, in whispers, next to the potbellied stove in Focus. I pull my coat around me tighter. "I promised I would immortalize her forever. Capture her in her varied, difficult perfection. I just wanted to help her. Send her off on her terms. Follow through on a promise we made to each other." I swallow, looking at Audra, trying to parse the smear in my vision she has become. "Then I painted it. She wanted me to." We are silent together for a moment, Audra and I, steeped in the blackness of the night.

"I am not the villain, here," I say gently. "*Mantis* is. You've got the wrong man. The wrong M." I laugh nervously, erratically. I hear

Audra laugh gently, too, and I feel like I'm finally getting through. It's like she's breaking from a fever. I exhale hard, relief creeping in.

"Max, Max, Max," she sighs. She steps closer, to console me. To end this nightmare. "Oh, Max, I know all about Mantis." She sounds sorry for me. She raises the gun and points it squarely at my head once more.

My mouth falls open. I don't know what to say.

This one final pocket of oxygen left to me evaporates. I feel like I can't breathe. She knows. She *knows*.

"The old Lupine Valley cook is close," she tells me, a small smile curling onto her lips. "The washed-up, high school football star—your pal—is near. I've kept in touch—the old-fashioned way. Letters. Postmarked from Boston." I swallow, feeling absolutely destroyed. More miserable than I ever have in my whole life. "Gee—I wonder if he thinks they're from you?"

"What have you done?" I whisper, tears brimming. She just smiles at me.

"Don't worry. He's next."

It feels like I've left my body.

Audra—the greatest demon, the queen. How could I have been so oblivious? So ignorant? How could Audra yet again be *better* than me? Even in this?

"You've had to lean on so many other people as a crutch—they've given you what little true art you've ever conjured. Misha. Coral. Chess. Oh, yes, I know all about Francesca. Second-years just *love* to gossip. And there are others. So many others. That's why your paintings have come out half decent over the years—because your subjects are worthwhile. Not your paintings themselves, you twat. They transcend you. They transcend you and your lack of vision and talent. Not the other way around." Her voice is a smug growl. She is the devil incarnate. The devil. *"You need them—they don't need you,"* she sneers.

Juniper on her cruelest night springs to mind. *You need her. She doesn't need you.*

"My mom made your career. That painting of her—*Animus.* Coral Dunn made you!"

It's like they sent Audra. My string of discarded lovers, Misha, Chess, these various broken toys—they flash through my mind; demons, all.

You had it right back in her studio, Max, old boy. Should have cut your own throat while you had the chance.

The startling voice comes from somewhere deep inside of me.

"I have something to offer you, Max." Audra's voice is like honey now. My eyes, which must be red as the devil, look right into her crystal-clear sepia ones, the ones I must blink and squint at to see. They look back into me, into everything. "In one form or another, the *you* that you have been will pass away from this earth tonight, Max. That much is certain. Max Durant as you know him now will not live to see morning. There is no getting away from this. Not this time. I've come for you."

I'm crying; I can't believe it. It is brilliant, toxic, the only thing I have left.

Audra tips her head to the side, her voice one of mercy.

"Now, this can happen in one of two ways. Are you listening?" She holds her finger up to me, wanting to make sure she has my attention. I nod, numb. "I can make it look like you attacked me. Drunk, jealous, ravenous, raving. And then I will hurt you. Not enough to kill you. No." I can hear the smirk in her voice. That smile of hers. The one I love. The one I want to destroy. "That would be no fun. Just enough to hurt you badly. And then the real fireworks would begin. I will tell everyone about the way you acted up in my studio. *I took pictures, Max, you fucking idiot.*" She laughs right at me. "I will tell them how you attacked me. Threatened me. Because of what I know. Because of what I found out." The meanness in her is intractable. "And I will tell them about every affair with every student you think is a secret. You think they don't talk, Max? A lot of them do. I've gotten them to talk to me. Bon-Hwa. Lin. Julia."

The face of each woman comes to me, a ghost. I was not a very nice man to any of them, in the end. Lin in particular could get me into big trouble. I grabbed her by her forearms a couple years ago during an argument. Hard. She took pictures of the bruises I left. She threatened me with them if I didn't leave her alone—and if I didn't write her a glowing letter of recommendation for a PhD program. We came to an understanding. Julia, I abandoned in New York City after an argument one night. She had to find her own way back to Boston. Bon-Hwa, I coerced into having an abortion.

I sit heavily against the trunk of the birch. Eviscerated.

"Most importantly, I will make sure the news about Coral gets out. I will make sure the connection between you and Coral's death gets out. I have proof. You will lose everything. Your reputation. Your career. Your job at the institute. You will lose what esteem you have. Your minor fame. The painting that launched your career, degraded. Everything that you have built, everything that you have made of yourself, everything that you think that you are—gone. You will have no legacy. The institute will scrub themselves of you. As will so many other galleries and schools you've touched in the past. You may even go to prison." Audra sighs. "A girl can dream." Tears continue to leak from my eyes. "I will connect the dots for them. In any case, no one will remember your name in five years."

She is destroying me. Turning me to ashes. My life. My career. The decades I've spent building my reputation.

She's right. It would all be gone.

There would be no coming back from that. Knowing everything that she knows, the connections she's made. And Mantis apparently won't survive her, either. There would be no one else to blame. They would believe her. I can't imagine it would be that hard to prove it, or most of it, at least. Where I was in early 1989. The fact that I crossed paths with Coral Dunn. The fact that Coral Dunn died and I left town shortly thereafter. And if these notes—like the notes I saw pinned in this forest…like the notes that are worked into her thesis pieces up at the house…if there are more of those, explicit—it would all be over.

"Or. Or, Max." Her voice is gentle as lavender. I look up at her. "You can concede defeat once and for all; save your legacy, and kill *yourself.*"

The offer, the option, the fact that it is coming from her stuns me. Punches me in the gut.

"Waving the white flag tonight would allow you to keep your good name intact. That would be the deal, Max, don't you see? An eye for an eye. Your life for Coral's. I'm not interested in much beyond that. Take your own life, and live on, through your work, forever." She lets this settle in the silence between us. "Refuse, and live in shame as an outcast—career, reputation, relationships, and body dismantled—for the rest of your life."

I think of my paintings hanging in various galleries and homes around the world. I think of how many might be taken down if the truth got out. How many would be shelved, stored, become dust collectors. I think of my glittering biographies taken down. Or worse, amended to inflect that my genius came with a large and irrevocable caveat. That my *genius* was really no genius at all; without my subjects, I am nothing.

She takes a step or two forward, bends down slightly, and looks me in the eyes. I can see her now, perfectly. We look at each other. And then her eyes flick up into the boughs of the birch. I look up with her. Accusing goldenrod ribbons billow in the breeze, soft, like dancers. Like crime scene tape. I close my eyes. I press the heel of my hand into my right eye socket, into the place where a seismic headache rocks me. I feel cracked wide open.

I told Coral so many things. How beautiful she was in winter light. How her tears made tracks on her face and inspired me. How her heaving sobs showed she was human in the highest order. That pain was good. Was beautiful. Beauty itself. That she couldn't be an artist without letting her true self out. That I could capture her in it. I could capture her in her radiant, golden glow, the one that ultimately consumed her. And wouldn't that be something? In the end?

He just returned one day, and Coral and I both understood. It was time. I stayed quiet as he returned from his exile. As he explained it to her. This was what she and I had been working toward the whole time anyway, even if we didn't know it.

We went down to this clearing with this boulder and this birch. Together. He told her what she had to do. And I didn't say anything.

I gave her comfort. Mantis told her to jump.

After, Mantis and I parted ways forever. He got to keep the truth about Ashley quiet, and I got the materials that would launch my career. We watched Coral go, and I gave her everlasting life. Through me. My work. My vision. Through *Animus*. We did that. Together.

I am crying so very, very hard now.

The soft scarf with the black tassels. The brown enamel lantern. The golden dove necklace. The raven, hung upside down.

Evie.

"Coral knew the truth of it," I say. Audra takes a few steps back from me as I ease and clutch the birch in my effort to gain my feet. "I made her beautiful."

"You made her dead, Max. Nothing more." Audra is holding a rope with a looped end out to me. Like a plaything. The foothold to a tree house.

I shut my eyes tight.

Just like before, a hand is taken to help someone onto the boulder. I hold the rope. I listen to her instruction.

"You would really tell them everything if I—if I didn't…?" The earth looks so far away from up on the boulder. My shaking hands slip the noose around my neck because I already know the answer. The fluttering strands of goldenrod in the boughs of the old birch lick my face, my shoulders. Audra smiles her crooked smile. She takes one hand from her gun and fishes something out from somewhere inside her dress—a pocket, a seam, I don't know. She looks at the small square of paper she now holds for a moment and then approaches me carefully, extending her arm up so that I can see it. It's a photograph. Of me. Of Coral. Neither of us is looking. I'm holding the door to my cabin open wearing a long shirt and paint-splattered workman's pants. Barefoot. Shaggy hair, big beard. I'm holding a cigarette. Coral is climbing the steps to join me inside. It's winter. So much white. And then her black coat. And then her red mittens. Blue cap. Her deep-yellow scarf with the black tassels. The one here in this clearing with us. It is undoubtedly her. It is undoubtedly me.

"An original Rowan Augustus McCue, this one. He gave it to

my grandparents at her funeral. Wanted them to have a picture of Coral with her friend from Lupine Valley." *Old Gus. Taking those goddamned photos when you knew it and when you didn't.* She pulls her arm away from me, steps back. Puts the photo away. Regrips the gun. "So, yeah, I'd tell. In a heartbeat, Max. Have no doubt. If you don't take care of this problem yourself, I will."

I can't allow it. I won't allow it. The disgrace.

I'm scared. Terrified. But I think she is telling me the truth.

It's a heavy necklace around my throat.

Audra's pendant winks up at me. She is radiant. Like her mother.

THIS IS CORAL, ISN'T IT, MOSS?

I jump from the boulder.

Audra

I thought it would take a lot more coaxing. More shaming. More threatening of his legacy. More proof, even. Easy enough to provide, but still. More dragging him through his own historical mud. Turns out all he needed was a steadying hand.

I've been standing here for ten minutes. The birch creaks in the cold breeze. It sounds belligerently loud in the horrible silence. Max doesn't flinch. I look at my watch. 2:16 a.m. I take Max's knife, which I secreted away from him down at the lake, and toss it onto the ground beneath him, blade open. *Snick.* I look at the knife, at the lantern. The bottle of gin. A desperate man making his way to a dying spot.

"Evie." The voice rises up from the darkness of the forest. I close my eyes and let my body drink it in: the voice, my name.

I turn and see Lance emerge from the darkness of the woods,

right on time. He pulls the black ski mask from his head, his brown hair squashed and messy as it frees itself. His cheeks are flushed with chill and exertion. He looks at me with tenderness, with concern, shotgun broken over his arm.

"Hi, my love," I say, voice steadier than I expected. I see that the duffel bag slung over his shoulder looks full. As he breaks into the light, the angle of his entrance finally allows him a vantage to Max, and he can't help but look up into the tree.

"Did you get everything?" I ask, my voice hoarse, hoping to distract him from the sight. His mouth falls open, eyes still glued to the body in the tree. I grasp his chin and guide his gaze to meet mine.

"Don't look, please. Don't look." I shake my head, feeling queasy, feeling a little light-headed. We lock eyes. I swallow. "It's not for you. It's not yours to take on." I stroke his cheek with my gloved thumb. He takes a shaky breath, refocuses. He squeezes his eyes shut for a few long moments, and so do I, resting my forehead against his. "It's done," I whisper. "It's okay. I'm okay." He nods his head against mine. We ease apart.

"I—I got the notes, the drawings, all of it." He nods, steam puffing from his mouth. "I turned off the lights on the trail." I can see it's taking everything in him to follow my request not to look up into the branches. Morbid curiosity. He unzips the bag and hands me a coat. I put it on immediately. "You're shaking. Are you doing alright?" Lance places his gloved hand on my shoulder.

"Fine." I feel numb. Lance looks concerned and pale. "Let's finish."

I make him stand facing away from the tree, looking out into the forest while I scale the familiar boughs and branches of the birch like a trained cat burglar, going from limb to limb, pulling down every singular piece of yellow fabric in the same way I put them up a few days ago. These flowing invocations of my mother. Of Coral. I ball the goldenrod jersey streamers up and throw them to Lance so he can bag them. I am careful, steady, fast, and soon I am on the ground again.

I look over at Lance waiting for me to come to his side then remember the folded piece of paper I took from Max earlier. I take the square of paper from my bra and unfold it. The painting that started all of this, a dreadful smear of amber, goldenrod, Tuscan yellows. The painting Max used my mother to make.

Animus. Max Durant. 1993.

I swallow and crumple the paper in my hand, using every fiber of self-control to hold wracking sobs at bay. Lance's strong back is to me. I can tell he's on edge. That he wants to come to me. I look up at Max, and a tear spills onto my cheek. I wipe it quickly away, take a breath, and approach Lance. I stand in front of him and show him the page.

"Burn that with the rest?" I ask. Lance nods, shoves it in his bag.

I survey the scene around us and look at Max the way he is. I know it may take a lifetime to scrub the image from my mind. I look to sweet Lance and hope he can rid it, too, after all this, and fast. I go around and turn off all the lights affixed to the trees in the clearing but one. The one on the birch. The one on the birch is the light that's always been part of the alternate trail that leads down to the lake, different from the one I took Max down on. I gaze up at the birch and at Max one last time.

Lance and I move through the forest together silently, sure-footed as foxes. We follow the permanent tree lights that exist every fifty yards until the tree line that leads into the heart of Lupine Valley. Lance's pickup is there.

"You ready?" Lance asks me. I look around the dark, abandoned commons and cabins.

"Ready," I say. We both climb into his truck. He drives me out of Lupine Valley and back around to the Moosehead Scenic Byway trailhead where I pick up my station wagon. Lance follows me on the pitch-black roads back to the main entrance to Lupine Valley. We amble up the dirt driveway until we reach the parking lot, where I leave the wagon with the keys inside. It looks so sad sitting there by itself as I get into the front seat of Lance's pickup once more before we drive back down the narrow, dark road.

The ride back to my house vacillates between tense silence and mantra-like repetition of the next steps of the plan. He drops me at the end of my driveway.

"See you after," I say. Our gloved hands find each other through the window and squeeze. We lock eyes, and I know something in mine must look like those of a drowning woman wishing desperately to be pulled from the deep end. But he can't help me past this point. The rest I must do on my own. His eyes are round pools of silent comfort. He squeezes my hand one last time then rolls up the window and backs out into the road. I watch his red taillights fade to nothingness, then I take the long, dark walk down the driveway in my mom's dress, holding my grandfather's gun.

When I get to the driveway pad up by the house, I see with great relief that Lance has done his duty; I see no yellow streamers up in the apple trees or down at the tree line. He stopped here before joining me at Lupine Valley like he was supposed to. In the coming hours, he will take all of that yellow fabric and burn it. He will throw my note from the lakeside in with it. He will box up and store Coral's notes and drawings from the trees for me. He will stow them and my hiking backpack with the thermoses in waterproof containers in the back of his large, wood shed. He will wait to hear from me.

I turn to face the dark, looming house.

Where I found so many of mom's notes and drawings. Messages from the dead.

I move through the blackness of the house into the kitchen. I take Max's phone from the pocket of my dress and put it up on the counter. I retrieve a glass from beside the sink that Max used earlier in the day and put it on the counter near his phone. I take off my gloves and grab a glass for myself, put it next to his. I splash some gin from my liquor cabinet in each one. Then, gloves back on, I dump them both in the kitchen sink and then place the glasses back down on the counter with the bottle of gin.

I go to my grandfather's desk a few rooms over, pull an old edition of e. e. cummings's complete works from the drawer, and remove a small, separate piece of paper that is pressed inside. I put the book back and return to the kitchen, placing the note near the tumblers. I lock the handgun and case away in the gun cabinet down the hall, and then I take my gloves off and climb the stairs to the second floor. Max's things are littered very organically about his room. Not too messy. Not too tidy. He didn't make his bed. Good. I go to my bedroom and quickly put mom's yellow dress away on a hanger in the back of my closet. Same with the gloves. I do my usual nighttime routine. I brush my teeth. I floss. I wash my face. I moisturize. I put on a pretty white slip. I climb into bed. It's 3:56 a.m. I toss and turn under the once-pristine covers to make it look slept in.

The house is silent. My room and the hallway outside are dark. It's been over an hour since Max hanged himself. I was smart enough to do some research on *his* computer in the lead-up to this, asking the internet how long it would take to die by hanging. I'd erased his search history each time I trespassed over the past year of course, lest he might see somehow what had been searched. But the police would look at his hard drive if they got any weird feelings about it at all. And there the keystrokes would be. My hard drive would have keystrokes about *autumn recipes* and *best gifts for a thesis advisor*. My computer would show that I was looking toward a celebration with my mentor. His computer would show he wasn't looking toward any sort of future.

I stay in bed as long as I can stomach it. It's so quiet. Too quiet. By myself, in the large, dark master bedroom. I have never wanted Lance by my side more. The night outside is deep, dusted with faint moonlight. I make it thirteen minutes. I press the home screen on my phone and see it's 4:09 a.m. My adrenaline and anxiety will let me wait no longer. I stare up into the ceiling, feeling electric, feeling sick.

It is important to go through all my planned playacting so it feels as real to me as possible. Method acting. I must do all of the steps. *The last several hours never happened. You and Max went on a hike on the Moosehead Scenic Byway, and then on to the lake this afternoon. Then you returned home and enjoyed dinner, and later, a final nightcap in the kitchen. You went to bed, too tired to stay up and continue drinking with Max, who was not ready for bed. Now you're waking up.*

I force a fake yawn and paw at the empty side of the bed, where Max likely assumed he would be by now. *I should check on things downstairs, make sure he turned off the lights and blew out candles before he went to bed in his room. Make sure he locked the door—I bet he went out for a smoke. That would be like him to go out for a smoke, drunk, and then not close or lock the door properly.* I make my face frown in consternation. It feels important to do this. To make it actual. I grab my phone from the side table and see it's 4:11. *I'd better go check so I can ease my mind and go back to sleep.*

I climb out of bed with a stretch and then go to the master bathroom, fill my little glass standing near the sink with water, and make myself drink half of it. I leave the little water glass next to the sink. Then I grab my robe from the back of the door and put it on, cinch it. I turn on the hall light when I get there so I can see, then pad down the hallway. Max's door is open. I peek inside and see that his bed is empty. *Still downstairs drinking? Lord help me.*

I turn on the light in the kitchen and find the two empty tumblers and the bottle on the counter. I see a small scrap of paper beside them. A note. A thrill of anxiety and fear tears through my body, and I momentarily pause in my progress. My heart is beating hard and fast. This is it. I feel terror for a moment. *This is the most important and most dangerous part, now. Go.*

What's done is done.

I force my legs to move again.

"Max?" I call in a shaky voice. "You there, Max? I thought you'd—you'd have gone to bed by now." I get no response as I approach the counter, the tumblers, and the note, kept pristine and fresh looking after all these years hidden inside the e. e. cummings volume.

Meet me in the place you showed me under the stars.

M

A romantic gesture perhaps, I lie to myself. *That would either be the lake…or the clearing with the boulder and the birch I showed him today.* I pretend that it worries me that he has left the house. That he has driven, on his own, all the way out to King City, possibly drunk. How could he have gotten there? I walk briskly over to the door leading out to the garage, flick on the light, and fling it open.

My Gram's old Toyota Tacoma is there. But my white Volvo wagon is gone.

He really went. He took my car.

I pretend to feel perturbed by this. Maybe even frightened. But perhaps it *is* a romantic gesture. At any rate, I have to go get him. His phone is on the counter, for god's sake. So I can't just call him and berate him to come home. I go upstairs and dress in an institute hoodie, jeans, socks, and sneakers. I grab my overcoat from the peg on the way out the door into the garage. I take out the old Tacoma and head toward King City.

My headlights flare into the white side of my Volvo, parked in the lot below the commons.

"Max'll get himself lost, even with the lights," I grumble to myself, aloud, trying for an ambiance of innocence in the air. I pick my way carefully across the short expanse of grass that leads to the lake path, the first guiding light already visible. *Just what does Max have in mind down there?* I feel sick at my own question, but I know I must ask it of myself. Emotion builds within me exponentially with every glowing beacon I approach and pass on my path.

One light. Deep breath.

Two lights. I stop without warning, feeling suddenly very alone.

Three lights.

Four.

Five. Tears well in my eyes, my breath ragged and steamy before me in the night.

Six lights.

Seven lights.

Eight.

The clearing.

The boulder.

The birch.

Max.

I scream, and I start to cry, and it all feels very real—even to me. I rush over to him, hesitating only for a moment as I approach, wanting to see that the knife is as it was, that there could be no tricks, no impossible loopholes. But the knife is exactly as I left it, though Max's body has turned about ninety degrees east. I swivel around to look at him, feeling ill. "Max!" He looks cold, like a side of beef. "Max!" I scream. "What—Wh-why? Max!"

I scream, real tears gushing out of my eyes, real sobs clenching and spasming my throat and chest. The realness is important. Whatever part of Max I'm mourning, it is helpful. My mother flashes to mind, her desperate, disturbed notes, her visceral, painful drawings of me, the baby she could not fathom, the baby she could not see, the baby she could not completely understand, and I cry harder. I can't tell anymore if it's fake or real, what I'm feeling. It feels pretty real.

What can I do?

I pull out my cell phone. I dial 911.

I say everything I should say. I sound exactly as I should sound.

Thirteen

Long Gone

Audra

The day is somber, the rain slashing down in a way that feels malicious, deliberate, the sky an angry, roiling sea of steel. Which is how Max would have wanted it, I'm sure. Dramatic. Across the street and down the block from where I'm parked, people are filing out of the Boston Basilica of Our Lady of Perpetual Help, hunched against the onslaught under umbrellas, dark coats, funeral programs. Same place Ted Kennedy had his funeral. Not bad.

I'm sitting in Gram's old Tacoma, watching everyone come out the same way I watched them all go in. I thought for a second about going in to Max's funeral when it was getting under way just over an hour ago. But I decided it wouldn't be for the best. Too much hubbub has arisen around me, around that weekend since his death. So I sat in my own kind of vigil, the rain thrumming the cab of my truck, the sound overpowering, unrelenting. I wept. I can admit that. It was a buildup of everything, I think. The stress.

The catharsis. Reliving my mother's own death so viscerally. And the fact is, I've spent the last few years of my life singularly fixated on him, getting close to him, springing this plan on him—him, him, him—so now his absence feels palpable. Strange. Impossible, somehow. Impossible that what I did could be done. Impossible that I was the one to do it. And now he's gone. Dead. And as his obituary reminded me, he was still a *talented man only at midcareer*.

He had more in him. I'm sure this is what President Dana Switzer spoke of in her eulogy. Max's dedication to his life's work, which was both his own art and the institute itself. There would have been indirect hints of the way he died, I'm sure—but only hints, would be my guess. I'm sure she never said the word *suicide*. She must have said things like *suffering, relief, trials, burden, burning too brightly, forgiveness, have mercy on his soul*, etc. All the usual phrases.

As soon as the news got out about what happened at Lupine Valley, it was clear to me that everyone had assumptions about why Max secretly traveled all the way to Maine to see me for a weekend, alone. Let them think what they want. I know the truth. I never let him touch me like that. I never let him kiss me. Over the past year, were there hugs he lingered in too long? Yes. Were there flirtatious comments or texts from time to time? Sure. I went along with it. I had to, to keep him close enough, to keep him within striking distance. But it went no further than that. I knew I had to keep the tease going if I had any chance of drawing him out of his comfort zone, if I had any chance at getting him to Maine. Max was known for having had affairs in the past, for being a little too friendly with students. Some of those stories—and new ones, too—came up again when he died. The *Boston Globe* has written a story about what happened, for Christ's sake. The *Bangor Daily News, Portland Press Herald*, too. In the first few pieces, as the details were still coming out, they mentioned these past indiscretions with a light touch, and they mentioned me in a separate breath and were fine with letting the readers draw their own conclusions.

Renowned art professor dies by suicide in Maine.

A Boston professor's trip to student's hometown ends in his tragic death.

I was honest with the police. I had to be. I had to stick as close to the truth as possible. They would find the veiled texts I sent in return to his not-so-veiled texts. Because of this, all the dirty laundry came out—or most of it, anyway. Max Durant, esteemed artist and professor at the Boston Institute for the Visual Arts, died by suicide while on a weekend away with a student he'd hoped might become a lover. Some conjectured he had ended his life over the guilt because other affairs from the past then came to light, brought forth by other lovers who now made it clear his predatory nature with students had been a pattern of behavior, not a one-off. I have received so many emails from friends and colleagues with an incredible variety of tones in the last two weeks. Some are furious with me, calling me a slut, a whore. Saying that Max only liked my work best because he wanted to fuck me or was fucking me. Those are the ones that hurt the most, actually. You can call me a whore, a slut, whatever—that's all meaningless. Because I know I was never with him that way. But a bad artist—that stings. Others have been more sympathetic, telling me that Max clearly had a history of seducing young women and that older, wiser people have fallen into such traps before. To take that part as a lesson. That set assured me that his death was not my fault. That I couldn't blame myself.

I didn't blame myself.

I made it clear to the other members of my thesis committee that I would need time to clear my head. A brief leave of absence.

That I would return when I felt ready. They were supportive of this. So I've been tucked away in Rockveil these last two weeks. Trying to forget that Max died where my mother died. That they both died in a place I'd loved; I'd seen it as magical before I knew the details of my mother's death. And it's a place she had seen as magical, too, before she and Moss and Mantis went there. The tree will go. I don't want to be reminded of what happened there any more than I need to be.

Some part of me felt bad for the small part of Max who could be kind, generous, funny when he wanted to be. I am not heartless. I wanted to punish him, but that doesn't mean I have no sense of humanity. If I felt nothing, I would be no better than Max.

I am better than Max.

The night he died, I let myself cry. For him. For Coral. For the way he destroyed her. For the way something she made destroyed him, ultimately. I even vomited. The cops hurried me into the powder room just in time. I puked until there was only yellow bile left. I was sweaty and clammy and sick and crying. I couldn't shake it.

They ended up taking me to the hospital. The one in Greenville. The one I was born in. The one Cindy was born in. At the hospital, they cleaned me up, assessed me, gave me Valium for my panic. At around nine a.m., the cops finally came in to take my official statement. I told them my truth. They asked me how Max "seemed" over his last few days. I told them that he seemed himself, for the most part. That he was a little preoccupied on the ride up, which was true. A little distracted or nervous. Flipping the knife open and closed, open and closed on the way to my house. They were inter-ested in the knife. Whose it was, where it came from. His, I told them. He—very uncharacteristically—bought it for himself when we stopped at the Dirigo Hill Trading Post. They jotted some notes down about that. They later checked that out and verified Max had indeed bought the knife himself. It made me glad Max had gotten bored and come into the trading post. When god closes a door...

I told them about our walk to the lake. I left out the part about getting him drunk and shoving him out into the lake in my rowboat. And the note at the shore, and Lance hunting him, shepherding him up to the clearing with the boulder and the birch. I left out Coral's words. Her drawings. I left out Coral entirely. I left out our talk in the clearing, the bargain we made. I told them that we talked and hung out in the kitchen for a while after our hike and dinner, and then at around one thirty, I went to bed. I woke up a couple hours later and found his note. Then I found him.

They came and talked to me out at the house a few more times over the next few days, but it was clearly a crossing-t's-and-dotting-i's type thing. They even kept the kitchen note for a day or two but eventually returned it to me. It was a suicide, plain and simple. I hadn't laid a finger on him, and everything about the circumstances of his death showed that. A washed-up, middle-aged artist who'd peaked many years ago and just couldn't take it. A man who manipulated and slept with his students. A man with a temper. I mentioned what happened in my studio. I showed them the pictures, which they studied with concern. They told me I was lucky that he hadn't turned his violence on me, that I should have called on them. I said I never imagined it would ever go this far, and that it had been scary and I hadn't known what to do. They'd patted my shoulder, expressed their condolences, said they were just so glad I was alright.

In the meantime, I've played my part well. Devastated. Shell-shocked. Keeping to myself up in Rockveil. But in a few days' time, I'll be reuniting with Lance, perhaps a little earlier than he'd expected. For another funeral. One I'll actually be able to attend. One I'm looking forward to attending. Lance's uncle Marcus Peters, my unwitting pen pal, died in a hunting accident recently. He was wearing white gloves way out in the woods and someone—god only knows who—mistook him for a deer.

But these things happen. I'm sure he'd tell you that himself, if he could. Sometimes you're the windshield, sometimes you're the bug.

It's getting cold in the cab of my pickup. I start the engine and smear the heavy rain away, turn up the heat. I look down the block and see there are no more mourners trickling out of the basilica. I pull out of my parking space and just start driving. I find myself drawn toward the institute and let myself glide slowly by, water skidding away from my tires as I look up into the big, plate-glass windows that face out onto St. James Avenue.

I keep on going, heading for Storrow Drive, then I-95 North. Traffic is thin as I pass Exit 286. By the time I cross the state line into New Hampshire, the rain is letting up. By the time I cross the Piscataqua River Bridge into Maine, the sun is out and shining.

Fourteen

Pleased to Meet You

Juniper

It's seven minutes past noon when I see the car finally pull into the driveway. I look through the curtains and watch her emerge from a not-very-new white Volvo, squinting into the bright winter day, sun hanging high and clear in the sky. I stay at the window, unable to move for a moment as she disappears from view around the front of the house to the door, carrying a laptop bag and a large portfolio. Any moment now, the bell will ring and I will have to face her. The last person to see my best friend alive. I will have to let her in. I close my eyes and take a deep breath and brace myself.

The bell rings loudly, and I move automatically to the door. When I get there, I open it and look at her through the outer glass. She's wearing a stylish, black wool coat, dark skinny jeans. Her auburn hair lights her face like a sunburst, like a lion's mane. She is beautiful. Her face is serious but not unfriendly. Since Max's passing, we have corresponded only via email or on the phone. I volunteered to take over as her thesis advisor. It only felt right. He was my oldest and best friend. She was his star student. And she has been through so much. What happened up in Maine—it was terrible. I cannot imagine how she must feel.

I push the glass door out toward her, a rush of frigid air sweeping into the house.

"Audra," I say, "come in."

"President Switzer, hi. Thanks for having me," she says, her eyes casting around my home. She's a good sport to have driven all the way from Rockveil, Maine, to my home in Providence, Rhode Island. But we thought it would be best to conduct her thesis defense in person. One-on-one—no full committee. The girl has been through a lot; I have been willing and happy to make such allowances.

"Call me Dana, please," I tell her, smiling in a way that I hope is warm. Welcoming.

We are quiet as she steps into the entryway and slides the shoes off her feet. The glass door falls shut behind her.

"I can take your coat," I offer. "There's a hook right here." I gesture at the wall to my left.

"Alright," she says and begins rearranging her things so she can slide it off. "Thank you." I hang her coat. She then hangs up a lovely, deep-yellow scarf with black tassels on the ends on top of the coat. It feels familiar to me, but I can't place it. I touch the fabric of the scarf slowly, as if moving under water, as it hangs from the hook. Audra studies me deeply, unflinchingly. I clear my throat and gather myself.

"It's a lovely piece," I tell her. She nods her thanks. "I have tea and coffee in here." I lead her into the sitting room attached to the kitchen. As we walk, I glance over my shoulder and see her looking around the space with the interest most students have in seeing a teacher's house, scanning for traces of a person above and outside of the one they are familiar with.

Audra sits on the couch before a coffee table set with crackers, cheese, cookies, a sliced pound cake, a pitcher of water, and two glasses. "Help yourself to this. Would you like coffee or tea?"

"Coffee, please. Just a splash of milk."

When I come back, Audra is eating a piece of the pound cake and has poured herself a glass of water. I set down her coffee and my tea. I take a seat in what my wife considers to be her easy chair, to the side of the couch.

"How are you doing?" I ask her, taking on the soothing purr of a therapist without meaning to. She shrugs and sighs; a deep sigh.

"Better. It's been a tough time. A weird time. It's a lot," she responds. "It's been about four months since everything happened, and sometimes it feels much longer than that. Other times, much shorter." She shakes her head. It takes her a moment to meet my eyes, but then she does. I don't see pain in her face. I was expecting to see pain.

"Of course. Of course, Audra." I nod.

"And I appreciate you being so…flexible. And understanding about my situation. About my wanting to finish up a bit early. I just need to be done, you know?"

"I can completely understand that. There was no reason to be a stickler under such—well, awful—circumstances. If you feel ready, you feel ready."

"I do." Confident.

We get down to it soon after, Audra using her laptop to refer to her opening remarks as she talks me through how her focus shifted over the course of her thesis experience.

"When I first started, I was working in these landscapes of the enlarged. Taking everyday items—but ones with significance to me—and blowing them up to a size that intensified their gravitas as well as their visible landscapes. The topography and emotion of things. An apple becomes an overwhelming erotic expression. A lantern becomes a harrowing stand-in for the passage of time. Etcetera." She takes a sip from her glass of water. "Meanwhile, there are these echoes—voices—within the objects themselves. Voices as objects; found objects." Up on the easel I've brought down from my own studio for her, she points to myriad layered scraps of paper hidden under layers of paint, scrawled words peeking out here, there, in a haunting, whispering way.

Deep within me, something sparks.

"Which creates this interesting texture and also a complicating intermedia component. So, I did a bunch of these. A bunch. But that was all before Max—Professor Durant—died." Her cheeks flush a little. "After that, I continued to fixate on the inanimate. In this case, the rope." From her portfolio, she pulls a dramatic painting in whites, beiges, brown, blacks, and oxbloods, the object itself difficult to discern until you let your eyes adjust to the darkness of the palette. There is, indeed, a rope buried in there. "The rope Max used to—the rope Max used," she settles on.

I feel alarm. Sadness. Sickness for my friend.

She goes on to show me iterations of this painting, one after the other, sometimes speaking, sometimes not. And as she goes along, something odd begins to happen. The rope is no longer a rope. The rope that was a rope is now Max. Somehow. A rope that evokes Max. A Max that evokes a rope. And then the rope that was a rope that became a Max becomes a Max hanging from a tree. It is, and it isn't. It invokes but does not solidify into something graspable.

It makes you conjure the terrible thing yourself. Fill in the blanks. *Look what you've done. Look what you made.*

I clasp my hands tightly to keep them from shaking. She keeps going.

"And then I had more. There was more in me." I want to tell her to stop. To please stop. No more. But I don't. I stay quiet. It is agony.

She starts to show me a new series. But a rope isn't the primary object this time. It's pair of white gloves in the first, and even the second, but elongated like wide-open plains. Then the white gloves that became plains becomes a deer, then becomes a woman, then becomes a man, a big man, then becomes some sort of insect, becomes a praying mantis.

For a long moment, all my senses evaporate to nothing. My heart pummels me from inside.

Audra has settled into her chair. She waits. Patiently. For questions. Further discussion. But I'm silent. Unable to create words. A smile cracks her face, the gap between her teeth on full display. I watch her reach into her jeans pocket and pull out a folded piece of newspaper. She tosses it at my feet. I swallow hard and slowly reach down and pick it up, afraid of what it might be. I unfold it, the thin paper shaking in my hands.

MARCUS ALVIN PETERS

1963–2018

Greenville—Marcus A. Peters, age 56, went to be with the Lord on October 28, 2018.

My stomach drops to my feet.

Mantis is dead?

Hot anguish and a confusing flood of relief overwhelm my every cell. My eyes skip through the paragraphs. *Lived in Greenville his whole life…high school football star…survived by his brother David Peters, sister-in-law Paige Peters, and nephew Lance Peters…passed in a tragic hunting accident…was wearing white gloves…the negligent hunter responsible for Marcus's death has yet to be apprehended. If you have any information, please call…*

I lift my eyes from the obituary.

Audra looks pleased.

"First Moss, now Mantis. Whewww," she whistles. My blood runs cold hearing the nicknames. Names that I haven't heard spoken aloud in decades. "Bad run for Lupine Valley alum, huh?" White-hot fear streaks through me. But so does recognition. Who else could it be but her?

The shock of it stiffens me. I forget to breathe.

I look at the curve of her cheek, the shape of her eyes, the outline of her nose.

Eveline.

And Coral. She's in there. Coral is in there.

Coral is in here—my home.

"I grieved your mom," I say, voice a broken croak. Audra nods, patronizing. "What happened to her was terrible—"

"What *did* happen to my mom?" she asks, her voice low, quiet. A challenge. I feel a subconscious animal fear prickle the length of my back. "I bet you know," she says now, crossing her arms in front of her. "You and Max were tight. Have been for decades. Since way back then. If that's the case, I'm sure you know what happened to my mom." We look at each other in silence. I swallow. My shaky hand reaches down for my water glass, nearly topples it. Then I manage to grasp it and take a few birdlike sips. Audra watches patiently.

"I—I didn't find out the whole truth until much later. I was the one who found her, you know. When they came back, and she wasn't with them—" My throat feels so tight. "I went and looked for her." Tears are crowding my eyes.

"Oh, I know, *Junie*." Her voice is controlled, so controlled. Like she's speaking to a panicking child. Junie. Jesus Christ. "I'm not saying you did anything too terribly wrong. But those other two?" She gives me a knowing look. "Probably got what was coming to them." A smile crinkles her face. I think of Ashley Pelletier. I think of the note Coral pinned to my door. My afternoon in the library, squinting at the microfiche. A baby strapped to my chest.

Eveline. Audra.

I press my fingers to my lips, sobs wanting to break inside of me.

"You've seen *Animus*." Her voice is gentler now. Almost sad. "I have, too. That's my mom. You must know that." I close my eyes. I know the painting well. The piece that launched Max. As soon as I saw it, as soon as he showed me, I knew. We didn't say it out loud, but I knew.

The door leading in from the garage bumps open, and we both jump. We look in the direction, on edge.

"It's alright. That's my wife," I tell her, clearing my throat, blinking my glassy eyes. I need to gather myself. "We're in here, Zeph," I call to her. She'll always be Zephyr to me. No longer has pink hair—it's gray now. But the nose stud remains. We found our way back to each other twenty years after we split. Together now for ten. We kept our promise.

"Sorry, sorry for the ruckus," she says sheepishly, wheeling around the corner, looking fresh and windblown. "I'm Zanibou. But I go by Zephyr most of the time." Audra looks surprised, almost starstruck. She plasters a warm enough smile on her face, gets to her feet and shakes hands with Zephyr.

"Audra. Pleased to meet you."

"Sorry to interrupt—I know you're in the middle of a thesis defense. Pretend like I'm not even here!" She smiles brightly, gives me a quick peck on the cheek, and then recedes upstairs with her phone and a shopping bag.

"Mom…left a metric ton of little notes behind." Audra swallows. "She mentions a Zephyr—your girlfriend." There is wonder in her voice.

"That's her," I say, a genuine smile coming to my face, some of the tension having been broken by Zephyr coming home, interrupting our rhythm. "She wrote those little poems all the time. Pinned them everywhere. All over the place." The intervening years have softened the edges of those memories, made the scary or mean or frantic ones less acute. I remember more of the playful ones. The ones she more often left for Moss. For Max. We sit in silence for a long moment. "So where do we go from here?" I breathe, my overwhelming sense of disorientation and shock returning to me.

"We graduate me. And we end the story here, today," she says. She is asking me to look the other way about what I know. Just as I did then. And she knows I will. Because no one ever really changes.

380

Epilogue

Happily Eveline After

Audra

I'm in the *Happily Eveline After* about seventy-five yards off Kress Beach on Moosehead Lake. The air is hot and breezy. It's July, and a more splendid Maine summer day has perhaps never before been seen. The sky is a faded lapis blue, the temperature is in the high seventies, the lake glints like sapphire. Motorboats and party boats speed and drift around the far side of the inlet, but over here it's just me in my rowboat. And I am happy. Happy and light. I'd been living with a crushing weight since I found out the complete truth about my mother, and it only went away after Max and Marc died.

What I still wonder about is how long Max and Marc watched. How long they stayed.

All I knew growing up was that she had hanged herself out on the Lupine Valley property. But then the notes appeared as I started renovating, as I started doing upkeep and landscaping and tree care on the land. Sometimes I found one-offs inside doorframes or pressed inside a book or under drawer liners, sometimes I found entire caches shoved into caboodles, plastic bags, walls, in little plastic sacks in the tree house wall, up in the gutters of our buildings in little plastic Easter eggs, or inside nooks and crannies of the snaking rock wall in our field. As I found more that talked about Lupine Valley, I explored there, too. And the more I searched, the more I found.

I wonder if my grandparents ever found any of them, and if they did, what they did with them. I wonder if Brady ever saw any of them or if she hid them so well, he never knew they existed. Brady Bouchard, the man who ran. He got married to a woman from Portland and gave full custody to my grandparents the year after Cindy died, leaving his father's timber business. He lives in Brunswick with that same woman now. I only know a few things about Brady: he owns his own car detailing place, he has two kids—half-siblings of mine, I suppose—he's a town councilman. But I don't really know him at all. He gave me up way back then, and I did the same. My grandparents just told me they were mine, and I was theirs, and that's all that mattered. They only told me about Brady later. I never cared to seek him out or meet him; he was too abstract for me. He never cared to seek me out and meet me. And that was that.

When I put enough of the notes together to figure out what, basically, had happened, it took me almost no time at all to find Max. The internet is wild like that. Max Durant. He was still an artist. He was still seeking approval and the spotlight. Everything I could cross-check, I cross-checked, and it all panned out. I made it my goal to get into the Boston Institute for the Visual Arts, where he taught, and I did. I crammed my final undergrad studies at UMaine, worked tirelessly to improve my craft, and applied. And it turned out I had the talent to get in. If I hadn't, I simply would have spent time in Boston and found ways to cross paths with him. He did enough public appearances. I would have made it work no matter what, but having the inside track made everything much easier. Word was he had a thing for students.

In the May BIVA email newsletter, the feature story was about Max. And about how President Jordana A. Switzer, PhD, had arranged for Max's painting *Architecture of Radiance* to be displayed in the Polk Room of the Boston Institute Gallery starting in the new academic year. As a tribute. The newsletter did not indicate if it would be in the Warhol spot or not. I remember just shaking my head, amazed and disappointed at Juniper's unending capacity for weakness where Max is concerned.

But now that it is all done, now that Max is dead, and Marc is dead, and Coral is avenged, my sleep is easy and peaceful. I hardly think about Max and Marc anymore.

I still have scores more of Mom's notes and drawings that were not used in my thesis. I got them back from Lance about two months after Max died, feeling it was safe to make the exchange by then. I think it's important to keep that stuff. I think it's important to remember some things. To remember what happened to my mother. To remember how one struggling woman tried so hard to get better. To remember how two men, one ambitious, one vengeful, abused her. To remember how I got here, and what I've done, even if the truth of her life and death exists only on these myriad disjointed, rough little scraps of paper.

Her Dark Things, though, might be displayed eventually. My mother might get her day in the sun after all. As for the rest of the notes and drawings, they are silent and buried far away in the basement, huddled under the forgotten ephemera of a woman long dead. But even so, they persist. The only remaining records of her agony, which I have no right to erase from this earth.

I look down at the knife in my hand, and I close it up as I sit under the glaring sun, skimming the weapon through the cold Moosehead water, the boat just drifting lazily and very slowly outward, farther. I should drop it in, let it go. Cast this last tangible part of Max off, this ill-fated thing that belonged to him, then passed to the police, then Juniper, now me. I look down at it, squeezing it tight and then draw my hand away from the water.

I can't do it. It's a good knife. Maybe the nicest knife I've ever owned. Max's beautiful souvenir. I put it in my jeans pocket.

I take the boat in and drag it up onto the beach. I make my way up the path toward the commons, following the subtle tracks only someone familiar with the land would know. I emerge from the woods and into the openness of the abandoned arts camp. I do a loop around the commons, and as I do, I hear a quiet hum then rumble—an engine growing louder, and I know someone must be coming up the road. It's a large, shiny, blue pickup truck. I hear Bob Dylan spilling out of the windows. I squint to see inside the glare-flaring windshield. Lance Peters gives me a smile and a wave from behind the wheel.

I wave and smile back, happy to see him smiling again. I've helped Lance mourn the loss of his uncle, with whom he'd always had a difficult and conflicted relationship. I've let him talk through with me countless times how the accident could have happened, who might have been out there, why in the world Uncle Marc would have been wearing those gloves. We also talk about how uncanny it is that his girlfriend back in the day had died the same way. Lance will whistle in exasperation and declare that there are more things in heaven and earth, etcetera, etcetera. And by the end of it we always settle on the simple fact that it could have been anyone. I hold his hands and look into his eyes, and I let him know: it could be anyone at all.

We've fallen back into things. Maybe even a proper relationship, you could say. We met in first grade, and there's been nothing for it ever since, in one way or another. We've been bumping into each other and catching up since I got back here last May. A lunch here, a movie there, sex in his truck here and there and there. Then one night several months before Max died, we went to Thelma's Landing, and we had some drinks, and some spigot inside me just opened to him. I ended up telling him what I had found out about my mom. I told him so much—almost everything. Everything about Max. And he didn't get scared away when I dropped into conversation that I wouldn't mind if Max Durant died.

He didn't bat an eye.

And when I expressed that I wouldn't mind doing it myself, he didn't flinch. And when I said I had a plan, he said how can I help. We were in love by then, and he would have done anything for me. And I for him. But beyond feeling an allegiance to me because of our relationship, I could see that he understood that I had been mortally wronged and that all this was, all I really planned to do, was to set it right.

"Hey, there, Evie." He smiles as he pushes the door of the truck closed behind him. Evie. *Evie.* Eveline. Audra was only a temporary, necessary measure. For Max. For the institute. I'm just Evie Dunn to Lance. Always have been. And he wants me to change my name back, officially. I probably will, despite the Dunn baggage. I created some of my own to carry. It's who I am. Audra Colfax served her purpose.

"Hey, there, Lance." I squint up at him.

"Thought you might want some muscle to start." He flexes for me in his old Greenville Lakers soccer tee. Still fits. Still fills it out quite nicely.

"Would I ever." We kiss, and he presses his hand tenderly to the side of my face.

We ride down to the clearing on his two ATVs with an ax, a chainsaw, a hatchet, some rope, some chain, and a few other things. We park at the edge of the clearing. We stand before the boulder. We stand before the birch. Lance puts his arm around my shoulders. We look at the birch in silence for a good long while. Maybe Lance thinks I'm praying. And in a way, he's right. I think about my strong, wiry, blond little mom. I think of her extraordinary, tenacious, unsettling talent. Her drawings. Her notes. Her small body in this tree draped in her favorite yellow dress. I think of suave, lithe, bespectacled Max. I think of his easy charisma in the classroom, the sparks of greatness in his paintings. I think of the rage and ego in him. I think of how desperately he wanted to be admired. I think of lumbering, brutish Marcus—cunning and calculating. A killer of women; one an "accident," one a "suicide." His smugness all these years as he tried to socialize with me through Lance. I think of everything these men— the Ms—have taken from me. I think of Max hanging in his smart peacoat. I think of Marcus bleeding out, face down in the dirt.

I leave Lance's gentle grasp and retrieve the ax from my ATV. I go to the birch and level a devastating hack into its papery-white side. I turn to look at Lance.

"It's time for it to come down. And I want all of the roots up. All of them," I tell him. I pull the ax from the tree. He nods and retrieves goggles, leather gloves, and the heavy-duty chain saw from his ATV. We are changing the history and the topography and the ecosystem of this land for the better. When he's most of the way through and the tree tips, Lance pulls the saw and backs up, shouting for me to keep clear. The birch crashes down through the branches and leaves of a few other trees, smashing into low bushes and brambles as it hits the earth with an enormous, muted smack. It falls downslope toward the lake, like an arrow.

We've been at it for about four hours, chopping and sawing off the limbs of the tree bit by bit, then chopping and sawing and stacking those into piles and bundles, then setting to cutting logs and discs from the trunk.

Lance leaves to grab food for us, and I pause in the still air, the earth moist and radiating humidity. I wipe my forehead with the back of my hand. I mindlessly pull Max's knife—my knife—from my pocket and flip it open and closed in one hand—*snick, snick.* I take a turn around the clearing, which seems so much bigger, so much brighter, so much lighter now. I look at the beautiful birch wood, a maddening proliferation. Now hundreds and hundreds of small, haunting birch trees. Mini gallows. I'm turning away from the black hole in the earth the tree once sat in when I see something. Something tucked into the space between the boulder and the freshly disturbed tangle of roots.

Snick, snick. Snick.

I turn back and squint, move myself closer to the hole. I get down on my hands and knees. There's a small, sturdy, clear-plastic box, red—like a child's jewelry box for a few bracelets or a collection of beads—pinging out of the blackness of the earth. The sudden red is a jolt, a cardinal flashing through trees, a fishing hook through the fingertip of a little girl.

Mom.

I stay looking at it for many good, long moments. I see that there is a folded piece of paper inside.

Jesus, Coral.

You are everywhere, Mom.

How many times have I found such a note of hers, folded and tucked, hidden in such a way over the past several years? All over the Dunn land? Inside my home? All over Lupine Valley? But it has been months since this has happened. It's almost too much to bear, to see her whispering at me from this earth, curling her finger at me to come closer. To look, one more time.

I shiver in the mid-July heat. I pull it loose. I find the clasp. It feels sealed permanently shut at first, but then it gives, the top lid flying back, falling over on its hinge. I look at the folded piece of paper inside and consider not opening it. I run my thumb over the paper again and again, dirtying it, stuck in some subterranean trauma rhythm, and in the other hand, *snick, snick.*

I open it up.

A cardinal shock, a flash of violence.

I only realize that the blade has sliced into my clenched fist when crimson dots the paper, my vision.

I'll tell Evie one day but Evie is so
small
of course Brady
is not her father
is not Evie's father Evie doesn't belong to him
is not of him
M
of course

Max Max Moss M Max Moss M
that devil in King City in that cabin
that devil put another devil in me
in that cabin in King City
made her a pretty little devil
too
the best thing he ever made
the best thing I ever made too even if she is
a
devil
like
him.

—March89. CD.

A Conversation with the Author

What inspired you to write *Dark Things I Adore?*

Wisps of ideas occur to me every now and again, but more often than not, I am led to a story by voice. A voice provides entry into a rhythm, into a way of noticing the world, then eventually into the things that happen around that perspective—which the voice ultimately filters and translates. The voice I started with in the very first iteration of this story ended up being an art student traveling to their professor's home on the Maine coast. This professor had a spouse who was an artist who needed rather grizzly inspiration for her works. And that's how it all began. Obviously, the trajectory of the story changed quite a lot from there, but at the heart of it remained art and this rather morbid question of what it might take for some to create it.

Some people need a regimented schedule to write (an hour a day, for example), while others are happy to write half of a novel in a single sitting. What does your writing process look like?

Oh, how I wish to be a regimented writer! There's something romantic about the idea to me, something very professional and noble. I have tried early alarms on cold, dark mornings; I have tried a promise of at least thirty minutes a day no matter what; I have tried sitting at a proper desk at which to *compose*. None of it is for me. Years of trial and error—and fighting my instincts—have shown me that I am and will only ever be what I refer to as a Tea Kettle Writer; I burble and heat and hum (thinking, ruminating, procrastinating), and then when it all boils to a sense of Must Write, I do just that—I write. On my couch. In my bed. Then I can go on day-long jags. But then there will be days and weeks (sometime months!) at a time where I don't write or only write fanfiction.

There are so many elements to this story—multiple perspectives, dual timelines, Coral's art, Audra's trap for Max. How did you keep them all straight? Is that something you mapped out before sitting down to write?

To this point in my writing life, I have never outlined or mapped anything out story- or plot-wise *before* starting. And I say this not as some sort of brag but only to point out the fact that I have little to no foresight about what I'm about to do when I start! And with *Dark Things I Adore*, things got more complicated with each draft. In early drafts, there was only one timeline, there were fewer POVs, and certain scenes existed in different places in the timeline. As things evolved and deepened in dimension and complexity, I found that I absolutely *had* to start taking notes on the fly. I took down notes in marble notebooks and Google Docs, drew diagrams on an easel-sized pad of drawing paper, and eventually created a spreadsheet *database* to keep it all straight! My next book, which is under way, will have some outlining because the core plot concept has started to solidify. The idea came before the voice this time!

Using Audra's thesis—and art in general—as a narrative thread is an interesting choice. How did you come up with it? Do you have a background in fine arts?

I'm a very middling visual artist, but I love art as a pure spectator and have *immense* respect for visual artists and what they can do. The painter Julie Beck is my current favorite. I think I was drawn to visual art in my storytelling in this book because there is something so physical, so tactile, so sensory about painting—the tools, the relationship of body to brush to paint to canvas, the magical-sounding color names—that it seemed to me a perfect medium to try to work with inside a novel. Everything about it feels very delicious and substantial and evocative. A fun challenge for a writer to do that ultimate thing: show, don't tell.

Audra rebels against the idea that she and Max are similar, though ultimately that proves to be true. When you started writing this book, is that how you imagined Audra's story would end?

No!

Juniper, a character who witnesses abuse but remains silent, is a fascinating example of moral ambiguity. How did you tackle writing a sympathetic but flawed character?

Ah, Juniper. Juniper has such an important function as a

character, of course—to be the reader's eyes and ears during a fraught and seminal time in the lives of a few of our main characters. I wanted Juniper to be able to convey what was happening without editorializing in a way that stunted the reader's relationship to the complexities of what was unfolding. Juniper is a portal. The reader gets to decide what to make of what they see through her. But as a *person*, Juniper, for me, feels almost painfully human, painfully familiar. For me, Juniper represents a kind of ongoing, internal Kitty Genovese phenomenon—the bystander effect. And it lasts the whole length of the book. Juniper reminds us that even when we're by and large "good" people, it's easy—scary easy—to watch suffering of various kinds and assume the problem is beyond us to solve. Or it's not our place, not our business. That the bad-vibes prickle up our spines is a misfire, that we're imagining trouble where there isn't any. Or that rocking the boat might lose us friends. Juniper is that sore spot of regret and frailty we all have from time to time, in big ways and in small ways, when we say to ourselves: *I should have said something. I should have done something.* But we didn't.

What draws you to dark, psychological stories as a writer? As a reader?

I've always been interested in things that are a little on the macabre end of the spectrum. As a kid, I remember watching *Unsolved Mysteries* and *Are You Afraid of the Dark?* and reading Goosebumps and Two-Minute Mysteries. I loved them. To this day I inhale podcasts like *My Favorite Murder, The Last Podcast on the Left, Dr. Death, S-Town,* and more. *I'll Be Gone in the Dark* and *The Stranger Beside Me* left me sleepless and triple-checking my door locks when I read them last year, but I kept on reading. Whether the stories are true crime or fiction, a person who embarks into any of these narratives goes in at the mercy of the inexplicable. I think that's a big part of the draw. We read and dissect and listen and force ourselves to imagine in an effort to understand the un-understandable. The split-second trigger that results in a crime of passion. The long years of build to a calculated horror. The grit of survivors who escape someone else's terrible plan for them. The bald, raw courage of loved ones left behind in the wake of a sudden and violent absence. *How?* We ask. *Why?* So we look to the evidence and materials around us and try to make sense of what's there. I think it's as expansive and mysterious as outer space, what goes on inside of any one person. I think that's why psychological stories are so popular, and always will be.

It seems that all the characters (Max, Mantis, Audra, Juniper, and even Lance) are guilty of something. Do you think any of the characters here are inherently good?

You know, I became increasingly aware of this as I kept writing and rewriting these people! No one comes out as a great candidate for any sort of humanitarian award. But! I don't think people are all good or all bad, of course. Not even Max and Mantis are *all* bad. (Though, to be sure, they are *mostly* bad!) So by this logic, all of them are inherently good(!). But the levels of goodness vary *wildly* from character to character. I think Coral might have the highest "good quotient" and then maybe Lance.

Can you talk about the different forms of complicity in this story?

There's so much! But I think all of it can basically be broken down into two major types: complicities of action and complicities of silence. There are characters who knowingly and deliberately *do* things that have major and horrible impacts on others. I think of Moss, Mantis, and Audra in particular. And then there are characters who understand and recognize various forms of peril and abuse around them and remain silent. I think of Juniper, Lance (who's a bit of a mix), and even Coral to a lesser extent—perhaps when it comes to Ashley Pelletier. I think one of the interesting things about all of this interplay of complicity is that a lot of the time it emerges out of a character's strong *need*—however selfish that need might be. Moss *needs* to be great artist. Mantis *needs* his past to remain a secret. Audra *needs* closure. Juniper *needs* the connectivity friendship affords. Lance *needs* Audra. Coral *needs* relief. So they each do what is within their power to do to achieve these ends. Often with tragic consequences.

What kinds of books are you reading these days?

I'm currently reading *Mexican Gothic* by Silvia Moreno-Garcia, *Rich and Pretty* by Rumaan Alam, and *Real Life* by Brandon Taylor. I recently finished *The Paper Palace* by Miranda Cowley Heller, which I loved.

Acknowledgments

A published book, I've learned, holds within it a stupendous eco-system of very kind, very talented, and very enthusiastic people. The making of a book—the making of a writer—is quite a magical, alchemical, and collaborative process. And I'm so grateful that it is. My book is better for it. I am better for it.

For loving my manuscript so fast and being willing to help me shape it so much; for our instant chemistry and your gracious patience; for always looking out for my best interests: Sarah Bedingfield, agent extraordinaire, thank you.

For your commitment to and enthusiasm for this story; for your ability to see and articulate narrative possibilities that I never could have dreamed of without you; for helping to make my book far better than when you first met it: my editors, MJ Johnston and Jenna Jankowski, thank you.

For giving me a shot and granting my work such a fabulous home among such fabulous company: Sourcebooks, thank you.

A special thank you to Molly Waxman, executive director of marketing, for being such a tenacious champion of this book in the marketplace and helping me to connect with other amazing writers and booksellers in the process.

For your instruction, your welcoming habitats, your power as homing beacons in my heart: the English departments of the University of Maine and the University of Notre Dame.

For your excitement, your cheerleading, your kindness, and your friendships: Joan Peters, Mary Peters, and my whole work family, thank you.

For years—years!—of belief, support, shop talk, love, and the simple fact of your profound presence in my life, the High Council, the friends: Megan Soderberg, Chris Tarbell, Tim Berrigan, Dave Kress, Evan Bryson, Beth Towle, and Drew Kalbach, thank you. For all my friends who happen not to be named here—but you know who you are—thank you.

For a lifetime of love, support, belief, and imagination; for being the people I got to start with—which put me way ahead of the game, if you ask me: my dad, Ken Lattari; my mom, Mary Lattari; and my brothers, KJ Lattari and Joe Lattari, thank you. Kerrie Lattari and Sarah Hardy, and the extended Lattari and Foss families, thank you, too.

For your incredible ability to see me and love me in a way I had not thought possible; for consulting as Plot Doctor when I was close to ripping my hair out; for keeping things light when the work felt heavy; for believing, believing, believing like it was a law of the universe, intractable, irrevocable: my husband and partner, Kevin Foss, thank you. I love you.

About the Author

Katie Lattari holds degrees from the University of Maine and the University of Notre Dame. Her first novel, *American Vaudeville*, a small press work, was published in 2016. A native of Brooklyn, New York, she now lives in Bangor, Maine, with her husband, Kevin, and their cat, Alex. *Dark Things I Adore* is Katie's debut thriller.